THE SHRIMP PEOPLE

REX SHELLEY

THE SHRIMP PEOPLE

TIMES BOOKS INTERNATIONAL
Singapore • Kuala Lumpur

Other books by Rex Shelley:

Words Mean Business
Cultures of The World: Japan

Published by Times Books Intrenational,
an imprint of Times Editions Pte Ltd.
Times Centre
1 New Industrial Road
Singapore 1953

2nd Floor, Wisma Hong Leong Yamaha
50 Jalan Penchala
46050 Petaling Jaya
Selangor Darul Ehsan Malaysia

Published in August 1991
1st reprint in September 1991

Printed in Singapore

ISBN 981 204 292 X

§

Fiction, Fact and Foreign Words

This tale is woven around a small minority in Southeast Asia: mixtures of the East and West known as Eurasians, mesticos, Serani or *geragoks*, the last term being the Malay name of a tiny little shrimp which their ancestors used to catch for a living nearly four hundred years ago.

It is all fiction. But the settings are in real worlds of the past. I have tried to keep the facts generally correct.

Foreign words and phrases are used fairly liberally, and their meanings are translated only where it is essential for the reader to follow the story.

I have used the variety of English known as 'Singlish.' Sometimes it is a variety that is or was peculiar to the Eurasians. Some of it is peculiar to Malaysians. Others are out of date.

I have combined Eurasian surnames, popular Eurasian Christian names and nicknames at random. Given the limited number of names, it is probable that a few of these random combinations are the names of real persons, dead or alive. There is no attempt to refer to any real person except for a few well-known public figures. I have deliberately misspelt some surnames whose pronunciation is not obvious from the English spelling.

I am indebted to Dennis Bloodworth for his criticism of my draft and his many suggestions which have helped to make the story more readable.

§

Contents

§

Prologue

'Perahu baharu, temberang pun baharu,
Baharu sekali masok Melaka.
Abang baharu, adek pun baharu,
Baharu sekali kenal biasa.'

(*The ship's new, the rigging's new,*
sailing suddenly into Malacca.
She's new to him, He's *new to her,*
Yet knowing at once each other.)

Old Malay poem.

Bedah stared at the sea, clutching the bundle of her clothes to her breast, her eyes wild with excitement, her mouth gaping open with wonder and awe. It was as though the sky had suddenly exploded into a huge dome above her. Like seeing the unexpected bright blue sky when one came out of the dark jungle into a clearing. But a thousand times wider. As far as the eye could see. And below the sky, the endless sea. Stretching far, far away in front of her. To eternity. Into space, meeting the sky somewhere beyond the horizon. Disappearing into the distance. Like the mountains of her land.

She had once gone downstream of the river that she had known from her earliest childhood with her mother after a week of incessant rain, and seen it overflow its banks. There was water everywhere. But this was a million times more frightening. Miles and miles of water in every direction.

Her toes curled into the soft damp sand, her mind shrinking from the thought of the unbelievable expanse of water. And it kept on coming. It kept on rushing in waves at the beach, splashing and churning up white froth unceasingly. One wave followed behind the other, to dash itself against the beach again. With the same tumbling and churning and the same rushing noise. Well, not quite the same. Somehow each wave broke differently on the shore. Like a swarm of ants pouring out of a damaged anthill. Like the endless clouds of mosquitoes by the river's edge. There was a constancy, yet a variation within it.

Pak Khamis watched her from under his drooping grey eyebrows smiling. "I told you it was big. Very big." But Bedah didn't hear him. She was listening to the roaring of the sea. Like distant thunder. But this thunder did not stop. Like the rain in the forests of her land. It was the constancy of the breaking waves that now terrified her. It dulled her senses, her hearing.

"Let's go," Pak Khamis said.

"No, wait," Bedah replied. She could not tear herself from the spectacle. She sat down on the beach. Pak Khamis sat beside her smiling. The wonder and awe in her eyes held him. It almost made the long journey from their mountain-jungle worthwhile. Anyway, they were in no hurry.

He sat silent for a few minutes. He could sit still and quiet for hours. He had sat rigid before, not even daring to breath too deeply from dusk to dawn, many a night waiting for a tapir or a tiger. And there was no need to talk when the other is busy with his or her thoughts. He knew when to keep silent.

Bedah moved her head slowly from side to side as if she had to reassure herself that the sea actually stretched all the way from the north to the south. Her ears slowly adapted to the sound of the surf on the beach. She put up her finger and turned to Pak Khamis, her eyes telling him of a new sound in the air.

"*Pekaka*," he said. He knew there was no need to keep silent on the wide open beach. This was not the dark, enclosed jungle where the sound of one's voice would reverberate and frighten away every living thing. The kingfisher appeared, flying over their heads from behind them in a few seconds.

"*Tidak sama*," Bedah said with surprise in her voice.

It was not the same white-breasted kingfisher that appeared occasionally in the foothills. It was the white-collared coastal kingfisher unfamiliar to Bedah. Pak Khamis explained the difference to her.

She relapsed into silence again, staring ahead of her at the horizon. Her eyes seemed to be straining to look that far. They had told her that if you went up to the top of the mountain ridge you would see mountains stretching out in front of you for miles and miles. It must be like this, she thought to herself. As far as the eye can see.

Pak Khamis pointed out towards the sea. There was a tiny speck of white on it. It looked like a bird hovering over the water to Bedah. "A sailing boat," he said in Malay.

"Ah." She had heard of them. Big boats. Not like the dug-outs they used on her river at home.

"We'll wait until it goes into Malacca," he said. He wriggled himself into another position in the sand and settled down watching the white speck as he had watched the *seladang* feed from a safe hide in the jungle many a morning.

As the boat came closer, Bedah's eyes opened wider and wider again. It seemed to grow and grow until it was almost three houses high. With three great poles and massive expanses of cloth sails.

"A white man's ship, I think," Pak Khamis said. He knew these things. He had been to Malacca three times before.

Pak Khamis watched the ship. In the wisdom of his fifty years he knew that things were changing rapidly. It was disturbing. It was not like the old days in the forests. Time was slipping by faster and faster these days. Some Malacca people even counted the time differently. This was the eight hundred and seventy-eighth year of his Islamic calendar, but the merchants were calling it the year fifteen hundred of the prophet Jesus Christ.

There were strange people in Malacca. Men from a far away place called India and people with yellow skins who had arrived in large boats from more than a thousand miles away bringing ceramic jars and many wonderful things. He had also heard some of the merchants talk of men with skins as white as the clouds in the sky. Like ghosts. And he had heard talk of the ships they sailed in. That must be one of them. Three masts. There were also Achinese and fierce men from Johor sailing the seas these days.

He had brought Bedah down from their jungle-clad mountains partly because he had wanted someone to look after the house he intended to erect on the outskirts of Malacca, partly because he wanted company for the long journey down to the sea with the precious rhino horn in his bundle of clothing, the horn which was going to provide him the capital for the trading venture he had planned to start, and partly because it solved his sister Rosiah's problem.

The girl was bewitched, Rosiah had said. She seemed to have eyes only for Harun. Harun was strong and sturdy but as reckless as the gibbons swinging in the trees with their meaningless chatter. She was ready for marriage, but Harun was not the boy they had planned for her. Besides, she had stood up one day when the men were organising a hunt for a rogue elephant that had been ripping up their fruit trees and houses at intervals for years, and had had the impertinence to ask to go with them. She was getting out of hand. Rosiah was convinced she had been bewitched.

So Pak Khamis had brought her down from the mountains. They walked for days on end. But he saw that as strong as she appeared to be in the jungles, the blazing sun of the open foothills and the plains tired her. He found a bullock cart going to Malacca on the last day and paid the man to carry them there. Bedah had slept almost all the way. She had run out of questions and gasps of amazement. She was tired. At sixteen she should have taken the journey much better, Pak Khamis though to himself. They had arrived late at night and Pak Khamis had told the bullock cart driver to drop them off at the beach. They slept on the beach that night, covering themselves with the thin cotton cloths they had brought. Bedah had awaken well after sunrise as the sun cleared the tops of the hills behind them in the west and its rays came upon them bright and warm.

And Bedah opened her eyes and saw the sea.

It frightened her for a long time. She did not understand the sea and its changing moods. She did not know the spirits that roamed the seas and the river mouth, as she had known the ways of the spirits of the jungle. There were new taboos and new ways of appeasing the evil forces that lurked behind the jagged rocks and in the deep blue depths of the ocean. But as time passed she learnt.

Pak Khamis built himself a house with the help of friends he had made on his previous trips. He also built up a steady trading business in rattan which were brought down from the jungles by the bullock carts. And he built himself a reputation as an honest and wise man from the mountains among the fishing people in the *kampongs* by the sea.

They treated Bedah as his child and soon the local women were making oblique remarks about Bedah. "You have a beautiful cage in your home. I have a beautiful bird. Can my bird not come peacefully to your cage?" Pak Khamis read the signs and knew that life would be easier if there was another man in the house. He would be able to devote more time to his growing trading business. Maybe he could even go into tin trading. He had friends who said they had friends from the Kinta valley.

It was arranged. Tahir became the husband of Bedah. They had four children. One every year, Pak Khamis thought. But he wasn't sure. He had his business to attend to. And he had been distracted by the widow Noriah on many a night. She was thirty and skilled in the tender ways of women. She also knew how to organise everything so very discreetly.

Then one day, Bedah's man, Tahir, heard of the attack by the rajah of Ligor, a vassal of the king of Siam, on Pahang and Sultan Mahmud Shah's assembling a force to crush the rajah. There were promises of glory and booty for the victors. He joined the Sultan's forces and was never seen again.

With the youngest still at her breast and the eldest racing around the house and *kampong*, a lusty healthy child of five, Bedah struggled on. Pak Khamis gave her a monthly allowance, but he had taken the widow Noriah as his second wife in happy accordance with his religious and social environment.

The spirit that drove Bedah racing along the jungle paths, shrieking and splashing in the swift mountain streams, gradually ebbed. It was not the physical effort. Nor was it the fear that if something happened to Pak Khamis she would be left stranded. She knew that she could then spend more time helping with the harvests and with the drying of the fish and shrimps as she was doing now and support her family, and that the villagers around her, however hard the times were, would never let her starve.

It was the loneliness.

The uneasy calm of her life was shattered in the year eight hundred and seventy-seven, the fifteen hundred and ninth year of the Christian calender the traders had talked about. The peace of the evening was shattered by the sound of explosions. The sky above Malacca town glowed red. The *kampong* folk who rushed to the beach said they saw two ships drifting, apparently unmanned, and on fire.

They huddled in groups in the *kampong* discussing what had happened till late in the night. One or two people had come in from Malacca earlier; they had whispered that the Gujerati traders were going to attack the white men's ships. Bedah had to ask to find out who the white men were. Some said they were from India. Some said they were Portuguese. People from a far away land who built huge ships. Their king, King Manuel, had sent an emissary with five ships to pay his respects to Sultan Mahmud Shah. He had a strange name. Diego Lopes de Diego Sequeira. Some said that these white men had really come to trade with the sultan. They would take over the trading which the Indian Muslims had been doing. There were many different versions. But the sound of guns and explosions of gunpowder now made it certain that the Gujeratis had attacked the Portuguese ships and had driven them away. Bedah went to sleep that night confused and frightened, her mind swimming with the complexity of it all.

She woke up still wondering about what had happened when

she heard the birds chattering strangely. She listened. Then she heard a soft groan. She went to the door. About twenty feet from the steps leading to her small verandah she saw a form of a man lying on the ground. He groaned again.

Bedah rushed up to him. The instincts from her childhood stirred in her. Man in her jungle had no enemies but the beasts and the spirits of the forests and mountains. She knelt beside him and looked at him in the darkness. Then, to her horror, she saw it was a white man. White. Pale pink-white like the underbelly of a pig. Like the ghosts of the forests. She recoiled.

His eyes opened. She saw there was a trickle of blood flowing out from the corner of his mouth. His eyes were pleading with her. He mumbled something. She listened. Her face nearer to his. "*Kuah, kuah* ..." he said. Gravy. Gravy? Maybe their language is like ours. Water. Gravy.

She held him by the shoulder and turned him over. He was almost limp. She could not see any wound like a thigh smashed by the charge of a rhino, or the belly ripped open by a bear. But she saw in his hand a short knife. It was wet with blood. He held it in his left hand.

Bedah rushed to the back of the house and got a coconut shell of water. She dipped her fingers in it and held them to the man's lips. He sucked her fingers. He sat up slowly and took the shell from her and drank it dry. He muttered something. She knew from the way he said it and the way his head dipped that it was a thank you. Bedah looked at him carefully. There was a mess of dried blood and ripped cloth at his right shoulder. It was not bleeding now, but she could see that he had been wounded badly. She stood up and stretched out her hands to him. He gripped her forearms and pulled himself up. His hands were large and powerful. He put his left arm around her shoulder and she walked him up the steps. His forearm was as hairy as a monkey's.

She led him into the house and lit a candle. With her knife she cut away the cloth of his shirt and cleaned the wound with a rag. He sat dazed and kept mumbling the same thank you words, nodding his head with gratitude. When she had finished, she got out a sarong and pointed to the well. He seemed steadier now. He went into the darkness. She heard the sound of splashing water. He had understood. She found some rice that the children had not finished and some salt fish and put them on a banana leaf. He came back from the well and nearly tripped on the steps. She motioned him to sit on the floor and gave him the food. He ate ravenously.

He bowed low to her when he had finished and whispered something. They were not the same thank you words. Then he saw his knife which she had cleaned and placed on the floor beside the banana leaf. He picked it up and looked at her.

There was no fear in Bedah. She had helped him and it was unthinkable that he should now attack her. She sat still and looked into his eyes. They were blue and clear and beautiful. He held the blade and offered the knife to her. With his left hand.

She recoiled immediately with the shock of his crudeness. His eyes showed surprise at her reaction. Then it struck her that the strange white-skinned people were like the Sakais and Semangs in the jungles. They did not understand the *adat*, the customs of her life. She put out her right hand and took his token of gratitude.

As she looked at him with his body naked above the waist she noticed the wound had started to bleed again. She found an old sarong, tore it into strips and bandaged his arm and shoulder. She had never touched a man like this before. Except Tahir.

She went to the back of the house and wrapped up two pieces of salt fish in a banana leaf. She picked up a faded *baju* of hers and handed it to him. He bowed again. Then she got a gourd of water and two guavas which she noticed lying on the floor. She took the *baju* back from him and wrapped all these up in it.

Then Bedah stood up. She held his hand and led him out of the house as though she was leading a child. She led him down a path she knew well to a small clearing behind the *kampong*. She left the path with his hand gripping hers with more strength and confidence now, and bending down she went through a tunnel of undergrowth to a place that was hidden from anyone walking the path.

He bowed again and whispered something. She raised her hand in the air making an arc with it, to indicate the rising and setting of the sun. He smiled and nodded. She went through the motion again and pointed to the house. He repeated her hand motions. He understood her. He would come to the house after nightfall tomorrow.

She tossed and turned on the mat all night. It was not the guilt of touching a man nor of what she had done for him. She had had no choice. It was fate. And she was not one to be frightened by the wagging tongues of the *kampong* women. It was the decision whether or not to continue to help the strange white-skinned man with eyes the colour of the blue-green sea.

But it was written in the stars, fated in the mysterious ways of the unseen forces. He was back the next night, ravenously hungry. The wound looked worse. She learnt her first words of the strange language that night. Obrigado and Pedro and Rodrigues.

Pak Khamis listened to Bedah's story frowning. Then he thought in silence for a long time while Bedah sat across him with Noriah beside him.

"You must look after him," he finally decided.

"I will arrange for a bullock cart to take you and him and the three oldest children to a beach a little south of here. It is quiet there. I have a friend who has a small shack there. We will look after Junid, the youngest," he said looking at Noriah.

He would give them two fishing nets and they would be able to earn a living catching shrimps. He called them *geragok*.

"What's that?" Bedah asked.

"Ah, my daughter of the jungles ... you don't know the *geragok* ... It is a very small shrimp. The tiniest thing we catch for food. An insignificant thing next to the beautiful big shiny silverfish. But when you dry them in the sun and mash them into a paste, they hold the taste of the sun and salt and the sea. And after baking the dried cakes of the paste over a fire and mixing them with pounded chilli, even the tiniest bit will bring waves of a wonderful new flavour to a whole scoopful of rice."

~ *Chapter One* ~

Old Joe

"Don't look now, but there's that old bloke from Singapore," Ray muttered under his breath just before he raised the glass of Swan to his lips. I made the fatal mistake. With my reactions slowed down by two glasses and curious to see a fellow Singaporean face, I looked over Ray's shoulder. I saw him at once. A grey-haired old man with a battered look on his face. Brown-skinned, a little wrinkled, badly shaven with an eager gleam in his grey-blue eyes. A rounded oriental, Malay sort of nose, high cheek bones, but his eyes and large bone structure did not look Asian. He was thin. Perhaps gaunt. But one could see that behind the dried skin there was once muscle in the old fellow's arms.

He caught me looking at him. I had perhaps let my look linger a little too long. He met my eyes, stared unblinking at me for a split second, and the corner of his mouth curled slightly in a smile. He started to move towards me.

"He's coming over, Ray," I said.

"Oh God." He was with us before Ray could say anything more. "Hey, Ray. Howyer mate?"

"Alright, and yerself?"

"Couldn't be better. Who's your friend?"

"Oh, this is Robert. He's from Singapore ..."

Before Ray could finish speaking the old fellow interrupted.

"I thought I saw a familiar face. Pleased to meet you. I'm Joe. Joe Coombes." He shot out his hand and gave me a firm friendly grip. "You're Serani, aren't you?"

"Yes," I replied, feeling guilty about it for some reason or other.

Perhaps it was because I should have recognised him as a fellow Serani at once. Ray chipped in with, "What this Serani?" and old Joe went into explanations about the Eurasians being called Serani and the derivation from the Malay word Nasarene, meaning Nazareth man, Christian and all that which I had heard and trotted out myself a million times.

"What's your surname?" The ritual had started. I winced and replied: "Machado."

"Oh! You're not from Singapore! You're a Penangite, aren't you?"

"No. I'm a true blue Singaporean. Don't smoke and keep short hair. My father was from Penang."

"Was he the goalie? Bobby Machado?"

"No. Bobby was my uncle."

He was away now. I could see his eyes sparkle and I knew it was coming. He would know them all. He was going to rush into it and enjoy every moment, every memory. He paused for effect.

"Let me see now … Your mother must have been a Rodrigues. Didn't Ben Machado marry Bertha?"

"No. My mother's name is Beryl."

"Of course! Beryl Rodrigues … the one with the big tits. Sorry lah. No offence intended. Just rememberin …"

He laughed, took a gulp of his beer and continued. I stood there resigned. I realised now why Ray had muttered "Oh God."

"Yes. Yes, yes … Bertha married Heng, that bloody rascal. But she was a bit of a flighty thing herself. Ditched the bugger, didn't she?"

"Yes, my Auntie Bertha left Uncle Heng."

"Uncle Heng? Is that what you called him?"

"Yeah … my mother didn't like us using his Chinese name."

"Teepical, teepical …" in his Singapore-English way.

I felt I had to do my bit for politeness sake. "Are you related to Anthony Coombes who's with the fire service?"

"Yah. That's my good-for-nothing nephew. Joined the Fire Brigade against his parent's advice. Straight after his Senior

Cambridge. Silly bugger. Wanted adventure, he said, and where did it get him? The only bloody adventure and excitement he had was chasing Malay women down the *kampong* paths in Geylang. Real bugger for the girls, he was. Chased anything that moved in a *sarong*. Do you know him?"

"No. But I met him once at a wedding."

"Let me get you buggers a drink."

Ray shot his "Oh God" glance at me while the diversion of getting drinks distracted Old Joe. But he was back at it as soon as we picked up our fresh, full glasses.

"Good stuff this, but nothing like a Tiger, ha?"

Before I could defend the Swans in our hands, he shot back: "And how is Beryl?"

"OK. Bit of rheumatism."

"She wasn't like Bertha. No, not like Bertha at all. She had the looks all right, and the ..." he shot a glance at me and saw my anticipation, "the body, but she was placid. Ah, that's the word. Placid. Right?"

"Yeaah ... I suppose so."

"Did you ever hear about the business of Heng and the De Souza girl?" He didn't wait for an answer. By now I could see that old Joe had had quite a few. "Now, that was a girl! Whoa, she was terrific, man. You know that smooth-skin type, eh?"

He almost drooled with the memory. "She was a flirt. No bloody doubt about that. Hey, you mean you didn't know about your uncle?"

"My ex-uncle."

"Dammit, ex or no ex, he's your uncle. Isn't he."

The old timers' stand. Once married, stamped, branded.

"Well ..." I muttered, feeling I had to say something, or mumble some reaction. After all he was an old bugger.

"It all started at Theresa Pestana's wedding. You know the Pestana family?"

"No."

"Sheesh, man. You should know. They had their own gharry in

the old days. Style man! Old Doris used to sit there with her head in the air like bloody Queen Mary going to Ascot. Hat and ribbons. She's the one who called me once at a dance. Just waved her fan at me. I was hot and sweaty in my tuxedo having a damn good time when I saw her wave her fan at me. At once I went. Yes, Mrs. Pestana? Then she let fly. But not gerderbak-gederbook. Just softly. Young man, I knew your father when he was alive. He would be astounded, astounded, man. I can still remember the word. He would be ASTOUNDED at your bold behaviour with that Scully girl. On the dance floor too. You're a Coombes, aren't you? Yes, Mrs. Pestana. Then behave like one. Leave her alone. Buzz off now and remember, I'll be watching you … The blerdy woman … tried to run the whole community like an empress. She even tried to fix the SRC. committee once … Where was I?"

"Uncle Heng, at the wedding."

"But she had style you know. Even the Europeans treated her like a bigshot. Do you know that once when the coronation procession was on, she just pushed herself into one of the European seats? Really, she was so bold."

He shook his head. I wasn't sure if it was disgust or admiration.

"Yah … it was at Theresa Pestana's wedding that it all began. Boy! That was a wedding! You know, one of the grand old-style weddings. Page boys, flower girls … the lot. Dancing. I tink it was Soliano's band that played. Real bebop man. Those buggers could really play. And it was full-suit, you know. No bloody Hawaiian shirts in those days. I remember my father had a special suit for weddings. And funerals. Every time he wore that suit, he used to take out his handkerchief in church and wipe the kneeler before he knelt down. And my mother used to get mad at him. The church is the house of God, she used to say, it's an insult to make as if the place is dusty. One day Father will see you wiping the kneeler, then die for you … Yah … It was full suits at the big weddings in those days. And we used to walk in with our tins of cigarettes in our hands. Tins of fifty. Players. But I used to smoke Capstan. It was cheaper. Old Henry Alvis always had Churchills. Or was it

Churchmans. He was always like that. Always."

He stopped to gulp his beer. Ray shot another of those looks at me. He offered to buy us a round of drinks in accordance with the immutable, inflexible law of his land that the round must be settled like bank clearing houses, striking off the pluses and minuses before the day is ended.

"Hey ... I sardennly remembered. Your mother Bertha could really dance."

"My mother is Beryl."

"Oh yes, sorry lah. It was Beryl who could dance like a fairy."

"My mother?"

"Yes. For Godssake, man, you young buggers don't know a ting about dancing dese days. Hey man, in dose days it was proper dancing. Not this jumping-jumping ting. Hold and go man. Chee-aase ...it was sheook ... style boy. And the tango ... I was damn good at dat. Tarp! Bend over. Tarp! Spin around."

He swayed as he relived it. Ray opened his mouth, but ...

"Yah ... where was I? Oh yes, Theresa Pestana's wedding, when Aloysious got drunk. The blardy fellow. Smashed ... tried to kiss Mrs. Galistan. You know, the tall one?"

I thought I should say something again. "No, I don't."

"Oh you don't know the Galistans? Well of course you were only a *kichie-brat* then ... The best part of the story was the night when Reggie got smashed and wanted to curse Archie Perera. The whole gang went in Derek's Ford Prefect to Bidadari to look for his grave. Everybody lighting matches to read the tombstones. We finally found Archie Perera's grave and Reggie pissed on it cursing to high heaven. What a night!"

"That was on the wedding night?"

"No lah! Dat was anarder night. Long before the wadeing night. Ah ... the Theresa Pestana wedding ... I first met Girlie Klaus that night. You know the Ipoh Klauses? ... Ah? You don't? The redheads ... the grandfadder was a preest?"

"A priest? Sheesh, I never heard that one."

"Well, I tell you ... Mary Jeremiah in the olden days married this European, dunno where he came from ..." He was off again on another long-drawn anecdote. I shut off for a little while but the stray phrase I caught sounded interesting, so I listened in again. He related how the foreigner had brought a "tin trunk," as Old Joe called it, with him when he married but never opened it in front of his wife throughout their thirty years of marriage. When he died, she found a full set of a priest's vestments in it. The ladies of the parish to a woman concluded, without the slightest hesitation, that Klaus had been a defrocked priest to their great horror and the twitterings and cluckings at the utter enormity of it reverberated round the parish for decades.

"Are you telling me that all the Ipoh Klauses come from a priest?"

"Yeah, boy. The old kraut was a priest!"

"Are you sure it is true?"

"Hey! Look here! Look me in the eye. Do I look like der type dat would lie to you? Young man ... you've got a lot to learn."

"Gawd! I was crazy over Dolly Koch once, to think that ..."

"Small world eh? Dolly's grandmother was Mary lah!"

"I know that."

"Hey ..." A drawled serious tone. "Your turn, sonny."

"Sorry, I'm not used to your Auzzie ways."

"Don't you ever call me Auzzie."

I bought the round. Ray glared at me. Really glared.

"Didn't Dolly Koch finally marry that young Perkins boy?"

"I don't know."

"Emily Perkins, son. Now there was a woman who could dance the Branyong. You young farts don't know these things. Bet you don't know a single word of Portuguese."

"Of course I do. *Dali*."

"Ha! Ha! Ha! ..." He roared with laughter. I read Ray's glance. "The old bloke is getting pissed." I added in my mind, "... with his monologue of memories." Yet I was fascinated.

He turned to Ray. "*Dali* means to hit. We used to use the word when the Chinese were around. They didn't know what *dali* was ...

I remember the night when 'Botak Gunting' and Edwin Theseira took on, or tried to take on all the bus drivers at Bukit Bintang. We were at a *satay* stall. That bloody 'Botak Gunting' was three-quarter gone ... he was always like dat. After a few drinks, he would get bold; mind you the bugger could drink ... Well, that night, he and Edwin and I had a good few ... then for some bloody reason I can't remember, he started an argument wit one of the bars drivers ... The barsket took out a sparner and went for 'Botak.' 'Botak' was blerdy fast ... he swayed ..." Old Joe swung his body to one side to illustrate, stumbled and would have fallen if Ray had not caught him. I caught Ray's "Let's go" look.

"He hit the bugger square on the face ... Barp! ... Blerd ... Then the other bars drivers moved in ... You see, it was a sort of a bars terminus, not like dose dese days ... just a place where dey turned round and ate mee or drank kopi ... They all got up and moved towards 'Botak Gunting' ... those were der days when they used narkle darsters. I saw their hans go into dere pockets. I was really *chuah* ... Boy! My balls were shrivelled ... Den sardenly, Edwin rushed up. He takes out a card and waves it. '*Saya Polis*!'

"Police, the bugger says ... 'I arrest you, you bloody gangster!' He grabs hold of 'Botak Gunting' and holds him. Den he walks off wit him down the road. We all knew dere was a porleece station just dere ... on der next roat. Those Chinese barskets stopped. Dey jus stood dere watching Edwin walk off wit 'Botak' ... and der bes part is, as he walks off, he hammers him one on der neck. A damn good one ... Dat was real fast tinking boy!"

Ray stood still. There was a short silence between us, an isolated silence with the rumble and grumble of the pub noise beating against us. "Gee ... that was good, Joe ..." Ray muttered.

I broke the mood. "I know Gunting's son, Clive. He's in the army ... a major. He married a Gwen Dias ..."

"Not the daughter of Dias-*hitam-manis*?"

"No, Mr. Coombes. Maybe the granddaughter ..."

"Hoi. Please. This is Australia. I'm Joe ..."

"Sorry ... Mr. Coombes."

"Shit! Ha Ha Ha ..."

"I guess we'd better go," Ray broke in, firmly, decisively.

"Go if you wan mate ... I'll send Robert back."

"Look Joe, they'll get you with the blower ... you must be breathing pure alcohol by now. Maybe I should take you back too ... Where do you stay?"

"Rossmoyne."

"OK. You can leave your wheels here ... they're used to it ... Pick it up in the morning ... C'mon. Lessgo ..."

"Hang on Ray ... I haven't told you about the wedding and this young man's uncle and the De Souza girl and all that ... The police took months cracking their brains about the thing ... that's a real mystery, Ray ... One day someone will write a bestseller about it."

"Joe! You're gone mate. Wrap it up. We're all going. C'mon Robert, let's go ..."

We led him to the car, still talking nineteen to the dozen, prattling away with much enjoyment about the land and times he had left behind him. It was a world he could not shake off. I wondered if I could. I had been fascinated by his rambling reminiscences and disjointed anecdotes; fascinated, I told myself, because this was part of my past too.

He turned round to me. I was sitting at the back. "Whatever happened to your uncle ... the hockey wizard ... Eric?"

"He's here in Perth."

"Good heavens! Fancy that! I've never seen him. How long has he been here?"

"Probably about five years."

"Fancy that! Eric being here and I've not seen him. He was a bugger ... He was the fastest stick in Penang. No umpire could see his crack at your shins when he decided you deserved it. Mind you, he would never play dirty, but if you started he'd *letak*. Gar ... he was good ... Way back in the fifties he won the all-Malaya cup for Penang ... two-nil ... both his goals. Selangor had that star bugger, Jamit Singh ... Man, you should have seen your uncle play."

"I have seen him. He sure was good."

"Not only on the hockey field, but he was a first-class fellow. He could sing, man; I remember his favourite song was 'Ramona' ... Those were the days ... after the game we used to drink. It was mostly Tiger I think. Then the dirt would come out ... You basket, you tried to take it through yourself ... Shit I was there racing down waiting ... you bloody well know Krishnan can stop you any time, you basket and so on ... ha, ha ... yes man, those were the days. I never scored any goals. I was the feeder, centre-half. That young Lesslar and I were a real combination. Yah, man, he was terrific. I could almost read his eyes in one split second ... 'not now' ... 'to the left' ... 'straight, straight to Paul' ... The bugger had fingers of steel. He used to stop the ball dead on the grass ... then he'd let fly ... Waarp! ... Hey, slow down, next left, then go over the Shelley bridge ..."

We finally dropped him off, with a thousand goodbyes and directions, to send love to all my relatives, some of whom were dead and gone. But I let it be. Ray grinned at me as I clicked the seat belt. "He's quite a guy isn't he?"

"Yeah, the old bugger," I unconsciously slipped into the dialect.

"You know Robert, those stories of his old days fascinate me. All those wild weddings, and those crazy guys screwing around, whacking at shins in the hockey field ... You've seen it all?"

An enquiring tone, expecting an answer. "Not really. Most of it was before my time"

"But that aunt of yours ... Bertha wasn't it? She must have been quite a sheila."

~ *Chapter Two* ~

The Rodrigues

Bertha; Beryl, my mother; "Bunny," my father, Eurasians of that time. The time I had heard and described of as the good old days until it made me sick. But I saw, lived in the tail end of those days. The weddings, the soccer games, the shooting, fishing, swimming … It came back to me as I lay in bed at the motel that night, waiting for sleep to carry me away.

James Rodrigues was a policeman. He joined "the force" as he used to call it, right after his Junior Cambridge. It pleased his old man. It was a proper thing to do. One either joined Shell or Stanvac or a good British bank or, best of all, worked for the government. A police job had prospects.

James Rodrigues joined the police force. He walked his beat night after night. He learnt how to handle the drunks and the prostitutes and how far to go with the gangs. He learnt about people. About Shari's style. Shari, the station inspector. He wasn't an inspector, of course. Just the name of the bugger in charge. He knew when Shari wanted action and learnt to read the signs Shari showed when he was too keen on pushing justice. He had sat at the coffee stalls with the older men and listened. Which gambling dens were to be left alone, unless there was trouble, of course. Which houses were to be watched closely. Which street stalls paid their dues to the 08 and which stalls paid to the 03. And he learnt who was who; both in the force and in the big complex world outside. And over the years, he saw the beautiful logic of Shari's swaying and selection. It was like the palace intrigues of the old Malay courts. He bowed or bared his teeth as the signs told him. He knew

ASP Robinson had the ear of the commissioner and that CID *badawa* Jones was a rake. He played up to both of them. James took it all in and watched Shari make his moves.

So James went up. Up in the police world. To corporal. Then to sergeant. And one day, he got the letter. He was to go to the PTS. The Police Training School. Inspector! Shari! He'd said the right words. Not just Shari. Old Robinson had seen how he had nabbed the bloody *Kling* bugger who climbed over the wall at Chong's. He'd probably read his reports and seen that there was no funny English in them. After all, he'd got a "credit" for English in his Junior Cambridge.

So James Rodrigues could afford to marry the girl of his schoolday excitements. He did all the right things. He told his parents. He knew that they would send the word over to Mary's family. He didn't know that it had been whispered and plotted and planned for over a year. They married. He was given quarters near the Sepoy Lines. He walked tall and proud. Not every Serani got a woman as fair and sweet as Mary Gomez.

James and Mary had three children. Beryl was the first. Then there was Eric and, after that, Bertha. After Bertha, there were no more. Bertha was the wild *gila* one. Bertha gave them their greatest joys of parenthood and, later, she dragged them through pains of parenthood that they never imagined, in their younger, blissful days, could be possible.

To begin with, Bertha would never settle in bed. They would put her down with Beryl and Eric, and James would sing to them softly songs that his mother used to sing to him. Some were Malay, some Portuguese and some English. "Go to sleep my baby, shut your pretty eyes. Angels up above you, peering at you dearly from the skies ..." But Bertha would lie there with her eyes wide open, darting from her father's face to the other children. Beryl would drop off to sleep first. Eric, thin and sickly, but always alive and alert, would talk to him a little then shut his eyes and sleep. Then, Bertha would sit up. She would scramble out of the bed and run to kitchen to her mother. "Aiyah ... Bertah ..."

Mary would scoop her into her arms and kiss her, giggling. James would walk in, exasperated, with a "Ha … Mary, you spoil her."

"She's my baby, Jim."

Bertha was not like the others. She was bursting with energy almost all the time. She laughed with an abandon that was infectious. She kept trying to do things beyond the capabilities of her age; not just keep up with her elder brother and sister, but to do better than them. Beryl laughed at her efforts. They amused James too but the old and wizened Mrs. Cardoza silently shook her head with incomprehensible mutterings.

When she was about four, her little mind crashed head on with James's. He decided one night that he had to straighten out her way of brushing her teeth. She attacked them with a fury, brushing the inside ones but neglecting totally her front teeth.

"Come here Bertha, I show you how to brush your teeth."

"Mama tole me ordiddy …"

"Well, you got it wrong, sweetie."

"I can, Pa."

"Come here."

"I tole you … I can."

He pulled her towards him and took her little toothbrush in his hand. "Now say 'eeeee.' "

Her lower lip curled down. Her mouth tightly closed.

"Come on, Pa says say 'eeee.' "

Her mouth remained closed. James began to lose his patience. He repeated his order several times with increasing intensity but Bertha would not give in.

"I'll smack you and tell the *momoh* to bite you."

Bertha shrank visibly at the terrible threat. She moved her little body forward, opened her mouth, baring her teeth and through her clenched teeth she managed to say "Uuu."

Her little mind had not given in fully.

Mary talked about her when the women were exchanging anecdotes of their children after church as being, "so stubborn lah."

It was not a completely critical phrase. There was a hint of pride in Mary's voice as she said the words, "so stubborn lah." There was the same dual-meaning comment when later, as Bertha grew up, she described her as, "Aiyah! she real tomboy."

From the time she started school at the Cannosian Convent, Bertha was a rough-and-tumble girl. She raced with the boys down the backlanes behind their house at Sepoy Lines. She learnt all the bad words the Malay boys used and could flick a marble with her second finger as well as the best of them. She could spin a top and fly the small flimsy kites one bought at the *kedai* for five cents. In her scruffy stained and frayed white dress, she hung around with the *kampong* boys after school was over.

One afternoon, when Bertha, Ahmad and Dollah were sitting under a large tree in her garden talking of this and that, the subject of fruits came up. The size of Pak Majid's *nangka*; the *pulasans* her Pa had brought back from Johor when he came back from a hunting trip; how many rambutans have you eaten in one sitting? *Jambus*, *dukus*, *chikus*, *langsats*, *sentols* ...

"Hey! You know got one big tree in the *bai's* house?"

"Sure lah. We not so stupit. I know long time arready."

"Yah. But now full, man. So many. All big an yellow."

And so they went to look at the tree with the "big and yellow" *sentols*. The fruits looked perfect. They were ripe for picking. A large branch hung over the five-foot corrugated iron fence. It really wasn't so high if one thought about it. Dollah had a strong back. "Yah ... but the top of the fence is so sharp lah" "... not if you found an old rag, say a gunny sack ... then if you put it over the edge, you could grip the top and pull yourself up, then catch hold of that thin branch." "Will break lah." "Sure will break if *gumoh* like you ... but I am not so heavy."

The challenge was too strong. They found the gunny sack near where the *kebun* burnt the rubbish. Back to the fence. The *sentols* looked a heavenly yellow. "Aiyah! ... so beeg!" Dollah bent down. Bertha was on his back in a flash. Ahmad helped her. The gunny sack was passed up. It did what they expected it to do. Bertha gripped the edge of the fence and swung herself up to the slim branch. They held their breath waiting for the crack. But it held. Bertha was right. She was light enough. Soon the *sentols* came down, thud, thud, thud on the ground. The boys filled their shirts with them. Some split as they hit the ground to Ahmad's great delight as they were ready to be broken open. It was one mad rush of picking the fruits, throwing them down and tucking them into their shirts.

Suddenly, there was a loud shout, "*Chelaka*! *Pencuri*!"

Up on the tree, Bertha heard it and saw the burly Sikh run towards the tree. She looked down for Dollah's back. But the boys had fled. The Sikh rushed up to the foot of the tree. As he arrived he ejaculated: "*Alamak*! YOU!"

Bertha recognised him at once. The sergeant at the station.

"Come down at once, you bloody girl!"

She hesitated for a second. Maybe she could sit him out. But her practical logic told her it was impossible to avoid the consequences. She slid down slowly, trying to think of another way to get out of her desperate situation. The Sikh grabbed her arm with his big hairy hand and started walking her away from the tree. "*Mampost*! The police station!" she thought to herself.

The walk seemed endless. He was almost dragging her. Her arm hurt. Then to her great relief she saw that he was moving to her house. But the relief was soon gone as she pictured her father with his face red with anger.

"Sir! I thought it was Salleh's sons … but *Alamak*! I was so surprise to see it was your naughty girl."

Her mother standing there with her face pained. Her Pa getting the feather duster from the pantry where it hung above the rice box. Lifting up her skirt. The swish, the stinging pain, one, two, three, she started counting … until it didn't matter any more. She grit her teeth.

The following Sunday she overheard her mother telling Mrs. Zhender, the fat one with the lovely smile, "Not a sound from the little devil. No screaming, no crying, no pleading …"

Her bottom was on fire when Pa had finished. She could see that he was still raging with fury. She did not know that half his rage was that his sergeant had caught her. His daughter, a petty thief! The inspector's daughter! Shit!

She started walking out of the house as her mother picked up the feather duster Pa had flung onto the floor.

"Where you think you going?"

"To return the gunny sack ..."

"Gunny bag? What the hell?"

"I borrowed a gunny bag. I must return it."

"What the bloody hell! What gunny bag?"

"Aramugam's."

"You stay here! Go to your room!"

"No Pa, I must return it."

"Let her go James ... Bertha, you come back at once after that ... You hear me? You come back at once."

She went to the fence. She had to jump up to get the sack. Then, she walked slowly and deliberately to Dollah's house. He was sitting on the wooden steps that went up to the verandah. "Hoi! You *chabot* ah?" he called out.

Bertha walked up to him without a word. Dollah began to frown. When she was right in front of him, she stopped. Her foot shot out. She hit him hard between his legs. Dollah doubled up in pain, groaning.

Bertha turned around and ran. She heard his cries of "Aiyoo, Aiyoo ..." and ran on. She threw the gunny sack down near the rubbish fire place where they had found it and ran home. She arrived home panting. Pa was in the verandah, his hands on the rail. She knew he was still mad with anger. She noticed how firm and muscular his arms were. She ran past him. It seemed to her that for a moment he turned as if to stop her and say something. But she ran on. She passed the kitchen. Ma was there wiping something. It looked like her eyes were full of tears. Bertha ran on. Straight to her bed. She flopped onto it and hugged her bolster. Her bottom was on fire. Her head was on fire. Her whole body was aflame. "Bastards!"

she whimpered.

When she was eleven the "dirt business," as they referred to it in later years, occurred. James got a call one day from the Reverend Mother of the convent. She wanted to see him about his girl Bertha. James tried to question her on the phone but she would not reveal a clue. As he put down the receiver, he remembered that yesterday was the convent's annual Sports Day. He should have gone. But surely that could not be the reason for the very Reverend Mother to want to speak to him. Neither could it be the fact that Bertha had just missed the overall championship, getting the runner-up cup and being quite thrilled about it. The old girl would have spoken in a cheerier voice if it was about Bertha's sporting achievements. Her schoolwork was sort of OK as far as he was concerned. He frowned. The phone rang and he was Inspector Rodrigues again, tough and decisive, and no longer Bertha's Pa.

The Reverend Mother came to her point at once. "I regret, Mr. Rodrigues, that I have to speak to you about one of my girls. She has always been up to some monkey trick or other, but this time she has gone too far." She glared at him as though he was responsible for whatever mysterious prank Bertha had got up to. It put him on the defensive.

"It was crude, Mr. Rodrigues. Quite disgusting!"

James stiffened. His Bertha was never crude. It looked like a slap at the family face. "What happened, Reverend Mother?"

"It was at the sports yesterday. All the events were over and I stood up to make my speech. I had a script on the prizes table. As I glanced at it to pick it up while I said my opening words, to my horror, I saw this on top of my papers." She tossed a bit of celluloid onto the desk. It first struck James as some brown, slightly curved cylindrical thing; then he saw it was a celluloid replica of a piece of human faeces. He nearly burst out with laughter.

The Reverend Mother continued but as he struggled to contain himself he only caught scraps of her tirade. "I, the Reverend Mother, in my state of shock, uttered those blasphemous words right into the microphone, 'Mama Mia!' A last warning … She's a lively girl but. ... not just the school ... sense of propriety ... family influences ... those Malay boys who were cheering for her yesterday ... Mr. Rodrigues, Mr. Rodrigues ..."

He muttered something about straightening her out and left with much relief.

When he told Mary about it, she broke into peals of laughter.

Bertha was duly scolded but she could see that it was a perfunctionary kind of scolding.

As the years went by, Bertha learnt how to deal with the harsh world around her. Beryl was easily handled. You gave her face and you could ignore her. Eric was different. Eric could be a real friend; unless you pulled a fast one on him. He would *ketok* you then. With lightning speed, his hand would shoot out and hit you on the head with his middle finger knuckle. He could even do it in front of Pa and Ma, moving his body so that his *ketok* could not be seen. But Eric was not a bully. You could rely on Eric; if you didn't try to be too smart with him.

She tried to work Eric's trick on the netball field. But that bloody Mrs. Chin saw her. So she gave that up. She had her own ways of getting even. After all, she enjoyed doing things in her style. Why should she try to do things in other people's ways?

Then one day, looking at her pimples in the mirror, Bertha suddenly saw that she was a beautiful woman. Yes ! A woman. She took off her clothes and for the first time ever, looked at her body. She knew all that hair on her *puki* (she hadn't learnt the English word yet) and the blood and all that meant that she was changing. Her Ma had never explained it to her. Siti had told her some things. It sounded so medical and irrelevant to her life of books and netball and flying kites with the boys. Now it struck her fully. She saw her breasts. She saw the scar of the barbed wire just under her left breast and winced. It had never been anything to worry about before. She saw her thighs, strong and full with the flesh and muscle of her running to and from school for years, her gorging of *siew yok, soup kambing, beryani, satay perut* and thousands of glasses of *ice bandung*. She saw how shapely they had grown from her pushing the concrete-cylinder lawn roller with Eric, thrashing around in the sea, gripping the necks of the Malay boys playing *chang kuda*, heaving at the rope, yelling her heart out pulling for the class tug-of-war team. She saw she was no ordinary girl; no ordinary woman. Aiyah! Bertha, she said to herself, softly, slowly, you are beautiful.

She turned around and looked at the back of her legs. She thought her calves, round, firm and shapely, were really super.

It was her calves that the feather-duster lashed against that night with her Pa trembling with rage and her mother standing in the corner shouting at him, "Give it to her, Jim ... the little bitch."

She was sixteen then. Wally Oehlers had got a crush on her. He was nice, but such a "cissy" in some ways. Thin like a *chaching kring*. But he could afford to buy her sarsee and smarties. He could also afford to take her to the pictures now and then.

That evening, they had been to the six-thirty. It was a wet night with an overcast sky. It was quite dark by the time Wally and Bertha got back to her house. He had kissed her before. She had loved it. Jenny, Mabel, Phyllis and Mavis had been shocked and impressed when she told them. She described her feelings to them to squeeze the most out of her triumph. That night Wally made a grab at her as he said good night. She melted into his arms. She had just seen the style on the screen. She kissed him with her whole body, thrilling more to the experience than to Wally. They held it for ever so long. Then Wally's hand moved to her breast, which was full and round. She didn't make the slightest move of protest. She felt her whole being tingle. Her mouth pressed harder against Wally's for a minute and she pushed him away, turned around and ran towards the house.

Then she saw her Pa. He had had dinner and was standing at the verandah rail in his *sarong*. In a flash she realised that he could have seen her in spite of the darkness because the neighbour's portico light was on.

"You bloody bitch!" he shouted, forgetting himself, forgetting that the whole line of quarters could hear him with the roaring violence and volume of his shout.

He hit her again and again on her calves, fuming, beside himself with anger. He had shouted at Mary when she started to protest that the bloody bitch was letting that Oehlers bastard play with her "*susu.*" Mary reeled with shock and added her curses on Bertha's head.

Bertha stood stock still. She braced herself and told herself that this was the price … it wouldn't be for long. These old fashioned folks of hers … bloody Catholics, out of bloody date.

Mary sobbed in bed that night. James held her close. "We've done all we can, Mary. Somewhere in her there's bad blood." "It's not what she did, Jim, that pains me. It's the way she defied us while you caned her … it won't do her any good. Oh God! What kind of woman is she going to be, Jim …?"

~ Chapter Three ~

Back to the Bar.

I had come to Perth for ten days. My company in Singapore was going into a joint-sales programme with Ray's company in Perth, selling LPG gas cylinders which we manufactured in Singapore. I was to work with Ray to develop and detail plans for our Australian sales drive. So we spent most of the time together and, after the day's work was done, we went off and had a drink somewhere.

"What about that place where we met Old Joe?" he suggested on the following day. "Some of the things he said amused me."

"OK," I agreed. So we went there. And Joe was there when we arrived. And again, I thought he had already been there for a couple of hours. He was not alone. He was with a man who looked very much like a Singaporean. Eurasian or Malay, I was not sure.

"Hey, Ray! Robert! Howyergoing mate?" he called out to us.

"Allrighty Joe. How's yerself?"

"Meet a Singapore friend of mine. John Peters. Ray and Robert."

John Peters was brown, perhaps you could say black; about my age, perhaps two or three years older. Dressed smartly like a regular business executive. Probably an accountant, I thought to myself.

We said our Hi's. "John's another Singapore migrant, but he's totally fresh. Just got here last month ... still cannot pronounce Hay Street. Ha! Ha!"

"But I've been here a couple of times on holiday, that's why we were sure that this is the land for us."

"Good on you, mate," Ray did his patriotic bit. "How'sit goin' so far?"

"So-so ... Have got myself a house and wheels, put the kiddies in school."

"How many have you got?"

"Three."

And so it went on for a bit. I kept quiet. I was waiting for Joe to lay out the family linkages. It came soon enough.

"You should know John, his mother was ..." It was all a blur to me. In the blur, I heard D'Cotta and Dragons and a Braga ... Leceisters, Kraals, Tessensohns, Clarkes, Pintos, MacCullys. I saw Ray too had switched off. But suddenly I heard him say, "He used to go hunting with James, your grandfather, Robert, before the war.

"He was one bugger. Damn good shot, but he'd always pick the best position for himself. Mind you, the bugger knew how to choose the best position. Old Pak Bujang told me one day that he soon realised Tony was always trying to get himself in front, so one day he purposely got the beaters to drive the pigs in a different way and poor old Tony never got a clear line that day. Your dad, Robert, was a good man with a gun too. Damn good eye."

"I remember all the *babi utan* we used to have. Hey but hang on. James Rodrigues was not HIS father."

"I never said dat! I jus sed he was a good shot."

"Ahh, sorry ... You were saying."

"Yeah, Tony was a bugger all right. He used to swear like a *china-bek-chak* all the time." He chuckled, and continued. "He was the fellow who really was the cause of your grandfather's embarrassment, before the war ... at the St. Joseph's church funfair."

"What was that all about?"

"Little Bertha ... so they tell me. There was this stall where you threw a ball and hit some bloody thing or other. James knew his girl, even at five or six whatever she was then, was good at throwing, so he lifted her up on the counter and let her have a go ...Parp! Parp! Two shots in succession, she hit the target.

"Whoa! everyone said ... even the Padre was impressed. He was standing there just behind James. She's got one more ball. She threw and missed. Then she says out loudly: 'Fukkit,' not once but again and again. 'Fukkit, fukkit, fukkit ...' Poor Mary Rodrigues was so *malu*. James gets her down at once and moves off quickly. The bloody *kitchie-brat* keeps saying, 'Fukkit, fukkit ...' They take her away to a far away corner of the field.

"Mary takes over. She does not scold the girl. She only asks,'Girl, where did you learn to say that word?' Bertha tells her, Uncle Tony. You know from that day James would never let Tony into the house. Not that he stopped going to Johor to shoot pig with him, but no more of the old drinks at James's place when they came back. They had to go to that Lesslar bugger's place, whassisname ...?"

"Hey, Joe," John spoke up, "You tell the story like it was your time. Bloody James Rottengeese was ..." Ray broke out into laughter. It wasn't funny to us. We had been through the Rottengeese version of Rodrigues a million times ... like the Tua Sung Tsern for Tessensohn, Holyfellah for Oliveiro, and those age-old twists.

John continued. It was obvious that he had known Joe for some time and the familiarity coupled with respect that the community accepted between generation gaps was obvious.

"Joe, you can spin out a story like you were there ... any time. Dammit, ASP Rodrigues was your fadder's time, man!"

"Yeah but you know the old folks used to tell these stories so many times, you could feel it happened to you. That story of Bertha I heard at every birthday party in Katong."

"You got the gift, mate," Ray chipped in.

"No lah! It's jus that you hear it so many times ... and the stories of Bertha were really repeated so many times ... there's the one about when she caught the ball."

"Whose balls?" John asked, trying to be funny. I winced. Ray tossed out his corny-joke-or-shaggy-dog-story-I'm-bored to-utter-death look.

The ordering of another round disrupted the conversation. But Old Joe was not put off.

"You know her brother Eric was an absolute wizard wit the hockey stick. At seventeen, he played for the Hornets."

"The Hornets?"

"Yes, a small group of top-class players ... they had no club. You young buggers these days are really spoilt. Those days we had to organise ourselves ... Get the sticks, make the jerseys, find the field. They played at the ACS field at Barker Road."

"You mean at the Barker Road Dunearn junction?"

"Yes, lah!" Joe said impatiently. He didn't like to lose the swing of his anecdotes. "Bertha was a little girl then."

"Lemme see ... twelve? Thirteen ...?"

"About that lah!" Again with impatience. John got the message. From the subtle adjustment of his stance I saw he was resigned to listen without interrupting.

"Sometimes they would just play against some *kuching-kurap* team ... to give them practice, before they took on the "Saylon" Sports club buggers. No spectators, no supporters, except a few wives and sweethearts. But in one corner of the field every evening there were at least six prams ... and the black and white *amahs*, taking their white babies for a walk and talking of their *mems* and *tuans*. And there were the older kids, like three to seven hanging around. The *amahs* used to break away from their long bloody stories sometimes and call out, 'Doan sit there Roland ... must not sit on hot cement.' 'Aiyah! Sodertty!' but the little European kids used so sit on the side and watch the Hornets ... specially the older ones. When Eric started wit the Hornets, Bertha used to go there every time he played ... One day she was like kneeling on the side-line when someone flicked a ball out. Tarp! A hard flick, man. It went straight to the face of one of those European kids ... but Bertha saw it at once. Tarp! her hand went out and caught it. Old Pennefather saw her catch the ball. He was shocked ... er ... impressed, I mean, lah.

"The game went on, but he went up to her. 'Hey girl, you're fast.' Afterwards he found out that Bertha was Eric's sister.

"Now," Joe paused for effect, like a practised actor, "the next day, or the next time the Hornets played there, a big Bentley drove up. A big burly European came out and spoke to an *amah* and then he went up to Bertha who, as always, was there, and he thanked her for saving his boy from getting hurt. It turned out that he was the commissioner! He asked Bertha her name, and the next day James got a call. Whoa! He was so shock! He went home and hugged Bertha and tole Mary the story."

"So! James got promoted?" John asked cynically. It looked like he too was getting bored at Joe's monologues.

"No lah! The real thing was that old Pennefather allowed Bertha to practise with the team and that's how she got her style. Hey man, she played for Singapore at seventeen."

"Bertha ... You mentioned her last night didn't you, Joe?"

"Yah! Robert's aunt."

"There was a mystery about her, wasn't there?"

"Yeah."

"What was it? I've forgotten."

I pricked up my ears. Ray had broken Old Joe's gush of reminiscences, or reminiscences of other people's tales. It snapped our group out of the listening-to-one-man phase. John turned to me, asking whether I had emigrated, or what was I doing there and all that sort of thing. We started talking to each other. He was standing beside me. In the corner of my eye and, with half an ear, I heard old Joe telling Ray something about Bertha.

"Confrontasi ... Heng ... the Silver Inn ... that bloody bitch. Mildred ... screwing her ... Jeez!" while I chatted to John about the friendliness of Australia, the hang loose and in some ways *tidak-apa-ness* of Western Australia ... "Would I like to bring up a teenager here? ... the big open spaces ... Spoilt lah! ... spoilt by the wealth of the land ... all those minerals ... all that bloody space. Did you hear the one about ...? But all said and done, between the education system in Singapore and the Chinese politics. Hey! Whaddyamean ...? ... Whaddyer spect ... wit 85 per cent? Doan get so het up, ssjus the fact that we can't beat them in maths. Christ, those buggers get four bloody 'A's in add mats ... Come on man, you use your advantages. We speak English ... .not 'Singlish.' Yeah, but ..."

"Yah! She was a good looker ... not just dat, she had the brains, only she never could concentrate when she was younger. To tink dat was the trouble in dose days ... too many distractions. You know, there's someting to be sait about the old *towkay* an his concubines. Used up all his bad blood, came out clean. Ate his *hokkien mee* at two o'clock after it was over an finished wit sex for the week ... The bugger could give his whole mine to his bizness."

"So, Robert, you'll only be here for a week?" "No, ten days ... well, eight more to go." "Why doan you come over one night, meet Syl ... Sylvia an the family?" "Goot to tok of ole times ..." John and I. Me, half an ear cocked to Old Joe's talking.

"You know Ray, it took me years to work the bloody ting out. It's only becos I tok to people alla time dat I finally found out what happened to Bertha and ..."

"I've been in accounting all my life ... not so exciting as sales ah?" "No, It's not the excitement. It's seeing results. Look at our fren Rudy, he chases a bloody story every day. He gets a high when he hits page one ... but he cannot look back at the end of the year. Every high lasts twenty four hours only ... or is it twelve? Or eight?"

"Yeah ... you've gotta keep reviewing. You know my old man used to sit at the dining table every year in his tuxedo, waiting for my Mum to tittivate herself for the GSC ball, an work out what he had earned an spent an saved every year. Then she would come out of the bedroom, all lipsticked an fancy, an wait for my Dad to finish his figures ... Sss something I remember. He did his review every year ... like what they tole us at the magement courses."

"The nerve of the woman. By God, Ray, the woman had passion, fire, an what-have-you, but yet she could be as cold as a bloody fish ..."

"ROBERT!" Ray almost shouted at me, "We've gotta go!"

I read his voice, volume, tone, body, gestures. Maybe I read more than the signals he sent ... but I thought Ray was saying, "Let's go! Old Joe is not going to tell us any more of the Bertha affair tonight. And that's all I can take of him, and your bloody incestuous Eurasian community, though you're a nice guy ..."

We left.

~ *Chapter four.* ~

Mary Rodrigues.

The fifties were a difficult period for James. First there was the Maria Hertogh affair. The first real riots that Singapore had ever experienced which arose out of a legal wrangle between Maria Hertogh's Dutch parents and her adopted Malay parents. It had religious, racial and political overtones. James remembered it as the Maria Bertha Hertogh affair, with her full name. "All the bloody Malays are on the rampage," were the words he used to sum up the situation to Mary. "And what's bloody worse, they are going for us when they can't find a bloody European." Mary was visibly shaken as James related the details of the riots; it seemed to her that a dragon had leapt out of the ground and was raging through the streets of Singapore.

It was not like the Indian mutiny that her father had told her about. That was a fighting between two groups of outsiders; the Indian Sepoys, as she called them, and the *orang puteh*, the white men. This was different. Despite the huge religious gap between them she regarded the Malays as "us." She spoke their language. Not very competently but in the language of the common people, understanding the nuances of words like *geram* and *takut* and *malu*. She knew their superstitions and, in fact, hung onto a lot of the same superstitions herself. With James being in "the force," she now had more Malay friends than she ever had. "But what is this word *merdeka*?" she asked James. "Is it Indonesian?"

"I think so. It means freedom," he replied.

Freedom? Mary was puzzled. It didn't seem to have anything to do with that Dutch girl Maria. But there were things she didn't understand, like the first planes without propellers. She had learnt to ignore the complexities behind them. She knew that, if they stayed around, she would accept them in the course of time.

James was most disturbed that the mobs were attacking Eurasians. It was frightening to him. They had never been treated like some different race before. Well … apart from the Japanese time. They were not accepted by the Europeans. They were not Europeans. That was fair enough. But the Europeans knew that they were loyal to the king. They knew that we understood them better than any other Singapore people. And we spoke English. Not John Chinaman's pidgin. But today, these Malay mobs were going for us. It set them apart. It isolated them. James was worried. Shit. This is our country …

He saw Mary suddenly start up. "James, is there any trouble in Stamford Road ?" … "Why?" … "Beryl and Bertha went to the pictures … to the Capitol." … "Gawd!" James gasped. "There are no buses running … no taxis. What time did the show finish?" he asked and immediately answered his question, "The three o'clock show, I suppose, that would have ended about five-thirty."

He looked across at Mary. She was pale with fear. "But there's no trouble there. It's just that they will have trouble getting back." Silently he thanked his Catholic God for making them brown. And he knew the girls spoke fluent Malay. They could pass off … or they could talk to the mob. Huh! Talk to the mob!

He went to the phone. Mary could not hear what he said. But she heard him speaking in a calm, quiet tone. Not like when there was a small crisis when the sergeant had bungled some thing or other. She knew her James kept his cool when the pressure was on.

"Think, Mary … What would they do? Go to Jerry's place?"

"No … I don't think they know how to get there. You have always driven us. I know. They will go to the church."

"But that is too far away."

"Not our church, the French church."

"Oh no! They wouldn't. That's not our place …"

"Oh I know! They'll go to the YWCA."

"Christ Ma! That's a bloody Methodist thing, isn't it?"

"Yes, but Beryl knows Peggy Reutens who lives there. She's been there several times. Peggy is from Penang, that's why she's staying there. She's come to Singapore to work. Her folks said that it was a safe place for her to stay."

"You mean they take in Catholics too?"

"Of course. It's not what you think. They are good people."

James walked slowly to the phone. Mary tried hard to listen without going up to the phone to show how anxious she was. She had to keep a calm front, she told herself, to help James.

He took longer than she expected. He made more than one call. After what she thought was half an hour he came back to the verandah where Mary was sitting, gripping the arms of the cane chair.

"I've asked a snipe to go there." She knew what he meant. One of the Humber snipes of the radio squad. "Their phone was not working. I don't know why."

The phone rang. James jumped up. But once on his feet he controlled himself and walked slowly, thinking what to do if the news was bad.

He came back to the verandah walking quickly. He put his hands on Mary's shoulders and said to her. "It's all right. You were right, Ma. They were at the YW." Mary let out a long sigh. "Thank God !" "Radio is bringing them home. I also told them to bring Peggy Reutens back here. We'll send a cable to her folks in Penang. They'll be worried like hell when they hear the nine-thirty news."

Mary's eyes filled with tears. "Oh James."

"Where's Eric?" James suddenly asked.

"He's in his room playing his geetar."

James went to the sideboard and poured himself a whisky. He went to the fridge and topped it up with soda. He returned to the verandah and passed the glass to Mary. He always did that. Mary didn't drink whisky but, every evening, since he took over "D" he poured a drink as soon as he came home and passed it to her for one first and last sip. It had become a ritual. Mary looked forward to that one sip. On some evenings, she would then stir herself and get out the bottle of sherry or Wincarnis for herself. But not often.

"It's very thin today," she said.

"Yah, I'm on stand-by."

That was the first of the surprises of the fifties. It was an earthshaking shock to James and his circle; not just his police circle but his SRC friends and the "Antedeluvian Association of Froth Blowers," an almost masonic type of club of camaraderie to which he belonged. Some Europeans were also members, he used to say quietly to his friends. They talked about it for weeks; the dragon that had been born so suddenly, so unexpectedly. "What the hell were the special branch doing? They should have predicted this sort of thing." "They were busy, man, tracking the Commies." James thought about this. "Yah, they're right, that's the real danger … mark my bloody words, Joe, that's where the trouble is going to be … the bloody Chinks."

James was right. The fifties saw him under pressure from the strikes and the demonstrations. The demonstrations and protests against colonial rule. The pickets. The students of the Chinese schools. The old distrust he had for the Chinese, which, he had explained to himself, was because they were far smarter than us Seranis, returned. The trust that the European officers had in him and the other Eurasian officers bolstered his confidence in the British. He was transferred to the "riot squad" and as he cleared unruly pickets and singing students, his anti-Chinese feelings which had been seeded in him by his parents, which had lain dormant and never ever boiled, grew. Some nights, sitting in the verandah with his *stengah* cold in his hand, inhaling his "Players" with the mosquito coil smoke, he pulled himself back and thought about people. The Chinese and Malay friends he knew. The wretched hovel he had to go into near Lorong Three; a flimsy thing of zinc sheets and cardboard, when he was looking for the 07 gang leader; the little Malay boy with his *sarong* round his shoulders crying after the fire at Jalan Eunos; the old prostitute beaten up by the sailor. These were people. Not Chinese or Malays. I must get a grip on myself.

It's the bloody commies we're fighting. Not the Chinese.

Mary used to come and sit by him sometimes. The dinner was ready. But she knew there were nights when James wanted to be by himself or wanted to talk to her a little longer before she called the family to dinner. Anyway, the kids weren't hungry. There was the wireless now … if only her mother had lived to hear what one could get on the wireless these days …

Some nights, James talked about things she knew well. But sometimes, he rambled on about promotions, or the Godammed unreliable Malay PC's, or the gambling dens or that Reg Watson, the OCPD, a real gentleman, which she listened to silently thinking about the price of pork, or whether the *ikan selah* would be fresh tomorrow and things like that.

But Mary knew that those were hard times for "the force." And they coincided with the hard time they were having with their children growing up. It was not Beryl; she was the sweetest thing one could ever hope for; nor Eric, he had his hockey and his "geetar." Most of the trouble was with Bertha, God bless her!

But still she was so sweet … Aiyah! *Apa boleh buat!*

And in the midst of all this, Beryl comes home one night and says she wants to get married. She should have seen it coming. She knew it, but somehow when it came she cried her eyes out until James got impatient with her. "Look Mary, It's Hubert Machado's son … I know he's no star but he's solid lah.'

James was confident in consoling Mary that night. But he fumbled and stuttered when the "young pup" came up to him two days later and did the absolutely traditional thing and asked for Beryl's hand. Yah! By God, those were the words he used! He told them years later. Ben Machado was almost trembling. James smelled and saw that Ben had had a drink, possibly two … but then you never know with these young blokes … some of them go all red in the eye with jus a small "Anchor" … probably had one at the "Colonial Bar" at "Tekka." James tried his very best to smile and put on his you-can-trust-me-I'm-not-like-the-others face that he had used so often with suspicious or frightened witnesses. Dammit!

I was trying to help the guy. Ben said his piece. Then James almost cracked with nervousness. He offered Ben Machado a whisky … that gave him some time … but when it was poured and the distraction extended by explaining the virtues of "Haig" … the terrible silence descended upon the verandah that had been his solace-place for years. Eventually, the ordeal was over. He gave his pompous "Yes." Later, he felt bad about the way he said it. He could have been more informal … perhaps a joke … a slightly "off" joke would have relaxed young Ben … perhaps when Bertha gets married he would be able to do it better …

Then the Godammed details started. Aiyah! The "banns," the hall, flower-girls, Ruth Fox getting all upset about her daughter not being chosen, Mary being "conned" by the Portuguese priest to have the full choir which cost so much more, getting the OCPD to lend them his car; he really should have stood his ground against Mary on that. The biggest bust-up was with the band. He told Jesus Otega one night at the SRC that he wanted him to play, but when he came home and told Mary, she said they had agreed on the Eber boys' band. He did not! Oh Yes YOU DID! I DID NOT! Last week, here in this very house, on the verandah! I can remember your words. OK Dottie, as long as they can play 'Jingli Nonah' and some Victor Sylvester stuff, *boleh lah*!"

"*Chelaka*! I did not !"

Finally the Eber boys' band played … "Jim, we've got to support our own people," Dottie had said. She had obviously come round the next day because Mary had rung her. "What the hell you wan to get a blerdy Filipino band for a Serani wedding. Your mother will die!"

Finally, even though Mary had discovered that half the *buah kelwa* she had bought were bad on the day before the wedding, and Basil Monteiro had had a puncture on his way down from Malacca bringing the *chinchalok*, and Beryl developed a pimple on her nose … not really on her nose, just near it, and Ah Fatt had not done his suit right and had to change the padding on the shoulders, and in spite of the argument he had with Bertha, their baby, he'd forgotten she was already sixteen then ... she had drafted his speech, he still remembers what he said to her, "Hey girl, this is my speech. Nobody asked you to write it out.. You think I am David Marshall making a policy speech! I'll bloody well say what I want to, and in my own way. I don't care if the deputy commissioner is there or not. I don't need your high-falutin stuff, Bertha. I'll speak from my heart." In spite of all the dreadful crises in the last few days it went off "wit a bang."

It was a wedding they talked about up to Easter. James had done it right.

Beryl looked radiant. His knees were shaking as he led her up the aisle. That bloody Ben turned round to look against all tradition, the Padre made a nice sermon, as far as the parts he heard were concerned. James remembered how he bent over the back of the seat in front of him after holy Communion and from the very bottom of his heart implored his God, his creator, to bless them and let them love each other and live a happy life. No wars, no poverty. Please God! He prayed with his whole soul that evening.

Yes, it was an evening wedding ... The church had agreed to evening weddings, that was good ... The whole crowd could move on to the hall for the celebrations.

They didn't have champagne, only those modern people served champagne ... like the Stewarts. They had champagne at Winnie's wedding. But we had all the whisky in the world one needed ... thanks to Bertie. He got the staff price from John Littles, or was it Hagemeyers or Guthries. Yah! Guthries.

Old Bertie. He'd been at Guthries for bloody years. Seen so many expats come and go. Quiet bugger ... until he'd had a few. The only thing about Bertie was his political views. He was probably the only Serani at the SRC in those days who stood at the bar and defended the PAP. "What about Byrne? Barker? Marcus? ... a founder member of the Peoples' Action Party." "Yes lah!" But Bertie was one of us ... the best spin bowler the SRC ever had.

Yah! That day he took the Delikan fellow ... the ball really jumped as though it was charmed. Shuuut! ... it suddenly shot out behind Delikan's bat.

It was a wonderful wedding. In the garden the young ones lit sparklers and whirled them around in circles and threw them up high, high, high into the sky. In the kitchen, they swore and cursed because the devil curry was not ready, the onions not sliced thin enough … quick! The *sambal lengkong* had to be replenished. They laughed when Auntie May dropped the *achar* on top of the ham; when Phyllis Demornay stopped Jenny from serving the last portion of *tau-yu-bak* because she said the kitchen people should have it. In the hall, the ladies laughed at the Padre's jokes about his sermon. He was a one, this Padre. Did they say the Portuguese priests joined the seminary when they were fifteen? All these years though, he hadn't learnt Malay, he still had his Portuguese accent. He really was a one … reminds me of Dolly's wedding. That fellow … what was his name? … Father Dias? I can't remember. Oh, you mean Dolly Paul's wedding? Yes lah! … whoa that was a one. Auntie Gladys danced the Branyong. Ha, Ha, ha … Yes, she was a live wire wasn't she? Talking of weddings do any of you remember Angella James's wedding. You mean Millicent's daughter? Yes lah! The fight? Yeaaaaah … those Danker boys. Disgraceful! … Hey Millie, what ever happened to your old beau, that Dutch fellow? Please lah, Dulcie … let sleeping dogs lie.

In the dance hall, the wedding really swung. The Eber band could do an imitation of Satchmo's "Give me a kiss to build a dream on" and some Doris Day smoochie numbers, and for the Dads and Mums the old Vera Lynn hits … Young Gerry Cordeiro was risking his reputation dancing the slow fox tightly, ever so tightly, with the Angus girl. Bertha Rodrigues led Danny across the floor, spinning, whirling, his eyes locked on her, gasping with excitement … Jack LaBrooy was jiving like a mad man, muttering his "tara-tum-da-da-da-deee-dah ba-ba-ba's" and other absolutely "in" mouthings as he held his arm up and let his partner spin and let herself go … go, go go … those were the buzz-words. Jack was a one. They watched him and wished they could dance like Jack, but wouldn't want to be as ugly as Jacky. Only Jean Rappa wished she had Jack's brains … but Jean Rappa was different … Phil winked at Doris as Henry spun her round. Doris knew, it took this wedding to jell that. Doris hugged her *Katek* Danny." She loved him … even though her chin pressed down on his head as they danced. She watched the Read girl smile at her in a knowing way as Kishore danced past her sliding smoothly as though he was skimming over ice …

They all had a good time on the floor at the wedding. They also had a "Damn good-bloody-night" at the bar … Herman told his story for the billionth time about this Chinese girl, Amy. They guffawed but when Balwant, "he's one of us, the bloody shaven *bai*," told his tale of the D'almeida girl in the Malacca hotel. It eclipsed Herman's yarn. And so they went on …the incident at Kota Tinggi, when the tiger came rushing through with the *babi utan*, Aloy hit him. He was damn quick … Where was that? Kota Tinggi lah ! Not that *kampong* where they have that *kramat*? Yah! Dat's der place … Pak Smail? … Yah! … where there's that *chempedak* tree that leans over. Yes lah! You mean you know Pak Ismail? … Well, well, well, it's a small world.. Did you say it's a "smail" world … Ha.Ha.Ha.

It was a great wedding. They relived the hunting escapades in Johor … the keluang shooting, always referring to flying foxes as "birds" … the snipe shooting. Man, you gotta be quick … the fight at the New World when Bautista hit that Chinese bugger. They relived the North-South Rugger final of 51 … the Fijians came up … their speed. That Joe Lullela fellow … whatssisname, Joe Lulleal? Lollala? Hey you're confusing him, LaLolla, Lolla jolly-body, with that Penang bugger who trained the north side … You know he used to get the young buggers and teach them the follow-through with a durian? They did have a good time at the bar. It was a great wedding … Beryl's wedding was an event of the fifties … they said no one would ever forget that night. That was a night, man! … But then they did not know that Theresa Pestana would be marrying within a few years' time. Beryl's wedding made Eurasian community history … but that was before Theresa Pestana married …

For Bertha it was a night of ecstasy. She collapsed on her bed thinking only of him … his smile, his voice, his touch, the way he held her when he danced … when he said she was beautiful … he told her that she was "Beautiful." Yes, he said, "beautiful!" … Oh my darling! For Bertha it was a milestone.

That was Beryl's wedding …

Chapter five.

Carl Westerhout

Ray had to go somewhere on Thursday morning so he asked Nick to pick me up from the motel. Nick had a car pool going with Dave and some other bloke from "shipping," so the car was full.

"G'day. This is Robert. Robert, this is Pedro."

"Nice day, isn't it?"

"You're from Singapore I hear. My grandad was out there during the war. Got locked up in Changi, then went to the railway. Had a helluva time. Won't buy any Jap thing now if he can help it."

"That's OK, if he can help it. Let's em off his own bloody hook."

"I guess the bad feelings against the Japs have all gone now in Singapore."

"Yeah ... but haven't they got new feelings about the 'economic occupation?' "

"No. The Japanese have not really moved into Singapore."

"Yet, mate. Don't ferget to add the 'yet' bit. They've moved in here. They'd take over the bloody country if it wasn't for Hawkie."

"Kill it, Dave. You must excuse our friend here, Robert; he's the political one in the company. If you want to know anything about any political issue, just ask Dave here. He'll tell you. It may take two or three hours, though."

"Yep, Robert. He'll give it to you. The complete story of one side."

"Huh! That's the trouble with this country, Robert. Nobody's interested in politics."

Nick intervened. "How's the boat, Pedro?"

We drove to the office through this morning chatter and the

morning traffic. As we walked out of the car park Nick suggested we get together that evening for a "glass or two."

I told Ray that Nick had suggested the drink when we finished that evening. But even as I was saying it Nick walked into Ray's room.

"I got Dave and Pedro stamping their feet impatiently in the carpark. If we don't go now they'll start their withdrawal spasms. You bring Robert, Ray? Where to? That's the only decision."

"We've been going to that place near the Burger King, just after you pass the Humes factory. How about that?"

"Oh yes, I know it. Yeah ... that'll do. See yer there."

"You don't have to go there to make up for your impatience last night, Ray," I said after Nick had left. Ray just grinned.

Later in the car he said, "Funny bloke, that Old Joe chappie. Interesting though. But what happened to your aunt eventually?"

"Dunno ... that's a family skeleton. So no one would tell me."

"Tell you what. We'll get old Joe really pissed tonight and give him the full pumping routine."

"That's no problem. It's keeping him on the same track that'll drive us round the bend."

"Simple, fellah! All we gotta do is tell him straight. Joe we only want to hear about Bertha."

"OK. We'll give it a whirl."

The bar was crowded when we went in. Dave suggested he get a jug. Pedro protested that it really cost more. "But it's my round and my money, so shut your mouth my Latin friend!"

We could not see if Old Joe was there. The conversation went straight into shoptalk. By-laws, regulations, the Danish gas regulators, aluminium ones, west farmers changing the pricing, the camping cylinder market. We stayed on it for some time. It came round to my turn. I decided to follow Dave's example and get a jug. It was so much easier when the place was crowded. I pushed my way into a gap at the bar and was just about to place the order when a voice boomed out behind me.

"So there you are, Robert. I thought you guys weren't here."

"Hello Joe! Awfully crowded today, isn't it?"

"Come and join us. There's a whole bunch of *geragoks* here tonight."

"We're with some other blokes from the 'orifice.' We may join you later. See how it goes."

Nick and his carpool group just stayed for one cycle, as I thought of it myself, now being quite used to the Australian way. That was five glasses that night. Ray bought a packet of crisps when he got the last round.

"Better eat, Robert. We're going to have a hard evening."

As if it would help, I thought to myself. Still, if there's a psychological effect.

We joined Old Joe's group. There were four of them, Old Joe and three strangers to me. One like Old Joe was brown and sunburnt. One looked like an Indian. Not really dark but with a brownish-yellowish skin like some Indians have. The type who could pass off as a dark Italian, Lebanese, Indonesian or what have you. Like my Dad used to say, in the dark bars in Singapore the girls asked him if he was an *ang moh* and in the dark nightclubs of London, they asked him if he was Chinese.

The third of the new faces was definitely Eurasian. He was fair. Fair skinned, that is. With dark brownish hair. One could take him as a Caucasian at first glance, but people like us and the South Americans, who are continuously conscious of race, would notice that his eyes and cheekbones were different. He was introduced as "Carl." The others were Cuthbert and Steven. They were all about Old Joe's age, perhaps a little younger.

"Robert here is from Singapore," Old Joe added after introductions and "Hi's," to lead the talk his way. "Cuthbert's now an old Australian, as opposed to new, Steven's from Malacca, a newie ... and this bugger Carl, I don't know where he says he's from."

"Come on, Joe ..." Carl slapped him on the back. "You bloody well know I'm one of your crazy mixed-up lot." The accent was not a Singapore-Malaysian one.

Ray had understood Old Joe's easy way and the way his friends could take ethnic cracks at each other. He butted in.

"Looks like a pom, speaks like a pom."

"But is not a pom," Carl finished it for Ray. We laughed. Carl went on the explain that he was a"dinky-die" *geragok* and assured us that his grandmother chewed betel nut and could speak Portuguese as fluently as she could speak Malay. He could even show us the graves of his ancestors in Malacca and on Fort Canning in Singapore.

"And," Joe added, "the bones of his grandfathers and grandmothers which were dug out of the Bukit Timah cemetery and moved to some God-forsaken place. Lim Chu Kang or Yio Chu Kang or Chua Chu Kang ... one of the bloody Chu Kangs, anyway. If I didn't come here I would be lying unpeacefully there."

"This really bugs Joe," Steven said. "He was hoping it would be Bidadari cemetery for him. But not Bukit Brown eh Joe?"

"Sheeesh."

"What so bad about Bukit Brown? I presume it's a cemetery?" Ray asked.

"It is. It is the Chinese cemetery."

"Joe cannot be buried there. He used to make love on the graves there in his wild young days. Right, Joe?"

"Yeahhha, ha-ha." A "yeah" sliding into a chuckle. "It was the safest place. No Chinese thugs would annoy you there. No one was around at night. And it was nice high ground."

"You are superstitious about the elevation above sea level for making love?"

"No lah! Not so damp, lah."

"What about the ghosts?"

"That was no problem. That was the beauty of it. Chinese ghosts would not worry us. They were busy enough with the Chinese. Eating all the food they were offered."

"Would Malay ghosts disturb you?"

"Of course."

"Bloody Joe's crazy ideas."

The talk drifted to subjects of migrants. Where Asian food could be bought. The older ones flaunted their knowledge and leapt into tales of the old days when things were so different. Six o'clock swill and all that. One could get liver and fish heads for almost free then.

Then Cuthbert said he had to go, "The old girl's waiting ..."

Steven took the opportunity and said he too had to go. His old girl was waiting too. They went off with "see yer's."

Old Joe opened up after they had left. "You know, young man," looking at me, "this bloke here might have been your uncle."

His head jerked towards Carl. Carl grinned a self-conscious grin, with a "huh" almost not articulated.

Ray's eyes lit up. "You mean he nearly married Bertha, Joe?"

"Yeah."

"You know Bertha?" Carl asked with surprise.

"Oh no. It's just that Joe here was talking about her the other night when he realised that Bertha was Robert's aunt. She seemed to be someone very special."

"Yeah ... she was in a way." There was a tone of finality in Carl's comment. But Joe would not let him off so easily.

"You were her first real love, weren't you?"

"Good Lord, no."

"Of course you were. Those other buggers were just hordie-ervers ... just starters."

Ray pressed on. "Joe was saying she played in the state hockey team when she was seventeen."

"Yes. She had looks, brains and a quick eye."

"And a beautiful body," Joe added.

"Yeah, so Joe said ..." Ray keeping the pot boiling. I was silent. Somehow I felt uncomfortable. I should have known all about the whole affair, if it was an affair, that is. Somehow it didn't seem right that these outsiders were talking about my family. And more than that, this Australian prodding away, hungry for more information, like a bitch smelling blood or scandal. But these thoughts just drifted by in me without unsettling me. I was a generation away.

Not just in the distance of ages but with different family and community attitudes ... well, different in some ways ... most ways.

"She played left wing. Not that she was left handed. She decided that there were few who could play this position and worked at it. Drove herself at it, in fact. She was a pretty determined girl, in many ways."

"Too determined for you?" Ray with a probing half-smile.

"I guess that could have been one of the reasons ... that was all a long time ago, mate."

"And the other reasons?" Joe moved in, following on Ray's interrogation.

"Incompatibility is the word they use nowadays."

"No, tell us, Carl. I have often wondered why the two of you broke up. You could have brought out the best in her, you know ..." Joe spoke in his best persuasive voice.

"Is one supposed to do that to one's spouse?"

"You don't do it consciously. It happens."

"Oh no! Not if the woman is a strong person."

"It's relative. It's who's stronger, isn't it?"

"In your case, with your brains and your education, and your strong silent force, Carl, you could have influenced her, moulded her to your benefit ... to your mutual benefit, I should say."

"It's got nothing to do with education."

"Indirectly it has. Doesn't matter whether you're a doctor or engineer or a "liar." It's having been abroad an mixed wit udder people, seen udder tings. Dat's what it is."

"Just maturing, you mean huh."

"But surely, Carl," Ray asked, "that's the last thing one thinks about when one is thinking of getting married?"

"Not if you're a crazy idealist."

"Tell us, when you got married did you think of how you would change your future wife?"

"Carl's still a bachelor."

"Oh dear ... I'm sorry."

"Hey don't be sorry."

Ray was restless. It wasn't going his way. He tried another tack. "Did you ever hear the full story about Bertha?"

"It didn't interest me then. But people have kept telling me all sorts of things. I don't know what's true and what's concocted. Do you know what actually happened, Joe?"

"Yes, I tink I do."

We waited. Joe drained his glass slowly, relishing the anticipation on our faces. "Ah! That was good."

"My turn," Ray said. "What about switching to scotch?"

"Yep, a double for me," Joe replied.

Two other "me-too's" and Ray was off to the bar with a faint smile on his lips. The plan was under way.

"Old James Rodrigues was quite upset at first at the whole ting … but later I tink he was secretly pleased wit it all. His daughter had the spunk in her, and it showed … and was an example to all those young pups that you could never be happy with a Chinese. That was how dey taught in dose days, of course."

Ray was back, with his hands full. Joe continued.

"As I always say, it all started at Theresa Pestana's wedding …"

"It did not!" Carl interrupted.

~ *Chapter six* ~

Bertha

The night, after James had caned Bertha on her calves, he tossed in bed for some time. Apart from Mary being so distressed at Bertha's behaviour, he was worried about so many things himself. The least among them kept returning to his confused, angered mind. Is "mama mia" blasphemous?

He had been around, in the coffee shops, street stalls, Geylang bars before, during and after his shifts as a PC and later as an inspector. He had seen the petty thieves, the pickpockets, the organised burglars, the car-stealing gangs. He had seen the tough and the frightened weaklings in the backroom at the station, standing up to or cringing to the threats, the shouts, the kick in the shins, the hard body punches. He had seen the distraught women; mothers of accident victims, wives of men disfigured almost beyond recognition by fire; children snivelling, weeping, staring wild-eyed with shock. At fifty-four now, he'd been around to more places on the island and been in more situations than most of his friends had. He'd been to the PTS upgrading and refresher courses. He'd learnt to handle men in the streets, assistant commissioners behind massive office desks, magistrates and coroners peering down on him over the tops of spectacles balancing on tips of their noses; face to face and through carefully selected, reread and corrected written words. He'd learnt to think and move fast and to sit back, forcing himself at times out of the unending ruts of a bewildered and emotion-blocked mind to rethink along the same path slowly and thoroughly. He had prided himself that he had grown so much since the day he first came home and stood in front of his mother in his PC's uniform.

But tonight, all this knowledge and strength seemed to have gone from him. And over a stupid little thing, he told himself. It's the personal involvement. But still he tossed in bed, unable to sleep. He went to the kitchen to get himself a glass of water. He passed the girls' room on the way. The door was open. They sometimes left it open on a hot night. He could see in the dim altar oil-lamp light that Bertha was lying on her back with her hands joined behind her neck, awake. "Goodnight, Pa," she called out. He mumbled a gruff "Night." He wanted to go in there and put his arms around her and hug her. But that was not him.

Back in bed, he felt the tension seeping out of him. He knew now that, whatever happened to the children, Mary and he must never blame themselves. They had done what they could. Before God they could swear that they had done their duty. But there was still more to be done for their "baby." He must get her on the right track of life. He'd have to think of something. But not now. He was too tired.

James was up at five-thirty the next morning. He brushed his teeth, sat on "the throne," as Mary described it, with a cigarette, and had his morning bath, pouring the cold water from the large ceramic jar onto his body. Like the Malays, he always had a cold bath early in the morning.

Old Muthu had made the tea. He poured a cup for himself, added a large teaspoonful of condensed milk and took it to the verandah. He sat there with a cigarette, thinking.

This was one variation of his morning routines. Sometimes he went out early to the station and took some of the men out to breakfast. If they had time, he preferred the Wayang Satu, an almost tumbled-down coffee shop where the *toseh*, he reckoned, was the best in Singapore. Often, it was *prata*. He himself was not as keen on *nasi lemak* as his corporal.

Sometimes, if he did not have to go to the station early, he would potter around the garden, killing snails crawling across the glistening grass wet with the early morning dew. Or he would weed out a flower bed, or even get out the *changkol* and move a Lantana plant, a Canna, pull out a dying Croton or just mark out a hole for Aramugam to dig when he came in at three after his work with the City Council was over. On those days he had another cold bath before he went to the station or the HQ.

He had time today, but did not chose to do any gardening. He thought about his children: Beryl, so fussy about dirt and little things; Eric so greedy, rushing from school to some mad fishing expedition or to hockey practice; Bertha, still a child in many ways. Because she was the youngest, he said to himself.

Then it came to him. We'll put her in "boarders." He knew that the Cannosians would not take her in as a boarder. The Holy Infant Jesus would. That convent was not associated with their church. But it was for her good. They'd have to change her school. And damn what people say about social climbing. They would still go to St. Joseph's.

But Mary would want to go to the cathedral sometimes so that she could catch a glimpse of Bertha as the boarders in their funny plain white dresses came in. Or as she went up to Communion. And as the boarders filed out of the church when mass was over.

Bertha would hate it, of course. But a year there would do her a world of good. He would have to convince Mary. Later. Yes, he sighed. That was the solution. Boarders, it would have to be. Poor little Bertha.

He rang Jerry Laporte when he had a moment to spare in the afternoon. He had not said a word about his decision to Mary. Not at breakfast nor when he came home for lunch. He wanted to check out the vacancy position first. No use getting her all worked up if there was no place. Jerry was the church organist. He knew the Reverend Mother. Jerry knew everybody that had anything at all to do with the church. His father had played the organ for umpteen years. And now Jerry's eldest, Brian, had started playing at third-class funerals. He was good. They really should let him play at second-class weddings. He was ready for it. James knew next to nothing about music. But he had his opinions.

"Jerry, *apa khabar?*"

"*Baik, tuan besar*. And you?"

"Fine. Jerry, I rang you to ask you to do me a little favour. I want to put our little Bertha in the convent boarders and I was wondering if you would be kind enough to just ask around a bit to see if there's any place for her."

"Your Bertha? But she's no more a little girl."

"Well, yes, she's growing up. Too damn fast, I think at times. But for one reason or another I thought a spell in the boarders would do her a lot of good."

"Why, James? She done something wrong?"

"Yah … in a way, but it's good for them to get away from home for a bit."

"Beryl and Eric seem to have done arright without going there."

"Yah … but Bertha's the youngest one. She gets it too soft at home."

"Well, you know the problem. I'm sure you can fix it, James. But not by putting the girl in the boarders. I strongly advise against it."

"Look, I know they're strict as hell and all that."

"It's not that. James, why don't we meet at the SRC this evening. I'd like to talk to you about it. And don't do anything until we've talked."

"Christ, Jerry! I only asked for some information. Next time I'll ask the CID blokes to find out. But OK. At the SRC. I can get there at five."

"OK. Five. See you there."

James put down the phone. Old Jerry's getting to be a real grandmother. Just like his old man. Wants to straighten you out. Do his charitable thing for the wayward of the parish. I'm not even in the "town church" parish. He bloody well knows that. Just like his old man. He remembered the time the old bugger, Laporte, saw him sneaking into the museum during school hours. Not that James was mad about the Raffles Museum. He liked the animals, though. Especially the *seladang*. But that was the best place to spend the day if you *pontenged* school. It was so cool and quiet.

The old bugger had told his father. It was none of his business, but old Laporte had to try to tidy up all the stray ends that God had forgotten about.

"Hey! What's bugging you?"

It was Alfie Matthews of traffic.

"Hey, hey ... Come sit down, Alf. Saw you at the Aviet's house that night but that old Mrs. Cook got hold of me. Thanks for squashing that ticket the other day. Bloody young twirp. George's son. Thinks he must pass every one on his battered Matchless."

"That's OK. You'd do the same for me one day, no doubt."

Meticulous Alf, recording his you-owe-me's.

"What's bugging you, James? You looked real worried or angry when I came in." That was Alf. Never gave up. You couldn't distract him with anything when he was determined to probe. The "Homicide" man, they called him. "Treats every bloody case like a homicide case." That's where he should be. They always put the wrong guy in the wrong slot. Or squash him into finally fitting into the shape of the slot. Changing his own shape. Bloody Alf. Probing. Might as well tell him.

James told him. Everything. They were good friends.

Alfie grinned from ear to ear as James came to the boarders bit and how Jerry Laporte wanted to meet him to probably try to dissuade him from putting Bertha into the convent boarders. Alfie kept grinning.

"Hey James, you don't get around enough any more."

"Busy lah. Why?"

"You obviously haven't heard about the Santa Maria girl. She was kicked out. Along with a girl from KL. Can't remember the name. Serani. One of the nuns caught the two of them in bed together. There was a big bust up. The bloody Frenchie Reverend Mother accused them of being up to 'wicked acts.' She fired them both. The best part was Mrs. Santa Maria telling the story. Said she never knew that women could do 'wicked acts' together! Gaww! I nearly burst out laughing."

James didn't laugh. It was a bit of a shock to him. In the

convent!

"So what's happened to the Santa Maria girl?"

"Oh, she's in the Cannosians now. Mother Theresa is very understanding. You're allowed to sin and be forgiven there. She knows she is not exactly God."

"Gee, thanks Alf. That's it. No boarders for Bertha." James felt a load fall from his shoulders.

Alfie stayed and talked about the latest in "the force." That barsket Karim got caught fighting in Bugis Street again. That bloody chap is always waiting to have a go at some drunk sailor. He really hates those white buggers. Hey, Sanderson is going up to DSP. Have you heard? Good for him. He deserves it. He does, but how the hell did that good-for-nothing, "Borak" Singh, get promoted? I don't know if it's the bloody PSC or HQ personnel lah!

When Alfie left, James reached for the phone.

"Say Jerry, I'm sorry. Something urgent has turned up. I can't meet you this evening … *Apa boleh buat*! … OK, OK. I promise you, I'll not do anything until I've spoken to you …"

But that did not end the regular pricks and irritations Bertha caused at home. Her suggesting that they should buy Edam cheese was one. "Now don't you get any high-faluting ideas from the Stewarts, girl! The next thing you'll be suggesting is that stinky blue godammed thing!" "I was going to suggest it," Bertha added to get her own back … "No way is my daughter going to be seen in public exposing her thighs! You're not some bloody Chinese dance hostess, girl! As long as you want to stay in this house, you'll not wear a cheongsam." "What if the slit is only two inches?" "Don't bargain with me, girl! The next thing I'll know it will be torn. So sorry, Pa … it got torn … I know you, Bertha." "But Pa, I show far more thigh on the hockey field. You know my friend Nyet Lin's father would kill her if she wore shorts like mine on the field." "Then maybe I should kill you, Bertha …" Eric's guffaw at the dining table stopped the subject from being taken further.

Christmas 1953 came and went. There was the usual big

gathering at Dan's place and the visiting rounds through the next two days. There were the curries and special Eurasian delicacies. James loved the pineapple jam tarts. There was turkey and ham. Curries, *sambals*, jellies, *agar-agar*, and glasses and glasses of whisky-soda. At Christmas they allowed the children a glass or two of wine at home. Beryl was already twenty-two that year. She was drinking freely. Eric was knocking back the beers. Only Bertha was under their family drinking limits that year. James kept his eye on her at all the houses they went to. But he was pleased to see she was not a "drinker." He had been worried. Four years earlier, he had caught Bertha and Mavis Santa Maria having a little session with the sherry. Bertha was settling down, he thought silently to himself.

Bertha rushed up onto the verandah one evening as Mary was sipping a Wincarnis and James was complaining that the soda was flat. "Get Framroz, Mary. They're always good." "Pa! Ma! They've asked me to play for the GSC!" "Wow! Bertha, you've made it !" "Who asked you?" "Sheelah Cornelius, the captain!" "Whaaa …" "The first game's against the SCC women's team. On the Padang! Wheeee …" "When is it?" "There's no need to watch her play, James. It's those bloody white thighs you want to see, isn't it? You dirty ole man …" Mary at her worst.

James didn't watch the game. He sat at the bar in the SRC and listened to the young Branksome fellow talk about his fishing trip to the Sisters Islands. James knew the area well. He had spent two years in "marine." "You gotta be careful of the currents there, son." "Oh I know, I always go with Hamid." "Not that Hamid in 'vice?' " "Yah! That's him … Whoa, Mr. Rodrigues, you know simply everybody in the police! But the *ikan merah* man …!"

Suddenly James felt a hefty slap on his back. Henry Marks was there. He kept his hand on James's back after the hard friendly thump. Esme Carlos and Nellie Choppard were with him.

"What the hell are you sitting here getting sloshed. You should have been out there seeing you daughter's brilliant stickwork."

"Absolutely brilliant," Esme added.

"Two goals, man! The only goals of the whole game. She really *sarpooed* those big European women. The first goal you should have seen, man! Sheelah passed it to her ... you know Sheelah's damn good at watching the field all the time ... she saw your Bertha ... out there on the wing ... waiting ... one sharp flick to Bertha. Bertha got it and went. Man, she went ... One, two, three, she got through them ... her stick, man ... real fast ... then she cut in ... that big Mrs. McMarthy was playing backs today, she's usually centre ... Bertha got past her ... then Tarp! ... high in the right top corner. You should have been there, man."

"A beuutifool one, James," Nellie gushed.

"Have a drink ... Esme ... Nellie, *gin merah* as usual? Henry?"

"Listen to me, James. That girl is damn good. Then the second goal ... about three minutes later ..."

"No Henry, about ten minutes later."

"Anyway, that Angus girl was coming down ... straight down the centre ... She saw the three European women ... so she passed to Millie ..."

"No, Henry that wasn't Millie. It was Sheelah. She had moved over to the left, justa little left of Millie."

"Oh yes ... Your Bertha read the game at once ... she cut in ... like a bloody streak of lightning ... She took Millie's pass. Sorry, I mean Sheelah's pass ... Stopped it with her hand and let fly ... Whoa, she really walloped it. She's got power too ... Straight in!"

"She was larkky," Nellie added with her typical Serani-Singlish, "dat Europin goalie not quick enough."

"No, Nellie," Henry wouldn't have his story ruined. "Nobody could have stopped that one ... not even Harkkie."

He slapped him on the back again. Joe Pawle came up, attracted by the excited voices of the group. Then "Punch Bogaars" joined them. More drinks. The play was retold again and again. Jock Mosbergen, standing at the bar next to them, couldn't restrain himself and gave his version of Bertha's dribbling ... "But most of all, Nellie, she looks around all the time ... She reads the game lah!"

The two fellows with Jock joined them. "Bunty" and Sithawalla.

More drinks all round. Sitha as they called him was the Indian Association left-winger. He gave his version. "She's got the eye, man. You mark my words, that girl will get to the state team one day."

Joe gave James another thump on the back. Joe had obviously been knocking them back with Ronnie Labrooy and Basil whassisname... Basil-Black.

"James, me boy, a star is born!"

James signed for another round.

He repeated Joe's words to Mary who was waiting for him on the verandah as he walked up the five steps at nine o'clock.

"Mary, a star was born this evening ... our Bertha."

~ *Chapter seven.* ~

Sergeant Neubronner.

"Hoi, Robert! You still here ... Hi, Ray. Come on, come and join us," Old Joe hailed us at the bar. There were two others with him; looked about his age group. Both had the Serani look about them. Joe introduced every one; "Chas" Neubronner, Dennis Carrier ... I noticed he used their full names. He also used my surname in introducing me. Ray was just plain Auzzie "Ray." Old Joe waved his hand around, "All now settled here." I was right. Old Joe had used their surnames in the good old traditions of his past, not because they were visiting and may have taken it as rather rude to introduce older people to young ones like Ray and me.

"We were just talking about your grandfadder, Robert."

"Robert's grandfather? James Rodrigues?"

"Yah!"

"I was in 'D' with him, first. Then, in 'riot.' I was just telling them about that May 13th day ... I was in the thick of it. I was there at the church."

"Church ?" Ray asked, his face quite puzzled.

Old Joe held up his hand like a policeman stopping traffic. "*Suma stop*! *Nanti*! Ray, I must explain that that was the day way back in 1954 when the Chinese High School students clashed with the police. It was one of the first of many clashes. OK, *tuan*, *boleh jalan*." Joe waved Neubronner on as though he was a vehicle, acting the part of the traffic policeman with his whole body and a serious expression on his face.

"It was a terrible day for me. I was a sergeant then. In the riot squad. Old man Rodrigues was OC of my unit. My bloody piles were killing me that morning. I told James. 'You'd better go off then, Chas,' he said to me. 'You'll be no bloody good to me if you're going to walk round with one hand on your arse all day.'

"I couldn't. I knew we were on full alert after all that fuss about the registration for the new national service. My boys would never have put their hearts into it if I was not there. Not to say boasting, man ... those Malay PC's had to have someone to be there alongside them. Some of the European inspectors could do it. But not all. You had to get to know them. See who were the buggers with spunk in them and who tended to hold back ... So I stayed on duty.

"Then we were told to move to Government House. There we waited. The special branch boys had found out that they wanted to hold a procession to protest. No police permit. We just hung around, our sticks and rattan shields all ready. I could see our boys were nervous. I talked to them. Playing politics lah! 'If you let these Cheena buggers take over, you are *habis*! Poke lah! *Chochok*.'

"I knew the Snipe waiting next to our red riot vans was getting the hot news. Slowly I moved towards it. Lighting a cigarette, as if I was just loitering around. So I heard the news before the OC called out. They were assembling at Fort Canning. They were coming by the lorry loads. Boys and girls. They were lining up along the railings. I heard Johnson, you know, that big size bugger who became director CPIB later ..."

"The fellow with the moustache? Played wing three-quarter?"

"Yah lah! *Itu dia* ... Heard him on the radio 'Send in unit two. They need help there. Rodrigues ... Can you hear me? You know the play ... go in ... if you have to.'

"We moved to the junction of Penang Road and Clemenceau Avenue. We got out of the van. James was in command. He got the Chinese bugger in the van to tell them to disperse. That little bugger was really shit scared. Sweating in the van, saying his 'ching-chiang-fong' thing in the loud hailer. They would not move.

"So James gave the order for us to move in. Stuuuupid bleerdy thing! We were tole to pull a rope and tie them to the railings. Crazy lah! I was so angry with Rodrigues ... if it had been an *ang moh*, he would have told us to move in with our sticks. Of course it didn't work. So the next order came up on the lights. You young buggers don't know, but in those days there were lights on the top of the turret of the riot vans. We had standard signals. Sorry, Ray, I really meant Robert.

"I saw it. Move in. Break up the crowd. My bloody arse was on fire. But I was cool, man. I moved with my boys. The students linked arms and started singing. The swines! They pushed the young ones in front. '*Gasah dia punya pantat*,' I told my boys."

"Hit them on their backsides," Old Joe translated quickly.

"*Hantam* lah! I yelled out. My boys gave it to them. They started running. Down Penang Road. '*Kejar*! *Hantam dia*!' I yelled and my boys chased them. My bloody arse was burning like bloody hell. But I ran wit dem. All down Penang Road. They ran into the Presbyterian Church."

I knew the church. A nice pretty place. My aunt Alice was a Presbyterian. Funny how years later it was reported in the newspapers that, in that church servants' quarters, some Indians murdered a man and cut him up, made curry out of his flesh, packed it into little take-away bundles and dropped the packets in dustbins all over Singapore … the Presbyterian church.

"We got a few buggers. Pulled them out. I got Salleh and "Smail" to take them to the van. I knew those were the *takut* buggers. The rest of us moved on. But when we got to the church wall, we found that the front line was all girls. I was ready to go at them with my boys. James was out on the road now. With his loud-hailer. 'Hold it! Stop! You cannot hit them.' Shit! I said to myself. If you wanna fight, you fight! I shouted at Rodrigues. 'Dammit! We've got to keep going. Fu…g women or men.' I doan tink he heard me. I'm not sure but I tink my boys pulled back on their own. Bloody softies. I was mad! Shit! When we've got the upper hand … I sat on the road … my arse was really killing me. I was so mad. We were winning …"

The group was silent. Neubronner was obviously reliving the action with all his emotions. "I can't remember the rest. We cleared them. We moved out as soon as the situation got quiet. A regular unit moved in. I went back to the van. I shouted out to Rodrigues, 'You stupid bastard!' Larky he didn't hear me. They would have fired me. Or I would never have got to inspector later.

"At the base, I cooled down ... because my piles were throbbing. Have you ever had piles, you buggers? James came up to me. He put his hand on my shoulder, 'Good work, Chas.' I could have hit him. But my pain had taken all the strength out of me. I remember how Jalleh came up to me. 'Sir, are you all right?' I explained to him. He found an Aspro. I'll never forget that day as long as I live. I've been in worse situations, like at the Hock Lee riots ... But that day was first blood."

Mr. Carrier, who had not said a word, commented, "Someone ought to put it down. How the Serani policemen held the force together in those days. You know it was because they had their bloody hearts in it. They were fighting for their queen."

"Don't give us that crap, Dennis," Old Joe put in his word.

"Weren't there any Chinese in the police?" Ray asked.

"Very few ... Very, very few."

I had listened to Neubronner's story rapt in attention. This was part of my past. I felt a little ashamed of myself that I didn't know the details of what had actually happened. I only knew vaguely that the Chinese school students had spearheaded the fight against the British. But they were communists. It was all a jumble to me. But somehow I felt some sort of pride in Mr. Carrier's comment that these men of my community had fought with their hearts and souls for something that they later found hollow and empty; in a way ...

We have changed so much. The same people, or should I say, the descendants of the same people play their part in the SAF now. I wondered if the isolation of being a community riding on the backs of the colonials had given them that spirit. From stories I had heard of the Japanese war, I thought it was a similar kind of loyalty, a blind loyalty. I guess you would fight to the death for a friend, even though you knew he was a bastard in some ways ... when there was nothing else ...

Old Joe continued the reminiscences. "That was the night when they flashed on all the cinema screens the call to all British troops to return to barracks."

But I was not listening to the bits and pieces of those days that Chas Neubronner, Old Joe and Mr. Carrier were exchanging. I suddenly realised that the man Neubronner had described was my grandfather. With all the current interest in minorities in Singapore, I had been asking the old people about my ancestors. The sea captain who had started it all. The Portuguese soldier ... He was more likely to be a soldier than a sailor, I was convinced, since the soldiers who got mixed up with the Malay women were forced to marry them; good and proper-like as the Catholic Church demanded ... the Portuguese guy who started the Machados ... me a Machado ... and the woman. I had delved into the romantic past of the sixteenth century but had forgotten the recent past, still living in the "oldies" around me ... in Singapore, Australia, Malaysia. Yes, there were still many who would not pull up their roots from the land that had bred them, that had given them the rich harvests of *geragok* shrimps and the ease of tropical life and had also treated them so harshly at times. I thought of the Jewish community in Singapore. Sophia Road, Wilkie Road, Niven Street ... They had left when the state of Israel was announced so many years ago ... People who had eaten rice and curry all their lives got up and went when the call of the past was raised after two, three generations? My people had left their land ... Malaya, Singapore ... but not all. So many had adapted to the new conditions, found themselves, in some sort of way, changed ... become part of the new systems, thrown their lot in with new ethnic powers, yet ... the vestiges of the "Serani" still kick their last dying pangs ... Huh! Me one of them?

"ROBERTO! Wake up! Wassamatter? You feeling all right?"

"Come on Robert, We should go." Ray looking after his charge.

~ *Chapter eight* ~

Mr. *Vandyke*

One evening sometime in the middle of 1955, Bertha came up to James as he sat on the verandah with his "Haig."

"Pa, may I use your typewriter?"

"Yes, of course."

James did not hesitate for a moment. He had an old typewriter at home. Like all the other men in the force, he did a lot of report writing at home, laboriously typing them out with two fingers on the typewriter.

"You'll find it in the *almeira*. And there's some carbon paper in the bureau drawer."

"Thanks, Pa."

He saw her at the typewriter that night. It was not James's nature to be "nosey," as Mary used to describe poking one's nose into other people's business. For the next few days, he saw Bertha at the typewriter every evening when he came home. One day he went up to her and standing behind her read what was in the machine. It was completely unintelligible to him.

"Good heavens, girl. What the blazes is that?"

"I'm learning to type."

"It's not so easy ... and the important thing is to get it right from the start ... the fingering."

"Sheelah Cornelius is teaching me, what finger goes on "p" and what finger goes on "w" and all that. And I've been practising with the typewriter cover over my hands."

"Hmm ... good ... good of Sheelah to teach you ... will be useful sometime. Wish I had learnt."

James did not think any more about this. He was too busy. They had just come through the Hock Lee riots and the business of the two thousand students staying in at the Chinese High School. This was the end of it. He had plenty on his mind.

About nine months later, Bertha came up with a surprise at dinner. Later, he realised that she had raised it at dinner, and not quietly to him on the verandah when he was usually in his best mood, because she knew Eric would be there to back her up.

"Pa, Mum ... I want to leave school and get a job."

"Good heavens Bertha!"

That was all James could say. He didn't have any argument at the moment against it. Mary was silent, looking at James to handle the situation.

"But what can you do? Why don't you wait till you've done the Cambridge and become a teacher."

"Heck! No. Not for me ... not teaching."

"It's a jolly good job. Look how well Ben is doing."

"OK. It's a good job. But not for me."

"What can you do?"

"I can type now."

"Ho! ho! ..." In half a laugh.

"'Course I can. I'll show you what I did this afternoon."

Bertha got up from the table and went to her room. It was her own room now that Beryl was married. She picked up the letters she had typed from the dressing table. She stood there for a few minutes before she went back to the table. She had decided that it would be better to let them think or talk among themselves for bit before she returned to the dining table. One glance at James from the doorway told her that it would be all right.

"Hmmm ... not bad, but I suppose you spent hours correcting them eh? Hey, these are letters of application for jobs."

"Yes, just practising."

"You didn't write them, did you?"

"Yes, I did."

He looked hard at her as he passed the typewritten sheets to

Mary. His little Bertha wasn't so bad after all. Hah! She didn't get them from a book? No, they weren't really perfect.

"Did Sheelah help you?"

"No. Look, Pa, writing a letter of application is nothing."

James looked at Bertha again and thought how she had matured. She was still as *gila* as ever in many ways but she did not embarrass them with her off-beat acts. She had been the talk of the SRC and the Indian Association, so Pillai had told him, with her successes on the hockey field. She mixed with older women there. It had helped her maturing. In fact, he had thought to himself a good few times, she was the one Serani female who understood what was happening in politics. His stories at the dining table and his own thoughts and analyses of the situations had no doubt contributed to his children's interest and knowledge in politics. The other Seranis would know at once if Reggie Hope hit another century, or if the murtabak man in Arab Street packed up to go to India for a holiday but they had little interest in politics.

He was involved. The police bore the brunt of the power-testing moves of both sides. His friends in the Special Branch gave him the low-down on the commies' approaches. He just had to be conscious enough of the sensitivity of the day, of the hour at times, to be able to operate, even though no senior officer would ever admit that there was any element of politics in the simple decisions of whether to arrest them, or use the hose, or tear gas, or the coloured dyes. It had not been the straightforward police work that he had been bred on. It was the police against people; doesn't matter what kind of people, he had often said to Mary, it's just terrible to keep at them day after day. The Chinese students had not yet raised their cry of "*pah-police*," instead of "*merdeka*," but James knew it had to come.

Bertha had heard more about these things than most girls of her age. She had cheered wildly when David Marshall had been elected as Chief Minister of Singapore. Because he was a Jew, she said. Any one can be anything here, no matter what race they are.

He had frowned on this premature statement of hers. But he

had kept silent. He had taken her unexpected fierce reaction in his stride when he had commented on the "antics" of John Eber and his attacks against colonialism in London. He had ended cynical denigration of the man with, "and the fella's a Serani." She had accused him of being unfair. His race didn't matter at all. He had kept his mouth shut though he wanted to tell her that whatever "communistic" ideas she had, it would never change.

Yes, he said to himself, Bertha has grown up. He saw Mary's uneasiness. He muttered a "Hmmmmm" and finally said, "Think about it seriously, girl. You know that you'll never get anywhere without a Senior Cambridge."

"Yes, Pa, I will ... but you know I'll never be able to pass in maths."

So Bertha left school and got a job. But James would not let her do it the way she wanted to. He stopped her from applying for advertised jobs. He got on the phone to his relatives and friends. He must get her into a good position, he said to Mary. They discussed it for three days on the verandah before he began his telephoning, or approaching friends at the club bar.

"Stanvac," Mary had said quite firmly. "That's where she should get into. Tommy Holmberg. Speak to him."

"I know Bill was looking for someone."

"Bill Hocquard? You don't want her to be a counter-jumper at Whiteaways, do you?"

"Not a salesgirl, Mary. Bill was saying they are looking for a typist."

"Oh. That's different ... Yah. She would probably be able to buy things at staff price."

"I'll try Bill. What about Singapore Traction? Betty Green would know."

"Yah. I'll speak to Betty. She knows what's going on there."

"I'll say she does, probably more than the Managing Director himself ... if I know Betty."

One of the possibilities they did not discuss came unexpectedly. He met Rachel Elias at the GH Cafe. She ran a boarding house in

Sophia Road. Her husband had left her the house when he died. "And nothing much else," she always added. She had put it to good use and ran a profitable business. James believed she also did some smuggling on the side. She had edged up the "classiness" of her "establishment" over the years and could now command good prices. It was a "European" place now. Roast beef and what-have-you. Cucumber sandwiches for tea. No reductions for not having dinner unless you gave three night's notice. It was Rachel who brought up the subject.

"James, do you know any girl who can type and do a bit of shorthand? Someone from a good family, you know ... One of my 'guests' (she never used the word lodger) is looking for a girl he can trust. Just a small firm. He's a nice quiet old fellow. I'm not sure what he does, but it's some kind of business. He travels a lot too. Never gives me any trouble. Except for some stupid nonsense about the curtain colours once."

James arranged to meet Mr. P.J.Vandyke. He had to check him out himself. He had asked his friends and it turned out that Herman Braga knew Mr. Vandyke. Then it turned out that Mr. Vandyke knew Robinson. And Robinson had helped him with a parking ticket. And, by the strangest coincidence, James had been in traffic then. Mr.Vandyke had been "in the Straits Settlements" for "donkey's years" and had lived up there in Georgetown, Penang, KL, Hongkong (Herman had met him there) and Batavia.

James brought up the subject of his daughter looking for a job quite casually and Mr. Vandyke had agreed to interview her. He actually said "meet her," James had told Mary when he got home. James was particularly pleased at how he was able to slip it into the drift of conversation so casually.

Later, Bertha told them that Mr. Vandyke had worked for Huttenback's and then with Henry Waugh. She thought he was some sort of engineer. But now the company, his own company, was doing some trading business. Mr. Vandyke travelled to Java, Hongkong, Bangkok, Saigon and often drove up-country on business. He had made her an offer on the spot after talking to her about this and that and everything but her school results or her typing. She had even felt it necessary to tell him that she had only just started shorthand lessons in the evenings. It didn't seem to worry him whether she could take down dictation or not.

Bertha liked it there. There was only Mr. Vandyke, herself and a *tamby*; only three of them. That is, if you did not include Rais. Rais was the driver, but he could read and write a little. So he did an odd job now and then at the office. It was like a small family. There was quite a lot of typing to do but Bertha could do it in reasonable time. Mr. Vandyke was very understanding and let her off exactly at five if she had a game. If it was just practice she didn't even think of asking him to let her off exactly at five. She was happy there. "Much better than school!" she told Mary.

Bertha was so nervous in the first week. Mrs. Chin her teacher had given her a farewell talk about the wickedness of the world and, though she and Eric had laughed their sides out at some of the things she said, "the old fuss-pot," the fear that offices were full of men waiting to pounce on and seduce young girls lingered. She wore her plainest dress on the first day. It was the dress she wore for Good Friday mass. Mum said that one shouldn't really call it mass because there was no Communion but she wasn't quite sure what one should say. "Service" sounded so Protestant.

Mr. Vandyke was ever so pleasant. He told her what to do. Showed her how things were done. Wrote out the words to say when she answered a telephone call and saw that she was settled in with pencils, blotting paper and all that. He was mostly serious but smiled at times and put in a joke now and then. But she saw that he had taken her whole body in when he first met her at the interview and when she arrived every morning. Like all men, she said to herself. She was pleased that Mr. Vandyke had turned out to be such a pleasant person.

And to top it all, he had agreed to her taking leave for a week when she went on tour with the GSC team up-country.

In fact, it was easier asking him for permission than asking for it at home.

"They've included me in the team for the trip up-country."

"Whoa! That's good, Bertha. Pass the curry, please."

"Oh! Good for you!' Eric slapped her on the back.

Mary was silent for a while. Then she spoke softly and slowly, "Eric can go with you. You've got some leave haven't you, Eric?"

"For Gowdssake! Ma! I'm not a child any more. I'm a grown woman."

"That's what's worrying Ma. Ha! Ha! Ha! ..." Eric laughed.

"James. She can't go alone."

"But I'm not going alone. There are a hundred thousand others going. It's all organised."

"Is Sheelah going?"

"Yes, of course, she's the captain."

That seemed to help a little towards calming Mary.

"Where are you going to stay?"

"The GSC have arranged it all, Mum. In KL, we're going to stay at the YW. At Seremban, they've arranged for members of the Negri club to put us up. At Penang ..."

"You're going as far as Penang?"

"Yah. Three places. KL, Seremban, Penang. No, four. Malacca too."

"You can stay with Auntie May in Penang."

"They've arranged it already, Ma. The convent has space in the boarder's dorm, so we're staying at the convent in Penang. There! Isn't that a wonderful place of chastity to stay in!"

"Don't be sarcastic, girl. The *petai sambal*, please, Mary."

"But there's plenty of room at Auntie May's place, now that Anna and Myrtle have married and left."

"It's out in the *ulu*, Mary," James said.

"Say, Pa, did you see that Blue Eyes which won the four o'clock on Wednesday?"

"Eric, you stay away from the horses, man. Stick to hockey. Whoa, this petai is damn good today, Mary. And the *kachang-botol* ... so fresh and crisp."

"But Pa, I don't play big stuff, lah."

"Any money put on a horse to me is lost."

"Ha! Ha! Whose talking?"

"Get away with you ...!"

James rang Sheelah Cornelius the following morning. She was a "steno" with the Borneo Company.

"Sheelah. I only agreed for Bertha to go because I trust you. You look after out Bertha. Don't let her get spoilt up there."

"For heavens sake, James. It's only a week's trip. Or not even a week. We'll be back on Saturday night. Besides, we'll be together all the time. You know that. You jolly well know how I look after my girls. And this trip, no one is going to get even the slightest bit tiddly. I assure you."

Sheelah knew what James meant. It didn't mean getting big ideas about luxury living or swigging BGA's or smoking *ganja* or anything like that. Neither did it mean mixing with Europeans or Chinese or Indians. James didn't have to ask. He knew that the GSC team would be playing against the PRC in Penang and all the Eurasian clubs in the other towns.

"I know what you mean, James Rodrigues. Your daughter will come back intact."

She was a little bit peeved by his call. Why don't they say ruined, these old people. She smiled and thought to herself, because they won't be ruined for the market but just "soiled." Not like the old-fashioned Chinese. We are different ... she smiled.

~ *Chapter nine* ~

Heng Boon Teck

"*Feng!*" Old Joe raised his right hand with one finger pointing skyward. "You ask me what Eurasian food is, I answer you in one word: *Feng*." He paused. Ray had asked him if there was anything special in Eurasian food. We were at the bar again with Old Joe. Ray had insisted we go. The whole thing was an interesting new experience to him. This odd lot of migrants, neither Asian nor European. And characters like Old Joe.

But it was not just the unusual people and their ways that made Ray want to go to the same bar again. We were both frustrated that night when Old Joe started telling us about the mystery of Bertha and Carl Westerhout interrupted him as soon as he started. Old Joe had taken much offence to Carl's flat statement that he was wrong. He had challenged Carl's statement but Carl had refused to elaborate and Joe sulked into silence. The night had ended drearily with the garrulous Old Joe standing there in our midst with his lower lip curled down. Not even muttering a "yes" or a grunt. So we went off. Disappointed.

Lying in the motel bed that night, I decided that Carl, who seemed to be a very disciplined sort of person, had deliberately upset Old Joe to stop him from relating his story. It was not just careless rudeness or the loosening of the tongue, or the wanting to have one's say that alcohol tended to provoke.

Tonight, Cuthbert and Steven were there. Carl Westerhout who had contradicted Old Joe about the start of Bertha's scandalous story was not there. Old Joe said he was expecting John Peters. Ray had worked the talk away from the Test with his food question. Joe had uttered "*feng*" with a flourish as though he was on stage presenting a star. He waited for the obvious question.

"What's *feng*?"

"It came from the Portuguese. It's the head of a pig cut into tiny pieces, as small as a peanut, in a curried sort of style. The whole head, you know. The skin and the flesh. Even those hard parts. It's really fantastic."

"Isn't there some liver in it too?" I asked.

"I donno. But all I know it is *sheok*!"

"I think there is," Cuthbert said, "must ask Dulcie when I get home."

"But Joe, that's not the only Serani food. What about *sambal lengkong*?"

"No, no ... That's Malay."

"Didn't the Serani popularise it?"

"There's devil?"

"What's devil? It sounds hot stuff." Ray asked. He didn't have time to ask about *sambal lengkong*.

"Yah. Devil is true Eurasian food."

"There's lots more lah. *Shmoo*, *babi chin*, tort cake."

"No, no ... *Babi chin* is surely Chinese."

"Baba isn't it?"

"And tort cake is Dutch?"

"Aiyah! None of you knows anyting about food."

"What's devil?" Ray repeated.

"It's a kinda' curry," I explained. "Chicken. A thin gravy curry. There's a slight sour taste. They put vinegar in it. Lots of onions. Garlic, mustard seeds, ginger and soy-sauce."

"You forgot the chillies, Robert."

"Oh yes. It must have large whole red and green chillies floating around in it ... or it's not devil."

"Hey, you forgot *kelwa* curry."

"That's Baba lah. But it's an interesting dish, Ray. It's a chicken curry ..."

"With pork sometimes."

"Not sometimes, lah, it must have pork."

"That's your version, Steven."

"Chicken ... and pork cooked with a bitterish nut from Indonesia."

"Surabaya. East Indonesia."

"The nut has a very hard shell. Like er, er ... almost like plastic."

"Like a coconut shell."

"A hole is broken on one side when it is cooked and the nuts are put into the curry. It gives it a very special taste. And you scoop out the inside flesh, a dark brown, almost black thing, and eat it with your rice. It's an acquired taste, really ... but quite delicious, I assure you."

"Yah man, *sheok*!"

"What about sugi-cake?"

"That's just a cake. You know there are a lot of foods which we think are Eurasian food which are really not. Our people have adapted some of them in various ways. But they are Malay or Chinese or Indian food."

"AH! Here's one. Vindyaloo."

"This one I've argued with my mother," I spoke up. "She insists that it should be said 'vindeealoo,' because of the wine in it. 'Vino' ... Portuguese. She says it's a Portuguese curry. But my Dad says it's an old Indian dish that's got nothing at all to do with the Portuguese."

"Now, don't tell me it came from Goa?" Steven with a frown.

We laughed at his attempt to resolve the question.

Old Joe moved into the silence after the laugh. "Hey, Ray is it true about the Bengal Bicycle Company?"

"Never heard of it. Never been to Bengal. Why pick on me, mate?"

"No lah. Nothing to do with Bengal. It seems that there was a bicycle shop here in Perth which was not doing so well. So they started selling rice and curry. They became quite well known for their curries. But they wouldn't change their name and it became a gimmicky selling point. The Bengal Bicycle Company for the best curries in Perth!"

"Hallo, Hallo, Hallo …"

It was John Peters. "Sorry Joe, had to take Syl to the super. Took longer than I thought."

"Ah ha! You see, Ray. He's already calling her the shortened Australian way, Syl," Joe said.

"Terrible …" I cut in. "It's awful to me how they shorten names here. Even a name like Ian is cut down to "Ee." Don't do it, John. Sylvia is Sylvia. Even in Singapore I stopped them in the office from spoiling that lovely Malay name Sukarti to Sue."

"And did you succeed, Rob?" Ray asked, stressing the "Rob."

"No."

"Robert, that's not just Auzzie. Even the Chinese and Malays do it. Isn't the Indonesian *Bang* a shortened *Abang*?" Old Joe said.

"I don't know. I only know that my uncle whose full name is Heng Boon Teck is known by everybody as Heng."

"Isn't that your aunt Bertha's husband, Rob?" Ray asked.

"Yes, Raymond," I replied stressing the "Raymond."

"That bastard …" Old Joe muttered. Ray looked at me and grinned.

"I don't suppose you mean it in the 'Stryne sense?"

"Well … in a way I do. Half and half … A lovable rogue, if you know what I mean."

"No, Joe, I don't," Ray egged him on.

"Take that night we went out with him. Ricky, Felix Newman, Roland Keet and some others … can't remember. We started drinking at the Ban Chuan. Then a Mr. Tong something or other saw Heng and hailed him like a long lost brother. It seems they had a wild night in Patpong together. Tong orders a bottle of XO. We had already downed a few beers. About eight of us … Tarp! It went just like that. This fellow Tong obviously had money. He gets another. It goes quickly, but not so fast. Anyway, Tong stops them as they bring a third bottle to the table. He suggests that we go to a bar he knows. Knows the *towkay* of the joint. Near Short Street.

Somewhere near there, lah. Whoa … This place is full of girls. Before you can say Jack Robinson, Ricky has got one on his lap. Heng starts that OhhhZom! game. Loses *yamsengs*."

"Try to keep out the dialect, Joe," Ray interrupts.

But Old Joe was away. He was not going to stop to explain "OhhhZom" and break the flow of his story.

"We ate some chicken legs and *samosas*. But we had a lot to drink. There was this girl, Mimi … you know, every bar had a Mimi in those days …"

"Yeah, Joe."

"Heng starts fondling her. Playing around lah!"

"Details, please."

"Get away with you!"

"Anyway the bar eventually closes. Tong hands out one 'Hongkong' to each of the girls. 'Hongkong,' Ray, meant ten dollars. There must have been nine of them, I reckon. He says goodnight quickly, because he's got his arm round Mimi.

"Then we see that bugger Heng is going off to his car with another. Barsket! He'd only been married for about a year then. Two days later I meet him at the club. 'Had a good time, you bloody fornicator?' I asked him. 'Crazy! I must tell you, I really got fixed that night,' he said. 'What? She fleeced you?'

"Heng told me the story. She said she wanted to go home. No sitting in the park or hotel room business. He agreed to send her home. Then she tells him she lives in JB. Bloody miles away. He's not upset. Heng's always on top of it. He takes her to the causeway. When they get to the Immigration, he opens his glove compartment and sees his passport is not there. Only then he remembers that he sent it in to the Australian High Commission to get a visa. There's big arguments between him and her and the Immigration fellow.

Then the young Malay official comes up with a solution. He says he will take her home if Heng lends him the car and waits there. Smiling as he suggests it. The girl tells him to get out of the driving seat, pronto, and beckons the Immigration fellow in. So Heng sits there waiting. One hour! Ninety minutes. The

Immigration fellow comes back, grinning like mad. Says she lived far away. Heng damn well knows she lives only near the market. Three minutes by car from the Immigration line. She told him. To add to it, the Immigration fellow tells him that 'she very good girl,' still grinning. I tell you, we had a bloody good laugh.

"Another time, we were waiting for Heng at the Mayfair when he comes in. A girl who had been at the Silver Inn was there. She recognised him and went to the door. 'Haaalo!' Ray, that's hello in your tongue. 'I donno you,' he says. 'Lasstime at the Siver Inn lah!' 'I never seen you,' Heng insists.

She lifts up her skirt, right up. 'Lemember me?' That girl really had a sense of humour … Yes, I'll have a Scotch. Thanks, Rob.

"Then the time we were at Michiko's. Poshish place. Japanese bar. Keith Farley had just won a lot at the races. He was treating us. You know Keith, never goes to cheap places, silly bugger. We are drinking and singing. Nobody notices that Heng has slipped out. In about two minutes, he comes back. He knocks my leg under the table. Hide it, he says. It's a packet of *nasi lemak*. So we keep one hand under the table and when the 'mummy' is not looking we eat one mouthful of *nasi lemak*. Just like schoolboys chewing peanuts when the 'teach' is not looking. That's Heng."

"So he broke up with Bertha?" Ray asked. He was getting bored with Old Joe's stories.

"She caught him. She had to go to some place in Balmoral Road to deliver some document to someone and as the lift comes down Heng is there in it holding hands with a woman. She was an Indonesian millionaire's divorced ex-wife."

"I hear someone fixed him," John said, "… rang her and told her to go there. Gave her the time even. Delivering the letter was her story, they say."

"Yah. I heard that one too. But Heng did not have any enemies. He was not that kind of guy."

"Doesn't sound like a coincidence to me," Ray said.

"Didn't she find him with Mildred De Souza too?"

"Yah …"

"Was that a fix too?" I asked.

"That was different. That was in Mavis Santa Maria's flat."

"In someone's flat? She caught him inside the flat?"

"Yah. It seems that Mildred had borrowed her key to use the flat. When the two of them came out of the bedroom, Mavis and Bertha were there. I think Mavis fixed it. Could be her."

"But she was a good friend of Bertha's, wasn't she?" There was a silence as Ray waited for Old Joe to continue talking. I decided to speak up. I felt the picture that Old Joe painted of Heng was not quite right.

"But, you know, Heng wasn't a bad guy. I don't think he really considered himself an immoral person."

"Whaddayermean?" Ray asked.

"That generation was half way to being Western. The generation before had kept concubines and kept mistresses. Second wives is different. Mistresses were playthings. In their minds it was a naughty thing. But just naughty, if you know what I mean. Like eating a Mars Bar when you're on a diet. Or like how the Japanese get roaring drunk and do not consider it a bad or unsocial thing. I reckon Heng's generation did not think that playing around with other women was all that immoral. And by playing around I mean screwing around.

"I'm not quite sure about the womenfolk then, but I suspect that they knew what was going on and shut their eyes. For one thing, their fathers had done it. And the last thing that they wanted to happen to them was to have a showdown and get thrown out."

"Robert is right. I even know of a case where the wife accepted her man back wholeheartedly after he had a full scale affair with someone. A Chinese woman, I mean. A Serani woman would never have accepted that," Old Joe said.

I continued, "Heng did everything else right. As a car salesman he had the reputation of giving you a square deal. He told you what the good points and the bad points were. He might have loaded the facts a little, but never sold anyone an absolute lemon."

"Only relative lemons, Rob?" Ray asked grinning.

"Look ... He didn't beat up his wife. Nor waste all his money on the horses. Sure he would have had a lot more if he didn't throw it around in bars and cabarets. But he may not have made so many sales if he had stayed at home and read 'Playboy' ... that's about the only thing he would probably read."

"Robert," Old Joe looked at me fiercely in the eye. "Are you saying that Heng still had a morality that was half old Chinese and half Christian, or rather Western? And that if Bertha had been able to accept that they would have lived happily ever after, till Kingdom come?"

"Yes. I'm saying that his running around with hot and cold women was not a terribly wicked thing to him."

"And that Bertha should have accepted this?"

"No. Put it this way. If she were an old school Chinese woman she would have."

"Therefore, you silly twisted boy, a Eurasian should not marry a Chinese?"

"I guess so ... in those days, unless one of them could adapt to the other ...?"

"And today, my learned friend?" Old Joe leered at me. He was enjoying it. I saw I had worked myself into a corner.

"Depends on the girl and the man ..."

"Can I assume," Old Joe very loudly and haughtily, "my worthy and learned friend, that the Chinese fifty, seventy, years ago did not understand or feel romantic love?"

~ *Chapter Ten* ~

The up-country tour

The station platform was buzzing with excitement. The GSC team was boarding the "night mail." Parents, brothers, sisters and friends were all there to send them on a successful tour. Husbands of the married ones, some clutching babies, and sweethearts hanging on to each other's hands till the last moment. Between them, was the usual mixed and motley crowd of third-class passengers. Families moving up to Malaya to a new job. Employees being relocated. Serious and sour-faced people going to see sick relatives or to funerals; small-time traders with little suitcases; an occasional and rare man or couple on holiday, for travelling to Malaya on holiday was then a luxury, even going by third, and the Emergency, the battle against the communists in the jungles, was now on. Many Singapore people had a distorted impression that almost a full scale war was being waged up-country.

Bertha arrived with James and Mary. She had met Patience Connor at the ticket machine buying platform tickets for her Ma and Pa. Patience had introduced them to her parents, the stern looking Mr. Connor and his plump wife who always seemed to have her bottom lip curled down. They had walked back together to the Rodrigues'. Bertha introduced them. Mary started calling Mrs. Connor, "Mrs. O'Connor" and Bertha cut in rather brusquely, "It's Connor, Mum, not O'Connor."

Mary had got terribly embarrassed at this. Because they were uppity Protestant people. They spoke with a *matsalleh* – white man's – accent. Patience was at the University. Mr. Connor drove a Ford V-8.

After the barrier, they ran into the excited send-off crowd. They knew most of them. Not all. "Vivvie" Ephraim hailed Mary. Her daughter was in the team. Polly Ephraim's latest beau hung around sad and sheepishly. The Van der Put's. Doug with his pipe. "*Apa khabar*, James?" James had been in school with him. Martha Beck and Leonard. Leonard with his bright Hawaiian shirt. "Why can't he see that his black skin does not go with those crimsons?" Mary had said dozens of times. Young Crabb with his sister. Elaine Beck, looking as pretty as ever. "Bet she'll come up and flirt with James," Mary thought to herself. Mary caught a glimpse of the Consigleire girl giving her boyfriend a quick peck on the lips. The way these young things behave in public!

Sheelah saw Bertha and came up at once. She ticked off her name in the little "555" pocket book she was carrying.

"Have you seen Laura?"

"No."

"Aiyah! That girl is always late ... Anyway I told her this time we cannot start the game late. The train won't wait."

"She's probably rushing from the hospital after her shift," Mary tried to speak up for Laura. After all, Laura Martens was such a nice girl, even though she was a bit harum-scarum at times.

"I must check if 'Poppy' has brought the extra stick," Sheelah said and started moving off. She was in a great flap. James grabbed her arm. "Look after our Bertha, Sheelah ..."

"Of course. I told you I would."

"Pa!" Bertha protested. Sheelah slipped away at once. The Bartholomews came up to them.

"Hello James, hello Mary, hello Bertha."

They did not shake hands. They knew each other well enough. "Your first tour with the team Bertha?"

"Yah. First time in Malaya too."

"Whoa! Big day for you, huh?"

"Yah."

"You're playing Negri tomorrow, aren't you?"

"Well ... Seremban."

"Yah. They call themselves the Negri Club ... watch out for that Van Geyzel girl. Jan's daughter. I've seen her play. She's tricky as ever. She'll change direction faster than you can think."

"What position does she play?"

"Half ... centre or right. You're sure to clash with her. I'm sure they've been reading about you in the papers. You'll be marked like hell."

"I've got my tricks you know, Uncle."

"That's it, Bertha. You've got to show those up-country folks how to play hockey," James chipped in.

"But Jan's daughter will show her a trick or two."

"Uncle Harry used to stay in Seremban, so he knows who's who. Don't you wish you were going with them Harry?"

"You bet! All these pretty girls."

"I meant going back to your old stamping ground, man."

"Excuse me, Ma. I'll go and look for a place and put my things there."

"We'll go with you ..." James said. "Come along, Mary."

"Well ta-ta," Harry Bartholomew and his wife said their goodbyes. But before they could get to the carriage steps, there was a loud shout across the platform.

"BERTA! WAIT FOR ME!"

It was Ethel, known as "Ettel," the way she was called at home.

James and Mary did not know her. Ethel Richards was taller than the average Singapore girl. Slim but shapely and muscular. Dark-brown skinned. A pair of glistening eyes that almost said "Stop! It's me!" if you glanced at them. A disarming smile. A chin delicately curved which seemed too feminine for her strong sinewy body. Legs that carried her towards them in long, strong determined strides.

Mary took her in. A cheap and nasty blouse. Hair needs combing. Filthy canvas shoes. A scruffy looking bag. Holding her hockey stick as though it were a truncheon or a club. Probably smells. But such a smile. A real *hitam-manis*. Yet, almost masculine in some way. Probably twenty-three or twenty-four.

The goalie. James suddenly recognised her. Devil-may-care woman with a crazy laugh when she made a spectacular save. Intense. Almost trembling with tension in a one to one situation. "She'd scare the hell out of me if I was in the dee and had an open run with only her at the goal mouth waiting." With her pads and her wild hair, Ethel could look very fierce. "The ting about her," LeMercier once said, "is dat when you are dare coming arp to der gol', looking to see which leg her weight is on, you get scarte' … because if the blerdy girl stops your shot she'll laugh like a blerdy ghostly *pontianak*." LeMercier had a way of saying things.

But James did not know that she was also the State team goalkeeper. He had met her in the days when he was posted to Joo Chiat Station. He could not recognise her now that she had grown up.

"Whoossat?" Mary asked.

"Ethel Richards, our goalie," Bertha replied.

Then James remembered. The Richards who lived in that ramshackle bunch of wooden shacks by the sea at Siglap.

"Your people, Rodrigues," ASP Chandler had once said.

He hated them. Those good-for-nothing *geragoks* there. The goddammed scum of the earth. Nothing but *chap-ji-ki* and shit. Always filthy-dirty. Always fighting, stealing. Always dead broke. Even when the sea was full of prawns. Letting the money-lender fellow screw them into the ground. Into the bloody mud. Not a *bai*, but one of their own kind too! That sniveling Williams. Always with some outlandish excuse or alibi. Bet he's got Indian blood in him.

This must the eldest girl. He'd seen her in her grubby white "jumpers," a sort of a one piece suit like a baggy swimsuit or boiler-suit but with short leg pieces, running from the coffee shop with condensed-milk tins of coffee hanging with strings from her finger, running like mad, spilling the coffee, jumping across the soft muddy patches to firm ground, with a confidence of knowing every puddle, laughing with her eyes sparkling.

When he first saw her, he cursed them inwardly for the way

they were bringing up their children. Leaving them to get their meals when they wanted to eat from the pots which had been cooked early in the morning. Letting them sit around watching the card games till they fell asleep every night. Shouting at the them in the foulest language when they distracted them from their gambling.

Cards. Four digits. Huh. And blaring radios. They really couldn't afford them. Must be stolen, James used to think. He had tried to explain to them that it was far cheaper to make coffee at home than buy it from the coffee shop. But they wouldn't listen. "But you doan know how many times the coffee we make at home is not finished." He had given up. He did not realise that buying coffee powder, sugar and milk needed more ready money than buying a few tins from the coffee shop in the morning. And when there was no money, there was no coffee.

He also gave up feeling sorry for their children after he encountered two of them on the mud track one day. That's it. It was her. The eldest Richards girl!

She was sitting astride the chest of a tiny Malay boy, her hands on his throat. He saw her face determined and savage. He heard the little boy's cries, "Aiyooh, Aiyooh ..." He had pulled the girl off grabbing her "jumpers." She turned round. He was in uniform. She took one look at him and bit his hand. He relaxed his hold with the shock; not so much the pain but the surprise at the way she reacted so quickly and bit him. She was gone before he could recover.

He pulled the skinny Malay boy up. "*Nama siapa? ... Tinggal di mana?*" The frightened child stared at him for a long time then mumbled, "Merwin." "Mervin? Mervin what?"

"Merwin Palmer."

James let him go as though he was contagious or covered with vermin. That bloody girl! Her own people. My people. Serani. Something boiled up in him. Some kind of rage mixed with disappointment. He was angry and confused.

From that day he avoided them if he could. He stopped trying to argue and persuade them.

He wanted to thrust the incident out of his mind. He also thrust out of his mind the sight of that same girl leaning against a wooden shack wall with her arm round a small Chinese girl, watching every movement of his as he walked past.

But all that was years ago. He didn't realise that he had forgotten it because somewhere inside him a thousand voices were screaming at him. He usually told Mary most of his encounters with the "unwashed rabble" as he sipped his "Haig" on the verandah. He had not told her that one. As he watched Ethel dashing up and greeting their Bertha as a bosom friend, he was glad he didn't. The male in him stirred to the woman that rushed forward.

"Berta."

"Ettel! Aiyah, why so late?"

The way Bertha replied registered in James's mind. He saw that his Bertha had a certain intimacy with the rough woman; yes, she was a woman now … probably twenty-four?

"Come on, Ettel … there's a place nex to me … here, dis one." Bertha pointed to the train door. She had switched her language to Ethel's. Like the way James talked to the rough-diamond detectives; bloody crooks at heart, only they're on our side.

Bertha went up into the train, but only for a minute, and came back down the steps. The station master, or some black Indian in a white uniform behaving like the station master walked down the platform. Somehow the people milling around cleared a path for him. It was as though the train would not go if one obstructed him. They heard a whistle. Sweethearts grabbed each other. Mary hugged Bertha. Bertha turned to James, "Bye, Pa."

"Whack them, Bertha. Five goal at least. Be good, girl …"

A grip on her shoulder. She was no longer a child to hug in public. James knew. Hope that bloody Sheelah looks after her.

Everybody got into the train. It was all ready to go. But it did not. They hung around. Waving shyly, Mrs. Consigleire shouted out, like a fishwife, Mary thought, "Doan fergait der *chinchalok*!" A Chinese woman in a black *samfoo* shouted something in unintelligible Chinese to someone on the platform. They all looked to see who it was. A fat slovenly-looking woman. She shouted something back.

That seemed to be the last exchange that would set the train moving. But it did not. It just stayed there motionless. James looked down the line at the signal. It was green. At the other end of the line there was nothing to see but the big black greasy buffer pistons. As a boy, he had examined them with curiosity. Now they were just big black things at the wrong end of the platform.

A hand wave seen dimly through the glass. Two of the GSC girls came out onto the open gap between the carriages. They looked up and down the platform. They waved. One of them, "the Beck girl," Mary thought, mouthed something hoping her family would understand it.

Then one carriage down from where they were standing, a young man rushed up to the train. He jumped onto the steps to a rounded young Eurasian girl. He appeared to kiss her and dash back to the platform.

"That Norris boy,' Mary said to herself, 'Just like a Norris; just like Archie used to be … so impetuous … Aiyah!"

The incident was forgotten in the next second. The train did not move. "Hell … Bloody engine cannot start."

Suddenly the train jerked. There was an "oh" gasp from the crowd on the platform. But it stopped again. Nothing moved. The carriage in front of them was there, as large as life, motionless, static, frozen. James shuffled. Mary looked at James. They saw Bertha make a weak wave with her fingers. Not with her whole hand, nor with her whole arm, as one would expect Bertha to wave.

Then another jerk, and another, and more jerks … and the train was off. They waved and called out. The girls yelled back. Yelled. On the top of their voices. A tension lifted. They screamed as the train moved on. The long dark substance of a whole moving train disappeared into the dark. They were off.

James took Mary by the arm. They nodded to the Connors, the Consigleires and to Uncle Harry. They found their cars. James saw the Connor's flashy Ford V-8 pull out in front of him. He was tired. "Hope that bloody Sheelah knows how to manage a team …"

Knowing, half-knowing the understatement of that level of his thoughts. Not wanting to hear some things. But somewhere in the dark of it all, knowing that this was a special night in his and Mary's life, when the baby staggers on the brink of the nest and drops down ... to fly ... or fall.

As they drove round the small roundabout at Tanjong Pagar, on their way home, James looked at the red-brick Fraser & Neave building and remarked to Mary, "Hey Ma, did you know that F & N started in 1833?"

Mary was silent. He took a glance at her and relapsed into silence as he turned off towards the Sepoy Lines. Years later when their precocious grandson, Beryl's little mite, asked them about Fraser & Neave they could not remember a thing. But James did remember that the the sign said 1833; the night Bertha left ... for the first time. "Founded in 1833 ..." he said.

The girls were quiet as the train picked up speed. Ethel, sitting next to Bertha, was restless. She had no "goodbyes" to turn over in her mind.

"Tired," she said to Bertha.

"Den, sleep lah," Bertha shot back. Bertha closed her eyes. Five goals. At least! Van Geyzel. Right half. Or centre?

This is it. Not just for the GSC and Singapore.

"Baby" Miles came down the aisle. "Ah dere you are ... Sheelah wants to spik to you. She's up dere." A jerk of her thumb over her shoulder towards the carriage in front. Bertha stood up. The swaying of the train was a new experience to her. It was strange, fascinating, challenging to her balance. She walked to the next carriage, feeling the rush of wind and noise as she crossed over the connecting steel floor out in the open air. The stuffy suppressed noise and fuggy atmosphere of the carriage returned, stifling, heavy, as she slipped into the next carriage. She saw Sheelah at once. "Ah, Bertha."

Sheelah asked her if everything was OK. Then she repeated some things which were told to them before. Bertha started wondering about the summons to see Sheelah. Maybe Sheelah was just checking all round. Then Sheelah came out with it. "Bertha, whatever you do, don't lend Ettel any money. You'll never get it back. Anyway, she won't need any on this trip. I'll see to that. You heard me?"

Bertha too was tired. She got back to her place next to Ethel. She leant against the back of the hard seat and let her body go limp. The train rocked her body. The noise like a hammering on a forty-four-gallon-drum was like the unceasing beat of a twanging base guitar … she was tired.

She woke up, or half-awakened to the same rhythm of the steel wheels on the rails. Somehow it was not a perfectly constant rhythm. Over the unchanging clunk-clunking, there was a periodic "ger-dunk." Just two or three "gerdunk's" and then no more … for awhile. Bertha tried to find a pattern in it as she sat on the seat with the fog of sleep slowly clearing.

The train started slowing down. It was the change in the sleep-extending rhythm she needed to wake her up. The train finally stopped. A large white sign with a station name on it in solid black lettering flashed past just before it stopped. It passed too fast for Bertha to read.

It was so still and silent when the train stopped. Some passengers stirred. Those who slept lightly. There were muffled voices from the platform. Muffled as they came through the glass.

A man with a light, a burning flame of light, started down the platform. Every now and then he stopped, stooped down and looked under the carriages. The brakes, Bertha decided. He's checking the brakes. But it wasn't anything important. His slow progress down the train seemed to fit in with the unexpected stopping of everything. The rhythmic beat, the clunks and the gerdunks.

It looked misty and damp outside. Hazy. A thin dirty-looking Indian man with his sarong tucked up so that you could see his spindly legs shuffled down the platform into her narrow field of vision. It was frustrating. This inability to look further on even with your face flat against the glass. The skinny-legged man walked past and disappeared. It looked as though the train's arrival had woken him up from sleep. It seemed, to Bertha in her first fogged thoughts, that he was looking at the thing that had roared into his bedroom and woken him up. And now the monster was silent and motionless. But this little scene was probably enacted every night when the "night mail" from Singapore came rushing in and stopped suddenly. Like an animal with all its raging spent.

The single yellow incandescent lamp she could see was weak and threw just a little light on her section of the platform. It made the scene so much more dream-like.

"Cigarette?" Ethel was now awake beside her, offering her a cigarette in the Chinese way of holding out one cigarette towards her. "No thanks. I don't smoke." No "decent" girl in the group of her cousins and her convent schoolmates smoked. Not that it was sinful. It was just like boy's shirts having the buttons the other way. Girls didn't smoke.

Ethel lit one for herself with a heavy "zippo" type lighter and took in a deep breath.

"Where are we?"

"Donno."

"Wazzatime?"

"Donno."

"You jus' gottup?"

"Yah ..."

Ethel smoked her Rough Rider silently for a minute. She leant forward and looked across Bertha. She saw only the dimly lit orangey platform with no movement at all across it. She leant back against her seat. When she came to the end of her cigarette, she stubbed it out on the floor of the carriage and slouched back, wriggled a little and breathed out a long sigh.

"Aiyah, so tired."

Bertha turned to Ethel. But she had shut her eyes again and appeared to be trying to go back to sleep.

Bertha turned her attention back to the platform. It was still the same. An orange slice of a part of Malaya. Where nothing was stirring. And the only sounds were faint voices and thumping noises like crates being rolled over. Even these faint noises stopped after a few minutes. The train seemed to have unloaded all it had to but was not moving on, as though it too was tired and had to stay there in this quiet ghostly station and rest.

Bertha dozed off.

When Bertha woke up again she smelt Ethel's cigarette. The plump middle-aged Chinese sitting across the aisle who had wrapped himself up in a red blanket was stirring. She looked out of the window. The very first streaks of dawn were appearing in the sky between the rubber trees. There was nothing to see but rubber trees. Bertha knew they were rubber trees in their regular lines stretching to infinity. She had seen them since she was a young girl along Bukit Timah Road. Or along the road to Changi. There were fewer places left in Singapore where you could see rubber estates now, she thought idly.

The train passed a track running through the estate. Two women were cycling along it. Without lights. The had their heads wrapped up and one could hardly see their faces. Tappers on their way to work, she decided. Then more rubber trees. And nothing else.

"Your first time in Malaya, ha?" Ethel asked.

"Yah ... not counting Johor Baru."

"Place is full of bloody Malays."

Bertha sat up in surprise. "Whaddaya mean?"

"I hate them. Terrible people."

It came as a shock to Bertha to hear Ethel say this. Her parents, uncles, aunts and cousins kept saying nasty things about the Chinese, or the *kling pusings*, and sometimes, but only seldom, threw criticisms or obvious personal remarks against some Malay or other. The never expressed a racial hate as Ethel had just spat out. It upset her. She remained silent.

"You probably haven't seen them at their worst in the *kampong*," Ethel added, noticing her silence. Bertha had seem them and played around the wooden houses, sat on the steps with her Malay friends, lay on the cool timbered floors of the verandahs in the hot afternoons talking, peeped into the bath shacks standing apart from the houses and used the smelly *jambans*. She loved the *kampongs*. The quiet easy way of the people. She kept silent.

"Give me John Chinaman any day," Ethel added.

Bertha was sure now that she should let Ethel's wild statements pass. She looked at the others around them. They didn't look like types who spoke English. But it made her uneasy.

"I grew up in a fishing village. Filthy place," Ethel said.

"But you've left it … haven't you?"

"Yah. It was demolished. We went to an HDB flat. No coffee shops and *kedai's* around. Well, close by, I mean. Only the building site to play in. More gambling than ever … Ah yah!" she sighed.

"I guess that was long ago …"

"Yah. Thank God."

Bertha only knew Ethel from the GSC. She was good fun though her language was dreadful at times. She kept referring to the convent as "an arsehole of a place." Patience once shouted back at her but Ethel only tossed her head back and roared her mad laugh. She knew Ethel worked at the hospital. But she didn't know what Ethel did. Ethel seemed to want to talk now but Bertha was in no mood to listen to her past and her hating this and that.

"Not long now. Sheelah said we would arrive just about dawn."

Ethel was listening to some Cantonese talking behind them.

"Yah, dose people are saying we're almost there." She saw the querying look in Bertha's eyes and added, "They call it Fu Yong, whatever it means …" Neither of them knew it was the romantic Cantonese word for Seremban; Fairy Hill.

The train started slowing down. Several people started collecting their things together. The sky was brighter outside now. There were roads and houses. And as Bertha was trying to imagine what kind of family she was going to stay with, hoping they weren't too much like Ethel's, the train stopped.

The girls were all out on the platform. It was damp and cold. Sheelah was talking to the men and women who were on the platform to meet them. The girls crowded around Sheelah. There were introductions and kisses.

A slim girl was introduced to Bertha. She looked European.

Ginger hair, Bertha thought. The light was still poor. A tall man came up. Mr. Van Geyzel. He too looked *matsalleh*. Van Geyzel; the name then struck her. That was Jean Van Geyzel. Ah! She was going to stay with them. Mrs. Van Geyzel appeared. That's "Jan," Bertha remembered. She's beautiful she thought. But there was little time to think. There were questions about Uncle Harry, and the journey and whether she knew the Armstrongs, or the Leembruggens, and explanations of the station in relation to their house, and a thousand distractions. She waved to the other girls and was soon in a warm car driving off to the Van Geyzel's house.

Jean Van Geyzel told Bertha the programme as the car drove through the town for a bit then past beautiful grassed ravines and almost perfectly pruned hedges of houses set well back from the road. They would have breakfast and just laze around till lunch. Then an early curry tiffin and a good sleep. The game was at five. They would leave the house at four-forty. "Isn't that cutting it a bit too fine?' Bertha asked.

Mr. Van Geyzel laughed, "This is not Singapore. We'll be at the field in ten minutes."

It was just about six minutes from the station to the house. They were NEB quarters, Mrs. Van Geyzel said.

"NEB?"

"Like your PUB, the electricity authority."

It was a pretty wooden house with a green lawn glinting with dew drops in the early sun and huge bougainvillea bushes around the house. Jean chatted brightly all the time. To Bertha she spoke beautifully. Almost like those girls you saw on the screen. She seemed to be the dead opposite of Ethel. She was slender and supple. Smiling all the time, perfectly polite and completely open and friendly. Bertha had to ask one question and the three Van Geyzels answered her in their different ways. She took to Mrs. Van Geyzel immediately.

There were many questions about Singapore. "It's ages since we were last there. The place is changing so fast. We go on in the same old way year after year here in Seremban." How was so and so ...

and the whoosits … and what is on at the cinemas now?

And they told her all about Seremban. "Pity you are only going to be here for one night. We could have taken you to Port Dickson. Or to Sri Menanti. Mrs. Danker in Tampin knew your father, you know. She'd love to see you. Stay longer the next time."

They could not be more charming. The curry tiffin was delicious. Vindyaloo and those brinjals. And at last she flopped into bed. "So tired," as Ethel would have said. She wondered if Ethel had struck such a nice host family.

"Call me Auntie Van. It's so much easier … everyone does."

It was a beautiful bright sunny evening. The field seemed to be a brighter green than their fields in Singapore. The sky seemed to be more blue. Sheelah and some of the other girls were already there. Ethel was strapping on her pads.

"Hoi, Berta. How's your family?"

"Wonderful. And yours?"

"Very nice people. He's the CPHI of Seremban."

"CPHI? What's that?"

"Chief Public Health Inspector. Hey, that's no small job, man. All the meat, food, all the coffee shops, dirty drains, hairdressers, so many tings lah are control' by him. Big shot, you know." Ethel was clearly impressed. But she was even more impressed by what she saw in the house.

"Everywhere, simply everywhere, dere are books. Not jus' books on meat and vegetables and smallpox and dose kine' of tings, but on poetry, fee-lohsoh-fee, geography, mats … everyting lah. Like a book shop. That fellow got plenty brains, man."

"Whose father is it?"

"That big girl dere, der one wit der ball now … dere, dere, dere."

Bertha looked across the field where the Negri girls were hitting the ball around. She recognised her as Debra Schoonmaker she met at the station. A big girl with a friendly grin. About her age.

Ethel continued her account. "I'd never seen a house like dat. Really so many books …"

Some of other girls came up. Patience related that her family didn't have modern sanitation. She screwed up her nose. Bertha wondered if Sheelah had planned it all that way. Ethel and her "books-house," Patience and her *toh-tie-man* house.

Sheelah called them together. Her pep talk. They were quite used to it. Only the older married women were getting immune to it. But everyone was attentive today. They knew their captain. She was likely to come out with a surprise strategy now and then.

"This is the youngest team we will be playing. For the size of the town they are really good. They have just missed winning the All-Malaya final after getting to the final for the last three years. There are some stars. So we've got to give it our best, girls."

There was more. Some, but a very few remarks to individuals. Then the surprise came. It startled Bertha.

"We're going to make a switch today. Bertha, you play right wing. Rosemary you move over."

Rosemary's jaw dropped. She knew she was not as good on the left. "Hah!" she stuttered. There were soft noises of surprise from the other girls.

"I know Bertha can adapt. We know they're going to mark her like hell. I don't think their girls and their half line especially is flexible enough. I'm gambling they won't rearrange their side. One more thing. Can we make an all-out try to score in the first minute. Come on. We'll really try … Well, that's it. About three minutes to go."

Bertha looked at Ethel to see her reaction to the change. But Ethel was not listening. She was watching the other team hit the ball around. She always did that. Looking for the people who would be confronting her.

"Hey, is that Van Geyzel girl playing in the haf' line or forwart?'

"Half. She told me."

"Man, she should be in the front. But maybe she will. Maybe dat's the way they play it."

"Ettel. Did you hear Sheelah telling us about the switch?"

"Whazzat?"

"I'm playing right wing."

"Dat bitch's crazy. Crazy lah. Dat's your ace card lah! Aiyah ..."

"It's OK by me."

It was a Saturday evening and there were quite a few spectators lining the field. Not just the Negri girls' supporters. The crowd was very much an assortment of different races, sexes and ages. The usual children running around behind the spectator lines were there. The fussy ones spreading a newspaper or a handkerchief on the grass before they sat down were also there in Seremban.

As they moved to their positions Ethel could see the reaction of the Negri team. They turned to their captain and looked at her when they saw Bertha on the right. Zena saw her girls' expectant faces waiting for the nod, the pointing telling them to change over. She decided. She put her thumb up just a little in front of her chest giving the OK sign. There was to be no counter change.

The game exploded into action as soon as the whistle went off. Sheelah started the crackling pace with a rough and aggressive bully-off. Then they saw she had the ball. Stella, on her left, was ready for her pass. But unlike Sheelah's usual play she took it herself, moving swiftly down the middle. She passed the skinny brown centre-half. The backs were close to the goal. She had a brief run. The ball fully in her control. Jean Van Geyzel moved towards her. Bertha saw Sheelah take a rapid glance at her but Bertha knew that she was too far to take a pass. Besides, that hefty thing was hanging round her.

With stickwork that brought the first "whoa" from the spectators, Sheelah beat Jean. One of the backs was in front of her now. The Negri forwards were moving down. She saw Stella by her side. Further away, Connie was moving towards the centre.

She passed it to Connie. Bertha had also moved in. She was just at the "dee" line. Sheelah had moved like lightning and the Negri team had been slow in falling back.

A Negri girl raced across to cut off any possible pass to Bertha. Jean Van Geyzel was running up to Bertha. Connie passed it back to Sheelah. She took it through the backs girl, moving right. Jean switched her attention to Sheelah. With a hard crack from Sheelah's stick, the ball went skimming over the grass to Bertha.

It was a perfect pass. And Bertha was there, ready.

Someone in the crowd yelled, "Shoot! Shoot!" Bertha flicked it up. It whizzed past the goalkeeper at hip height into the goal.

The GSC girls screamed. The small crowd roared with its wild, excited, delighted voice.

Bertha saw Mr. Van clapping very sedately. She heard scraps of words from the people on the edge as she walked back to her position.

"Hah. *Itu dia. Dia selalu main lep.*"

"*Tetapi* ... dat captain lah. *Betul dia punya goal.* Whoa *chepat sekali.*"

"Jeez! That centre-forward ..."

"Whoa dese Singapore women, so fierce."

"Good lah! Show our *sombong* girls."

"What man! That fellow Keet in the *Straits Times* says to watch the left wing ... That centre, the captain, she's the one to watch. God, man. She can go."

"Hey, dis game gonna be good."

The GSC girls played with their spirits soaring as the game continued. "We made it ... within the first minute." "I've never seen Sheelah sweep through like that."

But within the next five minutes, Ethel faced a series of attacks. As much as the sudden opening goal had raised the spirits of the Singapore team, it had fired the emotions of the Negri girls. They came at the Singapore goal in periodic waves. Then Ethel saw the ball rolling towards her left foot and, before she could react, she heard the clunk of it hitting the timber board inside the goal. The clunk she knew so well that made something churn in her stomach every time she heard it.

One-all. The pressure was on both sides. The game went on at a desperate fast pace.

At the half time whistle, Ethel spat her curses at the "blerdy umpire." Sheelah shut her up quickly. "Keep it up. We're winning.

They cannot take this pace."

"O God! I'm all in," Patience gasped.

"If you didn't smoke those bloody tings you'd have more stamina."

"Oh dry up! You sound like my mother."

"Sheelah. You were terrific! What a start!"

"Yeah, Sheelah. Do it again."

"I mean to."

"Shall we go back to the usual positions now?" Rosemary Howell asked.

Sheelah looked hard at her. She looked at the others quickly then looked at Bertha, searching her face for a sign. She saw it.

"OK. Let's confuse them again. Rosemary, Bertha, switch."

"That blerdy umpire ..."

"Oh shut up Ettel ..." Sheelah said laughing.

The second half started with the same crackling pace. Later they argued whether that Margie Skoon had tried to break through at the bully-off as Sheelah had done. "Yah, I tink so," Ethel thought, "But dat Braun woman should have been in the right place." "No way. You can't hope to do a shock thing like that when everyone is warmed up," Patience said.

The GSC got in the clincher after about fifteen minutes. It was what Rosemary called one of their "classic" moves, coming down one side swiftly and unexpectedly when the opposing team were hot with attacking. It was either her or Bertha. That day it was Bertha. Sheelah, standing back from the players at their goal as Negri kept pressing, found a stray ball and raced up the field. She saw Bertha run. So did Jean Van Geyzel. But Jean had moved too far from Bertha, one eye on the attack, one eye on Bertha, hoping she could back up her Negri girls. It was the setting for one of their classics.

Bertha took it, moved up a little, but as the defenders turned to her, she passed it to Sheelah. Sheelah ran down the centre. A voice from the crowd yelled, "Go, man, go!" It was Sheelah at her best and fastest. She was facing the backs now. Then a flick to Bertha and Bertha took it, turned her stick around and swung with all her strength. It went into the top corner. Goal!

That killed the morale of the Negri girls. But not the fighting spirit of Jean. As her team-mates seemed to slow down in speed and spirit Jean seemed to be everywhere in the last ten minutes of the game. Ethel kept her eye on her. Jean had a chance once but she tripped and got out of step. It allowed Molly to catch up with her.

When the final whistle was blown, both sides were too tired to cheer. The crowd gave a long roar. It had been a fast and exciting game.

Bertha flopped onto the grass. She was spent. Two goals to her. But she knew they weren't her goals. She had never seen Sheelah play with such determination and aggressiveness before. That night, she told the girls that. It was a wonderful start to their tour. She was happy.

Jean Van Geyzel ran up to her. She knelt down beside her and grabbed her by the shoulders. "Oh Bertha, you were wonderful! You're all they said you were!" She kissed her on the cheek.

Bertha sat up. A wave of emotion was running through her. Her friends, her family, never poured out their feelings, their spontaneous admiration about anything like this. This beautiful delicate girl was truly overjoyed with her performance. She was telling it to her straight out like that without any inhibitions.

It was a rushing into her heart that she had never experienced before. She could only say, "Oh, Jean ... Thanks," and feel so inadequate about her expression of appreciation of Jean's beautiful openness.

The older "Vans" were equally generous and genuine with their congratulations. The match was analysed in overlapping bursts from all in the car on their way back to the Van Geyzel's house. Everyone kept interrupting each other. But there were none of Ethel's harsh criticisms and rough words. Mr. Van said Sheelah was "Damn good," and Mrs. told him to "watch your language, love."

"Oh. Your Sheelah is fantastic, Bertha," Jean gushed. Bertha felt so proud of Sheelah. It was the way Jean said it.

But there was no time to talk about the game or to answer Jean's remark, "Hey, Bertha, that goalie girl is a good friend of yours, isn't she?" because they had to shower and dress for the dinner and dance. It was one mad rush.

As they came up to the steps leading to the verandah, Bertha saw a tall slim young man standing there waiting for them. "Bertha, my brother, Geoff."

He was fair skinned, Caucasian in features and as handsome as the most handsome film stars Bertha had seen on the screen. He stood looking down on them, looking into Bertha's eyes rather shyly and asking about the game. His half smile was something very special, very different.

But there was no time to talk to or to think about Geoff. Mrs. Van, in a great flap, apologised for forgetting to ask Bertha if she had a dress to iron. She snatched up what Bertha handed over to her and rushed off. Mr. Van shouted out in a loud but friendly-fatherly voice that no one must be late or they'll be left behind.

Bertha stripped quickly and completely in front of Jean in the bedroom. She saw Jean was startled. She went to the bathroom. When she came out, Jean had undressed and was waiting with a towel around her. Her skin was so white, Bertha thought.

Mrs.Van came in with the ironed dress. She hesitated for a second at the door when she saw Bertha was in her bra and panties. Jean was out of the bathroom in ten minutes, talking excitedly. "It's St. Paul's school hall." ... "It's ages since I've been to a dance. Do you have a lot of dances in Singapore?" ... "You'll meet all the Romeo's of Seremban, Bertha. I'm sure you'll slay them." ... "Hey that's a strong lipstick. But it goes with your colour, Bertha."

"Now, Bertha, can you do me a favour?"

Bertha turned towards her, expectant. "It's Geoff. Can you try to help me get him out of his shell? Will you ask him to dance to get him started? He's so goddamned shy."

That wasn't Jean's language. Maybe she's human after all. Not just that beautiful perfect doll. Bertha smiled.

"Favour? He's a dream! I'll dance with him all night if he will."

"Oh, Bertha, thank you ... you're so kind."

Bertha winced inwardly.

As the Van Geyzels and Bertha walked into the hall she felt the excitement of the night. The band had started playing and the hall was full of bright dresses and hanging balloons and laughter. The GSC girls still buoyant with their win were in the highest of spirits and swept away any gloom that the Seremban people might have had with their defeat.

There were introductions and wisecracks. More enquiries about relatives and friends here and there. The Seremban people were calling out to each other and going up to Sheelah and Bertha and congratulating them. And the GSC girls slapping that Lopez girl who scored Negri's goal on the back.

It was an open informal party. There were coupons to hand in for drinks but the food was there for one to eat one's fill. There were no special seating arrangements except for the committee table where Bertha saw Sheelah sitting. The older ladies were, however, establishing claims and building little groups at some tables. The GSC girls were with the families who had taken them in for the short stay and, as they dashed around to talk to each other, they met their friend's "families." It soon became one big friendly party. Fathers and mothers, aunts, uncles, cousins, grandmothers and grandfathers. The whole of Seremban seem to be here, Mrs. Van remarked.

There was rice and curry and ham and roasted chickens and salads, sambals, spring rolls, and every single dish that the Eurasians relished. Except the Chinese dishes that involved complicated cooking, or just had to be eaten hot off the fire and, of course, the special dishes reserved for occasions like Christmas.

The band was all Eurasian except for Dollah, the trumpeter. Bertha noticed that unlike Singapore there was no Filipino or Filipino mixtures in the band. They played the oldies that had been danced to for years. "Alexander's Ragtime Band." "The bells are ringing for me and my girl." "I'm in love with two sweethearts." And they played the jive numbers of the day. Of yesterday, the GSC girls giggled to themselves.

The Lopez girl was a spectacular dancer. Bertha admired her dancing and said so to Jean Van Geyzel.

"Yes, she's very good. But she's not really one of us."

"Whaddyamean?"

"She's a *Beng*."

"A what?"

"A *Beng*. A *geragok*."

Bertha flushed. These Ceylon Burghers! She had a good mind to retort that she too was a *geragok*, pronouncing it the way Jean did. But she kept her mouth shut. She remembered that the Van Geyzels were different. They did not have a little altar with an oil lamp in the house. Nor did they have any "holy pictures" hanging anywhere.

Bertha saw Ethel at the tables that were used as a bar among the older men laughing heartily with a glass in her hand.

"Let's go over and join Ethel and her new heart-throbs," she suggested. Jean seemed to shrink back physically. "You go on and join them. I want to say hello to my auntie Adele."

Bertha saw the reluctance. She left Jean for the rowdier crowd at the bar.

"Hoi! Here's your left wing star who got into the wrong place today! Come, come, girl … what are you drinking?"

Someone's father in high spirits. There were introductions. And the attempts to trace family lines. A red-faced older man, Mr. Toft, cut in to stop the dreary questions.

"It's easy, Jack, with these Singapore people. Everyone's related to a de Souza." They laughed.

"Did you ever hear the story of how a thief broke into a house at Queen Street.."

"Is that the street alongside the church?"

"Yes. He woke up the whole house and everyone chased him. As he ran, he pulled out a gun and shot into the gang chasing him. He hit two de Souzas."

When the laugh had subsided, Bertha added, "My father swears it's true."

They went on to talk about the GSC tour and there was advice from all the Malayans about the best food in each place they were going to. Bertha only remembered the "Inche Cabin" of Penang, thinking it was on odd name.

Ethel got into an argument starting with her flat statement that *kajang satay* was just plain lousy. She'd tried it.

A tall young man came up and asked Ethel to dance. This was almost immediately followed by another boy asking Bertha, as though he had been waiting for someone to break the ice and begin pulling the Singapore girls away from the bar tables.

Bertha looked around for Geoff Van Geyzel after the piece had finished. She saw him at the Van Geyzel's table and went up to him. "Jean has given me strict orders to ask you to dance with me."

He grinned and stood up. His hold was ever so weak. He moved slowly and nervously. Bertha tried to relax him with a joke and conversational starters. But he was stiff and silent as stone. Her dream melted away.

"My … He so hansome'." Ethel said to her after that. "Yah, but like a rag doll, lah. No spunk in dat fellow."

Nevertheless Bertha enjoyed herself thoroughly at the dance and when the band finally played "Who's taking you home tonight" at two in the morning, she let Reggie Lopez hold her close as the lights dimmed for the first time. She saw Mrs. Van watching her. So she put her head on his shoulder.

Sheelah, passing her on the floor, turned around and said softly, "Beerthaa?" in a half-teasing, half-warning tone.

As they drove home, Mrs. Van, still smiling and looking as fresh as ever, turned around to Bertha in the back seat, "The Turners will pick you up at seven-forty-five for the eight o'clock service. We go to the evening service. Mr. Van is a church warden."

Bertha understood. She really meant the high mass. They were not Catholics.

The team left in a chartered bus for Malacca after lunch. They were not playing on Sunday. Ethel had queried Sheelah about this. "Waste of chance lah." But Sheelah explained that there were still some families who would not like them to play on a Sunday. "Besides, it will allow us to have a late Saturday night." Ethel frowned at the explanation, but the logic of a late night kept her silent.

Sheelah made her speech as the bus wound round the curves through the mountain pass shortly after they got out of Seremban. Bertha remembered that this was where her father had seen the black leopard looking at him with its green eyes gleaming in the dark one night when he was hunting in Malaya many years ago.

"OK girls. You were really great yesterday. Now let's see that right through this trip. Tonight is early bye-byes for everyone. No going out. I don't care if you have godfathers or aunts in Malacca who want to take you out. No one is going out tonight. Got that clear? You can go out in the morning. But you must be back by three at the convent where we are putting up. Three o'clock. Sharp. And no bargaining. If you are going out you have to tell me. Now, if there are enough of you interested I'll see if I can get the convent school bus to take us to St. John's fort and to St. Francis Xavier's church ... and maybe the Portuguese village.

"That's it. Don't forget what I said ... keep the standard we set yesterday ... We'll show these Malayans what Singapore can do."

Ethel yelled something. Then someone shouted "for she's a jolly good fellow" and the singing started. They went through the "Camptown Ladies," "Polly-wolly-doodles," "Old-black-Joe" and through "I'm forever blowing bubbles," "I've got Sixpence," "Five Minutes More," "You are my Sunshine," "Tavern in the Town" and started on a long "Rasa Sayang" with the Leceister girl doing all the verses, even that naughty one about "*tengok tetek menolak baju.*" Then when they appeared to run out of ideas, Ethel roared out "Jingli Nonah" and they were off again. Patience sang something from a Gilbert and Sullivan and the singing petered out.

Bertha looked out of the window. This was Malaya. Not the endless rows of rubber trees she saw from the train. She looked with much interest. This was the country her Pa had talked so much about. Her mother had lived here for a few years somewhere in this region. A place called Bahau. That was during the war years. Mary had related her stories with little emotion telling them of the hardships of living at the jungle fringe at Bahau. The malaria. The *ubi kayu.*

But the Malaya Bertha saw through the bus window seemed so calm and relaxed in the afternoon. Goats, cows, buffaloes were resting everywhere. She caught glimpses of little boys climbing trees, Malay men tinkering with tractor engines, a dog chasing chickens, an obese Malay woman refolding her sarong around her, looking at the road vacantly. Even the villages they passed seemed to be asleep in the hot afternoon sun.

At every village there was a roadblock. A police checkpoint. She wasn't sure if they were policemen or soldiers. They carried guns. The Emergency was on. The commies were still fighting the British in the jungles. Sheelah had warned them that they could not carry food. "Aiyah! When will the British stamp them out?" But that afternoon there wasn't the slightest hint of any action or violence. The world had almost stopped. Only the buzzing of the bus engine. If it wasn't for the drone of the bus engine, she was sure that there would only be the sound of the breeze rustling the *lallang* and the leaves of the trees and the soft rush of water in the clear frothing streams they passed. God's day of rest, she said to herself. But that's only my God. Not theirs.

The Malacca girls met them at the convent. It was not in the programme. But the Malacca Eurasian Association whose sports wing they were playing against planned it as a surprise. They met the team. Some of the surnames were familiar to Bertha. Some were not. Sequeira, D'Almeida, Carvallo, Theseira, Minjoot, Brown, Aroozoo, Nunis, Nonis, Da Costa, Ferdericks ... Bertha was too tired to be sociable. She kept to her Singapore gang. The others had obviously slept on the bus. She had not.

She slept like a log that night. Ethel wanted to talk, but she just dropped off at once. The last thing she remembered was Ethel looking around for something to use as an ashtray.

It was another beautiful evening when they went on the field in their black and yellow outfits. There was a larger crowd than at Seremban. Ethel watched the opposing team knock the ball around before the game started. She always did that. "They're slower but have more power than the Negri team," she said to Bertha.

Sheelah tried to kick it off with a left side raid. But it became obvious that they were not going to let Bertha have the ball if they had to put a hundred girls around her. Sheelah read the scene. The passes to Bertha became fewer and far between. Sheelah took every opportunity to try and make a run herself. She got the first goal off a short corner on the left of the Malacca goal. While they marked Bertha, Sheelah slipped in and tapped the ball into the goal.

Their second goal came from one of Sheelah's breakaway runs, her stick sliding the ball between the back's legs. A short pass to Rosemary. And Rosemary gave it all she had. It nearly tore the net. The crowd went wild.

At half-time, Bertha saw Sheelah's eyes were shining. There was that aggressive, killing fire in her. Yesterday it seemed to be dampened by worry, by concern that they should make their kill at the first game. Today, it was Sheelah without that load on her.

"We'll give you one, Bertha," she said spitting out a mouthful of water onto the grass.

The whistle went. And it was there at Bertha's stick. Two girls were on top of her in a flash. She saw a third blocking the line of her intended pass to Stella. The ball went out. It was the GSC's throw-in. Bertha went up to the line. The ball had disappeared into the crowd. A hand rolled it to her. She looked up. His eyes met hers. She saw the strength of his look. She saw his fair masculine face. His thin muscular arm. His slightly brownish hair. She saw the gleam in his eyes. She almost froze.

She hesitated for a second or two looking at him. "Come on, Bertha!" She saw him looking at her thighs as she turned around to roll the ball back into play. Her knees went soft.

She was trapped. She could not move. They were marking her as though the whole game depended on how well they immobilised her. And Sheelah was running wild everywhere.

Bertha hung around waiting for that pass that would send her moving like a streak of lightning down the left line. In the corner of her eye she kept looking for him. To see his face again. "Bertha!" a scream from Sheelah. The ball was at her stick. An absolutely perfect pass straight to her. But her mind was not there. She had taken a glance into the crowd. At him. For the moment she couldn't think who was where. Had the Nonis woman moved inwards? Where was the pimply one? She "screwed it up," as Ethel said later.

As she walked towards the Malacca goal, waiting for another chance, she saw Sheelah glaring daggers at her. But in the next split second Sheelah had the ball and an opening. The Malacca girls had not come back fast enough. Sheelah took it. It was a solo thing. Bertha stopped in her stride as she watched Sheelah move. This was what made her captain and inside right of the state team. She went through three of them. The goalie came out to her. But Sheelah was too good for Sally Ferdericks. She dribbled through her and put the ball in.

Bertha looked at him as the crowd roared. He was looking straight into her eyes. The sun was behind him. She thought she saw him wink.

The ball was at Bertha's feet again. Somehow she let a Malacca girl get it.

Malacca was now fighting desperately. They got a goal. Then another. It was two-three and about eight minutes to go. Bertha felt his eyes on her. She took a pass and flicked it to Stella. She knew Ethel would give her a telling off for that. There was a chance. She had ditched it. Ethel watched every move Bertha made. She had a tremendous faith in Bertha's future.

The whistle shrilled. They had won again. Their second game. Bertha looked across the field at the dissolving crowd. Ethel was the first to speak to her.

"*Gila*!" she spat out.

Sheelah's eyes were still shining with the excitement of their win. She gave Bertha a knowing look. I'll speak to you later, it said.

The girls milled around. Some Malacca girls came up and talked to them. Bertha was introduced to a Trollope girl who wasn't there when they had arrived. They chatted. Then she saw him. Standing around with the Malacca team. His hands in his pockets, nervously leaning back on his heels, smiling and listening to one of the team; that forward Sequeira. Yes, the Sequeira woman.

Bertha summoned up her courage and pointing with her chin asked the Trollope girl who that fellow was.

"Oh, him. Carl Westerhout. He's been away studying overseas. Just back. Finished his course. Was going with Dafne Cresson before he left. Real strong. Poor bugger. She married a Swedish *matsalleh* two or three months after he left. We all thought it was a dead "cert." thing that he would come back and marry her. Nice fellow. Shy, though."

She saw Bertha looking at him. She was much older than Bertha. She saw the way Bertha was not really concentrating on the talk around them. Anita Trollope smiled in the corner of her lips, and with the smile still on her face for Bertha to see she asked, "Wanna meet him?"

"Yah."

"Come on."

They went up to him. "Hey, Carl. This is the Singapore left winger … Bertha Rodrigues."

He bowed and muttered something. Bertha said something. She did not know what. He spoke first. "They tell me you're the danger girl."

"On the field, yes. But they didn't give me a chance today."

"You're not dangerous off the field?"

Bertha smiled. She hoped it was in a knowing way. She wasn't used to these exchanges. Meeting strangers. Every boy she had been attracted to before was someone she had known since she was a kid.

She saw his eyes moving over her. As a woman knows, she saw, as she saw on the field, that he was strongly attracted to her. She looked at him and confirmed her first impressions. He was staggeringly handsome in some kind of way. Not every woman would think so. But there was some force, some magnetic force that drew her, mesmerised, to him.

"You going to thc dancc tonight?" he asked.

"Yah."

"See you there, Bertha."

She reeled with the intimacy of his using her name. Her folks did not use first names like that unless they were really close. To use someone's first name was not part of the normal conversational touching. Neither did they use surnames or other addresses in ordinary talk. One met Uncle George and said, "Hello, Uncle George," but one never repeated "Uncle George" as one spoke to him. Her Pa kept saying Mary to her Mum. It was a sort of intimate thing. His saying, "See you there, Bertha," had nuances to Bertha's subconscious mind that the Trollope girl might have read. It did not occur to her that he had picked up expressions in England which he did not realise were out of tune with the society he had come back to.

Anita Trollope's statement that he had been ditched by some Eurasian girl went round inside her head. It wasn't just a motherly feminine sympathy. It was a deep atavistic thing. To be thrown out because of a *matsalleh.* To be thrown out because of some sexy Chinese bitch or voluptuous Malay girl, in her reference, switching the race of it all, would have been different. She couldn't see that it was the conditioning of her society and times. Somehow she understood the pain he must have gone through. It drew her closer to him, in some way. Poor Carl.

"BERTA! The bus is leaving! Hurry up lah!"

To the bus. To the convent. Rushing to the bathrooms. The terrible light in the dorm. Having to ask Ethel if her make-up was "right." Smoothing down her unironed dress with her hands. Frantically. Stella dashing past, looking beautiful. Sheelah with her hair up; so stylish. So quickly dressed already. Shoes! Where were her red shoes? Sheesh ... I'm sure they are there in the right-hand, top corner of the suitcase.

Somehow she got on to the bus, to the dance hall. Whew!

Bertha's eyes scanned the hall for Carl. He was not there when she walked in. As they stood around she kept searching the crowd with one eye on the door. She finally spotted him at one of the tables talking to a mixed group of old ladies and young people. He was wearing a blue long-sleeved batik shirt. It was an informal "do." She studied the group at the table trying to see if there was any girl who seemed to be on familiar terms with him. She told herself it couldn't be if he had just returned from England. But what did Anita mean by "just come home?"

Then she realised she was not listening to the girls around her. She saw Sheelah looking closely at her. Iris Brown, one of the Malacca team, came up with a few other girls. She recognised "Baby" Sequeira, the forward.

"We're going to break up this little hen group. We've put two of you at each table. Here's the list." The girls crowded round the list.

"The table numbers go clockwise round the room."

"Bertha, you're on six." She looked at the speaker. It was Anita Trollope. Anita winked at her as their eyes met. She jerked her chin in the direction of the table. It was HIS table. That's why he had not come up to her when she arrived, she said to herself. He knew. Between he and Anita, they had arranged it. It was what she wanted to believe.

"This is Bertha, the Singapore star ..." he introduced her as soon as she arrived at the table and shyly nodded at him. He seemed to stand up at once and rush into the introductions to conceal his awkwardness.

"Mr. Aroozoo, Mr. and Mrs. Minjoot, Mr. and Mrs. Theseira, my aunt Matilda, Grace Theseira, Donny Carvallo, Gladys Carvallo, June Aroozoo, Christina Nonis ..." He introduced the older people first and then went round the table.

"They really marked you today, didn't they? Ha! Ha! ..." Mr. Aroozoo started the conversation going.

"He was one of the umpires," Carl said, turning to Bertha. His gaze stayed on her after he spoke.

"Yeah," Bertha said, "your Malacca girls were sticking to me like glue." She looked at the faces around the table. "Hey, you! You ..."

Christina Nonis smiled. "Yeah, I was right half today."

There was more talk about the game, a convenient common ground starter. Then the inevitable.

"Your father and I used to shoot pig together in the old days," Mr. Minjoot said. Bertha knew he meant wild boar. "Yah, we had good times ... and good shooting too. I remember once we tried to shoot a tiger."

"What do you mean 'tried?' " Carl asked.

"It was a real funny thing. We got the *kampong* people to hang up a deer. It was almost rotten. They built a platform and that big size European fellow ... Robertson I think was his name, your daddy's boss ... He went up on the platform with Jimmy Pinto to wait. We climbed some trees further away ... Waited for hours. Finally the tiger came. The European bugger picked up his gun and shifted his weight ... Kederbak! The platform fell down! I tell you we laughed so much. Even the tiger got scared and *chabot*. That was the last time we tried anything funny like that ... I told them, 'let's stick to what we know. Stick to the pigs, lah.' "

The food was ready. They went up to the buffet tables. Rice and all the Malacca delicacies. "Try Auntie Matilda's Curry Devil," Carl suggested. He kept by her side as they moved along the table. "Hey, Ettel, you really hungry ah?" "Goalie must eat lah! How can you have a skinny *chinkeret* goalie?" "Hey the *achar* looks super, man!" "This is the genuine Malacca *chinchalok*, I presume." "Not too much, Bertha," Anita Trollope called out, "after you can't dance ..." with a knowing smile.

The band struck up with "These Foolish Things" after dinner. Carl who sat beside her occasionally joining in the general table talk, stealing glances at her now and then, was on his feet at once. "May I have the pleasure of this dance." The full proper thing to say. To hide his shyness, Bertha thought to herself.

"My pleasure," she said with a smile.

And she was in his arms. He held her so close. She wondered if everyone would notice it. Maybe that's the way they dance in England. She let her body relax and let the music seep into her.

"You're a beautiful dancer, Bertha."

"And so are you."

They swept across the floor without talking to each other. For a few minutes the floor was quite empty and Carl took her smoothly with the slow-fox beat, doing all the Victor Sylvester steps in his dog-eared, black-cover book. He was delighted that Bertha responded quickly and perfectly to the little changes of pressure of his hand against her back, his left hand movements, the subtle twists of his trunk. He felt the whole room looking at him as they passed the Brown's table. But the floor soon filled and Carl slowed his pace. Bertha felt his grip on her hand tighten.

"Bertha, you're beautiful."

No man had ever said this to her so openly, so suddenly. She felt her knees go soft. She drew him closer and could only whisper, "Oh, Carl."

The night was one unending dream. They danced with each other almost through the night. He said he had to dance with Mrs. Minjoot once. Then as the band started "On the sunny side of the street," one of Bertha's favourites, he asked Iris Brown, who had come to their table to chat with Auntie Matilda, to dance. That's two we've missed, she counted. But Donny Carvallo danced with her and she showed him how she could jive when Donny swung her out holding the tip of her forefinger.

They came back to the table breathless. Donny was a wild energetic dancer. Between his panting he tapped Carl on the shoulder, after he had drawn Bertha's chair out for her, and whispered, "Sorry old cock."

Bertha was taken aback at this. She saw Auntie Matilda glaring at Donny. Her ears picked up everything. Her eyes saw everything.

As the drink flowed, the noise and laughter became louder and louder. Female shrieks and uninhibited throaty guffaws. The band sensed the mood and began to play sing-along pieces. Bertha hugged Carl on the dance floor as he sang "I'm in Love with Two

Sweethearts," asking him who the other was, assuming that she was one. They sang "I'm Forever Blowing Bubbles," "Girl of my Dreams" and "Bengawan Solo." Then suddenly it was over. The last dance. Carl kissed her on the cheek as it ended. She wanted to turn her mouth to his, but she knew Auntie Matilda, the Minjoots, the Sequeiras, the Browns, the whole of Malacca and Sheelah would see her. She squeezed his hand and rushed to the bus. She knew she would not have been able to go through a long goodbye of broken phrases, promises to write and all that.

Bertha got on the bus the next morning with her head still fuzzy. She had taken a long time to drop off to sleep, but when she did she had slept solidly and she still did not feel wide awake. She moved to the back of the bus. Ethel was there on the last seat.

She always sat on the last seat. On her first tour she had explained it in her way with, "I goalie, lah! ... Always watching your backsides."

"Berta, come sit here," Ethel called out thumping the empty seat next to her with her open palm. Bertha flopped down and shut her eyes. Ethel took one look at her and kept silent. The bus started to move off. Bertha was still dazed. Olga Struys and Damien Filmer's sister were talking loudly about Malacca and the game. Scraps of their conversation drifted to Bertha and Ethel on the seat behind them. Food, boys, Sheelah ... "So strict, lah!" ... Rosemary's dribbling past the Malacca back. Then a comment woke Bertha up.

"You know dat back, dat lef' back. Angella Jasper, she's not Eurasian ... she got no right to play for dem. Jasper is from Jaspal Singh, you know."

Bertha sat up bristling. She held herself back. But Ethel had heard it too. She shouted out loudly, "Den you tell us, what is rashian?"

"Like us, lah, Serani ..." Olga replied.

"Black, white, what? ... *Kopi susu*? Chinese and Malay *champorisation*?"

"You so clefer to ask, you tell us!" Olga shot back.

Patience across the aisle in her best accents chipped in, "The

Eurasian Association rules say you must have an European surname."

"So der!" Ethel shouted at Olga. "Jasper not *kwei-loh* name?" She didn't wait for Olga to retort. She was obviously infuriated for some reason which Bertha could not figure out. She continued, "I tell you ... Eurasian must eat *sambal belachan*, *chinchalok* and can eat Hylam pork chop or Chinese black chicken, or *kai keok*. ... some more ... man cannot be *sunat*."

The strange outburst seemed to settle Ethel. She leant back in her seat and sighed. Olga kept quiet. Patience turned to Bertha and grinned. Bertha glared at her.

After a few minutes Ethel looked at Bertha. She put her hand on Bertha's thigh where it was bare below her short skirt. Such a soft hand, Bertha thought, for someone who seemed so rough in many ways.

"Berta," she said softly. "You had good time las' night, ha? ... Las' night was las' night. Dey all der same ... for him too las' night finish already ... *habis*! ... you doan be so sad."

Bertha leaned against Ethel feeling her strong shoulder against her own. She sighed softly and shut her eyes again.

The game that evening against the Selangor side was fast but without the frenzy of the Seremban game. The KL team were older than they were. They were slower but had far more experience and better teamwork than the GSC team. Bertha knew it was going to be a hard fight.

She had one brilliant run midway in the first half. She seemed to fly down the left line passing the defenders with the greatest of confidence and ease. The crowd started cheering excitedly when they saw that there was a chance for a goal. Sheelah took her pass. She moved into the dee and "clunk," the ball hit the board at the back of the goal. They had "hammered one in," as Ethel used to say.

But it did not do them much good. At half time it was two-one with Selangor in the lead. Five minutes after they resumed play, Selangor got another goal. Then another.

Bertha had an opportunity after this and took it right up but the Orloff girl stopped her. Three times after that Bertha was stopped as she flew down on the left. The Mayo woman in particular seemed to rush at her savagely.

They lost. Ethel threw her stick down, depressed, when she came to the drinks tray on the grass after the game ended, "Aiyah!"

"Can't win them all, Ethel," Sheelah consoled her. "You stopped some sizzlers, Ethel."

There was no dinner or dance that night. Kuala Lumpur was different. They were going to have dinner at the SEA President's house somewhere in the Jalan Kenny area. He was a "big-shot" in Shell. Big house. Huge lawn, they said. Just drinks and dinner. No dancing. We're tired, anyway, they told themselves.

The crowd was different. They seemed to Bertha to be much "posher." She heard Millicent McCoy order a "gin and it" and wondered what it was. *Makan kechil* was handed around while they were drinking and talking. They were talking of what was happening in KL and no one tried to find links between their relatives and hers.

Bertha found herself alone after Colin Poulier left her. "Oh, I must catch hold of Ronnie Grenier," he said and mumbled something about a rugger game. She looked around. Sheelah was talking to a tall bespectacled Indian, about fortyish and Margie Labrooy. She went up to them. Greetings and introductions. Krishnamoorthy, call me Chris, from personnel, Shell.

"But Graham Greene does understand the Catholic psyche so well, Chris," Sheelah said. "Yes, but he overdoes it in *The Heart of the Matter* … you see …" "All this confessional conscience, this terrible weight our church places on us from birth." "Baptism, Chris." "Well … from our first communion."

"You must be a Catholic to really understand him, Margie."

Bertha stood silent listening. Her concentration drifted from time to time. Then she caught D.H. Lawrence. She pricked up her ears. Lady Chatterley. She had borrowed it but it did not stir her as it had stirred Mavis. They didn't mention the book at all. Sheelah and Chris were talking of language and words. "A snake came to my watertrough," and lots more Chris recited. "There's an unstructured rhythm," she heard Sheelah say. Margie said something like "the seemingly endless sexual energy that just flows out." She stepped back in her mind and watched and listened to Sheelah. "And she's not a teacher," she noted to herself.

It became a little more interesting when Jack Gonzales joined them and the subject moved to Malaya and politics and to Eurasians in Malaya.

"We're not unique. You've got to read the Indonesians on this … *This Earth of Mankind* … but the most interesting book I've ever . . ."

"Is *Half-Caste*, by Cedric Dover," a voice boomed out interrupting Jack from behind Bertha. She recognised it at once. Carl Westerhout.

"Carl!" several voices rose in surprise.

"Surprise, surprise," he said, looking at Bertha first and then the others.

"I thought I needed a break, so I borrowed Dad's car and drove up."

"And go back tomorrow?"

"No, I've taken a few days off."

"What brings you here?"

"The game of the year …"

"Come on, man … whassit?"

"Jus' felt like a break."

"Mus' be a woman somewhere."

Bertha cut in, "Are there women everywhere?"

He looked into her eyes and remained silent.

"You missed a good game."

"I know, I heard," and turning to Bertha, "And I heard that the danger-girl of Singapore got the first goal."

She did not bother to correct him.

"As I was saying when this young man interrupted us."

Carl turned to Bertha again. "Your glass is empty. Come on I know the barman." He took her by the arm and they moved away.

Bertha caught Sheelah's eye. She thought there was the faintest trace of a wink.

He took Bertha's glass from her hand as they walked and put it on a table. He held her by the arm and led her. Bertha was dizzy with the thrill of his sudden appearance. Only after they passed the bar did she realise that he was leading her out into the garden.

He held her and kissed her as they stood on the lawn. Full on the lips. Bertha surrendered her whole self to him with the kiss. He kissed her again and again. The sky and the trees around her seemed to be spinning around them. Then she felt a surge of emotion rush through her. His hand was there. The shock of realising it made her reel. It wasn't anger or fright. Nobody had done that to her before. She let her blood race through her body for a few minutes, then gently held his arm and moved his hand away. He did not resist.

"Oh Carl, Carl ..."

She pushed him back and looked into his eyes. "What a wonderful surprise. For me, Carl."

"Yes, my darling I had to come here and see you again."

He hugged her and spoke. "You were terrific today on the field, Bertha. You are really wonderful. The way you move. Your body. Your speed."

"You saw me!"

"Yes. I went straight to the field after I arrived. I'm glad I did. That was not the same you that played in Malacca."

"Because you hypnotised me that day."

"It was only yesterday, Bertha."

"Seems like years and years ago ..."

It was the greatest night of her life, she told herself a thousand times in bed in the convent dormitory. Oh, how lucky I am! Ethel had been nearly bowled over when she dragged Carl to her while Ethel was heaping up her plate.

"Ettel! Look at what I've got for dinner!"

She saw Bertha's eyes shining. And Bertha saw the happiness on her face as she glanced quickly from Bertha to Carl. "Oh, Berta, you so larky ..."

"I'm the lucky one," Carl replied, his accent sounding so markedly different from Ethel's.

"I'm so happy for you," Ethel said to her and kissed her on the cheek as she lay in bed in the dorm. Then she turned away and went to her own bed. In her heart, Bertha thanked her for knowing, for understanding.

She had her second surge of surprise the next morning as she walked out to the bus with her bag after breakfast. Carl was standing there at the side of the bus talking to Sheelah.

"Carl!" She rushed up to him.

He kissed her on the cheek but appeared to be very serious. Sheelah looked at Bertha. Then at Carl. Her face was stern. She put her hand on Bertha's shoulder and, facing Carl, spoke.

"OK. But you follow the bus. I don't want you out of my sight. Hear that Mr. Westerhout. All the way. Stay with the bus. Promise me."

"Yes Miss Cornelius," mockingly, "Thy will shall be done."

"What's this all about?" Bertha asked.

With a wide grin Carl explained. "I'm going to Penang. You'll come in my car. Captain has finally agreed! We'll follow the bus. Follow the yellow brick road. Lesssgo."

"Oh Carl ... Oh thank you, Sheelah."

Northern Malaya was beautiful that day. The sun was shining, blindingly bright. Even the crowded Ipoh road that they crawled through was fascinating to Bertha. The timber and zinc shacks and old shophouses. The log lorries with trailers. The wide open stretch of sand as they pulled out of KL. Tin mines, Carl explained to her.

The steep slopes. The dark green jungle. Just north of KL. Cars stopped by the side of the road. Somewhere beyond the road the occupants were wandering in the shady tracks between the trees. The rushing stream. They caught glimpses of it as they drove. It appeared and disappeared in short rushes of frothy white with the noise of running water. It was hot, but Bertha did not feel it. The breeze blew in, ruffling her hair. And Carl's. She saw how soft and thick it was.

"Carl, you've got the most beautiful curving eyelashes."

Miles and miles of jungle. Carl told her that there could be communists somewhere out there.

Tanjong Malim. The town was suddenly there. The bus stopped. The girls came streaming out. They parked and went up to them. "*Pipi* stop. Sheelah says we're going to have coffee and *char-siew-pau*," Ethel explained.

Carl was shy and quiet among the girls. They teased him about being the only thorn. Patience and Ethel sat at the same table with them. Patience screwed up her nose at the *pau's*. "You can have mine," she said to Carl. "I'll take it if you doan min'," Ethel had said and reached out for the *pau*. "I gave it to Carl!" Patience protested, "He's a growing boy."

"Oh yeah!"

Like a European, Bertha thought, at the way he said "Oh yeah."

Ethel's "Frien', frien', never min' ..." settled the question.

After Tanjong Malim, more hills. Then the flatter land. The padifields. Glimpses of *kampongs* whizzing past. Fruit stalls by the sides of the road. Hey, durian! mangosteens too!

Flat wide sweeps of blinding white sand. The occasional dredger looking like a house sitting in its private garden-lake. Rusty pipelines. The shimmering haze above the sand. The heat now becoming almost unbearable, in spite of the air rushing through the windows.

The limestone outcrops. Bertha was enthralled by the beauty of the limestone with the green growth on top.

More rubber. More padifields. More jungle. Tin mines getting fewer. It was all beautiful. So very, very beautiful to Bertha. This is where I want to live, she said to herself.

They talked. From KL to Tanjong Malim, through Slim River and Kampar, past Ipoh, past Taiping. She caught the sign, "Mambau di Awam." Hey! Mambau in the Clouds! What a pretty name, Carl.

She told Carl all about herself. Her family. Her passion for fish-head curry and *loh-mai-kai*. Mr. Vandyke. The Maria Hertogh riots.

Eric. Beryl.

Carl talked of his studying in England. Winter. Snow. Malaya Hall at Bryanston Square. Italy. The heat in the summer. Rome. The Vatican.

The bus stopped somewhere after Taiping for lunch. The bus driver knew the coffee shop *towkay*. They had a good meal. Sheelah sat with them this time. She was in good spirits. But Bertha saw that Sheelah and Carl could talk of things and interests they had in common which were new and strange to her. Like Shopan. She gathered he was a composer. Sibelius. Highden.

They were running late. As soon as they had eaten, they were off again. Carl hummed. She snuggled up to him. It was a Hillman Minx with a bench seat in front and one of those gears that stuck out of the steering column.

Ethel kept an eye on the car. She turned round regularly to see if they were there. At times, she dozed off and would wake up with a start and quickly turn round to see if they were still following them.

At Nibong Tebal there was a traffic light. Ethel turned around again to look at the black Hillman Minx behind them. Then she let put a screech of delight. It came spontaneously to her. "They're kissing!"

The girls rushed to the back. Olga slipped the window glass down and yelled at the top of her voice. No one knew what she shouted but everyone shouted her own remark and witty crack.

There was laughing and chatter as the bus lurched forward when the lights went green.

Ethel slumped back in her seat. She frowned. She couldn't see the sad smile at the corner of Sheelah's mouth.

When the chain ferry at Prai started, half the girls got out of the bus and rushed to the car. Carl saw them coming. He wound up the screens and locked all the doors. Bertha buried her face in her hands and pretended to be excruciatingly embarrassed. They saw her smiling behind her hands.

You'll love Penang, Carl had said to Bertha. She only saw a slice of the hill and the island as they pulled into the ferry terminal. One couldn't get a full view from the road at Butterworth. When the ferry was fully loaded and the ropes were cast off, the girls got out of the bus. Carl and Bertha got out of their car and went to the front of the ferry. Then she saw the island across the sea in the evening sun. The hill appeared huge to her. It seemed to be just one large hill. She turned to Carl standing beside her, "It's beautiful."

It was as beautiful as the Penang Carl had described in the car. He had told her how he had gone away to study law in England. How his father had saved to make it possible for him to do so. His old man was a Technical Assistant; a sort of engineer without the qualification and with a quarter of the pay, Carl said. The British had got the men they wanted and given them the knowledge to operate as engineers, but they set the course for Technical Assistants just a little below that needed for recognition as an engineer. Part of the colonial system that his dad (He called him "Dad," "Pa" to Bertha) had railed against when he'd had a few. But not in front of the Europeans.

He had studied hard with the pennies feeding his gas fire in a bed-sitter for four years. But he'd had a good time too. He had heard Nat Temple and had seen Victor Mature one day in a hotel lobby. He didn't say so, but above all he'd learnt that the "white man" was no different from us. And the tales Auntie Matilda and others had told him about every English girl having "b.o." were not true, he laughed.

"And after how many experiments did you come to this scientific conclusion?"

"No Bertha, I'm not the romeo type."

Bertha looked deep into his eyes. She wasn't sure. He had moved so fast with her.

"I thought of staying there for a few years. I would have been happy, perhaps found and married an English girl. Or more probably an Irish one ... But my folks were quite upset at the thought I expressed in a letter. I felt a kinda duty to return. It wasn't all that painful. I liked England but there some things that I could not get used to. Bathing in a long bath was one."

Bertha held his hand while he drove and talked.

"So finally I said goodbye to my friends."

"Boys and girls," Bertha interjected.

"And I boarded the *Canton* for Malaya. We had a wonderful time on the boat. Most of the locals had just graduated and were feeling carefree ... some were crazy. We played poker, chess, sang, and danced."

"With who?"

"Oh, there were a good few Chinese girls and one Malay girl returning with degrees. And there was Mrs. Ho. Some rich doctor's wife who had been to Europe on a holiday flirting with the young blokes ... Yah ... it was a good trip."

"Then one morning my cabin mate, Tajuddin, woke me up. Penang was in sight. I dressed quickly and went up on the deck. And there was Penang. My country, my home ... You know Bertha, I never knew I felt so strongly for my home and my people till I saw Penang and my Malaya appear."

"Breathes there a man with soul so dead ..."

Carl turned to Bertha with his mouth half open. "You know that?"

"Sure, not so stupid, you know ..."

"Wow you've got everything ... beauty, brains."

"Brains yes, my father's brains. But education no ... not yet, *akan datang*. You forgot to say speet."

"Speed, sweetheart," Carl said unexpectedly, emphasising the "d" which Bertha had not articulated fully.

Bertha looked at him. It did not strike her at that moment that his reaction showed a gap in their upbringing.

Bertha could not remember the game at the Dato' Kramat ground in Penang. Penang was a whirl of Carl and his kisses. His arms around her. His eyes on her as she played, as she danced with another man, as she talked to the Penang hockey team. His eyes never leaving her.

And Sheelah's eyes finding her's suddenly so often. Seeing

Sheelah reading her feelings. Seeing Sheelah watching; sometimes smiling in the corner of her mouth.

The beach. Carl trickling sand on her back. Racing to the jagged rock. She beat him. He was not a swimmer. Just-manage-type of swimming. Her laughing with him when she discovered that the lane running beside the church was Love Lane. The Robless girl, the left winger lived there. She was some relation of Carl's. His uncle Ignatious and Auntie Mona Reutens; their lovely house with all the flowers. The way they accepted her as a friend of Carl's without all the probing or sniggling that her relatives would have reacted to Eric bringing a strange girl to their house. His aunt Mona was so sweet and charming. Like the Van Geyzels, she made her feel completely at home, and she felt a special attraction for Auntie Mona that stayed inside her for years although she had only met her twice while they were in Penang.

But it ended all too quickly. She clung to Carl and told him she loved him with tears in her eyes as they parted that night. They left early the next morning, going in a procession of trishaws from the convent to the railway ferry. Ethel looking for a place where they could sit together in the train. The long wait before it started. Wondering if Carl had got to the chain ferry by then. To Bertha, the tour ended the night before when Carl held her in his arms outside the convent gate for the last time.

Sheelah let out a long breath of air as the train picked up momentum. They had done well. Bertha had lived up to her expectations. Especially at that first game in Seremban. She was sure that she had carried out her promise to James Rodrigues.

Next year ... next year ... maybe.

~ *Chapter Eleven* ~

Ben Machado

Ben Machado was born in 1929, and was brought up in the traditions of the Eurasian community in Singapore. But in many ways, he was different.

His father, Hubert Machado, started with Cable and Wireless as a junior clerk and worked his way up to chief clerk. His mother, one of the Hogan girls, was a telephone operator at Oriental Telephone but stopped working when Ben was born. He could not trace his family further back than his grandparents and he knew very little about them. He had asked when he grew up, but his parents seemed reluctant to tell him too much.

As he grew up, he started realising that he was different from his cousins and Eurasian friends. Not just that he was stuck with the nickname of "Bunny" because his ears stuck out, nor that he was fairer than the others. Firstly, he went to St. Anthony's Boys' School instead of St. Joseph's although they went to the Good Shepherd and not to the St. Joseph's church of the Portuguese mission. So his school friends and his cousins and the friends he met at aunt and uncle's birthday parties were two different groups.

And secondly, he was not as interested in sports as his friends were. They told him that his father had been the school high jump champion and achieved other distinctions in athletics. It didn't impress him nor inspire him. All he knew was that, when he was younger, he had to go to the billiards saloon and shout out to his father from under the swinging door that Mum says to come home now for dinner. The saloon used to smell of cigarette and cigar smoke and the Malay boys hanging around tried to jostle him and get him into a fight. It didn't frighten him. He knew he could shout out to his Dad who would send them running.

He started reading when he was about ten. And from then, he was always with a book. This, coupled with his lack of interest in sports, made his cousins call him "cissified." It annoyed him.

He started running along the beach at Katong in the evenings, pushing himself, increasing the distance daily to show them that he was no weakling. And subconsciously to prove it to himself.

Just after the war, when he was eighteen, Philomena Lazaroo, the eldest of headmaster Lazaroo's daughters, started a thin "Roneo" sheet magazine. She called it *The Thoughts of Youth*, taking the title from Longfellow's, *The Thoughts of Youth are Long, Long Thoughts*. It changed his life in some ways. He never realised that there were other people, he meant Eurasians, of course, who were interested in poetry and things like that. Phil herself was too old and haughty for him to open up to, but in her monthly paper he began reading into fields that he had never explored before. He contributed to it. Some readers wrote in and complimented some of his articles. It gave him a new confidence and fired his interest in the English language.

He never forgot one little poem in particular. About a boat lying in the mud in the smelly Singapore river waiting for the breakers. He learnt it by heart. It was written by a girl called Joan Pillai, whom he had never met and will never meet.

He remembered that it started with, "The old boat settled in its time worn timbers, and listlessly gazed out to sea; I know they are coming ... tar-um-tar-um-tar-um-tar-um, I know they are coming for me."

It was inevitable that he should become a teacher. It was a good job. Secure. It had much status. His parents were proud that their eldest had chosen to join the "teaching profession." Perhaps, one day, he might even become a headmaster like Mr. Lazaroo. They didn't dream that he could ever reach the exalted level of Inspector of Schools.

So Ben became a schoolmaster, going to "normal" classes while he was a student teacher, and eventually qualifying at twenty. That was old, Mr. Lazaroo told him. "In my time I started teaching at sixteen." Ben listened silently. "I must not say these things when I'm as old as Mr. Lazaroo," he decided. He was making a mental list of what a good teacher should be. A sort of ideal role. He wanted to get to the top. He devoured *Teachers' World* when it came in on the mail boat and when he saw the sign "Mail not arrived" outside the newsagent's shop, it was a big disappointment.

But his ambitions were dulled shortly after he became a fully qualified teacher. He found a new interest. Later, he referred to it as an addiction. He discovered the joys of poker and bridge. He saw them playing at the SRC once. He was fascinated. He got "bitten by the bug," as his father described it, adding, "the stupid bugger."

One day, at the Rozells' place, he played poker with Hector Webb, Ricky Francisco, two Chinese men and an European. He didn't know how Simon Rozells had roped the fellow in. Ben had a great night. At two in the morning, the European fellow was finished. He had no cash to pay up. Ricky had been drinking rather heavily during the game. He got annoyed. The two Chinese men backed him up. They muttered to Ricky something about not letting the *ang moh* fellow get away. Ben could only speak a little Hokkien but he understood. He was involved as he was the main winner.

The European read the threats and anger. He said he would hand in his boat. It was a small sailing boat. After much discussion, they all went in Simon's Morris Minor to Punggol. Hector said it was a fair deal. They argued among themselves how the boat should be divided up. Ben was the largest shareholder and he decided to settle it there and then by paying off the others. So Ben became the owner of a sixteen-footer.

There was much excitement about this. The European and the Chinese went off home. Ricky, Hector and Ben found a coffee shop that was open for the fishermen and discussed Ben's new possession over a couple of Tigers while they waited for Simon to return from the Upper Serangoon Road junction where he had gone to drop the European and the Chinese. He knew where they could get a "pirate taxi." Even at that hour.

Hector and Ricky both claimed to have had experience in sailing. They had all the advice anyone needed to sail the boat. It was an exciting thing. A prestigious thing. Ben jolly well knew, that no way in the world, could they have got onto such a boat. He was too tired and pleased with himself to argue. He let them plan the first outing on Sunday. They started off with the four of them and Noreen and Ruth and that Casmir Gonzales's sister. And they decided that Ben should bring Beryl with whom he was going out. That was too many. Not Noreen lah! She's too lady-like. And what about Gonzales? Forget him! He won't be interested anyway. He'll be out on his bike.

Simon returned and had his own ideas. Not that Gonzales girl. Christ! Ruth will kill me. Hey, Ben do you know her? Man! That's something. Hey, what about bringing Beryl's sister along? Hold it, man. It isn't the *Queen Mary*. And who's going to buy the beer? I'll get a couple of tins of sardines. No. Corned Beef. Much better. It went on and on.

The first "boating Sunday" was a complete fiasco. To add to their embarrassment, they had decided that it was going to be too difficult to limit the numbers. Ben came up with the idea that there could be one party on the shore and and one on the boat. They could take turns sailing. It was declared as absolutely brilliant. Hey, our Ben not so stupid lah! Simon insisted that the Gonzales girl had to be invited, and Hector countered in a most logical way that they would therefore have to "dilute" her by asking more girls. That would satisfy Ruth. Bertha was scratched. After all she was so young.

As it turned out, the group that came was about ten. Many could not come or doubted the wisdom of sailing in Ben's new boat or had no faith in Simon, Ricky and Hector's sailing abilities. But, Ben said, the "diplomatics" of it all were intact. After all, we did invite them. Didn't we?

The boat had a drop keel. This was mysterious thing to the four of them. They lowered it and raised it a dozen times and finally voted three to one that it was there for rough weather, like typhoons. Stood to reason. The drag it caused would be terrible. It would slow the boat down to a grinding halt. Maybe that's what it was. A sort of brake to use when you are coming in. Can't go skimming in at full sail and hit the beach, kerderbak!

So the boat capsized on the first trip out when they raised the sail. The four men and the Gonzales girl who was persuaded that it was safe against the advice of the others were all thrown into the water. The sardines and corned beef and beautiful crispy french loaves that they had bought from the Siglap Road bakery sank to the bottom of the sea, to Noreen's great annoyance. In their despondency later, no one was willing to try and dive into the sea to look for the cans of sardines and corned beef.

The girls on the shore laughed till their sides nearly split, of course. Ruth's special pleasure was seeing the Gonzales girl get drenched in her "fancy pants," as Ruth called them. Nothing fancy about them, Simon had said, only they're a little tight for her. Aren't they? Aren't they, Ricky?

It went through the whole of Katong by five o'clock that Sunday. By six, the story had got to Newton, St. Michael's Road and Queen Street. By seven, the remotest of Eurasian households in Singapore at Flower Road, Chestnut Drive, Zhender Road and Galistan Avenue had laughed at the stupidity of the four "idiots."

But Ben got a decent price for the thing within two weeks.

It wasn't "the sailing mishap with the yacht," Ben said later, that made him stop playing poker with the same frenzy. It was saving up to get married.

There was another incident in Ben's life about two years later that pulled him back from the brink of a wayward life as he hovered in temptation.

His love for the written word had continued to grow. But he found so few people in his circle who shared his enthusiasm and interest. He had met two earlier when he went to the University of Malaya at Cluny Road. Tessie Frois and Gerrard De Jong. They got on so well. All three of them. But Tessie moved in another strata above his. The Frois family had a pew in the St. Joseph's church with their name on a metal plate fixed to it. Gerrard De Jong returned to Malacca after he graduated.

He found a kindred soul in Sheelah Cornelius. Sheelah of all people, he said to himself the night after he discovered the breadth of her reading and her knowledge at the Casket Company while paying his respects to Uncle Walter. She had made some remark, he'd forgotten what, and that triggered off a hushed conversation.

He and Sheelah hailed each other if they met at Christmas visits, birthdays, weddings or christenings. Beryl did not mind this friendship with Sheelah. She had viewed their huddles in big parties or dances with suspicion at first, but she fought her jealousy. She knew Sheelah was a direct open person. She also knew she was attractive, dynamic and "very smart." If Sheelah wanted a man, she could get him. But she won't want my Ben, Beryl told herself. He's not good enough for her.

Ben admired her. When he heard the rumour that Mrs. Bullen, her boss's wife, had remarked loudly in the refined air of the Tanglin Club, "Sheelah Cornelius? She practically runs the Borneo Company," he had smiled. That was Sheelah. She must be good at her job.

There was also Cyril Vancullenberg. Ben used to meet him and talk of writers and books. But Cyril was too much of an introvert for Ben. Besides that, he was so steeped in the romantics that he would not look at what the world was writing today.

In his school, Rosalind Lam, a "normal trained" teacher like him, read voraciously. She went to the Raffles Library at least once a week. They talked in the staff room at times. And slowly, he got to appreciate her views and feel her excitements when she found a new writer. He remembered how she had raged about Steinbeck. That was already old hat to him. "Yes, that young chit of a thing, has quite an analytical mind," he thought to himself. He was twenty-eight then. She was twenty-one.

Beryl had created a bad scene with him about her. He was

taking a group of boys to Penang. It was a geography tour. They had also managed to get a soccer team of sorts from the group that was going. Rosalind Lam was one of the three teachers who were accompanying the group. Beryl was mad when she heard that "that bloody Chink woman" was to be one of the party. The tour had caused some unhappiness when he first announced it at home. "You mean you're going to waste your holidays AND spend your own money?" He had argued with her. It would happen again and again, he said. This is my job. This is what makes a good teacher. Sure I'll enjoy myself (he hadn't told her about Rosalind going then), but that's not the reason I'm going. You marry a policeman, you have to put up with his irregular hours. You marry a teacher, this is what you have to live with. Look at Huey Ess. He's at Purdy Camp every school holiday, year in, year out ... That's different. It's in Singapore ... Oh yeah! I can tell you a few things that have gone on with the Brownie mistresses ... Maybe he shouldn't have said that.

He put his foot down. He went to Penang with the group. She kissed him goodbye sourly with numerous warnings and threats. "Doesn't any wife know that that is not the way to say goodbye," he muttered inwardly, "they all forget how they clung to their men declaring their love when they parted before they were married." He scowled as he walked out of the house with his suitcase.

The third teacher was Mr. Arasu, the headmaster. He was a jovial man who controlled his staff and his schoolboys with an iron hand. But his iron hand relaxed now and then. He was relaxed as they met at the railway station.

It was a good trip. The boys had a marvellous time, and he enjoyed talking to Mr. Arasu and Rosalind. He got to know her, her tastes in fiction and poetry, her idiosyncrasies, her spinsterish ways, especially with regard to cleanliness. They began to understand each other and Mr. Arasu.

He had raised his hands up in the air when he walked into the house on his return and declared in a loud voice that he had not touched even the hair of a woman for one week. Beryl was not sure if it was a joke or not. She hugged him, happy to see him home again. Robert rushed up and kissed him and he took little Valerie out of Beryl's arms. He was happy to be home.

The school annual sports was held two weeks after they returned. It was known as "Sports Day" to boys and teachers. There was a lot of work to be done. And when it was over – when the cups had been handed out and the school had sung, "For he's a jolly good fellow" and given three cheers to the man from the "Ministry" who was invited to give out the prizes, the teachers gave instructions to the scouts and servants about clearing up, dismantling the PA system and putting away various things in the right places – they gathered in the staff room for "a little drink," as Mr. Arasu put it. It was part of the school tradition that Mr. Arasu had instituted. He wanted to get on the good side of the ministry official. If there was an important police officer's son in the school, he was invited too. And some of the people whom the school dealt with. He also wanted his teachers to relax after all their efforts. There were always at least three bottles of White Horse. And at least two dozen cold Anchors which were delicious after the running around, getting the boys into the right places at the right time on the field. There was orange crush and ginger beer, sodas and most of the teachers brought little tidbits to nibble. The invited guests usually stayed for one or two drinks and made excuses to leave. By the time it was dark, only the staff were left. It fact, it was the annual staff party in another guise.

Rosalind Lam was wearing the prettiest of dresses. She had to organise the prize table. She was up there in front of the crowd beside the VIP. She had to look good while Ben and the others were trying to get the prize giving going on time, sending boys to look for a missing house captain, getting the scouts to form a line to keep the eager-beavers back, telling Ah Kow to shut his mouth when he came whispering that two boys from Three-A had stolen a bottle of Anchor.

Mr. Arasu always called out to Ben and introduced him to the ministry official. Ben had the social graces. Mr. Arasu knew that he had to keep Gopal away from the VIP after Gopal had had a few. He whispered to Mrs. Chin that year to do this again. They had a good time after the guests left. Even grumpy Mr. Kwek was telling stories of his youth. Ben felt obliged to stand there and listen. Maybe he won't be so difficult with the time-tabling if I listen to his nonsense, he thought to himself.

Mr. Kwek was going on and on. "The fellow was in hospital with amoebic dysentery ... on a no-solids diet, just barley water ... and he asked me to smuggle in *mutton kurma* and *chapati* from that stall in Tanjong Pagar. He even specified it!" Mr. Kwek broke off to laugh. I'm sure he told that story too, years ago, Ben thought.

Mr. Arasu was going around with the bottle of White Horse in one hand and and a bottle of soda in the other recharging glasses, with his standard quip of, "and a little bit of the phoenix to rise from the ashes tomorrow ..." pouring from the Phoenix brand bottle.

Ben heard giggling and teasing among the younger teachers behind him. Bet they're forcing the clerk Lucy to have another again. He heard their awful "Singlish," as he termed it and started to get worked up about it. Must be the drink, he told himself. Do we get more intolerant with drink? Or tolerant?

Mr. Kwek started another story about Norman Beins. Ben excused himself and went to the toilet.

The light in the corridor was not on. He grunted his annoyance and went to find the switch. He knew it was behind the door of Six-B. It was dark there. He found the switch and pushed it down. But the light did not come on. I told Raja to check it, he muttered.

"Ban! What are you doing in the dark?" It was Rosalind with her irritating way of pronouncing his name. He was not irritated then. "Looking for a pretty girl," he said. She came right up to him. She put her arms round him and whispered, "Here's one. You haven't noticed."

He put his arms around her and was going to kiss her lightly on the cheek when he felt her open mouth on his, her tongue thrusting into him. He responded. She groaned softly in pleasure and rubbed her body voluptuously against him. Her hands were running through his hair. She was writhing in the ecstasy of the unending kiss. He could feel the passion throbbing in her.

He let his mouth linger on hers for a little longer. Then he reached out behind his neck, held her hands and gently pushed her away. Her eyes were blazing. They were bloodshot. Her lipstick was smeared all round her mouth.

They heard footsteps. "You go out," he whispered, "and tell whoever is there that the bulb's blown. I'll hide here."

She went out without even trying to wipe the lipstick off her mouth. It will be too dark for anyone to see, anyway, Ben said to himself. The silly girl. Hasn't she heard of "kissproof." He pulled out his handkerchief to wipe his lips. Then he stopped himself.

She was talking to Gopal. He knew the layout of the class. He did the English lesson there on Wednesdays. He moved in the dark to the door on the other side of the room, quietly opened the door and slipped out. He went to the toilet, listened if there was anyone there, and went in to wash his mouth. There was no mirror to check. He dried his mouth with his handkerchief without thinking. Then he realised what he had done and looked at it in the dim toilet light. It was clean. He walked back to the staff-room where the party was in full swing with long confident strides.

"Ben. There you are. Why don't you give us one of your funny limericks." "You've heard them all." "A *pantun* then ..." Zainul suggested. Zainul was the Malay language teacher. He was the joker among the staff. He always had a pleasant greeting and a crack for everybody. Ben had had an argument with Mr. Arasu about him only the day before. "Lazy blighter," Mr. Arusu had said. "He's not!" Ben objected. "Well, a useless teacher." "It's not his fault. That is the way he has always taught. Only the boys are different now." "Then he has to change. He went to some sort of in-service course ... fat lot of good it did him." "He's too old to change." "Nobody's too old to change ... Well, anybody who's any good should be able to change at any age." Ben got the last word in, but he wasn't quite sure whether it was in Zainul's favour, "... if he wants to."

"Come here Bee Wah. Sing us a song."

"I cannot sing lah!"

"Please no singing in the staff room!"

"Who you think you are, Ha? Mr. Alasu?"

"Shhh. He'll hear you."

"Naa'er min'. Late him!"

"Come on Bee Wah, I drive you back ... before you get the sack."

"Naa'er min' ... can go to St. Patrick's school an' work. Down dere got good *rojak* ... every day can eat *rojak*."

They laughed.

"And what mathematical theorem are you propounding to my colleagues, Bee Wah?" It was Rosalind pushing herself between Zainal and Mrs. Chin. She had redone her make-up. She smiled at Ben. He didn't know whether to smile or not. He was confused. Bee Wah said something else in her twisted grammar. She enjoyed making jokes like this, half ridiculing herself, half indicating that her English was not as bad as that. Or was she trying to make out that there was nothing wrong with her way of speaking? Ben confused himself with this thought and turned away from the group to refill his glass.

Mr. Arasu buttonholed him. He wanted to talk about that fellow Kalasasammy, or Kilasamarney, or pathy or was it thamby, anyway, his century on the Padang last Saturday. Man he was terrific ...

It gave Ben time to think. As soon as someone else came up to them, he excused himself on the pretence of going to the toilet and went out to the carpark. He started his car and drove home slowly. Very slowly. He decided as the little Fiat 600 passed the Katong church. I must get a hold of myself, stupid bugger.

It was about this time that he became a friend to Bertha. He had always admired her. He thought she was beautiful. She had the perfect body. Beryl was beautiful too. In a different way. She was the envy of most of her friends. "She's so well developed," as

Auntie Euphrasia said. But Auntie Euphrasia didn't see her thin Tamil legs. Bertha was the *gila* one. Beryl, the *manis* one. She suited him. But Bertha was still a very attractive woman.

His attitude to Bertha seemed to become more open, less strained and less tense about that time. Bertha also began to drop in unexpectedly more often. It was partly because the children were of that lovable, kissable, cute age – Robert said the funniest things. It was partly that Bertha was beginning to feel restless being alone with the old folks at home.

"How's the job?" he asked her one day.

Bertha told him everything. It was as though she wanted to talk to somebody about it. Beryl was in the kitchen cooking. He was sipping a drink reading *Teacher's World* when she came in. It was assumed that she would be staying for dinner.

"Good. But that Mr. Vandyke is a strange person. I've been there for nearly a year now and I still cannot tell you exactly what the company does. It loses money every year. But when I tried to cut down the costs the old fellow told me not worry too much. I told him I had seen the accounts. I know how to see them, you know, Sheelah has taught me. He said, 'Don't worry. I send my profits overseas.' I'm not sure if that's legal or not. But it's not my business. I do help him with the figures, but really I'm only the secretary. I'm not supposed to know what is right and what is wrong."

"You think there's dirty work?"

"Good heavens, NO … It's just that he keeps his money movements so secret."

"What does he do?"

"Oh buys and sells. Chemicals, machinery, equipment. He has contacts all over the world. That fellow's sure been around."

"But you're happy there."

"Oh yes. I wouldn't want to change. But I wish he'd change his brand of cigarettes."

She told him about the informality of the office. There were so many overseas visitors. She met interesting people from all over the place. Italy, Holland, America ... er ... Hongkong, Indonesia, lots of Indonesians, even some people from Africa. And it was nice to see faces that she had been typing letters to or spoken to on trunk calls suddenly appear in person at the office.

Mr. Vandyke travelled quite a bit. He telephoned her every day when he was out-station and gave her instructions. She liked it then. She was her own boss then. And now he let her use his car and Rais when he was away. She was thinking of taking driving lessons.

"Will you teach me, Ben?"

"No! And that's final. It is the best way to ruin a friendship, or break up a marriage. No."

"Aiyah ... you and your theories."

He was very good to her. "Tells me when I look nice, you know. Better than a husband, huh? And he teaches me. I think he teaches me something every day. Even if it's not like teaching properly. Like when he grumbles at some other company ... or gets frustrated with civil servants because he says it in a way that makes you see what is the right thing to do. Get what I mean?"

And recently, twice, he took me out when he entertained a customer. They were Indonesians both times. "Once we went to the Islamic and the second time to Dhoby Ghaut. You know the Nasi Padang place there? The Indonesian chap said the *nasi padang* was better than in Padang even! He's kind. A bit stingy. Loses his temper sometimes ... but not so often. I suppose old people don't lose their temper so often."

"That's nonsense. Some get worse when they get old. Like Mr. Kwek at my school ..."

"At first he had a lot of dealings with Africa."

"Africa?"

"Many different countries. You want stamps?"

"Stamps?"

"Used postage stamp lah."

"Ah ... no thanks."

"As I was saying first it was mostly Africa but, recently, it's

Holland mostly."

"Do you have to work late at times?"

"Very seldom. I think I've worked late about three times in all these months I've been with him. He sends Rais out to buy food. *Char-siew fan* or *mee goreng*. He always wants *teh aliah* himself. Says it's good for the stomach. Aiyah … He's got so many theories on food and all that."

"Does he drink?"

"Yah … a lot I think. Some days he comes back after lunch a little high. He's very jovial then."

"Is he married?"

"No. I told you he's staying at Rachael Elias's boarding house. Not cheap, you know, that place."

Beryl's voice interrupted them. "Come and get it. *Tau-yu-bak* and Beryl's patented *sambal belachan* with garlic."

"Wow!"

When Bertha returned from her Malayan tour she was at the Machado's the next day. There were a thousand stories to tell. But nothing of Carl. Bertha had in fact gone over to get him off her mind. He haunted her day and night. Bertha and Ben plied her with questions. Who were these Van Geyzels? Ceylon people, lah. I don't know, but they're very nice people. In fact, perhaps, a bit too nice. What do you mean? Oh, always so polite. Artificial, like? No. That's not true. They are genuine.

And how is Peggy Reutens? Did you see her? No.

"Hey you must have met the Samon girl in Penang. She plays for the club if I remember correctly."

"Yah. Just remember the name … You know her?"

"Yes. I met her when we did that school trip to Penang. She's a teacher at the Pulao Tikus school."

"Ha!" Beryl interrupted in a teasing way, "It's all coming out now."

"And the Mettahs? Uren, Fred Uren? Did you meet him?"

"No."

"Bernie Ritchie?"

"No."

"The Ward girl? Very tall?"

"No."

"You didn't meet anybody in Penang. What were you doing?"

Bertha blushed. Both Beryl and Ben saw it.

"Oh! Oh!" Beryl said.

Bertha kept quiet. Ben looked at Beryl. She told him with her eyes not to probe any further. Ben knew. Beryl would get it out of her sooner or later. He knew his Beryl.

Sheelah came over one day with a book for Ben. Saul Bellow.

"Hey, this *Jaudi* fellow can write. Solomon lent it to me. I asked him if I could pass it on to you."

"How's Solomon."

"Just the same. Head in the clouds. Fantastic ideas on the novel that must be written of Singapore, David Marshall, Lee Kuan Yew and all that. Great schemes to make millions."

"But nothing happening, right?"

"Yah. But he'll get somewhere one day."

Beryl came in from the bedroom where she had been trying to put Valerie to sleep.

"Take her, Ben. Sing her to sleep."

He took Valerie and went into the bedroom. He left the door open without thinking. He heard Beryl asking, "Sheelah, what happened in Malaya with Bertha?"

"Can't tell tales out of school."

"So … there must be a tale to tell?"

"You're been reading too many Earle Stanley Gardner."

"She's my sister, you know. I know something happened. Boyfriend huh?"

"Shut the door, Ben … We don't want to be put to sleep with your singing."

Ben shut the door reluctantly. He would have loved to listen in to the way Beryl was going to work on Sheelah. He knew that somewhere along the line Beryl would ask, "Eurasian?" and "Catholic?"

A few days later Simon rang him at the school. He rang back when he had a free period.

"Hey Bunny, we're short of a hand tonight. Bridge. Don't worry, small stakes. A few drinks. All nice and easy, like."

"OK. But I'm ever so rusty. Haven't played for ages."

"Hector Webb's place. Seven-thirty."

"Fine. Dinner?"

"Have dinner before you come, man. No one's going to feed you."

"Hope you won't end too late."

"No ... We're all settled down now."

"Thanks, Simon."

"OK. See you there, captain."

Ben smiled at the reference to the yacht affair as he put down the phone.

They had a good evening. Ben played better than he expected to. They finished at about ten-thirty. Simon went off and Donald Kloer got a lift from him. Ricky stayed for one more drink and they started talking of *merdeka*, the independence of Malaya coming up. It wasn't Donald's subject. He left.

Ben was about to leave when Hector asked in a serious tone.

"Tell me Ben, is there anything going between Bertha and her boss?"

Ben sat up. The question shook him.

"Why do you ask?"

"I met a Dutch bugger at the SCC last week. I played cricket against their team so they gave us lunch. He started talking of this Vandyke bloke whom Bertha is working for. Something about business, I donno' what lah, but then he makes a remark, 'He's got a good looking broad in his office. Seems he's got something going with her.' I tried to pump him a bit. You know, making out as if I was interested. Asked him if he was sure of it. Well, he didn't say so in so many words, but I'm pretty sure. Thought I'd ask you."

"Thanks for telling me. Good that I know what people are saying."

"It's not people. It's just that bloke."

"Maybe that's what the Europeans are saying."

"Hmmm ..."

Ben left and drove home thinking. He decided to sleep on it and talk to Beryl in the morning.

But when he got home, Beryl was up. She met him at the door with a bottle of Woodwards Gripe Water in her hand. He looked at her. It did not look like a crisis. But then with Beryl he never knew. She was always so calm in a crisis.

"Valerie?"

"Yes, she's all right now."

"Was it bad?"

"No. How was the game?"

"Fine."

"Doesn't look fine from your face."

"It's just that I heard something odd."

Beryl stood waiting. He told her. She looked at him for some time then looked beyond his shoulder. With the faintest nodding movement of her head she spoke. "I think I understand."

"Understand what?"

"It's not like Bertha ... I heard some of what she was saying about her job the other day when I came up from the kitchen to lay the table. I heard you questioning her. You sounded like a suspicious lover. My guess is that Mr. Vandyke knows that there's all sorts of types coming into his office. Those travelling husbands who forget themselves when they are away. Or those bloody Europeans who think every one of our girls can be had for the taking ... I think he has deliberately given the impression that he has something going with her ... for her sake."

Ben was silent. He had not thought of that. He was a little annoyed with himself for thinking of other things and not trusting Bertha.

Beryl looked at him and as if reading his mind said, "I don't think we should tell Bertha about it. Anyway, it's none of our business." She said it as if it was a matter of the most importance to

Ben and her.

At school, Rosalind did not change her attitude outwardly towards him. But he could see a difference. They talked to each other civilly but did not have long discussions on books any more. Unless it was in a group. And that was seldom.

He was very busy at school and even volunteered to take on more work for a while. One day Sheelah was at the house having "pot-luck" with them. They did not have enough for three that day. Sheelah suggested that she go get a vegetable dish from that roadside Cantonese food stall around the bend after the Cardoza's place.

"Good idea. I'll go," Ben said.

"My car's blocking yours. No point moving two cars. I'll go."

"Okaydoke ... I'll come for the ride."

"Leaving your wife and children for a pretty face!" Beryl mockingly wailed.

Sheelah ordered. Her smattering of Cantonese was better than his. While it was being cooked she turned to him.

"Ben, are you getting satisfaction in your job?"

"Sure. Why?"

"You are so interested in 'lit.' It must all seem so simple to you."

"Tell you what. It's not easy trying to ram Macbeth into solid boned Chinese heads."

"It's not Chinese heads. It's ears that aren't used to the sounds of Shakespeare."

"Hey, you should be a teacher ..."

"What I was thinking was that you should try to take a degree in English."

"I haven't got such high and mighty ideas."

"You've got ambition." She saw him pause before he replied, and added, "Sure you have. Don't try to fool me. Well, the world is changing and you should really think of studying for a degree."

"Where's the money going to come from?"

"Scholarships."

"Huh. You have to be Chinese."

"Don't be so bloody minority-persecuted. You bloody well know that if you're good enough you'll get a scholarship in Singapore."

"Yeah …" drawled, as if to end the subject.

"You heard me. Think about it."

"I'm not good enough to get a scholarship. You should see my Cambridge certificate. There are enough of run-of-the-mill 'goods' to made me look like a holy man. No a single 'very good.' "

"Well, you're not a very holy man."

Ben laughed. He thought it would end there.

Sheelah paid. There was no protest as his Chinese friends would have protested. Sheelah paid sometimes and he paid sometimes.

Sheelah continued in the car.

"As I was saying, these days you'll get nowhere without a degree. If you can't get a scholarship, then sit for the London U BA …"

"Hey … that's a thought."

"Hard work though."

"Yes, Mum! Thanks for the idea. Will chew on it."

~ *Chapter Twelve* ~

October twenty-fifth 1956

Ben called out to Beryl one evening, as a car pulled up outside their house. "Hoi, we've got visitors ..."

"Maybe it's for next door," Beryl said.

"No it isn't. Looks like a Eurasian car."

"Ha! Ha! my master of fancy words."

"Well, it's dirty, small, scratched and hasn't got any ridiculous things hanging from the mirror, or tissue boxes in the back."

Beryl came to the front door and stood beside him.

"A Malacca number," she pointed out.

Then a body got out of the low Austin Mini. To their surprise it was Bertha. She was grinning from ear to ear. Her face seemed to be glowing. "Hoi Beryl! Hoi Ben!"

A tall man got out from the driver's seat. He turned towards the house looking almost furtively at it.

"Who's this *orang puteh*?" Beryl muttered under her breath to Ben. In the fading evening light, they could not see his face clearly. But his hair was not jet black like theirs.

"Sorry to spring a surprise on you like this. I brought a friend to meet you," Bertha said. She stopped and turned around to wait for the man. They could see from his gait that he was a young man. As he came up to her, Bertha took his arm and the two of them came to the door together, Bertha clinging to his arm.

"This is my sister Beryl, and her husband Ben. This is Carl Westerhout from Malacca." They nodded to each other. He seemed shy. Bertha continued to hold on to his arm.

"Come in, come in ... all the way from Malacca eh?"

When the initial exchanges were done and Beryl had offered them and brought in drinks – it was an unspoken understanding that she served when strangers came to the house, and Ben got the drinks for close friends and family – Ben tried to break the ice with one blow.

"So … you must be the mystery man … Bertha, is he the cause of your big red blush the other day?"

Bertha laughed softly. Her eyes were sparkling.

"What's this all about?" Carl asked turning to Bertha.

"I blushed when they asked me why I didn't meet all their friends in Penang … the other day … couldn't help it, Carl."

It was a Malacca licence plate, Bertha thought to herself.

But Bertha explained it all fully, telling them how she had met Carl and how they had driven up to Penang under Sheelah's watchful eye and everything that was not too private between her and Carl.

Beryl looked at Ben while Bertha talked almost without stopping. He caught her eye. It was a happy contented Beryl. He even thought he saw her thinking, "this puts an end to all those Mr. Vandyke rumours." But most of all, he could see how proud Bertha was, how she related the tour story so openly to them and how pleased Beryl appeared to be.

"You must stay and have dinner with us."

"Thought you'd never ask! Shall we go and buy something?"

Ben wondered if Beryl should have asked them to stay for dinner. Maybe they want to be by themselves, he thought. But he did not say anything. Beryl should know her sister. Later, he saw that as much as Bertha wanted to be alone with Carl, she was so pleased to be together with them and Carl.

Their whirlwind romance, for indeed it was a lightning quick thing by the standards of James and Mary, was talked about at the Catholic Centre after mass and at the SRC after the soccer and hockey games. Mrs. Balhatchet, who was regarded as an authority on matters of marriage by some, seized upon the situation to appeal again for a return to the old systems of marriage. This started controversial discussions in houses from Pasir Panjang to Bedok.

She wanted them to go back to the custom of the groom's family paying for the liquor, while the bride's family paid for the rest of the reception, including the virgin-white wedding cake. She held forth at the Vaz's wedding anniversary, an ideal forum for such topics, that the Rodrigues should reinstate the practice of the groom's family paying for the bridal gown, the bridesmaids' and flower-girls' dresses. The groom's family should also pay for the band. That was the way it was, and the way it should be, she insisted. And the signet ring. There must be one for the groom. The bride's parents must pay for that. There were numerous other details.

Mary was in the kitchen helping out when Myra Tessensohn came in and related how Mrs. Balhatchet was carrying on. Mary stood stock still. Slowly, she walked out to the drawing room where the old dear was holding forth. She still had an apron on her. No one noticed her come in, drying her hands on her apron.

"Mrs. B," she said in a clear voice, knowing full well that Mrs. Balhatchet hated the abbreviated appellation, "I hope you're not referring to my daughter's possible wedding?"

"Oh! Goodness me! Where did she come from!" Mrs. Balhatchet feigned surprise and remarked, with the "she" accented in a way every woman present understood. Mary continued, her face frozen without expression, "You may prattle away on weddings at much as you please, Mrs. B, but I'll be obliged if you will keep your antediluvian views out of any plans our family may have."

She walked away, back to the kitchen, coolly. There was a tittering when she had left. The women looked at each other and at Mrs. Balhatchet. Mrs. Balhatchet said nothing. Her face was a deep red. After a few seconds, she turned to Edna Watts, "Help me up, please, Edna," and with Edna's help rose from her chair and left the room.

It went round from the drawing room to the pantry, from the dining room to the porch outside where the men were drinking, from the kitchen to the servants' quarters, to the bedrooms upstairs where clusters of teenage girls were giggling and swapping spicy tales.

Mary had only a few comments to the kitchen group. "They'll be thinking up there in Malacca that all of these are our ideas when they hear of it. We cannot let them think we Singapore people are always grabbing."

Many couldn't see the sense of Mary's interruption or her comments in the kitchen. Others stood up for her. "It's time we got out of the old-fashioned grooves. Good for Mary." There was so much to discuss.

James was mad with her. He lashed out with his tongue all the way back in the car.

Bertha only heard of the incident two days later while having lunch with Mavis Santa Maria. She confronted Mary when she got home that evening.

"Have you gone mad Ma! We're not even engaged!"

"Tell that to Mrs. B!" Mary retorted.

It worried James for days. That's not like Mary at all. She's getting old and intolerant. And jumping to conclusions ... all the time ... all the bloody time.

Bertha felt that she had to tell Carl when he came down again in October. A dark scowl ran over his face. She saw his brows knit in anger. He glared at Bertha. The fierceness of his look frightened her. She put her hand out to him, "Darling, it's just the old women's nonsense ..." Her voice trailed off. He had shrunk back from her touch.

They both knew. He had not proposed to her. He had said he loved her. In her heart, Bertha took this as a total commitment but she had not breathed a word to anybody. Now she was frightened.

"It's nothing to do with me ... Carl ... believe me."

He turned away. She was not sure he believed her.

It was a bad visit. Then fate intervened in other ways.

Carl had driven down on October 25th, 1956. They had met at her house and hugged and kissed panting with delight. Bertha told him that they were going to have dinner with Beryl and Ben that night. He had grown to like Ben. Ben thought about things. He could talk about other things and not just about hockey, soccer, boxing, hunting and dirty jokes. Ben was no ordinary man to Carl's mind. Carl knew that he and Bertha would be alone together after the feast. Perhaps they would go and sit on the beach. Or to MacRitchie reservoir.

Bertha had told Carl about the incident with Mrs. Balhatchet a little before they were due to leave for the Machado's. Now he stood there silent, fuming, boiling. She left him alone. She sat on the chair in the verandah while he stood against the rail, his hand gripping it. Not saying a word. She looked at his back outlined against the grey-blue sky of the fading day.

He seemed to stand there for hours.

The phone rang in the dining room. She heard Mary come up the steps from the kitchen to answer it. Bertha wasn't sure but she thought her Ma walked slower than she used to after that incident. She knew it caused a major row between her and James.

She heard the tinkling noise as Mary put down the phone. Then she heard Mary pick it up again and telephone someone else. A very brief hurried conversation. Mary seemed to be doing all the talking. She heard Mary ring someone else. Then another. Her anguish at Carl's rage turned to curiosity. She was about to go into the dining room when Mary came out to the verandah.

"There's bad trouble in town. Pa rang. You're not to go out. I've told Beryl. Pa says it's bad. He said that Carl is to stay here tonight." She said this in a tired way. She had lived through her husband's involvement in the Chinese High School riots in 1953, and through the Hock Lee Bus riots last year. She knew what it meant. But this time it seemed a heavier and more painful load to her. She was glad that Bertha and Carl were with her tonight.

Carl spun around. He snapped out of his depressed and angry mood.

"What's happened? Have the police decided to storm the Chung Cheng High School?"

It had been all over the papers that day. Students of the Chung

Cheng High School were protesting with a sit-in strike. The particular issue was not important to Carl. The dark clouds that were gathering were the increasing violence in clashes with the colonial police.

"Yes," Mary replied, "and a big crowd have gathered outside the school. Within the school compound there's a chain of parents linking hands. It looks very bad."

"And the Chinese High School?" Carl kept up with the politics in Singapore. He showed an intense personal interest in some aspects of the political scene that surprised Bertha when she found out. She was equally interested, but in a detached observers' sort of way.

"Don't know. James didn't say. He didn't have time. All I know is that there's also a PAP rally at the Beauty World tonight. They are connected."

"Shit!"

It was not like Carl. He never swore or used the rough words like "bugger" which her cousins used freely. He was refined. A gentleman. Bertha knew. She was sure.

Mary looked from Bertha to Carl and back again to Bertha.

"There's plenty to eat. ... I'm so glad you are here with me."

Bertha stood up and went up to her mother. She knew that Mary never said things like that. Never expressed her personal emotions on matters like this. Something was troubling Mary deeply.

"Can I help, Ma?" she asked.

"No. You stay here with Carl. There's nothing much more to do."

She shuffled back into the dark dining room. It was dark now. None of them had thought of switching on a light.

"Ma!" Bertha called out. "Please on the verandah light. The small one."

She went up to Carl and put her arms around him. He did not stiffen as she dreaded he would. He put his arms around her slowly, gently.

Mary called out in a voice softer than usual half an hour later.

Dinner was ready.

They sat down. Mary placed Carl in James's chair. It was macaroni and cheese over a bed of *ikan kurau*. Eric's favourite dish. A Western dish tonight. They didn't have soup as a regular course with their western meals. They had dessert. Soup was only served when there was a special dinner.

There was no conversation. Carl said, "Mmmm good," but it sounded as though he only wanted to break the silence.

"Where's Eric?" Bertha asked.

"He's on nights this week," Mary replied.

"Eric's working at the Harbour Board," Mary explained to Carl. "Apprentice engineer."

Bertha had told him this already.

"Salt?" Mary was trying.

Carl put his knife and fork down on his plate. His hand went across the table and grasped Bertha's wrist.

"Oh, why do we have to be born in this time to face all these changes, social changes, political changes, pain, violence ..."

Mary looked at him. She was unaccustomed to such statements with such emotion that swept across so many things.

"It's not just you that are seeing so many changes. We've seen the world turn upside-down in our time. We've seen the war," Mary said.

She stopped. She saw them listening, so she continued.

"In fact, we've seen two wars although we were toddlers during the First World War. And it wasn't a war to us here ... but the last war was a real war to us. Bertha was six the night they bombed Singapore. Hit Robinsons ... The thing is that we never expected it. Even the British never expected it. It was all so sudden. Let's hope all this upheaval is not going to be the same all over again."

"You were here during the war ... in Singapore?" Carl asked, with his mouth full.

"Oh, Let's not talk of the war!" Bertha interjected.

"Not only the war. You mentioned social changes. We've seen so much ... electricity, motorcars, fridges, radio," Mary said.

"Those are not social changes, Mum."

"Well, they caused changes," Carl said.

"You know, Bertha's Aunt Dolores couldn't adjust to the electricity when it came. She wanted to put the switch just half-way on, like a gas light. She kept trying to put in on half-way, or to dim it a little when she went to bed ..."

Mary's stories helped. They talked of those days. Carl said his grandmother actually had a little pounder thing which she took everywhere to pound the ingredients for her *serai*. And she wore those large pointed gold hairpins in her *kondek*. Bertha knew what he meant. There were still Baba women in Singapore who wore them.

"I had a set of those given to me by my mother but they were lost during the war," Mary said.

"The war again. Why does it always keep coming up?" Bertha sighed.

"Because it was there Bertha," Carl said in the tone with which one addresses a child. "We can't wipe out the past. And we shouldn't try to bury what we don't like. Besides, there're things about the war that should never be forgotten."

"Like what?" Bertha asked.

"Like the way the First Malay Brigade fought against the Japanese Eighteenth Division here in Singapore ... on Kent Ridge."

"Never heard of it."

"Singaporean who doesn't know her history?"

"I'm not the bookish type."

"That's my point. If you don't read then you must talk about these things. The past, the war."

"But past is past, *sudah habis* lah!"

"You are what you are because of your past, your parents, their past. You cannot get away from it."

"Doesn't matter. No need to know. I know what I am now and have to make the best of what I got."

"But Bertha, knowing your past helps you to know what you are now. Your past blood is European and Asian, your culture is a mixture of both. All that makes you."

"My blood cannot change. That's why the old folks say 'She got bad blood.' Some sense in that. But culture? I can stop being Eurasian tomorrow."

"At a price, at a cost of losing some of the strong points."

"What strong points. There are none."

"Take a simple one. You can sing? All Serani can sing."

"Aiyah Carl, Chinaman, *matsalleh*, *Malaikwai*, *Kerlingkwai* all can sing ... only Filipino can sing better."

"That's just it."

"They've got music in their blood, man."

"Does music come with your blood? Or environment?"

Mary stood up. "Carl's right. We shouldn't change what we've got. You two carry on arguing. You won't change the world. I wish I could change it for you ... Muthu! Can clear already!"

Mary went to the radio and switched it on. Then she went into Eric's room and came out in a few minutes with an armful of crumpled bedsheets, pillow and bolster cases.

Bertha and Carl went out to the verandah and sat there. Bertha switched off the light, lit a mosquito coil and drew her rattan chair close to Carl's.

Carl was silent. Bertha sat for a while holding his hand.

The air was still and her body was sticky.

"It's wonderful to have you here with me tonight. All by ourselves. You know Carl this is the happiest place of the house for me. I've lived here since I was born. I was born here. In this very house. Most of my cousins were born at KK, but Mum wanted to be in her own bed, with Grannie beside her. And Mrs. Frances, the midwife."

"Right here?" Carl asked softly.

"Yah. And on this verandah I first walked. Probably first talked. But what I do remember is Pa telling us stories here as I sat on his lap with Beryl and Eric crowding around. We spent so many nights here listening to Pa and his police stories. I think he told those to us to make us see life."

Carl let her hand go. It was too hot to hold hands for long. He put his hand on her arm.

"And Beryl used to tell her school stories to Pa before dinner. I remember them because they seemed wonderful to me then. I wanted to go to school so badly."

Carl smiled. He leant over and kissed her on the mouth.

"Oh Carl, it's so wonderful to have you here … Will you come and kiss me goodnight in my bed tonight. In my own bed."

"Like your Pa used to?" Carl asked. Bertha's eyes shone. She didn't hear a trace of the cynical tone of Carl's question.

The music on the radio stopped. They got up and went inside. Mary was there before them. They listened. Bertha looked at Carl's face as the news and announcements came over the air. Mary stared blankly at the large plastic radio cabinet.

They heard how the police moved in at dusk at the Chung Cheng High school into the crowd of five hundred confronting them. They heard how the crowds attacked the Katong Post Office and the Geylang Police Station. The stoning of cars and buses. How the crowd from the Beauty World PAP rally moved to swell the crowd outside the Chinese High School to four thousand. How police cars were overturned and burnt.

There was more. It was worse than anyone expected. The riots had spread to Rochore Road and elsewhere. As they listened the radio was drowned by the noise of an army helicopter passing low over the house.

Mary sighed when the music came on again.

"I'm going to bed. Not too late you two … Goodnight Carl, Bertha."

Bertha kissed her on the cheek. "Goodnight, Ma."

Carl watched her. This girl hovering at the edge of her nest. Not yet away. Clinging to her mother. "Ma" of her childhood days and "Mum" at different times. Her father probably still calls her "girl" or "baby." He felt old.

The phone rang. Bertha picked it up. Mary opened her bedroom door and waited. Carl saw that she was holding a rosary in her hand. "It's only Sheelah, Ma." Sheelah only rang to ask if they heard the news. Did they know anything more? Was everyone OK? She rang off without any further talking.

"Sheelah? The captain?" Carl asked.

"Yes."

"Why did she ring?"

"Dunno … Probably thought we would have some more news."

Bertha looked at him. He seemed to have doubts about whether Sheelah would ring to just ask if they were OK.

"Sheelah's a wonderful person," she said. "I owe her a lot."

"Yes, she's wonderful," Carl added.

They went back to the verandah. Bertha thought of her father. He was still in the riot squad. That gave her confidence. She knew that it was probably the safest unit to be in at the moment. She knew that the men in their patrol cars, the men at the smaller stations, were the most exposed.

"What a night to meet you, Bertha …" Carl said softly.

"Yah …"

"The bloody British!" he muttered.

Bertha sat up in surprise. This was a man who looked like one of them, spoke like them. He had just come back from their country.

"The commies, Carl."

"OK, OK, but they only have strength because of the bloody British."

"But our government is in control now."

"Hah. Who holds the gun?"

"The police. The British army. But it will be our Lim Yew Hock who will decide tonight … who decided today."

"Huh! You believe that?"

"I do. I know."

"Huh."

Bertha waited for more. He was silent. She was sure of herself on this. He seemed so emotional, so scattered in his thoughts. For all his education overseas … What went on inside him to make him like this?

"Let's go to sleep, Carl. We can't set the world straight here ... Not tonight anyway."

She got up and went to her room without another word. He could hear her having a bath. He could almost see the water from the dipper falling over her beautiful body. He knew the lay of the house. It was the same with all these old houses. Two bedrooms connected to one bathroom. Two sets of steps going down to the bathroom. Bolts on each side of each door.

When the sound of her bathing stopped, he went to Eric's room.

Bertha lay on her bed in her sarong. She could hear the sounds of water thrown over his body. Falling off his body. The galvanised steel dipper being placed on the wooden shelf. Faint creaking of the wooden grid on which he was standing while he was drying his slim white body. The loud creaking of the steps up to her room. The crunching squeak of the top step.

He came to her bed and sat on it, his hips almost touching hers.

Softly, his voice, "Goodnight, my love." His mouth on hers. Still with a taste of toothpaste. His body cool after the bath. A wet patch between his shoulders.

~ Chapter Thirteen ~

December twenty-first 1957

Carl kept coming to Singapore at two or three month intervals. They grew closer to each other, yet they argued a great deal. Especially about politics. Carl seemed to be so irrationally anti-British to Bertha. Her father on the other hand was so pro-British and Bertha believed that she could see both sides. She knew she did not feel involved. She watched the changes in a fatalistic way. Like watching a film of your future and not caring what happens.

When Carl came down in October 1957, she sensed that something was brewing inside him. He was tense and quieter than usual. When he left, he seemed to hold her for a long time before he turned around and walked down the verandah steps.

There was no word from Carl after he left in October. He didn't promise to write or call, Bertha recollected later. It just seemed unnecessary that either of them should make such promises. For Bertha, telephoning was quite out of the question. It was a thing one did in emergencies. Or for very special occasions like fiftieth wedding anniversaries. Even then, a cable would be less extravagant. Writing was not in Bertha's style. As much as she described herself to people she met as not being a "bookish" person with no hint of *infra-dig* (James's word), she was to her own mind not a writing person. She only knew, and lived with the spoken word. Perhaps without the fine styles of the dialogue she heard on the films, but with full control of her vocabulary, exploitation of nuances of accent and tone, and sensitivity to the unspoken messages she received in her variety of the English language.

She had the same control of the spoken Malay language. A

parallel vocabulary limitation, an unorthodox pronunciation of some words, but she could communicate freely in Malay.

She had read Carl with his English accent. She could read the emotions conveyed by the hawker she talked to, the Chinese educated she had to deal with, her neighbours with their garbled grammar and mix of mispronounced English and Chinese.

When she started working she had much trouble with the foreigners she had to speak to. Not the Dutchmen, Japanese or Germans. Some of them struggled with English, but those who spoke it well she understood completely.

It was the Englishmen, the Australians, the Irish. They used words and tone of voice in a different way. The same words she knew somehow held unfamiliar implications and nuances she found difficult to follow. But over the months she learnt.

It was the written word that she was uneasy with. She could not write to Carl. She could dash off notes to Mr. Vandyke saying things like Mr. Kruger rang to say that if the toys were not loaded on the twelfth, he would have to amend the letter of credit and the extra costs involved would be to Mr. Vandyke's account. Mr. Vandyke always used code words for his equipment. She could write things which were like giving someone a message over the phone. But nothing more than that. She knew she could not write to Carl.

Writing a "thank you" letter to the Van Geyzels which Sheelah had insisted on was a terrible strain on her. Eventually, she had rung Ben to give her the words over the phone. No. She knew she could not write those kinds of notes.

She felt lost. Isolated. Not a word from him. Then she heard that Sheelah was going to Malacca with the Singapore team. Ethel told her. Ethel could not go because she had no more leave and she could not afford to take no-pay leave. She telephoned Sheelah and asked her to ask Carl to write. If she met him. No, nothing special just that he hasn't written lately. She felt guilty about the deceit of "lately." Sheelah seemed to question her but she avoided Sheelah's probes. Sheelah must have heard of Mary's outburst at the wedding anniversary. And if anyone knew, it was Sheelah. She had watched her like a hawk all through the up-country tour; after Malacca, that is. When she put down the phone after talking to Sheelah she was sorry she rang. Just an uneasy feeling.

End of November. No news. No phone call. No letter. Nothing.

December. Ma was making pickles for Christmas. She always made them early. You had to catch a dry spell of at least two days, she said. Pa always joked about "twenty pickle days to Christmas." A standard family thing. Like Ma saying every Christmas to Eric that he ate pickles like *sayor*; like vegetables.

The rain poured down on Singapore all through December. She spent many evenings at Beryl's place. There was something oppressive about the whole place. The rain. The politics. The City Council elections were coming up. James was tense. The Eurasians were divided about the PAP. The pessimists added to the gloom of the wetness and dampness of everything. No letter.

It was just before Christmas. The twenty-first of December. She came home one evening and saw a letter on the dining table. Ma put the phone messages there. A Malayan stamp.

She poured herself a glass of water from the fridge and went to her room to read the letter. She kicked off her shoes and lay on the bed. She didn't know his handwriting, but she was sure it was Carl.

Ordinary paper. A hand not easy to read. It said:

"Dear Bertha,

This is going to be a difficult letter to write. I have been through much anguish and soul searching ..."

She put it down on her stomach. "Oh No. No. No. No ..."

"I have had to make a terrible decision. This is my country. My people are here. I was brought up on rice and curry and with the sweat pouring off me. But after being in England for four years I have changed. I have had to decide whether I have changed deep in the insides of me or whether this a transient thing. I hope you understand this.

"It is a basic thing. On top of it all is the politics. The Hofmeisters and Coutts' are leaving. Migrating to England. They are not the only ones. I hear some are even thinking of going to Australia. They must have gone through the same soul searching as I have gone through. I tried to talk to Mr. Coutts to see what he thought, why he was taking his family away. But he was as vague as hell. It was probably an intuitive decision.

"England is a place where anyone can breathe. But it is still a foreign country to me in spite of the time I spent there. And I can see it was a critical time of my life. I hope I don't sound like an old man thinking about these matters in this way. But it is my future. And your future.

"I now know I must leave Malaya. It pains me. I thought of taking you with me. I love you, Bertha. But I don't think it will work out.

"We are so different. The attraction of opposites is absolute bullshit. People coalesce because there are common touchings. We like many things in the same way. But there are also great chasms in some of our attitudes and ways of living.

"I don't want to hurt you, but I have to tell you all this. I cannot take you with me. It is too much of a risk to your happiness. I am so different from you. I rage and fly on different planes from your rages and flights. At this point in time I cannot feel sure that I can make you happy for the rest of your life. I am sorry. I mean it. I know this will hurt you, but I would hate to hurt you day after day for the rest of your life.

We could meet again and say goodbye. But it will only make our pain more difficult to bear.

That's all ... I'm sorry to have hurt you, Bertha."

She bit her lip as she read the last line. Something was burning inside her. Something was going to explode somewhere inside her. Oh God! God! ... Carl! Carl ... Bullshit!

Her heart seemed to burst. She doubled up in pain and groaned. Then her tears came. She clenched her fists and turned round to lie on her face. "Bastards! Bastards! All of them."

Mary heard the groan from Bertha's room. She listened. She heard the sobbing. She heard Bertha spitting out a curse. Her heart tightened. Oh God! Oh Mother Mary! Oh Lady of Fatima! Please don't hurt our Bertha. Our baby!

She knew. She knew in her heart on that day they talked and had dinner together. That night of the Chung Cheng High school riots. She saw something she couldn't put her finger on. It was the differences. She knew her Bertha. She had too much of her own mind. Since she was a baby. Oh God, let her pain go quickly!

The phone rang. It was James. More trouble. Ong Eng Guan at the City Council meeting. Inauguration of the mayor. The first elected mayor of the City Council. Mary knew that the inauguration would be used to stir up more antagonism against the British. Tell Beryl, James said. Eric. The Priors. You know who ... Stay at home. The bloody bugger even threw out the old mace today. Said it was a colonial symbol. I'll be back late. But don't worry. It's not as bad as the Hock Lee thing. They're not fighting desperately now. They've won.

"When will it all end?" Mary thought to herself. She was her placid self again now. That stupid outburst against Mrs. B had faded. James had forgiven her. But Bertha. Bertha ditched by that Westerhout boy. Oh God! Help her. Please God. Please Mother Mary.

I must trust in James. We've done all we can, he keeps saying. We've done our best. He's right. He's right.

"Time, Mary and distractions," James said when they discussed it the next day.

There were plenty of distractions for James, and thus indirectly for Mary, as Ong Eng Guan rocked the City Council Chamber with his inauguration, the students defying the police and rushing into City Hall, culminating in the act that shocked James the most; ordering the mace to be taken out of the Council Chamber.

It wasn't just the little accountant behaving like a pig, but that his party the PAP which had won the City Council elections was likely to win the State elections. The English educated including the Eurasians were worried to death about the future of Singapore. James feared reprisals against the force if they came in.

Bertha took these events in in a daze. Her world had been shattered the night before. But she had decided as she cursed him. She was not going to plead with him. He had hurt her so deeply. He was not going to hurt her a second time. She cursed him because that was her way of reacting. There was too much pain in her heart to allow hate to grow. Somewhere in the depths of her subconscious, a voice told her that hate would destroy her. Not her. No bloody bastard is going to crush me. The bastard! She slept through till the morning on that terrible night. Mary did not call her for dinner. James could see that Mary was knocking her spoon and fork together more often and louder than usual to let Bertha know that they were eating. Just in case she wanted to eat. But Mary did not call out to her.

She was dressed and out of the house when James got up the next morning. For a few minutes, he stirred his tea and thought of her doing "something rash." "Something rash" was the way he thought of it. But he decided that his Bertha could weather her storm. He cringed at the thought of the pain that was raging inside her. His "baby."

She appeared at the office on time.

The office consisted of two rooms. The general office and Mr. Vandyke's room. Mr. Vandyke's room was partitioned off with glass all round above waist level. He wanted to keep his eye on what was going on outside. He walked in with his *selamat pagi* and heard Bertha return an unusually soft greeting. He went to his room and looked at the cables and letters.

He made his phone calls looking at the diary in which he had made notes during breakfast. But today, he kept looking outside at Bertha. By ten-thirty, he was quite sure that there was something seriously wrong. He called her into the room. And as he did when he had something very confidential to discuss, he asked her to shut the door when she came in.

"Bertha. There's something wrong. What's the matter?" Straight and to the point. "Tell me."

She looked at him. She saw the genuine concern in his eyes. She hadn't spoken to anyone about it. Her eyes welled with tears. She put her head down into her hands and sobbed.

Mr. Vandyke walked around the desk. He put his hand lightly on her shoulder. He was silent until her sobbing stopped. Then he took his hand off her shoulder and said softly, "Tell me, Bertha. I'm not just your boss. I am a friend. You have to tell someone."

She looked up through her tears. "It's very personal."

"A man?"

"Yes"

"Dead?"

"No."

"Someone you love?"

She just shook her head, dazed.

Mr. Vandyke kept silent. He walked around the desk to his chair. She had stopped crying now. He took a tissue out from a drawer and passed it to her without a word.

"He let you down?"

She nodded.

He leant forward with his elbows on the desk, clasping his hands together. "Bertha. Will you listen to me? Just a little."

She nodded.

"You make up your mind now. Do you still want him … or not."

She clenched her teeth. "NO!"

"Then you must find all your strength. I'm sorry for you. I hate to see you like this. But I understand."

He let it sink in. She just sat there wiping her nose, her eyes and her cheeks wet with her tears. She felt as though all the strength had gone from her.

"Now listen. Can you concentrate?"

She nodded looking at Mr. Vandyke's blue eyes.

"Rais will drive you home now."

She shook her head. "I haven't finished … Please listen. Rais will drive you home now. You will get your birth certificate. Then he'll drive you to a photo studio. I'll tell him to go to the one I know. You'll get two passport photographs. Tell them you want them urgently. Offer to pay double. Are you following me?"

Bertha looked at him, puzzled. She nodded.

"Then come back to the office. I'll send the *tamby-wallah* for a form. An application form for a passport. Fill it in and get Rais to take you to the Immigration Office. I want you to get a passport as soon as possible. I'll telephone a friend I have at Immigration. Remember this name, Mr. Desmond Tay. Repeat it to me."

"Mr. Desmond Tay."

"Bertha, listen. Are you listening?"

"Yes, Mr. Vandyke."

"I intended to go to Jakarta to deliver some very important papers. I can see that you are too upset to look after the office if I go. So I'm sending you. Do you hear me?"

"Yes, Mr. Vandyke."

"All you'll have to do is to hand them over."

Bertha was silent. Her mind reeled.

"I'll get the plane ticket changed. If we can get your passport in time, you go tomorrow. If not, the day after."

He looked at her to see if it had all sunk in.

"There will be someone to meet you. He is a trusted friend."

Bertha stared at him. She had never been on an aeroplane. She had never been to a foreign country. Malaya was different. It was part of their country. Somehow she thought of the Van Geyzels. Someone to meet her at the station.

She shook her head like a dog tossing the water off its body. It was another shock. A distraction.

Mary gaped with her mouth wide open when Bertha rushed up the steps and asked her where her birth certificate was. Her jaw dropped lower when Bertha told her she was going to Jakarta. In an aeroplane! She rushed to their bedroom and opened the camphorwood chest. She struggled with her fear of her Bertha going to that backward country. Malaria pills! Smallpox!

Mary rummaged in the camphorwood chest looking for the

birth certificate. There were yellowed papers and little bundles of cheap jewellery. As Mary took these out a knife dropped out of one rough parcel.

"What's that?" Betha asked.

"Oh, some knife that Pa says is a family heirloom."

Her mind was elsewhere. She turned to Bertha and said, "Smallpox. Cholera injections. You'll need them Bertha."

"Don't know. Mr. Vandyke knows what to do. He'll tell me."

The wicked men out there. The water. It isn't safe. Electricity? Mary's mind was spinning. But suddenly she saw it. The best thing that could ever happen! Take her mind off that fellow. Oh Mother Mary! *Deo Gratis*! Must telephone James.

Bertha asked Mr.Vandyke about the injections and vaccination. He smiled. "I didn't forget them. I have friends there. You don't need them."

James stood frozen to the verandah floor as Mary broke the news to him when he came home. The mixed emotions of surprise, fear for his "baby," bewilderment at the fact that she was going to go in an aeroplane, the pride that Mr. Vandyke trusted her with those important papers, so important that they could not go by registered post ...

"Chrrrrist!" he gasped.

"James ... Your language."

He put his hands on Mary's shoulders. "Is she all right?"

~ Chapter Fourteen ~

Whisky and Fish Moolie

"This doesn't sound like a curry to me. Listen … lamb, shallots … What's that?"

"Those little red onions."

"Garlic, mustard, vinegar … ah, the vinegar you mentioned, chillies, soy sauce, thick, soy sauce, thin, cloves, pepper, oil, *belachan* … that's the shrimp paste you told me about?"

"Yah."

"Well, I know a thing or two about curries and this doesn't look like a curry to me … there's no turmeric, or fennel, or cumin seed … or coriander, cardamoms, *garam massala*."

"Well, there it is in the book."

"Interesting …"

Ray was reading from *The Asian Microwave Cookbook*. The curry devil recipe. We were at John Peter's place. He had asked Old Joe, Ray and me to his house for drinks and dinner. Somewhere in the North Beach area. It was a bigger house than the houses of other Singaporeans I had been to. He was an "accounts man" in some large company. Obviously a senior job from the looks of his house and his Fairmont. Ray picked us up from the bar and drove us there. On the way, he had asked about curry devil. So when we got there, after the introductions, I asked Sylvia if she had a recipe to show Ray. She produced *The Asian Microwave Cookbook*.

Sylvia was slim and pretty. Fair skin and brown eyes. A tinge of brown in her hair. High cheekbones and a nose that revealed her Asian ancestry. She was charming, smiling and beautiful, I thought. She spoke perfect English. Not "Singlish," yet the accents of many words and sentence stresses were not English English, or RP as my father called it.

She was introduced as "Syl." I fought my private war and called her Sylvia all through the night. Like my Dad, working insidiously all the time to push his ideas.

John poured whiskies all round. I noticed he poured five glasses. Sylvia sat down with us picked up a glass and lifted it at Old Joe's "cheers."

"Now that is Serani woman," Old Joe remarked, "drinking whisky."

"Very few Chinese women drink," John explained to Ray, "even today."

"In the old days even less," Old Joe added.

"But secretly at home the old Chinese ladies often had their glass of neat brandy ... or stout, didn't they, Joe," I said.

"Yah. But not secretly. It just wasn't proper for a young thing to drink in public. And they didn't like alcohol."

"At what age did they start then?" Sylvia asked.

"Dunno. Maybe it was the medicinal idea of brandy and stout that made them start. After giving birth they used to drink DOM."

"That's Eurasian for Benedictine, Ray," John explained. He continued, "Drinking and smoking gave the Serani girls a bad name in the eyes of the Chinese and Malays."

"Yah. Our girls were considered 'loose' in the early days," Sylvia said.

"Also because they went out with the Europeans."

"Because the Europeans were considered immoral?"

"Maybe."

"Was it just Europeans, or was it the soldier-boys and sailor-boys?" I questioned.

"I think Robert's right," Sylvia said. "If our girls in those days had only gone out with the Europeans, the 'master race,' they would not have had such a bad name."

"No, no, no." Old Joe had to have his say. And in fact he had some good points.

But he went on and on about the western style being more open than the Asian. Holding hands in public was a thing only the shameless Eurasians did. We didn't have the traditions of the Chinese or the Malays to hold us back. Or slow down our taking up the new ideas. We did have Victorian ideas, but without a long history.

"That's rubbish," John interjected. "Seranis have a long history."

"Another thing," Old Joe continued, ignoring John's comment, "our girls went out with the soldier-boys because they spoke English and had something in common in their way of life. Something like home, lah. The Chinese were still so 'chinkified' in those days."

"What about the Babas?" Sylvia asked. "They spoke English. They had thrown off their Chinese traditions ..."

"No, they had not. Not fully."

"Did the Babas religion have anything to do with it?"

"What religion? They did not have a proper religion."

"You know, the other night when Ray asked about Eurasian food we did not come up with very much." I changed the subject.

"I said *Feng*," Old Joe interrupted.

I ignored him. "The Babas on the other hand created so much by marrying the Chinese and Malay foods ... and Indian. So did the Hylams. Hylam pork chops, chicken curry."

"Wait, wait, wait. The Hylam buggers invented that Hainanese pork chop because they did not have their hearts in European food. They just couldn't do it the European way," Joe said.

"That's not true. They did learn the European cooking in most things."

Sylvia went into the kitchen and in what seemed to me an incredibly short time announced dinner. It was rice and fish moolie and *kangkong* with, of course, *sambal belachan* on the table.

"A real live Eurasian curry?" Ray asked.

"No. Indian," Sylvia replied. "The veges' should have been cooked with chilli, but seeing we had a 'native' with us tonight I left it out. The fish moolie is very mild. Not that I made it mild for you, Ray. It is a mild curry."

"Smells wonderful."

"And you must eat it with a spoon and fork. Your way of eating rice with a fork is quite silly and impractical to me," Old Joe added.

"Now that's a good hostess," I said, "leaving out the chilli because of your guest. I am sick of my Singapore staff ordering *Soon-hock* and that fancy steamed sharks'-fins when they are entertaining a visitor from overseas. The fellow would be happy as Larry with sweet-sour fish and 'Chinese beefsteak,' but they order the expensive dishes for themselves, and not for their guest."

"That's completely irrelevant, Robert," John said.

"Jeee ... This is good!" Ray said. "Tell me, are there any books on Eurasian cooking?"

"Not that I know of," Sylvia said.

"There's not enough to make a book," I said.

"Are there any books on Eurasians?" Ray asked.

"A few," John said. "There's a book by Harry Crabbe."

"Not that book. It makes out as if the Eurasians thought of nothing else but the colour of their skins."

"No, Joe. He does paint a picture of a type of Eurasian of that time. It was published in the sixties but the incidents and ideas he wrote about were of the fifties, I think. It is true what he wrote. True for a certain group of Eurasians."

"There's a book by Muriel Leicester. She's here in Australia," I said.

"I haven't read it," Sylvia said, "but I hear it is worth reading. As Anthony Burgess said, a writer must get out of his environment to write about it. That's why there are so many British writers living on the Continent ... And there is a slim book written by a Mr. Augustine of Kedah."

"But he's a Malaysian."

"Is there a difference?" Ray asked.

"Yes. Now."

"When did it become different?"

"Don't know. After *merdeka*?"

"No, Syl. Probably after 1965."

"Isn't there something written by a Portuguese priest? Father Pintado?"

"Yes. That's a list of names … surnames."

"Dr. Myrna Blake has written a few things. I reckon her work is the only serious study of the Eurasians."

"Oh no. There is something published by the Singapore Institute of South East Asia Studies."

"But that's utter crap!" Sylvia was definite in her opinion.

"Did you know that the Oral History unit has a good few tapes on Eurasians talking about themselves?"

"No. That should be interesting."

I changed the tack of the conversation. "You know, Sylvia, that point you made about self-exiled writers is true. Even our talking here … Is it not because we are away from our environment? I've never talked so much about Serani than in these last few days here in Perth."

They didn't seem to have heard me. Sylvia changed the tack again. "One should never forget that the Eurasians all started from a European male and an Asian female. That is of the greatest importance."

John interrupted. "Aiyah, Syl, you're not going to get all sexist again."

"The woman brought up the children. She stamped her Asian ways into them. We would have been different if the inter-marriages were not loaded one way. Probably more European in our culture."

"Point taken. But the Serani woman didn't emasculate her man as the Peranakan woman did. He could not be tied down," Joe said.

"They weren't such strong women, Joe," I said. "They didn't have the steel of the migrant Chinese women."

"Steel. That's the word Dr. Blake used in the title of her article on Eurasian women, *Steel Orchids*," John said.

"A bad title. The orchid is not flamboyant enough a flower. It needs to be something flashy, stylish, strong in colour. Not even the shoe-flower," I said.

"What's shoe-flower?" Ray asked.

"Hibiscus."

John switched the subject slightly. Maybe he didn't like the women bits. If he was a true Eurasian he would have been quite male chauvinistic. "The community grew out of rejection by the local people. And the Europeans. If these forces were not there to unite them the Eurasians would have split into so many little groups and got absorbed."

He went on to the differences between the Eurasians from the Malacca, the *geragoks*, who had descended from the Portuguese, the Ceylon Burghers, who came from Dutch stock, and the English Eurasians as I call them. And some from India. Very few. Differences in food, religion, customs and speech. It was like familiar background music to me while I thought how lovely Sylvia looked. "Yeah. Accent tends to stratify people," Ray said.

"But *belachan* unites them!" Old Joe said. He had had enough of this type of talk.

We moved away from the dining table, back to the lounge. John had a bottle of cognac. They had their fun telling me about Australia. The fishing at Mandura. Yanchep Park. Roos.

Sylvia told us how when they saw their first wombat she took a picture of it excitedly from about a hundred yards away. Then it came nearer. So she took another at five hundred yards. And so on. Eventually it came right up to them. She went to the bedroom and showed me the series.

Just before we left Sylvia asked, "How's your mother, Robert? I used to meet her at my auntie Zoey's place."

"Fine. Normal ageing aches and pains."

"And your auntie Bertha?"

I looked at Old Joe and couldn't help taking a quick glance at Ray. He was listening like a quivering deer.

"Don't know. Haven't you heard how she disappeared?"

"No. I heard she left her good-for-nothing husband, taking the car."

"Ha! Ha! Yes, that reminds me," Joe chuckled. "Must tell you this before we go. You know he was a car salesman. Sometimes he used to tell the seller that he would take his car for a few days. He'd lend him his car. Only way to get the best price. Show it to many people, or some *temberang* like that. When Bertha left him he had this Jaguar. She went off with it. The fellow sued him! That was bloody good I thought."

"Didn't they catch up with her?"

"No. And mind you a Jag was not a common car then."

"It isn't now either."

"The police never found it. Al Matthews told me that in Malaya, shortly after it disappeared, the up-country police reported that a bugger who was suspected of being the boss of a kidnapping gang was driving a Jag of the same description. Although Al was in 'Traffic,' he heard it from the CID blokes. He got them to try to check up on the chassis number. But they wouldn't. They didn't want to arouse suspicion."

"Kidnappers?"

"Yah. There were all sorts of rumours about Bertha after she disappeared."

"You mean she was not officially divorced?"

"No. That suited Heng. Best of both worlds. Immune from the marrying ones."

"You mean up to this day, no one knows what happened to Bertha and where she is now?"

"Right. Don't know whether she's alive or not. She'd be about fifty-one, fifty-two if she was alive."

~ *Chapter Fifteen* ~

Dr.Edwin Cornelius

Sheelah Cornelius was born with a silver spoon in her mouth, so the Bukit Timah folks said. It was not quite true. She was brought up comfortably in what was an upper middle-class family in those days. But it was not in wealth or luxury.

Her father Edwin Cornelius was a doctor. He was a Queen's Scholar. The Queen's Scholarship was the most prestigious award one could win in the Straits Settlements. He studied medicine in Dublin.

It was a good Catholic place to go to, his parents told themselves as he waved from the deck of the huge P.&O. steamer. But his mother worried in her heart that he would bring some European bride home. It would have pleased his father if he had. But his mother knew that "none of our people could be happy with one of those European women."

He started going out with an Irish girl and mentioned her in his letters. Mrs. Cornelius was alarmed. She knew her son was attractive to women. He was tall, with a big bone structure. When you stood there at the wicket gripping your bat and saw him running towards you with his long arm in the air you realised what a large man he was. He was six-feet one. He could "pass off" as an Englishman, his mother often said to herself. He was fair with a touch of brown in his hair.

But her prayers were answered. He returned home a fully qualified doctor without an Irish girl on his arm. The community was proud of him. But it was a quiet pride voiced in drawing rooms and at the club bar, not shouted out in public. Years later, Edwin compared the pride his people had in him with the pride the Hainanese community had when that young Foo lad, their first engineer, came home. There were parties and press interviews.

He had hardly started at the GH, when another fear arose in his mother's breast. He began dating a Chinese nurse. Mrs. Cornelius met the the girl and her fears were magnified when she found how lovely she looked. And she was "so very bold, for a Chinese girl."

But once again her nightly pleadings to heaven on her knees were answered. They broke off, and Edwin finally married Olive Perera's daughter. They had six children.

Eleanor was the first. Edwin and Rita fussed over the baby, spoilt her and panicked when the slightest thing went wrong. Pushed by Rita, he applied his medical knowledge almost to extremes to get her back into good health at the smallest signs of illness. Rita added her own family's "well established" cures to his scientific methods. Eleanor was dosed with gripe water, Phillips milk of magnesia, castor oil, enemaed, rubbed with camphorated oil, *minyak urat*, and sprinkled with holy water as Edwin and Rita decided what the illness needed.

They had seen their follies when Sheelah was born eighteen months later and she was christened and given her silver serviette, ring, spoon and "pusher" and allowed to grow with only an occasional Aspro or *obat perut* without too much fussing. She grew up into a strong, happy and laughing child.

But Rita kept telling Edwin that he was treating her like a boy. Because he wanted a boy, she explained. She was "educated." She had gone through the "normal training" and became a primary school teacher. She read widely and understood some of the mysteries of the human subconscious. She could see drifts and underlying motives.

Edwin laughed at her analyses. Sheelah was a normal girl, full of energy and curious about everything. She didn't distinguish between what little girls should do and what little boys should do. And Edwin, in his wisdom, tried to keep the illogical and unreasonable restrictions of the old folk away from the upbringing of his children.

When she was about fourteen or so he even started taking her with him to the boxing at the Happy World, to the disapproval of Auntie Pearlie and others.

He had stopped playing cricket when his duties as an MO became more onerous. But whenever he had the opportunity he was at the Padang watching a cricket match or a soccer or hockey game. Then he started getting really interested in boxing.

He had his favourites. That Eurasian boy, "Young Frisco," is going to go far, he said to them at the SRC. He had to defend his stand on many a night pointing out the faults of "Speedy Bautista." They discussed the power of Nai Som Pong and that negro fellow, Joe Diamond. They knew them all. The local boys, the Filipinos and the foreigners who came and went. It was an exciting sport to watch.

And Sheelah loved it. She was allowed to stay up late on Friday nights and sit on the hard concrete step-seats and yell with the crowd. It was the speed of the action that thrilled her. And the desperate need to win. To lay the other fellow flat out on the canvas. To show them who is the better man.

She charged with that spirit across the netball court and fired her teammates with it at every game. It didn't matter if it was just a game against the "A" class or against the Blue House team. She had to win. Later, when she played for the convent, her drive was even stronger. Miss Jenkins had to call her up once and lecture her on the true spirit of sportsmanship and tell her that there was no call to use unladylike words such as, "We've got to kill them! Smash them! *Hantam* the RGS!"

Rita fed her interest in geography with the *National Geographic* magazine and in English with A.A. Milne and Enid Blyton between nursing the babies that seemed to come very two years or eighteen months. There were always books around the house. And there was always good music from the big brown RCA radio.

Rita's efforts sank in. Sheelah raced up the steps of the children's library in Stamford Road every Saturday and rushed out excited with what she had taken out. But not her efforts to cultivate a fine taste in music in her children.

It annoyed her when Sheelah put on that "Tooler-rama-rama" piece again and again on the gramophone. And the needles she used up every day! Then, just before the war, the girl went mad on "The Lambeth Walk" which was really an adult dance.

But Rita was happy. She sat back one night after finishing her corrections and thought, how lucky she was! How her Creator had blessed them.

Edwin had been moving up in the world. He had bought a Marvelette when he joined GH and a Ballila when he was confirmed as an MO. Now he had left the government service and was established as a GP and, as the family had grown, he had recently bought the Fiat seven-seater. The one with the two pull-down seats at the back like a London taxi. For some reason or other he had stuck to Fiat. Gilbert Snodgrass always gave him a good deal and a good price for the old car. The workshop right on Orchard Road provided good service. And the children loved the ice-balls that the *tamby-fellow* who stationed his cart at the workshop gate handed out to them while Edwin was settling the servicing bill. He paid the fellow when he had finished and sometimes had one himself.

He had come home one day and told Rita that he had resigned from the government service. He wanted to be a GP, not a specialist. And there was no future for the non-specialist in the government. Rita was never consulted for the major decisions. He was a strong and determined man. She had learnt from their courting days that he would make all the key decisions himself. She accepted that. And she backed him up on all his decisions.

Like when he began as a GP, she had made it her duty to advertise for him by word of mouth. She smiled now as she remembered the little catchy thing she had thought up. "You must see my husband if you have no patience and cannot wait. He has no patients now." She was always turning words around. It embarrassed the children when they started growing up. They called her twists "corny." She had her standard ones when she met someone new ... She was a Perera before she got married. A blind

Perera. Without an eye. And when she married she became a Catholic. Because there was no way Edwin or the parish priest or Mrs. Cornelius would approve of a "mixed-marriage." So from an Anglican she became RC, Rita Cornelius.

She had not liked his decision to move into the Bukit Timah Road house. It was so far away. At the Keng Chin Road junction. The trolley buses stopped at Newton. The children would have to get into a "mosquito bus" from there. And they could hardly speak any Malay. They didn't know a word of Chinese, of course.

The hawkers would not pass that way. The road always flooded when there was heavy rain.

But she kept her thoughts to herself and, in the course of time, grew to like the house and the area. Maybe it was because she got Father Bonifacio to bless the house as soon as they moved in. Old Mrs. Cornelius shook her head and said to the old man that it's always the converts who were the most fervent.

After being there for about four months, Rita began to tell her friends that it was not a bad place. Away from the crowd of Serani at Bukit Timah and Hooper Road and Winstedt Road and Monks Hill Terrace. And we are not disturbed here by hawkers like the tock-tock man nor by the ting-ting man. Occasionally, a *kachang puteh* man would pass. And quite often the *wade* man. I think he passes here on his way to the *toddy* shop at Newton.

Edwin loves a *wade* with his Tiger in the evenings. And this man always has the freshest, crispiest, green chillies. My Indian tailor doesn't mind coming all the way here with his fashion books and cloth samples whenever I want to make a new dress. It's quite nice here.

The only one who complains is poor old Mrs. Stoppard when she walks from Newton with her bottles of salt-fish pickles and *achar*.

The Hendricks live across the road. We hardly ever really speak to them. She's got one big voice. Shouts out to her girls from the kitchen. With the choicest of words at times. Behind us is a quiet Japanese couple without children. On the other side of this field next to us is a big *towkay*. Lots of children. But all older than ours. I think he's got two wives. Chua something-or-other. Three or four cars. We have never spoken to them with this field between us.

The field was where the Cornelius children met and became good friends with the Chuas. One day, Rita was at the hedge trimming her congea bush when she looked into the field and to her great surprise saw her little Sheelah there among the hulking big Chua boys. The girl was holding a cricket bat almost as big as she was, standing in front of a wicket. She was alarmed and spoke to Edwin about it when he came back from the clinic. He laughed. That girl will make friends with anyone, he said.

Sheelah made friends with the Nakajimas. Wandering down the earth road on many a hot afternoon while her mother was having a brief nap after a hard morning at the school, she had noticed that the Nakajimas had an absolutely enormous *bling-bling* tree in their garden. Then it started to fruit. Now it became quite pretty with the fruit hanging there in bright green bunches from the trunk and boughs. After studying the beautiful tree very carefully for four days, she discovered to her amazement that the Nakajimas were not picking the fruit. So one day, when she saw Mrs. Nakajima in the garden, she pointed out to the fruit. Perhaps the old dear had not seen them. Mrs. Nakajima could speak very little English. But she got the message. She opened the gate and let Sheelah and her scraggy dog in and motioned with her hands that she could pick as much as she wanted to.

Sheelah tucked her skirt into her panties and started to fill her dress with *bling-bling*, stuffing the fruit down through the opening at the neck. She bit into one and seeing Mrs. Nakajima watching her she offered her one. Poor Mrs. Nakajima had such a shock at the sour taste. She spat it out. Sheelah laughed and the scraggy dog barked. She rushed home with the *bling-bling* and related her exciting little adventure to Rita. Rita later made a *bling-bling sambal*, put some in a dish and walked over to the Nakajimas to give it to them to try. There was much bowing and smiling. Mr. Nakajima came out. He could speak a fair amount of English and they were able to converse. The upshot of it all was that Sheelah was given absolute exclusive rights to the *bling-bling* tree and the Corneliuses and Nakajimas became friends. And a little bowl of *bling-bling sambal* was carried over to their house by willing little hands and feet quite often. Strange Japanese sweets were rushed back, tasted cautiously and found to be quite delicious.

Climbing over the hedge to the field became a regular thing. The Chua boys tired of cricket and started hockey. And Sheelah pestered her parents for a hockey stick, promising to do her homework every single day without fail forever and ever and accepting it as an advance present for her next birthday. So the wonderful wild hockey games in the field next door began.

Life was good in those days. There were parties at the house and they let the Eurasian Association Youth Movement hold a fund raising concert there once. Eleanor and Sheelah and even Max and Percy were given parts to the director's secret annoyance. Eleanor and Sheelah looked so terribly sweet in the colourful kimonos Mrs. Nakajima had given them as New Year presents. No one knew what Japanese girls had to do with that part of the sketch, but it didn't really matter.

And Edwin was having fun with the Volunteers. Sheelah could never get over his puttees. Not only were they as complicated as a *saree* but she was sure they were ticklish. It was such a tickly sort of flannel. And there were dances at the Volunteer Drill Hall on Beach Road and the children were so delighted at seeing their father out there on the Padang in parade.

Then the clouds of war gathered. The closing of the Fiat showroom and workshop was a proper nuisance. What are we going to do about spares? Did they actually put that nice Mr. Mariani in jail, Edwin?

And on the night of December the seventh, 1941, in the early hours of the morning, the bombs fell on Singapore. Rita and the older children were bewildered. Are they going to take the Nakajimas away, Dad? But aren't they Singapore people now? And Echigoya will be closed. Oh dear! And you mean there won't be any more "ten-cent" store, Mummy?

Sheelah watched her Dad move the pins he had stuck on a board with a map on it every night after the news. He explained it was where the fighting was. Up-country. Where Auntie Elaine and Yvonne and Royston were. The pins moved further and further south every night.

Carpenters came into the storeroom at the back of the house next to the servant's room and built a large table sort of thing. With a floor underneath it. They began to sleep there when the sirens went off more often. It was fun. But Mummy was very frightened. And Jacinta who was still a baby cried every time she heard the siren. Even the "all-clear" siren.

Then one day they had to pack up and Edwin drove them to the French convent where dozens of children and their mothers were milling around. That's all Max remembered.

Sheelah was fifteen when Singapore fell to General Yamashita's invading army. She knew what was happening and remembered the events which occurred in rapid succession. Years later, only a few of the major shocks and pains, and a handful of insignificant items remained in her memory.

She remembered Rita's shock and near-hysteria when she went up to the second floor classrooms of the convent and saw a European soldier shoot an Indian soldier dead on Stamford Road.

Her father came in for a few minutes haggard and tired with his work at the hospital. He had been pulled out of the Volunteer Force to help out at the GH. She heard him telling her mother that the Indian soldier was probably a deserter. Australians too were deserting. The Indian was probably from the 45th Infantry Brigade, he said, who had arrived in Singapore on the 3rd of January and almost immediately sent to the frontline into jungle country unfamiliar to them. They had been wiped out in Johor. The poor man was probably a straggler. It's not only the Indians and Australians. There was some kind of row, he heard, at the Rex Hotel last night. The British held a meeting to protest to the governor about the state of the defences. So I hear, he said.

She remembered the sudden silence of the surrender. And the unexpected explosions a couple of hours later as an ammunition dump near the convent erupted in flames.

And while the Japanese occupied Singapore, Sheelah and Eleanor were kept confined to the flat that Edwin had found for them in the city. It was like being imprisoned in one's own home. Rita was insistent on this. She had left Edwin to rule the house for all these years, but this was different. A woman understood the dangers. They were teenagers, attractive and "well developed," she said. They cooked and sewed, swept and cleaned out the flat and the toilets. Rita would not let them out. Not even for mass. She went to mass daily and prayed for them, for Edwin, for her mother and her father, for Elaine, Yvonne and Royston in Malaya.

The Japanese administration found that they had a problem with the Eurasians. Not that they suspected them as being completely loyal to the British. But they did not know whether they were Europeans who should be interned or Asians who should be re-educated into becoming citizens of The Great Asia Co-Prosperity Sphere they were trying to nurture. They pushed some into the camps with the British and other unfriendly aliens. Those who were obviously more Asian than European were left alone. But there were those in-between ones. They solved the problem by issuing the in-between ones with labels which everyone referred to as red stars, although it was really a white star on a red background. The common description seemed to fit in with everything being upside-down.

To the community, it drew the lines of internal conflicts which had been squabbled about in numerous petty ways for years. The European-Eurasians and the Asian-Eurasians, an onlooker would have said, but the distinction was never so crudely expressed within the community. Years later, old Augustine Tranquera used to say, after he had a few, that it drew the battle lines clearly for the first time but other enemies were all around us and we who did not have red stars felt sorry for those who did. "I reckon we were drawn closer together cos of those bloody red stars."

It was only when her father died suddenly of meningitis in 1949 that her mother told them what her father did during the war. It brought a rush of emotion and tears of pride to Sheelah. Rita said that he used to go out very early every morning just before dawn towards the end of the occupation. Between sobs, Rita told them of the thousands of Javanese labourers the Japanese had brought to Singapore. When they got sick and too weak to work, the Japanese turned them out into the streets. They gathered along the Rochore canal with sticks and wires. Each man found a rusty old soup can, balanced it on three stones over a fire and cooked the dead rats and rotting vegetable matter he fished out of the canal. They were living skeletons with just a thin layer of skin stretched over their bones. Most of them had sores filled with maggots.

Edwin went to these wretched people every morning before it became bright enough for anyone to notice him because the Japanese might not have condoned it. With his limited stock of medicines, he tended to them, knowing that the man he was treating may die within the hour or, at most, last a week. But more than the medical attention, he brought to them hope. And perhaps a touch, some vestige of faith in their fellow men.

"He used to pound *jambu batu* leaves and make some kind of mixture because he said that was the only thing he had to try to stop the purging."

"He made me promise not to tell anyone while he was still alive ... while he was still alive, he said ..." Rita broke off weeping.

~ Chapter Sixteen ~

Sheelah Cornelius

Sheelah was thirty in 1957. Still single. Rita often sighed at the thought. She's pretty, is such a nice person, has a good job. Yet none of our boys have fallen in love with her.

Her aunts and uncles, friends and acquaintances all had their theories. The young men had their thoughts.

"So snooty lah!"

"She won't go out with you, *badak*. She only goes out with Europeans."

"Hey. You wan' take her out? On your bike? Go and buy a car first. Mus' be bigger than hers for sure. Then go and pawn your marder's jewels. Dis girl you doan take to Marine Parade. Must go to Raffles Hotel. And wine, man ... Fergait it! I introduce you to Stella."

But Sheelah knew. They were frightened of her. She had ceased to care. At one time, she held herself back and didn't make statements about Lim Yew Hock or Lee Kuan Yew, and kept away from classical music. And she avoided raising subjects like the bestsellers, the value of the pound, the future of the Eurasians, the education system in Singapore or Percival's blunders during the battle for Singapore.

She could talk about every hockey game in Singapore and Malaya but got bored with cricket and soccer. There was no interest in boxing anymore. She didn't mind comparing cars but the Hill Climb and car rallies could not hold her attention for long.

She tried to draw Drysdale out on the subject of his ambitions in the force and his prospects but she soon saw that he wasn't very interested in his future himself. Fishing was his passion. Richard Pasqual was crazy about her for three months. He was on the sidelines at every game. They went swimming at Changi. She saw him drooling over her body. He was interesting though. He wanted to be a cook. A good cook. His sisters and cousins ridiculed his interest. Sheelah admired him for sticking to it. She also admired him physically. But although she enjoyed all kinds of food, cooking didn't turn her on. She could afford an *amah*. Rita came over regularly and taught the *amah* new dishes. Rita also started off new *amahs* for her. You couldn't keep them these days, everybody said.

"She's too godammed choosy," her Uncle Cosmas said to Rita. "That Hope boy and Malcom Foley were really keen on her. But she thinks she's the cat's whiskers. She'll learn."

"She's too pushy, Rita," Auntie Kate gave Rita her experienced advice. "I've seen it so many times. That kind of girl who acts like a sergeant major all the time. Clara tells me that every time there's a gang of girls and boys trying to decide what film to see, she bullies them into agreeing with her choice. And she's always interrupting ..."

"She doesn't, Kate," Rita said.

"Or she must have her say ... her two cents worth."

"Yah. She tends to speak up."

"Like those European women, lah."

Bertie O'Keefe believed that she would never marry "one of our boys." "I really think most of them are too limited for her. She needs a really strong man. All the good guys are married. While they were out looking for wives five, six years ago, she wouldn't look at anything but the hockey goalposts. Remember how she wouldn't even go to the nine o'clock show because it might slow her down? Just plain hockey mad, she was."

"So, my Sheelah is to going land up a spinster?" Rita asked Bertie.

"Or marry a rich Chinese who already has a wife," he joked.

"Cheh! Don't talk like that!"

"Could happen. Anything can happen with a woman."

Rita smiled coyly. She was a widow after all.

They knew who had been "running after" her. They knew everything that happened in the community whether it was in Katong or at Upper Serangoon. But they didn't know what happened in the European social circles. By this time, European included Americans, Australians and others because the old colonial types, rubber planters, and military men, were ceasing to dominate the social life among the expatriates in Singapore.

It irritated the Eurasian gossips that they hadn't a clue on what Sheelah was up to when she occasionally slipped out in conversation that she was at the Cricket Club or the RSYC. And the lack of tidbits on which one could build up some logical or at least plausible explanation or prediction gave rise to completely fabricated rumours.

Rita worried about all this.

And Rita's worrying began to annoy Sheelah. Sheelah also began to try to correct some of her mother's other habits like making dreadfully loud sucking noises when she was enjoying a crab curry or walking around the house in the "morning gown" Rita had copied from Hilda Cohen's, or still calling orange crush, orange smash and Jakarta, Batavia. Her visits to the old house became less frequent. She was also seen less often at relatives' birthday parties and weddings. Or at funerals, where long lost friends hailed each other happily in hushed voices.

Ben and Beryl's was a place of solace to Sheelah. She walked in just after Christmas 1957 to see Bertha sitting on the sofa talking excitedly. Bertha had just returned from Jakarta.

Both Ben and Beryl were listening attentively.

"Oh hello, Sheelah. Sit down. I'm just back from Jakarta."

"Had a good time?"

"I'd say ..." Beryl replied for Bertha.

"How long were you there?"

"Well that's one thing. I was to go for only a night, but as I was leaving Mr. Vandyke told me to stay for a week. Because he was expecting a parcel from Surabaya and if I stayed on I could bring it back for him."

"Did he go with you?"

"No lah."

"And how was Jakarta?"

"Filthy. But a nice place. People are so friendly there. It's like the Singapore Ma used to describe."

"Where did you stay?"

"In a dirty little hotel. But the sheets were clean and I had a bathroom attached. Anyway, I hardly spent any time there."

"Gadding about eh?"

"Yah. Had a good time. One of Mr. Vandyke's business friends looked after me. A big strong Sundanese man. Hadi. Very nice fellow."

"How old?"

"Dunno ... Maybe thirty-five."

"Handsome?"

"Yah. Really handsome fellow. Smooth. But a gentleman. No hanky-panky type. He treated me like a queen. Took me everywhere. I even went up to Puncak."

"Where's that?"

"Just near Jarkarta. Up in the mountains. He said it's just like the Penang Hills. He's been there. Or Maxwell Hill. Super! Cold but so nice."

"How high is it?"

"Dunno ... But it's beautiful. You can see the valley down below for miles. We stayed in his friend's bungalow. There was a cook and servants there so it was just like a hotel. And every morning, before we went out, he asked me what I wanted to eat. Whoa, like being a princess."

"Where did you go to every day?"

"Oh nowhere. Just walking around ... talking. Hadi told me so much about Indonesia. I felt so ashamed that I knew so little about that huge country just next door to us. I know more about England than Indonesia."

"Yeah. That's true for all of us in Singapore," Ben said.

"Oh yes. This I must tell you. The first time I went to the

bathroom there, I saw goldfish in the *bak mandi.*"

"Goldfish? *Bak mandi*? Children, I suppose."

"No, no. The *bak mandi* is the water tub. They put goldfish in there to prevent mosquito breeding. I was so scared that I would pour out a fish on my body."

"Good curries, I suppose."

"Yah. *Sheok.* I tried so many different things. *Usus gajah*, sort of fried beef with an egg on top."

"*Usus* is intestines isn't it?"

"Elephant's intestines?"

"No lah. Just a name. *Nasi rawon, nasi liwet* ..."

"And *Rijsttafel*, I presume?"

"Of course. And satay. Their satay is different from ours. And, Beryl, the most super *emping*."

"What's *emping*?" Sheelah asked.

"Aiyah! You Serani don't know *emping*? It's a kind of *keropok*."

"*Belut blado* ... an eel dish. Real good. *Pedas* as ever though ... And they eat more Chinese food than the Malays in Malaya I think."

"That's probably only in Jakarta."

"Their own style Chinese food. *Halal*, of course. *Bakmi* seems to be a favourite. Kind of a *mee*. And there's one thing I must tell you. Never had anything like it in all my life. *Adpokat*. It's a soft fruit. They mash it into a drink and put some strong coffee with milk on top. Beautiful. Like a custard."

"Avocado," Ben interrupted. "I've heard of it."

"How's that it is not eaten here?"

"Probably because the British did not like it," Ben suggested.

"Hadi was surprised I could speak Malay. He asked me if I was Malay or Portuguese. He did not understand what Eurasian was. He told me that there many mixed bloods in Indonesia, both among the Dutch when they were there and among the Indonesians. I met one. He looked just like an Indonesian. Rudi Schindkunz. Young fellow. Tall and damn good looking. Strong looking. Hadi said he was a very clever man. I think he was. Seemed to be very widely read. Spoke English very well. But with that funny Indonesian or Dutch accent."

"Hey, you did have a good time, didn't you? And no work?"

"That's the wonderful part. Nothing. Just waiting for the parcel."

"You missed all the Christmas parties."

"I wouldn't have missed that trip for all the Christmas parties in the world. When I have money I shall go there again."

"Didn't go to church, I suppose," Beryl asked.

"No. Doesn't matter lah, Beryl!"

"Don't talk like that."

Bertha told them about everything she did, she ate, she saw she admired and she hated. She held back some of her thoughts. She didn't tell them how her heart was still aching for Carl all through Jakarta and Puncak, how she knew, at the end of the week, Hadi had become very fond of her but had not given a sign nor said a word. She saw it in his eyes. She knew. And she didn't tell them what she thought of the parcel.

It was about twelve inches long and three inches in diameter.

Brown paper-wrapped. It didn't feel very heavy. Could have been a roll of biscuits. No sound when it was shaken.

On the plane back to Singapore, Garuda because Mr. Vandyke knew one could always get a seat on Garuda, she thought of the hectic week. It was the best thing that could have happened to her after the trauma of Carl's cruel letter. Thank you Mr. Vandyke, she said to him.

The customs checked her bag thoroughly. She thought it was because she had come from Jakarta. Then they examined the parcel. Shook it and listened, as she had done. Weighed it in their hands, as she had also done. They smelt it. Squeezed it. Then, they asked her to open it.

She undid the string and peeled off the scotch-tape carefully so that it could be stuck back again. She was just as curious as the customs men were. There were now three men watching her unwrap the parcel. There was a lot of newspaper stuffing inside and, when this was opened, a small piece of metal about three inches long was revealed. There was nothing else. Just that little piece of metal. It was a tube. Shiny. Hollow.

The customs men looked into the tube. One blew through it. They tapped it. It puzzled them. "What's it for?" they asked. "I don't know," she said. Then she began to get worried. She added that she thought it was a spare part of something. And she fabricated a story.

"My father's friend in Jakarta asked me to bring it back. That's all I know."

"Who is your father's friend in Jakarta?"

"I don't know. He came to the hotel and gave the parcel to me." She saw their restlessness. So she added, "I'm sure it is some sort of spare. You can't get anything in Jakarta. Many of my friends bring out damaged parts so that they can identify them in Singapore. They can't even get the parts catalogues."

A big man with a moustache who had been looking at the wrapping asked her, "Who's your father?"

"ASP James Rodrigues."

"Oh. Mr. Rodrigues! You are his daughter!"

So they let her through. She wrapped it up roughly and put it in her bag.

Mr. Vandyke had sent a message that the car would meet her. She saw Rais waiting. He told her that he was to drive her home. Mr. Vandyke said he was busy otherwise he would have met you.

She examined the little tube in the car on her way back.

She knew a thing or two about metals and machining. Because Eric was at the PSA doing an apprenticeship to be a ship's engineer like her uncle Ashley. He told her some things and she had listened to his friends talking. Bertha was not like the other girls who shut their minds when the subject was obviously something technical. Or something women were not normally interested in. Like engines, motor bikes, guns, brands of whisky.

She rubbed her finger over it, shut one eye and looked down its axis to see if it was bent. Felt the ends. They were hacksaw-cut, she was sure. And filed off after that. Mild steel. Not stainless or plated.

Cleaned and oiled.

She was convinced it was just an ordinary small tube cut off in a hurry.

So she turned her attention to the paper. Learning from the customs men she smelt every part of it. Only the smell of old newspapers and oil. A trace of *kretek* perhaps. She gave up, wrapped it neatly and was about to put it in her handbag when she thought of handing it over to Rais for Mr. Vandyke. No, that's not my instructions, she reminded herself and put it away.

When she handed it to Mr. Vandyke the next morning she said to him, "Mr. Vandyke, next time you ask me to bring anything for you, you must tell me what it is. The customs questioned me."

"What did you tell them?" he asked interrupting, his eyes narrowing.

"Nothing. Said it was for my dad." He smiled. "Good girl. You have developed commercial discretion. Never tell anyone anything they don't need to know."

The words rang a bell somewhere in her head. Norbert Fenton used that phrase once. "Need to know." Or "need to know basis" was the phrase he used. Norbert was in the army.

"What is it anyway?" Bertha asked.

He looked at her without replying.

"What is it?" she asked again.

He looked hard at her. "OK. I'll tell you. But you must keep it a secret. There are all sorts of strange things in this world. We have to live with them. Even though we do not understand them at times." He saw Bertha frown. He smiled and continued.

"It's part of a gun."

Bertha's eyes narrowed. She looked blank for a moment then she made a decision. She had been standing in front of Mr. Vandyke's desk. She walked briskly to the door, shut it and returned to the desk. She sat down on the chair in front of Mr. Vandyke.

He watched her with some discomfort. His eyes were filled with anticipation waiting for what she was going to say.

"That's not true, Mr. Vandyke. I know something about metal

finishes and something about guns. That is not part of a gun."

"Bertha, you surprise me. I never imagined."

"Is it the wrapping?"

A wide grin of relief and delight spread over his face.

"Bertha, you're wonderful. Just the girl for me!" He leant forward and continued.

"I've been looking for someone I can trust. Someone with a good general knowledge, who notices things and above all, someone who thinks. And that person must be able to keep secrets. I think that's you ..."

He let that sink in. "I've thought you had all this in you and your reactions to this little parcel business now convince me. Bertha, you and I are going places."

Bertha looked at him like a hawk. "I deal in many items of defence equipment. Not guns but other things. You've seen the code words in the cables. It is a business in which no one gives away information for free and no one talks."

He paused to light a cigarette. And suddenly she recognised the peculiar smell of his cigarettes. She had always thought it was some expensive, though evil smelling Dutch kind of cigarette. Now she knew. It was the Indonesian *kretek*.

"You have shown discretion, sharp observation and quick thinking in the little business with the parcel ... I am so pleased, Bertha ... Now I am going to remain mysterious for the moment. But it doesn't mean I don't trust you. I can't tell you now."

His face was serious. "I promise you that I will tell you about this in four months time. Go back to your desk and put it in your diary. If I forget, ask me. It is a promise."

"Thanks for the trust Mr. Vandyke. And for telling me about your business. I understand the 'need to know' basis of operating."

His brows raised. She stood up. But before she walked out she asked, without waiting for the answer, "A decoy?"

The whole world was changing. The pain of Carl ditching her. The wonderful Jakarta trip. Now this. She sat at her desk for a long time thinking. Then she stirred herself into action, took out her diary and marked the page four months ahead with "ASK HIM."

While Bertha's situation at the office had taken a sudden turn, Sheelah's job continued at the same even humdrum pace. But there were rumblings deep down inside Sheelah. She had been there for more than ten years now. She had risen from typist to the sales supervisor's steno. And on to a division manager's secretary. The division had grown and she was now in a way a small office manager, though her designation was still secretary. Sheelah had learnt a lot in those ten years. One thing she knew now was that she held a position that was held by much older Eurasian women in other companies. And most of these women who were secretaries to division managers or general managers were still single. It was almost a pattern. But it was not that. It was the fact that she had virtually reached her limit in the Borneo Company. The move from secretary to executive was quite impossible. Sheelah knew she had everything a senior executive needed except a university degree. She was happy there. She basically was not very ambitious. But the static humdrumness of it all rankled in her. Maybe it was something to do with sex and love, not the job.

She was earning good money. Very good money by Eurasian standards. If she had told anyone what she was earning it would have gone round like a forest fire. It would have put off any guy who was thinking of wooing her. Or it would have attracted the "money diggers," as Rita called them. In the late fifties, when only the rich Chinese could afford to go to Europe for a holiday, Sheelah was able to go away once in two or three years. It made her different from her circle. It brought her closer to the expatriate circles because she had been to this play or musical and knew the Lyons Corner House at Marble Arch and all that. There could be some common small talk to start off with strangers she met from Europe. Or Australia. But although she had periodic social contact with the expatriates, she still had not met an American. Nor a Canadian. She "lumped them together," as Rita would have said. But in her heart of hearts she did not really want to move in that circle of transient Europeans.

She was as successful as a girl in her circumstances could be, but the feeling that she was just coasting along kept simmering inside her. It was there. But it was not disturbing enough to do something about it. One night, at Zainul's brother's wedding, sitting drinking ice cream soda and wishing she could drink a beer with the three expatriate men who were there, she sat back and said to herself, "It's the Malay culture we have inherited. The *tidak apa*, the laid back attitude, the *apa boleh buat* ... the fisherman's philosophy." They fought the elements when they had to. But they knew they could not take them on when the sky was black, the winds howling and the sea frothing angry. Yet they laughed and danced more often than the Chinese or the Europeans. Life was always good. The pains that came were inevitable. That was the way of the seas and the gods.

Apart from the job, she was soaring to greater heights on the hockey field. The GSC was building not only a Straits reputation but a regional name under her captainship. She had found that Rodrigues girl, coached her and fired her with a drive that was almost invincible. With their crack left-winger and a goalkeeper that was almost mad with her antagonism against the opponents whoever they were, and that stalwart, Patience, playing cooly with her mind, a perfect centre half, the team would go up and up. Only the Indians. We've got to learn from them.

Ah ... Bertha. She was surprised at the girl. Bertha turned out to be not only an extraordinary winger but as an extraordinary person. And Ethel ...

No one in the GSC but Sheelah knew that Ethel worked as a labourer in the GH kitchen. Ethel had so much confidence in herself but she knew that the last thing she should tell the GSC girls was she was just a bloody kitchen hand. Sheelah understood.

Sheelah pitied her plight. But she knew she should not show it. One day, when Sheelah was looking at the jerseys after a game sorting out those that needed mending, she saw Ethel watching her. When Ethel caught her eye she came up to Sheelah and said, "Most of them only need a stitch or two. Who does that?"

"I send them to a tailor in Middle Road."

"Save your money … I'll do it."

So Ethel started doing the minor repair-stitching for the team's jerseys and skirts. Sheelah saw that her workmanship was good. One day, when she was telling the office *peon* to take down the curtains for dry-cleaning she suddenly thought of Ethel. With her skill at sewing she could sew curtains for people. Sheelah started asking her friends and getting small jobs for Ethel. Ethel came to the office to pick up and drop off the work. There was no other way Sheelah could contact Ethel. Mondays at five o'clock. That was the agreement. Just a snappy exchange of information. No social chatting. Ethel came and went. And delivered the goods on time. And no one complained.

One day Ethel said to her, "Thank you, Sheelah. Dis work helps me to get some extra money. Dis year I can buy my useless blerdy Ma a bottle of brandy for Christmas. That will make her happy."

On the next Monday, Sheelah said that the GSC would pay for the work Ethel did on the jerseys. Ethel's face blackened. "I tole you I would do it for der club. I doan wan' money." It was shot out with annoyance. Anger, perhaps. Sheelah regretted that she had raised it.

All this was kept as a secret between Sheelah and Ethel. Sheelah kept the secrets entrusted to her. Whether by her boss or her friends. "She's an introvert. That's her problem," Mrs. B said to Faith Moss. "No one will ever know what goes on in that mind of hers. Mark my words, Faith, that's the type of girl she is." Faith clucked. "Sk, sk, sk …" But there was no point talking about Sheelah Cornelius. Half the time you didn't know where she went, or with who or what she was up to.

Then one day, Faith picked up the hottest news one could ever hope to hear. Like Mrs. Stoppard, Faith earned a little "pocket money," as she called it, selling pickles. But she did a "Roumania" pickle better than anyone else in Singapore. She knew. She was at the Eber's and they had vistors. The D'ranjos from Penang. Mr. D'ranjo was a chief engineer on a Blue Funnel boat. He was rich.

The D'ranjos went to Europe every three years for their holidays. Like the Europeans. He was talking loudly as Faith waited for her change. "Guess who we saw in Paris ... As we were having breakfast in the hotel. They were paying their bill. Kathlene and I were sitting where we could see the desk. Carl Westerhout. That Malacca fellow. And guess who was with him, Sheelah Cornelius. You could have knocked me over! ... After breakfast Kathlene asked the receptionist, 'Weren't those people from Singapore?' She said 'No ... Not from Singapore but near your country ... Malacca. You know them? Mr. and Mrs. Westerhout?' ... What a coincidence!"

Faith dropped the "shillings" on the floor. She was almost trembling with excitement. She went to Vicky Desker's immediately, "Vicky! I've just heard something terrible. Ghastly! Absolutely shocking! Really sordid!"

The news went around Eurasian Singapore. It so happened that Faith had heard it on a Saturday, so it went around faster through the Saturday evening crowd at the SRC and the coffee groups at the Catholic Club at Queen Street and Joseph Bakers after the three masses on Sunday. Sheelah Cornelius! Well! Of all people!

Maisie Boyle was not one of the girls who "nattered away" over innumerable cups of coffee. In fact, Maisie never knew what was going on. She was a simple person. Who went around with whom did not matter to her. But the whisper surprised her. She had followed Sheelah Cornelius's hockey successes with a community pride in the *Straits Times* and *Free Press*. So the whisper stuck in her mind. She was standing at the bus stop on Monday morning when Bertha came up. Maisie was later than usual that day. They were nodding acquaintances. But she knew Bertha. The wizard left wing of the GSC. She told Bertha about the whisper she heard yesterday. Then the trolley bus came. Bertha was waiting for the Tay Koh Yat bus. She waved awkwardly. Maisie did not look at Bertha's face.

Monday was Ethel's call day at the Borneo Company Building. With a bag slung over her shoulder in faded blue denim jeans, Ethel walked out of the lift and down the parquet paved corridor to Sheelah's plush office. As she approached she saw Bertha Rodrigues standing up in front of Sheelah's desk. Bertha was shouting at Sheelah. Ethel heard the words with shock and horror.

"You stinking fucking bitch! Bastard! Bitch! … Swine! Pig! … You two-faced bloody bitch. BITCH!"

Ethel moved at once. She rushed up and clamped one hand over Bertha's mouth and grabbed her arm in a grip of steel with the other. She saw Sheelah's face pale. She saw Sheelah swaying with the shock of Bertha's loud abusing and cursing. She saw the open mouths of the others in the office beyond sitting up straight in their chairs. And she felt Bertha's body trembling uncontrollably with rage.

She dragged Bertha still shouting at the top of her voice to the lift. She pressed the buttons and thought, "Damn, the curtains are due today …" The lift was empty. She grabbed Bertha by the shoulders and shouted at her. "Berta'! Control yourself!" But Bertha was still shouting, "You bloody Bitch! Bitch!" She slapped Bertha across the face with the full force of her heavy hand and her swinging arm. It made no difference. The lift stopped. She dragged Bertha out of the lobby into the streets to a backlane behind the Borneo Company Building. Bertha was still shouting "Bitch! Bitch!" She pushed her against the backyard wall of some shophouse backing on to the lane. "Bastard! Bastard!" Ethel forced her body against Bertha's. Their hips were touching. Then she pressed her mouth on Bertha's, as the last syllable of "Bastards" was spat out. Bertha struggled. She felt the warmth of Ethel's body and mouth. She moved her head to free herself. But Ethel's wet mouth was there, her tongue penetrating into Bertha. Suddenly the tornado that was roaring inside her dropped. Her insides churned. She seemed to fall down and down through space. Only Ethel's soft mouth on hers … Oh Ethel … Ethel, Ethel … Oh God!

~ Chapter Seventeen ~

A Wedding

Two weeks later, Sheelah won a large prize in the Irish Sweepstake. It was illegal to sell the tickets in Singapore but it had been going on for years. How that particular sweepstake became popular in Singapore no one could explain. There were nasty rumours that the De Lasalle Brothers had first introduced it.

Sheelah had the contacts to move the money in the right way after putting some aside in Lombard's. What she brought to Singapore she declared as casino winnings. She had proof that she had been to France, Paris and Monte Carlo earlier in the year.

She resigned from the Borneo Company and started a small business of her own. Nobody quite understood what it was. She said she was a representative of a British publisher and she bought and sold rights and translation rights on their behalf. What everybody knew was she now drove around in a brand new Sunbeam Alpine. The car that had the electrical switch for the overdrive.

The old folks shook their heads and said that the ways of God are not what they used to be. For Sheelah was the guilty party. It was clearly her fault that Bertha blew up and created that dreadful scene at the office. More dreadful in view of Sheelah's senior position there. Just like her mother, they said, recollecting the incident between Mary and Mrs. Balhatchet. Just like her mother, hot-headed and impulsive, they said forgetting that neither Mary nor Bertha had ever lost their temper in public before. It was in her blood, poor girl.

What they didn't know was that Bertha had telephoned Sheelah the following day. "I just rang to say I'm sorry ..."

Sheelah didn't say a word. "Did you hear me?"

"Yes."

Bertha put down the telephone.

Bertha was now busy with something else. Mr.Vandyke had called her in on that Monday and told her he had fixed up with a driving school for her to get driving lessons. He wanted her to get a licence so that she could run errands for him. It pleased her. Learning in company time too. And to top it all Mr. Vandyke had said that he was going to get another small company car. They were getting so many visitors now. He could let Rais take them around in the Morris and he or Bertha would then drive the new car when the Morris was tied up. He was thinking of getting a little Austin. He wasn't sure yet. Bertha told him that her cousin had one and was quite happy with it.

The driving lessons distracted Bertha a little from the thoughts that churned inside her. One of the most painful was stopping her regular hockey practice and games. She could not face Sheelah after that terrible scene. She had not gone to the GSC field in Serangoon road since that day.

She met Ethel now and then and a bond developed between them. But there was a gap because their different interests and circles kept them apart, limiting the intimacy between them. Bertha also kept in touch with Mavis Santa Maria.

Bertha continued to go to Ben and Beryl's place regularly. Sheelah stopped her visits, to Ben's disappointment. And because of Beryl and Ben, Bertha continued to attend the family functions and move in the Eurasian social circles.

In December 1958, she went to old man Francis Bodwin's sixtieth birthday party. A birthday-cum-Christmas party, he said. It was at the Bodwin's Jalan Masjid terrace house. It was a small house but there was a long backyard garden and they had put up an aluminium awning at the back behind the kitchen and servant's room extending the roofed area. The place was packed. There were the usual greetings and kissings. Mrs. Capel greeted her warmly and chatted with her. Bertha wondered why. But Mrs. Capel had no ulterior motive. She just wanted to talk to some of the young ones that evening. She had a drink with Jimmy Wyatt and Ivy Lewis. They avoided asking why she was not playing for the GSC any more. Then dinner was ready. She helped herself to the food liberally, taking lots of *sotong* and fish-roe *sambal*. She knew the *sayor lodeh* at the Bodwin's was always terrific. Then she got bored. She went to the back garden and sat beside Mrs. Burgess on a shaky plank seat. They talked a little. Then Mrs. Burgess lapsed into silence. She was not one of the talkative Eurasian women. That's why she was out in the garden alone. The silence suited Bertha. It was also cooler out there. It was a full moon and the garden looked nice with the periwinkles they had planted along the wooden fence.

Bertha was wearing a pink suit. A coat and trousers with a white blouse. One of her fancier outfits. It suited her brown skin, Beryl had said when she first wore it. She wondered how long Ben and Beryl would stay. She had come with them.

Then a shadow fell across her. A young man was standing there. It was someone she was introduced to as they walked in. A Chinese lad.

"Full many a flower is born to blush unseen …" he said.

He bowed to Mrs. Burgess and turned back to Bertha. "Why are you hiding yourself in the garden, miss?"

"Oh … I was just hot and tired."

"Come on inside. Peter is going to play the piano. I will sing to you. Soft, sweet songs."

"Like 'Coming round the mountain?' "

"More like 'Come OUT of the garden, Maud.' We met at the door. I'm Heng."

Bertha looked at him in the moonlight. He was fair-skinned and had big brown eyes. He was an attractive man. He had a thick head of hair which was gleaming with brilliantine and fairly hairy arms. He was wearing a cream Filipino *barong* shirt. His smile was disarming.

Bertha got up. "Excuse me, Auntie. I'll go first." she said and walked back into the house with Heng.

Heng was oozing charm. But it was not in a sickly obvious way. He had a certain confidence and a swagger and to Bertha's mind spoke so nicely. They were blocked by the crowd from going to the piano in the dining room. Heng asked her about herself. Bertha had perked up when he came up to her. She told him in her style that she was the daughter of so and so and sister of … He interrupted her.

"But Bertha, tell me about you, not your sisters and cousins whom I'm sure you reckon up by dozens and your aunts."

Bertha laughed. "*Pinafore*?"

"I think so … maybe *The Pirates*."

"I wouldn't know anyway."

"But you recognised it as not my original."

He then asked her what she did.

"Well, I work, I've recently been to Jakarta, I used to play hockey, I'm not alcoholic."

"Don't mention that word! The other day we were at a restaurant, the Cockpit, when I told the waitress that I wanted to buy the band a drink. 'They're not alcoholic,' she says!"

They laughed. "Are you alcoholic?"

"Good heavens no. My weakness is beautiful women …"

"Like me huh?" Bertha surprised him with her finishing his sentence.

"Are you not the famous Bertha Rodrigues who knocked the hell out of the Johor ladies ?"

"Yah. But I've stopped now."

"Why?'

Bertha looked into his eyes. She thought she saw that he knew why. But she was not sure. She felt uncomfortable. He put his hand on her shoulder. It was a light touch.

"Come on, we can get through now. I must get Peter started."

"You know him?"

"Yup!"

"How come you know the Bodwins?" she asked.

Heng looked at her. She saw that he had read the unvoiced part of the question, "You not being Eurasian." He smiled.

"Hey, I know almost every Serani in Singapore. They say I'm almost one."

"Eat *belachan* eh?"

"Yah, of course. And can speak some Portuguese."

"Really? Speak to me, then."

"*Bosoku*!"

"You naughty boy! I'm sure that's the only word you know."

"Peter! Come on, man. Get it going. I wanna sing."

"Yeah, Peter."

The singing started and a crowd gathered round the piano. Peter knew what to play to kick off the singing. "Top of Old Smokey" was a sure thing. Then "You are My Sunshine." They were off. The requests were shouted in Peter's ear. Or someone started the first bars of a song and Peter found the key he had pitched and transposed to the key of the voice. Lynette Dunsford was there with them. She had a lovely voice. Peter knew her speciality. He played "Smoke Gets in Your Eyes."

Edgar Ross turned to old man Bodwin. "It always happens. Live music. Did you hear the gram playing this just now? No one listened ..."

Lynette's singing started the run of "slow ones." Peter played "Two Lovely Black Eyes" for the oldies. Heng knew it and sang into Bertha's eyes. She was enjoying herself. She always loved the singing. Beryl had a much better voice, but she seldom let herself go as Bertha did at parties. Heng put his arm round her as they sang "If You Were the Only Girl in the World" and kissed her lightly on the cheek after they finished, "Who's Kissing Her Now."

"Who's taking you home tonight?" he whispered to her.

"Peter! There's a request here for 'Who's Taking You Home Tonight,' " Bertha called out laughing.

"No lah! I was asking you, Bertha," Heng said in a loud stage-whisper. Everyone laughed.

Heng took her home that night. He stopped at Katong Park and kissed her. Bertha gave him her open mouth. She felt his hands on her. It was a long time since her blood had surged like that. It was a beautiful night. Heng was the perfect gentleman, she thought. So far and no further.

It was late when he started the car again. "Supper?" he asked. "Why not?" Bertha responded. They went to Bugis Street. Heng told her that she must hold his hand as they walked through the brightly lit street stalls so that other men would not lunge at her. Bertha smiled and held his hand tightly. The street stall man knew him. They had a delicious *quay-teow-goo-bak*, talked, and he took her home at four in the morning. He kissed her goodnight with passion.

Bertha had never met anyone like Heng. He was good looking. He had brains and a fluency with the English language. Unlike Carl he was hardly ever serious with Bertha. He appeared to be always relaxed and carefree. Dwelling on the nature of man, or the mysteries of religion, analysing the pattern of a musical piece or literary examination of a good book were not matters that concerned him. If you like it, enjoy it. Don't try to take it to pieces and believe that you will enjoy it more. If there's no money in it, don't waste your brains thinking about it. These were his philosophies, though he would hate you to call them philosophies. He went through life with the very minimum planning for tomorrow and thoroughly enjoyed the moment he was living in.

It was refreshing to Bertha. He was such a contrast to Ben and Carl. Or even to James, her father. Because James did worry about things that could happen. James was not what Tessie would call a thinking person but he did ponder about many things. He was as relaxed as Heng was but carried more in his head and heart than Heng did. And Bertha was like him in this.

It was not that Heng did not have the capability to think. Nor was he too lazy to think. When he decided to put his mind to something he was able to concentrate and find solutions. He played good poker. But it did not interest him too much. He preferred to stand at the tote board and take a decision within half a minute.

He was a man's man. He led a fast social life. So he picked up the latest news and scandals, the best racing form tips, the snappiest jokes and became even more popular as they all knew not only would they have a good time with him but he would be able to tell them what was the best buy in this or that and there was always something to learn from Heng.

He was gentle and attentive to Bertha. He treated her like a lady, she told Beryl. And he did this with confidence and a style Bertha had only seen in the films. He did not have Carl's shyness. Like Hadi, he was much older than she was but she could see that Hadi was never as sure of himself with the opposite sex as Heng was.

He mixed with "his own kind," as Mary would have said, and with Malays, Indians, Eurasians, and Europeans. He had learnt to adapt to the group he was with and Bertha felt there was no gap between them as she had felt with most of Ben's teacher friends. She did miss the interesting things which Carl and Ben talked about, books and psychology and all that, but Heng showed her the ways of the business world that were equally fascinating and exciting to her. Heng hardly ever read. He listened and retained what he heard. He listened to the BBC Overseas Service and could surprise her now and then with morsels of knowledge about bestsellers and musicals.

He took her to the best places in town. Mary had taught her children all she knew about European food and manners. But Mary did not know very much about the different types of brandies, cheeses and wines. She learnt from Heng.

And he drove her around in the slickest of cars. He did not try to fool her that they were his. He explained his style of borrowing the cars he had undertaken to sell.

Heng spent money freely. He didn't tell her that he spent everything he earned and sometimes a bit more. From him she learned that it was actually possible to mortgage a car.

He had a reasonable voice. "No' bad," as Ethel would have said. He sang softly to her as he drove her home from dinner or the pictures. He always knew the words. He could strum the base chords to accompany singing on a guitar.

He dressed flashily. He was especially proud of his shoes and would often tell the company he was with how much they had cost him. And how much discount he had obtained.

Heng proposed to her within four months of their meeting and Bertha accepted.

Mary raised the race question as Bertha had anticipated. "But he's Chinese."

"So what?" Bertha replied.

"She means it doesn't matter to her," James said sarcastically. He had stopped telling her off like a child.

"Is he Catholic?" Mary asked.

"Yes," Bertha replied and went on. "What is better, Eurasian and Muslim or Chinese and Catholic? What is more important, Ma, Eurasian or Catholic?"

Mary had no answer to that. Bertha continued, looking at her father, "We don't want a wedding. A big wedding, I mean."

"Besides ... with all this upheaveal, and you losing your COLA, Pa ..." Bertha added after a minute.

The new government had cut off the Civil Servants' Cost of Living Allowance.

James raised his eyebrows. He had looked forward to the day when he would lead his second girl up the aisle. To the congratulations. To the slapping on his back and telling him that he had made a wonderful speech again. Mary looked at James.

"Heng and I have talked it over," Bertha said. "In fact it is quite funny. He said that by his customs the man's family hold the big dinner. By our custom it is the father of the bride who pays. So he said we'll either have both or nothing. That way the families won't quarrel."

Neither James nor Mary thought it funny. At least he is Catholic. Thank God for that, Mary consoled herself. Then she thought of Mrs. B and smiled inwardly. "As you wish, Bertha, there will be no fuss. Times are changing. No need to stick to the old ways."

James looked at her. He couldn't understand why she had accepted Bertha's decision on the wedding so placidly.

So Heng and Bertha got married quietly in the church. They had a small reception. James saw to that. "Come over to the house after the church," he said a week before. "Ask Heng's folks and a couple of your friends." She agreed. Because it would make him happy.

So James and Mary secretly organised a buffet lunch. "Must not have only rice and curry," Mary had said. "Must also have some Chinese food." And James bought champagne. And a bottle of good brandy. I'm sure Heng's father will appreciate it, he said to himself.

It turned out to be a bigger party than Bertha had expected. Beryl and Ben and the children. Heng's parents and his sister wearing a cheongsam with a slit that caught Mary's eye as soon as she saw her. Peter, the pianist, the best man. Ethel and Mavis Santa Maria. Mr. Vandyke. The priest. Uncle Bobby. Martha, Elaine and the Armstrongs. Eric's latest, Jacquelene Goddard. Inspector Matthews, Henry Marks and Hardial Singh who had known her since she was little, with his fat smiling wife.

Hardial Singh got a little drunk and insisted on standing up and toasting Bertha and Heng. "May you have lots of little ones and may they not pluck my fruits!"

Muthu the cook gave her a present that morning before she went to the church. There were tears in his eyes as he bowed and presented it to "missi." It was a little Indian trinket.

The wedding was unforgettable because of the incident with the car keys. Peter was giving James's car keys to Eric. He had to go to the *kedai* to get more ice. Eric was standing at the top of the steps on the verandah. Peter threw them to Eric but they went right up onto the roof. There was a great to-do. The ladder was not long enough. Heng had the brilliant idea of driving the Morris Minor up to the steps and putting the ladder on the roof of the car. An old gunny sack was needed to ensure that the ladder would not slip. Ropes to tie the ladder. Hands to hold it. Warnings and worried words of caution from the women.

Hardial Singh volunteered to go up the ladder. They said he was too heavy. He insisted that he was not. James had to take him aside and give him another whisky to console him. "Since you are the one who caused all the problem, you should go up," Eric told Peter. But eventually Eric went up the ladder and with advice from dozens of voices, the keys were retrieved and the situation was saved with another block of ice from the *kedai*.

It was a good wedding, after all, James said to Mary that night.

Heng had rented a small flat at Lorong Stangee from his friend Cheng Bok. They rented the barest necessary furniture. Heng's mother had insisted that they have their own bed and had bought them a double bed with a Dunlopillo mattress. They were settled.

~ *Chapter eighteen* ~

Dinner in Perth

It was my last night in Perth. I had asked Ray and Sue, John Peters and Sylvia and Old Joe out to a Chinese restaurant. Old Joe had decided which restaurant. To my surprise, Ray brought a couple of bottles of wine. I was not used to wine with Chinese food. In fact, I believe that one should not drink wine with Chinese food because of the changing tastes as the meal progressed. It was some Western Australian riesling. I though it went well in spite of my prejudices.

Sylvia looked marvellous in a blue dress with bare shoulders. I couldn't take my eyes off her all night. I had met Sue briefly a few days ago. She was a big-structured, open, friendly, down-to-earth person. I liked her.

Old Joe had a batik shirt on. It looked incongruous here in Perth where sports shirts, open neck things seemed to be the informal wear.

The conversation started with Chinese food. Old Joe had his opinions. I discovered that Sylvia knew quite a lot about Chinese food. And about microwave cooking. And about the different types of soy-sauce. Ray told us about "long soup" and "short soup" in Melbourne.

"One day someone will find the perfect mix of Chinese food and French food," John said.

"It's been done," I said. "There's a fancy restaurant in Singapore which does it. It doesn't work."

"Because they haven't yet found the perfect mix," John countered.

As we were on food and there were four Seranis there, it was inevitable that the talk gravitated to Eurasian food. We each raved about dishes and who did what best and lamenting that some things were slowly disappearing. If the wine Ray had brought had not been as chilled and nice as it was, I would have fallen asleep.

I don't know how it arose but I suddenly heard the name Heng. It was John Peters talking to Old Joe, "You know I believe Heng attracted Bertha because he had that Eurasian flamboyance and touch of *tidak-apa-*ness."

"Like what the Malays have," Sylvia added.

"After all most of us descended from the Malays."

"Or the Indians, I'm thinking of the Ceylon Burghers."

"How is it there aren't more Eurasians descended from the Chinese," Ray asked, "seeing that there are more Chinese than any other race in Singapore and that they didn't have Islam to deter them from marrying Christians?"

Old Joe explained. We expected him to. "First and foremost, Ray, it's only now that the majority is Chinese. Second there were hardly any Chinese women around. That's how the Peranakans came into existence. And maybe there's a third ... Maybe the Chinese and European mixtures were absorbed by the Chinese. As they were in Hong Kong and Taiwan. They have a very strong culture."

"What Ray really asked is about the community. The half-castes were rejected by the Malays. They could not be reabsorbed by a half-caste marrying a Malay. So the the half-castes clung together," Sylvia said.

I had heard all this before. I was beginning to fall asleep again, when I heard Ray speak to me in a loud voice, "Robert what have you got to say about all this?"

"It's all been said," I replied. "I'm more interested in what happened to my wayward aunt."

"Wayward?" Old Joe queried.

"Well, you make out as though she was."

"Wrong, Robert. Unusual and mysterious," Old Joe said.

"Unsolved mystery," I said. "Can't you tell us more about her,

Joe?" I had got used to calling an older man by his first name. I wondered if I would do that if Old Joe was my uncle Eric.

"I told you, I don't know. No one knows the true story. I have little pieces of the jigsaw but they do not give the whole picture."

"Well then give us more pieces however jagged the edges are," Ray said.

"Did I tell you about the parcel?"

"No."

"Well you see the old bugger Vandyke sent Bertha to Jakarta. You see I know more things than most people because I used to drink with Heng."

"I see ..."

Old Joe told us about the parcel. She had told Heng.

"Then the day came when Bertha saw the 'ASK HIM' in her diary. So she asked the old bugger. He smiled and said, 'I knew you had had a terrible shock. I wanted to give you a break, a distraction. So Hadi and I made up the business about the parcel and the silly fellow put that stupid metal piece in it.' Bertha was incredulous. 'You mean you spent all that money on my trip and the extra days ... just for me.' 'Yes, Bertha,' he said."

"Looks fishy to me," Ray said.

"That's just what Heng said."

"He was up to something. I'm sure," I added.

"I don't know," Old Joe said. "You fit it in. Here's another piece. When Heng started his womanising ..."

"Yuk! What a word!" Sylvia interrupted.

"Hush, Syl," John said.

Old Joe continued, "As I was saying, when Heng started his monkey tricks again we all knew and as they say it's the wife who is the last to know. I remember poking around and questioning Bertha in a very roundabout sort of way to see if she suspected anything. But I could not be sure. Because she had two very good friends and if they heard anything they would have told her."

"But if everyone knew they were her good friends, Ethel or Mavis would not be told," I pointed out.

"Yah. So I wasn't sure. Then one day I met Heng in the Ban Chuan Bar. He was not himself. He had had a shock that afternoon. He had gone off with this Indonesian Chinese divorcee for a bit of slap and tickle at her Balmoral Road flat …"

"What moral?" I tried to be funny.

"Shut up, Robert," Ray cut my snigger off.

"When he comes down from the flat and the lift door opens on the ground floor, Bertha is standing there waiting for the lift. He is alone. Heng quickly thinks up the excuse of a buyer living there. Bertha says she is delivering a note for Vandyke. She asks him what flat he went to. He gives a number and she says, 'Then it should be that lift.' But what really worries him is that he thinks someone set her on to him. Heng is a guy with no enemies. He knows that. It only makes him more worried."

"Did she have a go at him that night?" Ray asked.

"No. She never referred to it again."

"Who do think tipped her off, Joe?" John asked.

"Her friends?" Sue asked. She had been listening to all this shaking her head. It was like a television melodrama to her.

"Could be. But someone would have had to tail Heng to know where to go. That was part of Heng's big worry. It was the first time he had been to her flat."

"The plot thickens!" Ray said sitting up and rubbing his chest with his big hands. "What more monkey tricks have you got in your bag, Joe?"

"The Pestana wedding."

"Oh yes. You mentioned that before …"

"Well, this I heard form Lydia Baptist who got it from Sarah Baker."

"Who got it from Jane, who got it from Winnie, who begot Seth, who begot Malaleel, who begot Henoch …"

"Shut up, Robert!"

"As I was saying before this young man started his blasphemous quoting from the Bible … I believe Bertha got hold of Mavis one day before the wedding and arranged with her to *chochok*. Mavis had a chat with Mildred De Souza and made her believe that Heng was crazy about her. He was having domestic trouble with Bertha, Mavis told Mildred. Poor man …

"So at the wedding she started giving him the 'come hither.' On top of that I believe that Mavis got Larry Poulier to fix his drinks. Gave him thick ones all the time. Though that I find hard to believe. Heng would have noticed it. Unless of course they put something else in … But it's not as easy to get hold of Mickey-Finns and that sort of thing as it appears to be in the films."

"Get on with it, Joe!"

"Anyway the upshot of it all was that Mildred flirted outrageously with Heng in front of everybody in the dance hall.

"Ester de Britto was standing next to me at one time. She said under her breath, I'm sorry for Bertha. But Bertha was putting on a brave front. She was chatting to all the old ladies. And dancing now and then. Laughing. I couldn't understand it."

"Neither can I," Sylvia said.

"Did they have an affair after that?" John asked.

"That's how it blew up."

"Through the grapevine information … Now Robert no wisecracks! … I pieced the story together. It appears that Mavis began to have heart-to-hearts with Mildred. And Mavis offered her flat to Mildred for one afternoon. She took the bait. Mavis let Bertha in with another key and they waited for Heng and Mildred to come out of the bedroom. Heng had put his car keys on a table in the hall as he always did at home. Bertha saw them at once. Mavis never even knew she had picked them up until later. Those were the keys of the Jag. I understand that Bertha did not throw a fit. She coolly called him a few choice words like …"

"Never mind Joe, we can guess."

"And she walked out. Heng thought he had got off lightly until he went to pick the keys."

"Huh!" Sylvia huffed.

"And she was never seen again."

"So did she run off with that Vandyke bloke?" Sue asked.

"Good heavens, no!" Old Joe replied appearing to be shocked to my surprise. He almost seemed to be on the defensive on Bertha's behalf.

"You see, what was incredible was that Bertha had made such a scene with Sheelah."

"What scene?" Ray asked.

"Oh. Didn't I tell you?" Old Joe related the blow-up-in- the-office business.

"All very sordid ..." Sue commented.

"Did they make up at all?"

"No way!"

"And did Bertha stop playing hockey for Sheelah's team?" I asked.

"Yes. But after she married Heng, the Chinese Swimming Club had a new left winger. Bertha Heng. She was off again. Whacking in the goals. She was damn good. Fast, man."

"Didn't her team meet Sheelah's team?"

"Right! And I tell you there were so many Seranis there in the crowd that day. I was there."

"Of course."

"Shut up, Rob!"

"Sheelah pulled her trick again that day. We should have expected it. She'd done it so many times. As the teams lined up for the start we saw it. She had rearranged the positions. She was playing right half. She stuck to Bertha like a leech. She knew just how Bertha would move. Bertha didn't have a chance. The GSC lost one player that day. In the sense that Sheelah did nothing else but mark Bertha."

"Who won?"

"Can't remember."

Sylvia's face hardened around her mouth. "And so all the elders said 'You see! A mixed marriage doesn't work?" she muttered sarcastically.

"Don't be like that, Sylvia," Old Joe said.

"Those days are gone now. That was the old generation. We are different now," I said to Ray and Sue, pointing to John and myself.

"Me too," Sylvia added turning her chin up.

Ray gave me a playful punch in the shoulder. "Come on, Robert. Buy us a last drink and we'll go."

"Wonder if we can get a brandy here?" I said.

"Chinese restaurant, sure can," Old Joe said.

He waved to the waiter and spoke to him in Hokkien. The man looked blank. Sylvia spoke to him in Cantonese. A smile broke over his face. They talked. He went off to the back and came back with glasses and a bottle of brandy.

"Well done, Syl," Ray said. Then he noticed that doubles were being poured. "Whoa! Go easy, mate."

"That's part of the deal. He said he had no licence to sell brandy. But as we were his personal friends we could have brandy. It would be added to the bill. The personal friends bit is what we have to say if any official comes in. But he said that since the bottle was out we might as well have doubles."

"Tell me," Ray asked after sipping his drink, "why did you blokes come out here?"

"Greener pastures," Old Joe replied.

"Don't give me that," Ray started to speak but Sylvia interrupted.

"Most of the Malaysians came because they were not happy with the political situation there. Especially the teaching of Malay in schools ..."

"But the Singaporeans?" Ray interrupted.

"Those of us who are here were not happy at home. You know the PAP government came in as a socialist government but now the poorer ones haven't a chance."

"If you haven't got brains," I said.

"Take the Eurasians," Sylvia said. "Two generations ago they were the privileged class. The palace slaves. They held the good jobs in the police, on the ships, in the schools. They were far better educated than the others. Now they are one of the poorer groups ... generally."

"Just lost their privileged status."

"So find your fortune in Australia?" Ray said.

"No. Get a far better standard of living for a reasonable effort on the job," Sylvia said.

"You, Joe. Why did you come here?" Ray pointed at Old Joe.

"Partly because my daughter was here and partly because the facilities for old people are much better ... considering cost, of course."

"And you, John."

Sylvia answered for him. "Several reasons. First the children. They'll get a better education here."

"Without the discipline," I interjected.

"Second we don't have to learn another language."

"But the Eurasians could all speak Malay before?"

"Somehow they can't now ... Or the teaching of Malay in Singapore schools is bad."

"It's also that Malay is hardly spoken now."

"Nonsense!"

"And lastly the job opportunities are open ... whether you have a degree or not."

"And it doesn't matter a damn if you've got first class honours or not."

"And you, Rob, why don't you emigrate here," Ray asked me.

"I reckon I can compete with anyone at home. I don't like the way teenagers behave here and I like my Singapore food. I'm probably not adaptable."

"Oh yes, you are. You've adapted so fast in your week here. Why, you even pay for your round now."

"Huh."

Ray continued his questions. "So the emigration has cleaned Singapore out of the Eurasians who don't like the place? All those still there are there because they want to be there."

"Or have no money to migrate ..."

"Or cannot get their papers ... migration papers, I mean."

"Or have married Chinese," I added.

"That's the solution," Ray said. "All this worrying about the colour of the skin. If the Brits and the Ports had married Chinks you would all be a dirty yellowish white and there would be no problems."

"It's thc last generation who worried about colour, Ray," I said.

""No, not the last." Old Joe said. "The one before the last."

"He's right," Sylvia said.

"Anyway, it's the brown ones who are going to be around when the hole in the ozone gets bigger ..."

"Well, Robert, thank you for the lovely meal," Sue started the goodnights and thanks. The brandies were finished anyway.

And I had had enough of Serani talk to last me a lifetime.

~ *Chapter Nineteen.*~

On the Run.

Bertha pressed the accelerator down as soon as she saw the black diagonal at the back of the speed limit sign. The Jag responded at once. She breathed a sigh of relief. It was also a sigh of pain and sadness. But she could not dwell on her plight because she had never handled such a large and powerful car. Neither had she driven on a trunk road before. She had to watch the signs. The traffic. Remember, the damn thing just leapt forward whenI put my foot down.

To make it more difficult for her, the light was just beginning to fade. She had driven the car back to their Lorong Stangee flat and packed her things. She didn't pack much. The anger was boiling inside her, but she knew she had to keep it under control. She fought with herself telling her rational mind that she must think, think, think.

She searched Heng's side of the desk and his side of the wardrobe for money. She found a wad of ten dollar notes. Probably three hundred she thought. There was no time to count. She took all her best things. As she threw them into the old case Mary had lent her to move her things to their flat, the totally irrelevant thought struck her that this was the chance to throw out what she had been wavering about discarding for months. She saw her hockey stick behind the door. She picked it up. It was almost a reflex action.

She decided that she must have a shower. It would give her thinking time. It would cool her down.

Passport. Jewels. A kitchen knife. Scissors. Screw-driver. What else? Paper. Pencils. No, no need for any book. A pillow case. It could hold things. What else? What else?

With her suitcase and her hockey bag with the stick slung between the handles, she slammed the flat door shut. Damn! I've still got Mr. Vandyke's car keys!

But the last thing she wanted to do was to telephone anyone.

She drove up the Bukit Timah Road to Johor Baru, trying to think as she drove.

I've got to think. But one roaring voice was screaming inside her. I've got to get away. Get away. Get away from this place. These people. Bastards! Bastards! All of them. Carl, the bastard! Heng, the swine! Pig!

A thousand irrelevant thoughts kept rushing through her mind. The bastards! They cut Pa's pay. The bloody PAP! Now Pa has told the *kebun* to go. He has no job. Six kids.

With her mind seething, she caught a glimpse of a large woman lifting up the top of her *samfoo* outside a rural coffeeshop near Bukit Panjang to breast feed her baby. The image lingered in her mind for a while. But she had to pass a truck forcing herself to think of the width of the Jag. She knew she had to remember it was a large, wide car.

Woodlands was there before she realised it. The customs and police. Her identity card. And she was through. Away. To the left. The coastal road. Past the mosque. Past the Istana. After that timber sawmill, the road would be clear. After that it would be all new to her.

As she stepped hard on the accelerator, she told herself that there was no need to hurry. Heng would not raise any alarm. He would go off and drink in a bar to think. He always did that when he had had a row with her or he got himself into a jam with a back-to-back car deal that went wrong. He would also be sure that she would come back to him. The bastard would probably be planning his sickly sweet apologies.

Six-thirty on the car clock. The luxury of a car-clock. Seremban or Malacca? Seremban. Two hundred miles. Average forty with this car. But in the dark? Pa came down with Joe Coombes in five hours after his last hunting trip. But Joe knew the road. Yet, he only had a Ford Prefect. Seremban. Better than Malacca. They'll think I went to KL. Doesn't matter. Heng would hesitate before he makes a report. He'll know Pa would hear of it as soon as any sergeant on duty sees the name. At any station.

Ayer Hitam? Is that on the main route?

Petrol! Oh God! I forgot to check! Oh God … Thank God.

She was on the open road now in the lingering grey twilight of Malaya. The slow fading of light of the Malayan sky dimmed, with the unwinding and dying of the fierce heat. The birds rushed out of the trees at this time. Especially the starlings. Screaming and flowing past in waves. The first hoot of the owls. There were still owls hooting in the twilight in Singapore. Bertha could recognise the hooting.

As she drove past the scattered clumps of wooden houses, she saw in the corner of her eye the men squatting around in small groups of two or three in their *sarongs* talking. The children hanging around the front steps waiting for the call to dinner. A woman with her *sarong* up to her armpits, her shoulders bare, her hair wet, struggling with two kerosene tins of water walking from the stream or the well back to her house. Walking fast. She was probably late. The family had to be fed.

The buffaloes. The goats. A bat, out early, flying straight at the car and turning up at the last moment. Insects dashing themselves against the windscreen. Leaving their death smudges on it.

Somewhere, into the depth of her soul, the calm and beauty of the evening seeped. The tension of the terrible afternoon eased. Tears welled up in her eyes. The dam that had held back the flood gradually crumbled. She took one hand off the wheel to brush the tears roughly from her eyes. They just flowed slowly without pain. Her stomach growled. She realised she was hungry.

I should have taken that Mars Bar from the fridge.

The headlight high beam led her. Like a moth led blindly to the light, she followed it. She had to concentrate. Bends suddenly came into view. The white line. Catseyes. That's what Jerry called them. Thank God for catseyes. Gleaming in the centre of the road.

Leading me.

Oh God, what would I give for a bowl of *wan-tan mee*. Or *mee rebus*. White milestones suddenly in the dark. A glint of the night sky light on steel as she passed a railway line. Thirty-miles-per-hour signs. A village. She kept her foot down right through the village. Must average forty.

She fought her body, craving for food and sleep. Her mouth was dry. She shook her head as her eyes tired. Only the determination raging inside her and the constant rippling vibrations of the engine kept her awake. The feel of the tyres on the road in her hand gripping the wheel. Then the milestone said ten miles to Seremban. Seremban. I'm almost there. Where to? Where's that hotel? Century? Century hotel? On the left. Off the main road. Turn left after the railway station. Opposite the stadium. Lemon Street. That's it! Lemon Street. Where the bus station is. That's the way Mr. Van Geyzel went. Century Hotel. Century Hotel. Lemon Street. After the railway station.

As she pulled into the hotel she remembered that her passport was still in her maiden name. She had kept postponing changing it. I'll use my maiden name she thought to herself.

But no one seemed to be bothered when she registered. A large room with the same yellowish-brown stained meranti furniture one saw everywhere in Malaya and Singapore. One picture on the wall was the only attempt to make the room look different. She unpacked the very minimum. And then she realised that she had forgotten her toothbrush. And toothpaste. A shower, gulps from the thermos flask of iced-water and straight into bed. She was too tired to eat, she convinced herself, putting the thought that she didn't want to be seen by anyone out of her mind.

She slept soundly, dreaming she had a halter round her neck. No one was holding the other end. But the halter was there. And there were men with oversized yellow boots, like Mickey Mouse shoes, dancing all round her. It was as though the Gods above, or her subconscious mind piecing together unremembered observations and random thoughts, was pointing towards the dark path ahead.

~ Chapter Twenty ~

Urgent Leave.

Ethel stood at the bus stop in her jeans and rough white tee-shirt. It had been a hard game. That Lakshimi was so tricky. Her wrists always turned so fast that the stick hit the ball at an angle one least expected. There was no point watching her stick or the way her body turned. You just had to wait for the ball. The bag seemed extra heavy on her shoulder today. She tried to think of the *murtabak* she decided to eat tonight at the coffee shop near her flat as a special treat to lift her spirits. *Murtabak* was an extravagance. Two *pratas* and the curry gravy were her usual when she chose to eat Indian. Or a *mee-goreng*.

Her spirits were down. Somehow she felt that Bertha was not herself again. That "blerdy Heng bugger." She knew the type. He just got her "on the rebound" as Jimmy used to say. But it's not my business. You never know the whole story. Why take sides. She still didn't know the whole story of Bertha's yelling at Sheelah like a Johore Street whore in the plush office. But it was not her business. She didn't ask. She admired Sheelah and she felt for Bertha like a sister. Donno why. Like I donno why I love silk and sleek racing horses even though I've never even touched a horse. No need to think about these things. The bus is late tonight. That filthy fellow blowing his nose stuff out into the drain! Aiyah!

An MG Magnette stopped just a little in front of the bus stop. A big built Malay man got out. He walked straight up to her deliberately and quickly. "Miss Ethel Richards?"

"Ye … s," she muttered.

"We want to talk to you. It's about your friend Miss Bertha Rodrigues. It's very important. And urgent." He looked at her as she reacted. "Will you meet us at the street stall over there?" He pointed to a Malay street stall in a backlane across the road. "We'll park the car and meet you there. Will you come? It's important."

"Yes."

Ethel's eyes narrowed. He was quick and direct. He must have known she would hesitate if he suggested that she get into their car. They needed her for something. Connected with Bertha? Or was that just the bait? Anyway she had nothing to lose.

Ethel stood around until the two men appeared. The other was a small man. With a small moustache. They were both well dressed in bright uncrushed shirts and trousers with the creases still visible. But not flashily dressed. The big man had a gold watch on. Looked expensive.

"I'm hungry," Ethel said as soon as they came up to her.

"Yah. We'll eat and talk." They exchanged glances. Ethel saw their eyes say, "she's going to be difficult."

There were tables and stools in the backlane. She ordered *soto ayam* and *tahu goreng*. She saw them register that her Malay was good and that she was not satisfied with one dish. They both ordered *mee rebus* and *ice bandung*. It was still early. The sun had just gone down. It was humid and hot.

The big man spoke. "I am Hartono. My friend is Mohammed." Jawa descent, she noted to herself. "Please forgive us for pushing ourselves on you like this. But it is important."

He sipped his bright pink drink. The service was immediate at these street stalls. "We know that Miss Bertha Rodrigues is a friend of yours. Miss Bertha Rodrigues is in big trouble at this moment. Not her fault. We want to help her. But we also need your help."

He paused, but Ethel pushed him with, "Go on."

"We will explain later why. But we know that she stole a car today."

"Stole a car?"

"... and is driving north up-country at this moment. She is very upset. It happened like this ..." He told Ethel about the trap Bertha had set. "But she didn't think of what she was going to do next."

And how she had stormed out of the flat and taken the Jag. And how she had later left her place at Lorong Stangee and gone over the causeway. "We don't know where she's driving to ..."

Ethel listened to every word, eating her *soto ayam*. She asked, "How do you know all this?"

"We knew that her husband was heading for a collision with her. So the boss asked us to follow her and keep an eye on her. We also kept an eye on Mr. Heng Boon Teck. We saw Mr. Heng Boon Teck and Miss Mildred De Souza go into the building. Then we saw Miss Mavis Santa Maria and Miss Bertha Rodrigues go in. We had put bugs on both cars. So when she took the Jaguar we were able to follow her, first to the house and then over the causeway."

"Your people are still following her? Now? At this very minute?"

"Yes."

"Why?"

"We will explain later."

"So? You want me to tell her to come back to her husband?"

"No."

"Then what? What you want me for?"

"I'll come to that. The point is that Mr. Heng Boon Teck reported to the police about an hour ago that his car was stolen by his wife. So she can't come back to Singapore unless she gives herself up."

"If I know her, she won't."

"We agree."

"So what? What is this all about?"

"Please be patient. This is all for your friend Bertha Rodrigues' good. Please eat." He motioned with his hands. Mohammed had already started eating. Hartono did not touch his food.

"We have a plan that may surprise you, but you will not lose out. It is this. We want to take you to Malaya to meet Miss Bertha Rodrigues. And we want to ask both of you to do a job for us in Malaya. It is not a difficult job. We will pay well."

"But I'm working at the hospital."

"We know that. We can arrange for you to get no-pay leave.

We have friends there at GH."

Ethel's eyes opened wide.

"It is a lucky coincidence. We want someone to do this work and have been looking for the right people for some time. And now we know Miss Bertha Rodrigues needs time to sort her problems out. She can do that while doing the work for us. But we need two people."

"What is this work?"

"I will explain later."

"How did you pick on Bertha?"

"Mr. Vandyke is a friend of ours."

"Mr. Vandyke?"

"Her boss."

"Oh yes, of course … the Dutchman."

"Yes, that's him … He has agreed to let us make our offer to Miss Bertha Rodrigues."

Ethel was silent. Her mind was swimming. But she ate her *soto ayam* and her *tahu goreng* while she was trying to think.

Hartono continued. He was talking slowly now. She could see the way he was looking at her watching for the smallest sign of her reaction. He was talking slowly because he saw the confusion in her.

"Tomorrow morning you apply for Urgent Personal Affairs leave. It will be approved. We will take you to Miss Bertha Rodrigues in Malaya. By car. When you are there you can apply for a longer no-pay leave. It will be granted."

"For how long?"

"Three months."

"THREE MONTHS! *Mana boleh*!"

"Not so loud please. It will be arranged. It will be like a holiday to you. And there's good money."

"I don't understand. The only ting I can do is to cut vegetables and wash pots and pans. Narting else."

"OK. This is it. You have the choice. You take the UPA and leave tomorrow. Three days. That's what you're allowed. We take you to Bertha Rodrigues. You and she talk about it. If you don't like it, we will bring you back."

Ethel looked straight into his eyes. She saw a fire in them. She believed she saw honesty. But she hesitated to agree.

He saw that she had finished her food. "I'll order another *tahu goreng*. We'll share." Then he started eating, taking great mouthfuls of *mee*, ignoring her while he ate.

Mohammed ordered the *tahu*. They shared it.

"How can I trust you?" she asked.

He put his fork down and looked at her. "How can I answer that? ... Only one way ... You can speak to Mr. Vandyke. Tomorrow morning. You have Bertha Rodrigues' office telephone number. Right?"

This was all coming too fast for Ethel.

"So many tings you said you will splain later ..."

"Yes. Tomorrow. The first thing is that you think about it and say if you agree to our taking you to Miss Bertha Rodrigues."

"What if I don't agree."

"That is your choice. You have the chance to help her."

Ethel looked hard at Hartono again. The worst that could happen is that they'll kill her. Or rape her. Why me? I'm not so great. There's more than that in this. But I must tell somebody that I am going away. Ma? No. Oh no. I know. Sheelah.

"You must not tell anyone about this. Because it is important for Miss Bertha Rodrigues." She did not show surprise at his words that seemed to follow her thoughts. He must have thought it out and anticipated her line of thinking.

He's like that fellow Rudi Lee from Medan, Ethel thought to herself. Always using the full name. But he did not give me his full name.

"I'll let you know tomorrow. Tonight I have to tink," Ethel said.

"No, Miss Ethel Richards. It will be too late. We have to arrange the car and a lot of things. It may also be too late to meet Miss Bertha Rodrigues. If we don't move fast we may lose track of her."

"What is the money?"

"At least one thousand dollars a month and all expenses paid. If you do well there is bonus."

Whew! Ethel said to herself. That's three or four times what I'm am getting. Is that the bait? An empty promise?

"How can I be sure that you will pay me?"

He shrugged his shoulders. "We can't be sure that you are the right kind of person. We take a risk too."

That was no answer, she told herself.

"So?"

"*Sebenta.*"

"Ah! You speak Indonesian? You knew I was Indonesian?"

Ethel was silent. She was not sure whether he was pleased or worried. She only knew a few words of Bahasa Indonesia. She thought she would throw that out. It worked. But now she wasn't sure how it had worked.

"OK. I'll go."

That was her way. Immediate impulsive decisions.

She considered adding a threat. But she knew she had nothing to threaten them with if they let her down. She'd take the risk, like deciding to rush out at the oncoming forward advancing alone to the goal.

There were details. Not the details of the mysterious job. But details about picking her up from her flat tomorrow morning and taking her to the hospital. She had to pack. One bag. No food. Because of the Emergency regulations in Malaya. He asked her for her IC number. And don't forget your IC tomorrow. We'll check with you in the morning anyway. Thanks. You must be tired. This must have been a shock and strain on you.

Once she was in her room her mind started racing. Must tell Sheelah. But they will be picking me up in the morning. There may not be a chance to ring Sheelah. Bertha's mother will know her house number. She walked to the coffee shop nearby where there was a phone. She started dialling and noticed a man come up to the phone and stand very close to her. It was Mohammed. She stiffened with shock.

"No need to tell anyone, Miss Ethel Richards."

I have to." She decided to put her foot down. Mrs. Rodrigues came on the phone. She asked for Sheelah's number, being careful not to repeat it for Mohammed to hear.

He realised what was going on. The name Sheelah had no doubt registered.

"Better not," he said.

Ethel looked over his shoulder around the coffee shop. It was still early and there were quite a few people there. She saw a *mata-mata* in uniform. This is it, she said to herself. If they are going to play this with force, Mohammed will have to move now. I must show them I'm not scared.

"Sheelah, Ettel here. Jus' rang to tell you that I'm going up to Malaya for a few days. So can't play tomorrow or Saturday. Three days. Will see you on Monday when I get back. If anyting happens and I am delayed I will ring you. Sick relative. Sorry, I'm in a great hurry. Have to go now. Bye."

There was no game tomorrow, nor on Saturday.

Mohammed looked at her stone-faced. She turned to him. "Tell Hartono. Tell him I must have my security also. I also tink. And tell him that I will not ring Mr. Vandyke. No need to. *Selamat malam*."

"*Selamat malam*," Mohammed responded, still stone-faced. She smiled at him.

She never liked men with that kind of small moustache.

They were there at the *kedai* the next morning, as arranged. She had her bag. As soon as she got into the car, Hartono gave her a leave form to sign. She didn't ask how he had got the form. She saw that everything was correct. As far as she knew, that is. She leant back in the back seat after that and relaxed. One of them was using a fragrant after-shave. Smelt good. Nice and fresh.

Then it was handing in the letter. Explaining it with the old sick and dying relative story. Taking it to the other office in the Admin. block. Mr. Chong seemed to have expected it. And it was done.

Back to the car. "We go now," Hartono said, "but first we drop Mohammed off at the bus stop. He's not coming."

As they drove up the Bukit Timah Road Hartono said, "I will tell you about us and all this later ... as we drive. After we have left JB. There's too much traffic now ..."

Bukit Timah, Bukit Panjang, Yew Tee. The villages drifted past the window. They were still villages, though Bukit Timah had started looking like a suburban neighbourhood centre. Ethel let her thoughts stray. She wasn't worried. She wasn't that type. She had decided, so now it was left to fate. She brooded over her circumstances of the moment and was gradually pulled back to her past, her present position.

She had put herself in the hands of these men. Or this man. Mohammed was obviously just the side-kick. Because she had nothing to lose. No future to jeopardise. Only, perhaps, her job. That wasn't so great anyway. And because she could see the world knocked people about so harshly, she knew how much helping another meant. People had such few unselfish friends. And such few grateful friends. Somehow she felt that people like Sheelah and Bertha were not like that. If she could help them, it would be something worthwhile.

In her opinion, Bertha had not been ungrateful to Sheelah. Neither had Sheelah done the dirty on Bertha. It just happened. How, it didn't matter to her. But she was sure that Bertha's outburst was against her very nature. That woman had such wild passion in her.

Funny, how she had turned to Sheelah when she was looking for someone last night who would care if she disappeared without reason. Because she was doing something for Bertha.

Was she? Or was this all a very strange plot which had nothing at all to do with Bertha, in which she was a dispensable pawn.

Yes, she was dispensable. If she was rubbed out tomorrow her mother would weep. A little. Not only because she would miss the occasional present Ethel gave her. Ethel had refused to give her money since that terrible row four years ago, when she discovered that the money she had saved by depriving herself of so much, including basic necessities, was being squandered by her mother on gambling and drink. Mostly gambling. It wasn't the row or her losing her control and swinging her bag at her mother. It was the collapse of all hope, the crumbling of an image that broke her heart after the fight that night.

Now she had adjusted to it. She had no responsibility to the woman. But she bought her mother an occasional present of liquor. That made her happy. It was no use giving her money. Some shark would win it from her sooner or later. Let her get drunk, the stupid woman. But she'll be happy for a while.

So life goes on. One day, maybe, I'll meet a guy who will really love me. Not want me like Hock Boon or Rodney. Someone like Siva but not so bloody conceited. Someone who treats me like a person. A proper ordinary person. Not like ... It's no use going over all that again.

I wonder how many men will be sitting in their small rented bedrooms hoping they would meet a girl like me tonight?

She heard Hartono breathe a loud sigh of relief as they left the customs. She looked at him. He was beginning to relax. It wasn't the traffic that was on his mind and made him tell her he didn't want to talk. Was it the police check at the causeway? It was too late for her to worry now, anyway.

They passed the Istana with the tall tower. She remembered Rodney telling her how the Japanese general, Yamashita, used it as his observation post during the battle of Singapore. The story stuck in her mind because, she said to herself, if people with all that education and brains like the British generals didn't think of knocking it down with a shell from their big guns, it only goes to show that it's not brains you need. It's thinking fast. At the right time. And believing what you think.

"Want a coffee?" Hartono asked.

"Don't min'," she answered in her brief way.

"Scudai's coming up. We'll stop there. It's a long run after that."

As he stirred his *kopi-susu* he started talking, watching her eyes closely for her reactions to what he said.

"First, I'd better tell you about myself. I am Sundanese."

"Sundanese?"

"Ah! You know very little about Indonesia. Good, now I know. Sunda is a region in the West of Jawa. So I am Jawanese and Sundanese. Have you heard of the Sunda Straits? That's the straits between Jawa and Sumatra." He paused.

"I went to school in my hometown and when I was about thirteen my father went to Jakarta. I learnt English there."

"Your English is very good. Better than mine."

"Cannot be! Then I joined the army. It was the best place to work. Indonesia is a poor country. There are not many jobs. I only got the job in the army because my father had a friend from his village who had influence. After some years, I was transferred to the Intelligence section. It was interesting. I learnt a lot there ... You want to eat something? I see *goreng-pisang* there."

They ordered *goreng-pisang*. "*Pisang Raja*. Good ... While I was in the intelligence a friend asked me to help him. He worked for one of the *cukongs*."

"*Cukong*?"

"The big Chinese *towkays*. Big, rich. Much more powerful than the *towkays* here in Malaya. His boss wanted information on a competitor. My friend had to get it. He tried to tail him but he found how difficult it was. People who read detective novels think it's easy. But it's not. So with some of my friends we got the information he wanted. It was nothing very secret. He wanted to know when the fellow saw Sutowo. How long he was there. And simple things like that. A few months later, he was back for more help. This time we asked what it was worth to his boss. So we asked for about one third of it. And so on."

Ethel was listening with concentration. Intelligence Service. What was this all about?

"Then a friend in my unit and I decided to leave the army. We had discovered a need. And a business opportunity. Something like private detectives for the business people. So we went into this business. That's how I came to Singapore. A lot of the information they wanted had to be obtained in Singapore. Who so and so met in Singapore for example.

"The funny thing was that we also found out accidentally about naughty husbands and wives. My friend wanted to use this, but I said no. We keep the aces until we need to play them for bigger fish."

He offered her a cigarette and lit it. Ethel saw that he was not using the same expensive looking lighter that he had used the night before.

"The business started growing. We needed more people. That is very difficult. You have got to find the right kind of people for this work. Then you have to train them. And I tell you, to be frank with you, you have to test them.

"A better way is to study them before you employ them. It costs money and time. But the facts can be picked up by more junior people. Later, we go into it and study the person."

"So that's how you found me?"

"No. We found Miss Bertha Rodrigues. When she was in Jakarta. Then we noticed that you and Miss Mavis Santa Maria were her good friends. I don't mind telling you now that Miss Mavis Santa Maria is not very good. Not much brains. And not reliable, I think. Also always late for meetings. Meetings with friends, I mean. So Miss Ethel Richards ..."

"For God's sake call me Ettel."

"Ethel Richards ..."

"Ettel lah!"

"Ethel then. Er, er, er ... This job. We have a client who wants us to give him details of a piece of land in Malaya. It is a lot of work. But not difficult. He wants to know every detail about the paths, streams ... even trees. At first, I thought he was crazy. Why not get a surveyor, I thought. But I know these *cukongs*. Everything must be secret. Especially in Malaya. They don't like the Malayan Chinese. Not don't like. They don't trust them. Then Pra ... my partner thought of the possible reason. Now we think he wants to build a big hotel there in the jungle."

"Jungle?"

"Not exactly jungle. Belukar, rubber estates ... We think he wants to make it a kind of a safari park. Leave nature alone. Show every detail in the rough maps of the paths in the brochure."

Hartono was watching Ethel closely.

"So we want to ask you and Miss Bertha Rodrigues to spend about three months there preparing the rough maps."

"But I doan know anyting about making maps."

"It's not making maps. It's filling in little details on maps we give you. We'll show you how. It's easy but it's living there in the bush for a long time. We'll give you every bit of help you need ... Actually, that is why we are successful. We always provide our frontline people with solid back-up."

"I see ..." Ethel murmured, trying to think.

"Malaria." she muttered and looked at Hartono.

He smiled. City girl's reaction. "No problem. Nowadays there are pills ... Let's go. We have a long way."

Back in the car, Hartono elaborated on the work. "We want an area of about ten by ten kilometres covered ..."

"What's that in miles?"

"About six by six."

"Not so big, ah?"

"No. We have divided it into a grid of two comma five kilometers square ..."

"Comma?"

"Ah, it is the European way."

"The European?"

"I mean on the continent of Europe. Holland, Germany ... So there are sixteen squares. If you take four days to do one, it will be sixty-four days. With some rest days, about two or three months."

"A lot of walking."

"Yah. But you are a strong girl. I've seen you play hockey. Very good."

"You watch hockey?"

"No. I went only to study you. I like football."

"Huh."

"We have found a small house. It is very simple but there's a well there."

"No *jamban?*"

Hartono continued to tell her more details, assuming that she had accepted the task in her mind. Ethel began to imagine herself in the little shack.

"About once a week, one of our friends will come to see you and take away what you have done. He will also bring the food and whatever you want."

"So we have to cook also?"

"Yah. No servants there!" he laughed.

"I can cook. I doan tink Berta can."

"We have also thought of that. When our friend comes he will bring something from the village. And we will give you tinned food for when you don't want to cook."

"I must eat rice every day."

"Ah! I forgot to say, we will also give you two bicycles."

Hartono slowed down as they passed the thirty-miles-per-hour sign before they came to a small village. Ethel noticed this. Not like that bus driver on the last trip. He was reckless. They came to a roadblock manned by two men in uniform who seemed to be most disinterested in the vehicles they stopped.

"As I said we have to keep all this secret. So we want you to wear *baju kurong* and *sarong*. Malay clothes."

Ethel frowned. But, on second thoughts, the image of herself in a *sarong* amused her.

"We will have to give you some training. I will do that. Maybe four or five days."

"What training?"

"How to record the details and other things."

"What udder tings?"

"Oh ... I'll tell you later."

"That is you favourite word hah?" Ethel said smiling.

"*Esok*! But we Jawanese are not like the Malays ..."

"Malayans? ... with their *besok* aller time."

"No, I meant the Sumatran Malays. It's true we wait for *esok* but when we want something we work very hard at it. Don't forget, our country has never been as easy as Sumatra and Malaya. We have too many people on our island. And volcanoes."

"Tell me about Jawa."

Hartono told her about the mountains. The beautiful mountains, he said. The volcanoes. The fertile land. But the country was getting poorer every day. They were actually producing less food per acre than before. The economy was bad.

"And your leader, Sukarno?"

"He's a wonderful man. You know, he speaks not only several Jawa dialects and Bahasa Indonesia but also Dutch, English and even some French and German. And he is a very clever man. Only he can keep the PKI in control. And stop the army people from fighting each other ..."

"PKI?"

"Partai Komunis Indonesia ... Dangerous people."

He told her how the *ra'ayat*, *rakyat*, he pronounced it, respected and loved Sukarno. "Bung Karno," they called him. Brother Karno, shortening Sukarno in familiarity. Many rural people thought he was the reincarnation of Raru Adil, the mythical prince with a magical sword who would come down from heaven and save them.

"But didn't he help the Japanese during the last war?"

This seemed to touch a raw nerve in Hartono. He told her how Sukarno was imprisoned by the Dutch and released as Indonesia fell to the Japanese. That Sukarno had appeared to work with the Japanese occupation administration and used them while he was building up his influence and planning a unified Indonesia. The fighting with the Dutch after the war. Independence with the help of America in the United Nations. Differences between the leaders.

Ethel dozed off.

~ Chapter Twenty-one ~

Singapore-Eurasians

Ben was reading one evening, when Beryl came out of the kitchen. He was sprawled on his favourite chair when she had gone behind to make her very special lady's fingers in a *belachan* sauce dish. She thought he was looking tired. He had been to some district meeting to organise a mass drill display. He said he had met Joy Ferroa of McNair Primary there. She had lent him a book. A book about Eurasians.

"Joy says that her ancestor Tomas Ferroa is mentioned in it."

"What you want to read about the Serani for? Who wrote it? Serani don't write books ..."

"Some German fellow."

"How can a German fellow write about Serani!"

"Don't be silly, Beryl, anybody can write about anything provided they study the subject."

"You can't write about Chinese poetry. Not if you studied it for a million years. It's the feeling, lah."

"That's poetry, Beryl. This is a serious sociological book."

"Probably mixes us up with the Ceylon people and Anglo-Indians and calls us half-castes."

"Aiyah! Don't be like that."

When she came out of the kitchen she knew something was wrong. One look at his face was enough for her to tell, after all the years she had followed his highs and lows. Ben was sitting up straight on the chair now. He had a pencil in his hand. There was a notebook beside him. She knew he was in one of his rages. Like when they transferred Gregory Teo out of his school.

"What's the matter, Ben?"

"This bloody idiot!"

"Please!"

"This chapter on Singapore Eurasians ... utter crap."

"Let me see ..." She took the book from him. "Ah ... There's the bit about Tomas Ferroa. Ah ... and Jose D'Almeida, that's Grace's ancestor, you know ... Sush! Bar girls?"

"It's true, Beryl."

"But only the black sheeps ..."

"Sheep."

"Slip of the tongue ... Servants? Oh! For God's sake! No Serani will work as a servant ... except perhaps for a Serani. But for a Chinese! For God's sake!"

"See what I mean?"

"What else? ... The Portuguese, I presume he means Eurasians, moved to the Tanglin area? Is that true, Ben? I never heard of that."

"I don't know. I never heard of a Serani living in Tanglin either. In those days. But read what he says further on. The typical Eurasian lived in the Tanglin area. That book was written in ... Oh it makes me sick. And this typical Eurasian worked in a military hospital. There were no more military hospitals then!"

"Eh, eh, eh ... Listen to this. 'They had no proof of their European origin.' The face, man. Didn't the fellow see any Serani?"

"Hallo, hallo, hallo ..." Joe Coombes had walked in.

"Brought the *tembok* you wanted, Beryl."

"Hello, Joe. Drink?"

"Ta, the usual ... What's all this excitement?"

"It's this book. All about Serani."

"Serani? Who in the world wants to write about us?"

"Well it's not only about us. It's about Eurasians all over South East Asia. But it's this chapter on Singapore Eurasians that is full of utter rot."

Beryl was still reading, "Listen to this, '... the Anglo-Eurasians and the Portuguese Eurasians, who had hardly anything in common.'

Aiyah! Joe Coombes you have nothing in common with us Portuguese Eurasians."

"Oh. Am I Anglo-Eurasian?"

"Yes, you speak fancy. You go to the French church."

"Oh, so that's it?"

"And this. Listen to this, Joe '… The Portuguese Eurasians were admitted as guests at functions strictly reserved for whites.' There's more '… They wrote books about the problems of being Eurasian,' that's the Anglo-Eurasians."

"Who wrote books on Serani, Ben?"

"Dunno …"

"And he says that the majority of Eurasians wrongly claim to have descended from the Portuguese …"

"What is true," Joe said, "is that the old Portuguese blood has been diluted. No doubt. But the ancestory is there."

"You think the old people would have accepted any Goanese coming here with a name like Da Costa into their midst?"

"Let's have a look," Joe asked Beryl and stretched out his hand for the book.

"Here, read this," she said as she handed it over, pointing to a paragraph.

Joe put on his best reading voice, " 'Between 1920 and 1940, more than 50 per cent of doctors in Singapore were Portuguese Eurasians.' Surely, Ben, that is not true. I don't mean about the Portuguese Eurasians. Fifty per cent were Eurasians? Cannot be lah!"

"Hey … Wait till the Government sees this shit. Sorry, Beryl. But it is shit. 'The Chinese rulers' of Singapore. Where did you find this book?"

"Joy Ferroa lent it to me. She found it at MPH," Ben replied.

"Not that bit, Joe, on top."

Joe read from a paragraph higher up. " 'They, the Serani, believed that the new rulers would rigorously eradicate the last vestiges of Europe from Singapore and that the community of Eurasians would be left in a void.' " He stopped reading and looked at them. "Who is this clown? Of course the PAP went on a yellow culture purge after 1959. But that wasn't European culture. That was *Playboy* and all that crazy new stuff?"

"Yeah!"

"Ferchrissesake ... They didn't rename it Lee Kuan Yew Theatre, did they? We've still got the Victoria Theatre ... And Winstedt Road, Orneat Road.. And all that funny walking to and fro between the Supreme court and the Cathedral."

"Your drink's there, Joe," Ben said.

Joe mumbled a brief "ta" but he ignored his drink. He kept on scanning the book. "Position of power! I ask you when did the Serani ever have a 'position of power'? Hey ... not only we get the shit ... listen to this. 'The Malays specialise in preparing and selling food.' Hey I must send this to Rahim ..."

"Hang on. That's Joy Ferroa's book. Not mine."

"Stay for dinner, Joe. Pot luck. With *kachang bendi sambal*."

"Yah. Dunno if I can eat now. This is the bloody limit ... Special Portuguese Eurasian bomohs! ... SHEESH! Listen, 'As a consequence, special Portuguese *keramats* have shot up everywhere ...' Oh boy! This really takes the cake! Listen, 'On Fridays or on the thirteenth day of the month they move about very cautiously.' For God's sake, who is this idiot?"

Ben had been grinning and listening. He was delighted that both Beryl and Joe had agreed with him. It cooled him down. He had to point out what Joe had missed.

"Did you see that bit about the Portuguese in South East Asia, he means the Eurasians of course, throwing out everything that is purely decorative?"

"Oh cripes! I spend half my life telling my good woman to throw out her sentimental junk. She's a real *ma burok* with the old things. You damn well know, Ben, every Serani house is cluttered with useless old bric-a-brac and ..."

"It's these accoutrements that help the Serani to stay Serani," Beryl interjected.

"Even that word is part of it," Ben said.

"But I didn't come here to discuss Serani, Ben."

"Thanks for the *tembok*. I forgot to thank you," Beryl said. Joe had told her that they had a spare one in the house. A small one. Just the size that Beryl needed.

"I came to ask if there's any news of Bertha. I heard from Alf Matthews that Heng put out a report on her stealing his car yesterday evening."

"Can a husband do that?" Beryl asked. "I thought everything was common property."

"Ah, but Heng's report said that Bertha was in collusion with persons unknown. The bugger's a *lawyer buroh*, you know."

"James told us. No news all day today. The Malayan police are looking out for the car. Either KL or Malacca, they said," Ben said.

"What about Seremban?" Beryl asked. "She has friends there."

"I don't think she went alone," Joe said.

"No, Joe. I am sure she went alone in one of her rages."

"Rare rages," Joe added.

"No. She has been getting edgy these last few months."

"Whaddyer 'spect," Joe commented.

"If she was alone she would not make KL," Ben said after a little while. "The police found out from one of the neighbours that she left about four o'clock."

"How did they know?" Joe asked.

"Eeeeh ... It's not every day a Jag is parked outside Lorong Stangee, man."

Joe saw Ben's counter of his statement. He added, "Heng only took over the car that morning. Alf told me."

Joe looked at Beryl, "Do you think she'll come back?"

"Yes," Beryl replied. "But she'll not go back to him." She looked into the distance and spoke again. "Ben, I think we should offer to let her stay with us when she returns. The old folks are a bit trying these days."

"We'll see ..." Ben mumbled. But she knew he would be delighted to have Bertha. She wasn't sure if she would. Not all the time. But she's my sister.

The phone rang. Beryl went to it. "Hello, Pa." A silence as she listened. "Ipoh! But she's never been there!"

Beryl returned to the drawing room. "That was Pa. The Malayan police have tracked the car. But they haven't found it. Or her. The petrol station people remembered a Jag stopped for petrol."

"A good looking bird, is what they remembered," Joe said.

"Kajang and Slim River. And someone saw the Jag on Kampar Road in Ipoh. I'm surprised."

Ben had been frowning. "Something funny. Surely the police have noticed it. If you fill up at Kajang, you won't need to fill her again at Slim River."

Joe put in his thoughts, "She probably didn't fill her up to the top. Maybe she was short of money. Or she didn't realise how much the Jag drank."

"Hmm ... maybe," Ben said.

"Guess they're checking the hotels in Ipoh," Joe said.

~ Chapter Twenty-two ~

Meeting in Malaya.

Bertha woke up early. She was desperately hungry. It never occurred to her to order breakfast in her room. She dressed quickly into jeans and a rough shirt and went downstairs to the dining room. She had seen where it was the night before. Breakfast first. Then think, she told herself.

The room was almost empty, except for two Malay men sitting at a table with coffee cups in front of them. She noticed how full the ashtray was. Service is not so good here, she noted. She ordered a full breakfast. Porridge, bacon and eggs and everything.

As the Hainanese boy walked away with the menu, she looked across the room at the two men. One had left. But his pack of cigarettes was still on the table. She caught the eye of the other, a large man. He was looking at her. He dropped his eyes at once. His green shirt would look good on Heng, she thought to herself. The bastard.

The waiter appeared at the door walking directly to her table. Now what, she said to herself. Run out of tomato juice, I guess. But his message was quite unexpected.

"Miss Rodrigues. Phone call. From Singapore. A Mr. Vandyke."

Mr. Vandyke? It startled her. How did he know where she was? She got up from the table at once and went to the reception desk. It WAS Mr. Vandyke.

"Bertha, don't be alarmed. I have found out where you are. But only I know. So don't worry. I also know what happened yesterday. You did the right thing, Bertha. Now listen. I have friends in Seremban. They are waiting to contact you. I have given them clear instructions. You can be quite frank with them. A Mr. Siswono will contact you. He is now at the hotel. He is wearing a green shirt. There is another man with him. They are there to help you, Bertha. You will also meet another man, a Mr. Hartono, later and he will put forward a proposal. I think you should accept it. But it's your decision. Are you all right, Bertha?"

"Yes, Mr. Vandyke. Thank you. But how ...?"

"Siswono will explain. I must ring off now. All the best."

"Thank you, Mr. Vandyke."

The man in the green shirt smiled at her when she appeared at the dining room doorway. She went up to their table. The other man was back at his place. "Mr. Siswono?"

"Yes, pleased to meet you Miss Bertha Rodrigues."

There was a brief silence. He smiled at her trying to show a benign friendliness. "May we come over to your table and talk."

"Yes. Please."

"This is Adam." He indicated the other man.

"Were you waiting long for me?" Bertha asked.

"Adam waited first. From seven o'clock. I came later."

"Seven! It's nearly ten now ... I'm sorry."

"Not your fault. In fact, you must be very confused about us. So let me tell you quickly. Mr. Vandyke's friends found out about your trouble yesterday afternoon with Mr. Heng Boon Teck. He was very worried so he asked his friends to keep an eye on you. They followed you all the way. And that's how Mr. Vandyke knew you were here."

"Followed me? In a car?"

"Yes."

"I never saw a car tailing me ..." She tried to think back.

"I think Mr. Vandyke's friends put a bug on the car while you were at your flat packing. That's what I think."

"I see ..."

"Please eat your breakfast. You must be hungry."

"I am. Excuse me." Bertha wolfed down her porridge and her eggs, her mind going through the implications of Mr. Vandyke's phone call and searching for the Indonesian connection.

"We are Indonesian," Siswono said.

"I thought so … from the name," Bertha remarked.

"We work for a good friend of Mr. Vandyke's. A Mr. Hartono."

"I see … Mr. Vandyke mentioned him," she said.

"We know your country fairly well. But not so well. You must excuse us."

"My country?" she asked. "You mean Singapore?"

"No. Malaya."

"Well … It's the same. Both are different from Indonesia."

"You've been to Indonesia?"

"Only Jakarta."

"It's very backward now. But Jakarta will rise up again one day."

"I found the Jawa people so friendly."

Both men grinned broadly. They're easy to please, Bertha thought to herself. But the smiles were spontaneous and genuine.

Siswono had very obviously switched to small talk while she ate. He turned to Adam and said something to him in Javanese. Bertha got the gist of it. Adam was asked to call someone called Azziza.

Adam left the table with an "excuse me, please" and a bow. She heard him talking loudly but briefly on the phone at the reception desk.

"Mr. Vandyke said that you would help me? I'd be grateful."

"Oh please, don't thank us. It is a pleasure to meet you. But I know. You want to know the details I suppose. I'll tell you. Please excuse my eating while you are talking. Oh! … talking while you are eating." He chuckled at his slip.

"That's OK. I'm almost finished."

"You want to order anything more? You have two meals to catch up with."

"No thanks. That's fine."

"More coffee?"

He called the waiter. Adam came back. More coffee was poured.

"The first problem is the car. I have to tell you that there was a police report yesterday evening that the car was stolen. So the police will be looking out for the car. A Jaguar is easy to find. We will take the car." He grinned. "And we will have some fun leaving a false trail for the Malayan police." Adam chuckled. He really enjoyed the thought Siswono had raised.

"Have you got anything in the car?"

"I don't know. I think I took everything of mine into the hotel. I'd better check ... But what happens to me then?"

"We will take you to another hotel. And register you under another name. Kuala Lumpur is best for the time being. It is a big place."

"I have friends there," Bertha said.

"Not to worry. I'm sure that Mr. Hartono has worked out something."

He offered her a cigarette. Bertha looked at him as he did so. It was quite unusual. Most people didn't expect a woman to smoke. She refused. "I don't smoke, thank you."

"Mind if we do?"

"No. Go ahead." She waited for more details of their plans for her.

Siswono looked at the door. A young woman had come in. Bertha almost gasped as she saw her. She was her height, her colour. She had her hair done in the same way. Her lipstick was the colour Bertha used. Only Bertha had not put on any lipstick that morning. She wore a similar tee shirt and blue jeans. Her features were similar but anyone knowing Bertha well would not have mistaken her for Bertha. This was it, she said to herself. The decoy girl.

Azziza grinned from ear to ear. Half-laughing, she put out her hand to Bertha. "I'm Miss Bertha Rodrigues today." Bertha grinned back at her. "Then I must be Azziza." She saw that Siswono and Adam were enjoying the exchange.

Siswono turned to Bertha abruptly. "How did you know she is Azziza?" "I heard Adam on the phone," Bertha replied at once.

He glared at Adam. Then he turned round and smiled at Bertha,

"You are very observant." Bertha shrugged her shoulders. "I am pleased that you are so sharp," Siswono said.

They discussed the plan openly with Bertha. Azziza was going to drive to KL, stopping on the way to buy fruit. And to get petrol at Kajang. At KL someone would empty the tank and she would pick up petrol again at Rawang. At both petrol stops she would chat and joke to the attendants. Probably buy something.

"Bertha doesn't smoke," Siswono said to Azziza.

She would stop again at Slim River to pump her tyres. The car will disappear at Kampar. Someone would take it to an estate where the number plate would be changed. They didn't say what would eventually happen to the car. It didn't interest Bertha either.

Bertha went to the car after breakfast and checked if she had left anything in it. Nothing. Azziza left in the Jag.

Siswono then said that he would wait with Bertha till about three o'clock when he expected Mr. Hartono to arrive.

"Where's he coming from?" Bertha asked.

"*Dari Singapura*," Siswono replied. He appeared to forget himself and replied in Malay. Bertha noted it.

"You can either stay in the room, or I can take you for a drive to the surrounding rubber estates," he said.

"Isn't it not safe to stay in the hotel?" Bertha asked.

"I can fix them so that they'll say you've left the hotel already. The car's gone."

"I have a suggestion," Siswono said as though he had had a bright thought suddenly."You rest here till twelve. I'll come back and pick you up for lunch. Then we'll go for a drive after lunch till three."

She agreed.

"What kind of food do you want to eat?" Siswono asked when he met her at the hotel. He handed her fifty dollars to pay the bill. "Give me back the change," he said in a matter of fact way. "And don't forget to take the receipt."

She hesitated about lunch. "Don't worry about eating Chinese food. I'm almost *Haji-Bir-Ham*." he said.

"What's that?" she asked.

He grinned. "That's what they say in Jakarta about anyone who eats ham and drinks beer. But I am a good Muslim. It's only that many of us over there believe that some of the less important rules are outdated. We can be just as good Muslims without sticking to the unnecessary old rules."

It was on the tip of her tongue to ask him how he decided what rules were out-dated, but she left it.

They ate at a small Indian coffee shop somewhere on the Rasah Road. She ate with her hands and enjoyed the food. The *dahl* was especially good, she said to Siswono. He told her that he didn't like Indian food very much while they were eating. They use funny kinds of oil, he said. We are not used to it. She apologised for choosing Indian. He waved her apology aside. "You're my guest," he said.

"And you're a very good host," Bertha replied smiling.

Then he drove to Port Dickson. It was a beautiful drive, Bertha thought. Not just rubber estates. There were wide open stretches with few trees and hardly any villages. "This area was a bad one at the height of the Emergency," he told her.

The tide was up when they reached Port Dickson. The sea was rough and the waves dashing against the seawalls. It looked inviting. "But the beach is not so good here," Siswono said, "It's better further up but still one has to go far out to swim properly."

"On the left is Tanjong Tuan. Far up there on our right, northwards is Morib."

"Oh yes. I've heard of it. The KL people go there to swim," Bertha said.

"Bad beach," Siswono said. He was silent for a while then he continued, "The British forces landed there after the Japanese surrendered. Because they had planned the invasion there. But when the boats came in they got stuck in the mud. It would have been a massacre if the invasion had been carried out. The Japanese would have mowed them down. They didn't have the right information. Information. Essential for military operations."

"You interested in soldiers and war and all that?" Bertha asked.

"Yes. Still a little boy at heart." He laughed.

Bertha stood there on the beach. The wind blowing her thin skirt against her. Her hair flying out wild. The afternoon sun was hot but with the sea breeze it was a wonderful feeling standing there. Only the far horizon and the frothing water at the end of the beach filled her mind. Siswono stood silent enjoying the view and the breeze.

His call came all too soon for Bertha. "Well. We'd better start back."

"Oh … this is a beautiful country," Bertha said as they drove back. He smiled, keeping his eyes on the road. "That's the trouble with you Singapore people. You are losing the feel of the soil and the sea," he said.

Talks like Ben, Bertha said to herself.

When they got into Seremban he stopped in front of a block of shophouses. They went into an air-conditioned restaurant that looked like a posh coffee shop. Bertha didn't see the name until she sat down and read it on the ashtray. Tong Fong. She ordered tea. Siswono also asked for a plate of sponge cake slices. She knew that one only paid for what one took in here.

"Now. I must tell you something so that you do not get too much of a sudden surprise," Siswono said sitting up straight in his seat. A faint smile in the corner of his mouth. "Mr. Hartono will be bringing someone you know with him."

"Who?" Bertha asked immediately. Mr. Vandyke came to her mind at once.

"Can't tell you. Like your Christmas presents."

"But Christmas presents are always nice surprises."

He just grinned.

"Huh! Won't tell ah!" Bertha said.

His back was to the door. Bertha could see the entrance. She was half way through her cake when she saw Ethel Richards walk in. Ethel saw her at once. "Berta!" she called out and rushed up to her. Bertha stood up and Ethel crashed into her. She hugged her.

"Ettel ... What you doing here?"

"Oh, Bertha. I'm so glad to see you." She released her hold and leant back to look into Bertha's eyes. "Are you all right?"

"Yes." She hugged her again.

Then Bertha saw the big man standing there smiling. Watching them hug each other. She looked at him over Ethel's shoulder and asked "Mr. Hartono?" He smiled and nodded.

~ *Chapter Twenty-three* ~

Hartono

Hartono changed the plan to go to KL. Waste of time, he said. And we want to stay away from the big roads. We'll go to Batu Pahat. The rest house there is good. Three days. Or two. Then we can go to the pondok.

Ethel understood what he was saying to Siswono. But Bertha was quite puzzled. Hartono looked around the restaurant. There was only one other table occupied. Two men and a woman. A chubby little boy about five years old was rolling a marble across the floor. Probably the couple's child.

Then Hartono described the plan to Bertha. The house in the jungle. The maps. He would teach them how to fill them in. A weekly visit from Siswono. Or someone else. If it was someone else, he would identify himself by saying that he was Hartono's brother-in-law, married to Hartono's sister. Remember that.

Bertha was stunned by the unexpected plan. She looked at Ethel and saw her calm face. Ethel must have been told already. She had obviously accepted it.

There were a lot of details. For one thing, they would have to dress as Malay women. *Sarongs*. *Bajus*. And behave like Malays. No pork. "You know how ..." he said looking at Bertha and Ethel in turn. "Nothing *haram* must be done. Not just if you see anyone looking. Make it a habit. Just in case anyone is watching. No *makruh* either."

Bertha understood. Not only the taboos of the Muslim religion, but also those of Malay customs will have to be observed.

"Ha!" Ethel said loudly. "No smoking then?"

"That's OK. Nowadays even some of the rural women smoke."

That may be in Indonesia, Bertha thought to herself, but not here. She kept quiet for Ethel's sake.

"I'm worried, Hartono, about us living alone," Ethel said with a friendly familiarity. "Tigers, robbers."

"Communists," Bertha added.

"We have thought of that. Now don't get startled. Because it's nothing. Just a reserve in case you need it."

The girls looked at him, waiting for him to continue.

"We're going to give you a gun. Just in case."

"But I can't use a gun." "Oh! No! I can't shoot," Ethel and Bertha spoke at the same time.

"I'll teach you. You are both sportswomen with a quick eye. You'll learn fast. Two days is enough."

He went to the bag he had with him, opened it and took out a paper parcel. There was a gun wrapped in it. A pistol.

Siswono picked up the gun. He weighed it in his hand. He pointed it against the wall and looked down the barrel. He rotated the wrist of the hand which was holding the gun.

"Good," he said. "I've never seen one of these Glocks."

The two men discussed the gun and their ideas of what would have been the best gun for the girls. They seemed to have forgotten the presence of Bertha and Ethel while they talked.

Bertha saw Ethel's nervous glances around the room. She could see that Ethel thought that the two men were being reckless bringing out the gun in the restaurant. But Bertha knew that in Malaya with the Emergency on many planters and miners carried guns.

"Sorry!" Hartono stopped the conversation turning to the girls. "Siswono here was quite a hunter before. He's always interested in guns."

Bertha heard the names of the models in English. She knew enough to register that these were not hunting guns.

Bertha was not quite satisfied. "What about the communists?" she asked.

"One little nine-millimetre gun won't stop them," she added.

"That's almost finished," Hartono replied.

"Yes it has." Bertha said. "But there are two areas still active. Somewhere in Perak and South Johor."

Hartono looked at Siswono. He was clearly surprised.

"How do you know that?" he asked.

"From my father's friends' talk," Bertha said. Hartono turned to Siswono, "Her father's in the Singapore police."

"And, what's more, only recently did they get that woman tapper who used to drag a gun tied to a string around. If you were hiding in the bushes and watching her you wouldn't see her dragging the rifle. She controlled four hundred men. Somewhere in South Johor."

"I never heard of that," Hartono said. Bertha could see that he was impressed with her information.

She continued. "If she saw the British soldiers she would start tapping a rubber tree. The *orang puteh* wouldn't know if it was the right time or if the tree had been tapped earlier. She was quite a character. They were looking for her for some time."

"I'll talk about the communists later," Hartono said.

Hartono decided that they would go to Batu Pahat in two cars. Bertha went with Siswono. Bertha tried to get more information from Siswono as he drove.

"Hartono's your boss?" she asked.

"Yes." Just that. Nothing more.

"You known him for a long time?" she tried again.

"No."

"How long?" Bertha asked.

"Oh about three years," Siswono replied, nonchalantly.

"You knew him in Indonesia?"

"Yah." Siswono turned to look at her as he spoke.

"Same town?" she asked again.

"No ... Miss Bertha Rodrigues, I cannot tell you too much about him. But I can tell you what kind of person he is."

"Company secrets, I suppose," Bertha remarked expecting an answer.

"Well ... We sell information so we are stingy giving it for free." He laughed.

"Then tell me about Hartono, the person," Bertha said.

"Why do want to know?" Siswono asked.

"If he's going to be my boss, even if it's only for a short time, I'd like to know," Bertha said.

"Yah ... of course. Well, he's much older than I am."

"I can see that.."

"And very much wiser. He's been around. He had a hard time during the war. It made him a very tough and committed man."

"How old would he have been during the war?"

"Maybe seventeeen, eighteen ... nineteen, twenty."

"What sort of hard time did he have?"

"He calls it good luck and bad luck. He decided to leave his village and go to Jakarta towards the end of the war. But as soon as he got there he was picked up by the Japanese and sent to Singapore to work."

"Oh! One of the 270,000 they sent overseas."

"Yah ... but he was weak from his long trip ... with hardly any rice. So he soon got too sick to work. They threw him out into the streets to die."

"God!" Bertha was horrified that he was one of them; the miserable wretches who sat beside the Rochore Canal.

"But he says a doctor came to him one morning and gave him some medicine. He says it was something wonderful that someone had taken the trouble to even speak to him. No Singapore people helped them ..."

"Because," Bertha interrupted, "They had no food themselves."

"But isn't that the test? Whether or not you are willing to share with another human being. *Orang*, Miss Bertha Rodrigues, not *binatang*."

Bertha was silent. Siswono continued. "Now he laughs when he tells us how he tasted the medicine and found it was nothing but *jambu batu*. *Tipu*! Swindle ... He laughs and says he got angry as if he was paying. But it was the doctor talking to him and he didn't understand half of what he said … that made him alive again."

Siswono was silent. He frowned and stared at the road ahead. "Ah yes, I remember. He said he was nineteen then."

"Did the medicine cure him?" Bertha asked.

"I suppose it did … to some extent, I guess … Miss Bertha Rodrigues. Do you mind if I speak Bahasa Melayu?" Siswono asked unexpectedly.

"No. *Silakan.*"

He switched and spoke fast. "It stirred the last bit of spirit in Hartono. He decided that he must live. But it was not all good. He decided that he would steal or even kill if he had to live. So he got up and went down the street and saw a Chinese hawker selling *kueh mankok*. He just went up and took two and ate them. The hawker stared at him. But he didn't do anything. He went back to the canal and started thinking. The food had given him new energy. He forced himself to get up again that night. You know they used to squat beside the canal. Just squat and stare at the slow flowing black water for hours. He got up and went to a coffee shop. He saw a man selling *pisang goreng*. He grabbed two and ran. But the excitement was too much for him. He fell. When he looked up he saw a *mata-mata* there. He was arrested and taken to the station." Siswono paused.

"At the station, there was a Malay inspector. He looked at him and realised who he was. I mean one of the canal-side people. He spoke to him in Malay. Hartono could not understand all he said but he knew what it meant. He was going to let him go. When Hartono tells the story, he says this is where more good luck came. The Malay inspector told a police car driver to take him to a place called Betting Kusa. They left him there."

"Betting Kusa?" Bertha was puzzled. She knew her Singapore.

"At Changi," Siswono said.

"Never heard of it."

"That's where the RAF aerodrome is now."

"Oh … Near Tanah Merah?"

"Don't know …"

"Then what happened?" Bertha was impatient.

"It was by the sea. At least it was clean there, Hartono says. He was able to find dead fish that the fishermen had thrown away. And catch small crabs. Seaweed. He survived. There were no Japanese there. The Malays living around soon found out that he was a vagrant there. These were *kampong* people, Hartono says. Not town people. They gave him little things. The most important, he says, was not food but clothes. Once he was dressed, things became different. He didn't look like a bum."

"Hah! Clothes more important than food! Crazy ..."

"Yes. It allowed him to move around without suspicion."

"Strange how things are ..." Bertha commented.

"But this is interesting. Hartono would not ask for work. He says he started helping the fishermen when they came in. Pulling their boats up onto the beach. Sorting out their catch. Washing the boat. And, eventually, they started giving him some food or fish or money for his help. Because out there everyone knew he had no home. They all knew he slept on the beach. And they knew he was one of the Indonesians that the people who went into town had talked about."

"Yah ... not like city people."

"That's why Hartono will never forget the Singapore Malays. Especially the inspector."

Siswono paused and after a long silence muttered, "... He survived."

"I guess he hates the Japanese," Bertha said.

"No. He doesn't. If there's anyone he hates it is a *komunis*."

"Why?"

"I don't know."

"Then what happened?" Bertha asked.

"He survived. If Hartono was telling it he would end by saying that it was bad luck because he got to know every inch of the ground around Betting Kusa. Every tree, he says, every rock. And all that knowledge is wasted. They have changed the whole place now ... the *kampongs* and orchards, the coconut trees he knew ...

all gone."

"He is not bitter about it now?" Bertha asked.

"No. What it did to him was to drive him to build reserves all the time. Not just physical reserves. I mean not just things. Or money. Physical reserves like muscles. And knowledge ... also discipline. He drives himself to achieve things that will not go if he is thrown out into the streets again. He has studied English. He speaks it so well."

"So do you, Siswono," Bertha said using his name.

"Yes, but I was taught. I had proper schooling."

"Hartono didn't?" Bertha asked.

"No. It was self study ... Ah, but he did go to some classes."

"He went back to Jawa after the war?"

"Yah ... He's a very strong man, Miss Bertha Rodrigues. I really admire him. He goes into every detail in whatever he does. He can teach me so much."

"Good boss ah?" Bertha smiled.

"Yes. You can work for a man you admire. I should say you can only really work for a man you admire."

"Yes, Siswono, that's right," Bertha added to Siswono's thought.

"So you can work for him then ..."

"He never asked if I would agree to the plan," Bertha said looking at Siswono's eyes.

"Do you have a choice, Miss Bertha Rodrigues?" Siswono took his eyes off the road and looked at Bertha. There was a half smile in the corner of his mouth.

"*Tahu, suda tahu*. But please. Will you stop calling me Miss Bertha Rodrigues. Bertha is my name, *tuan*."

Siswono threw his head back and laughed. The *tuan* had amused him immensely. Maybe it was her telling him to call her Bertha, she thought.

Hartono booked two double rooms at the rest house. Mr. and Mrs. Ghazali and Mr. and Mrs. Da'ffar, he wrote. As they walked down the corridor Hartono said to Bertha, "That was just for the staff. You and Ethel share one room. Siswono is my missus." He laughed. Loudly.

They spent four hectic days together. Hartono went through every detail with the girls. Always looking at Bertha, as though she was the leader. But he never said it. Just before sunset, Siswono drove them to some deserted place and Hartono taught them how to use the gun.

It was thrilling to Bertha and Ethel. The feel of the steel in their hands. The cold yet reassuring metal. The force of the explosions. The kick that went through the arm into the whole body. Telling yourself that this time you're going to hit the can. Tensing the forearm. Keeping it rigid. Then the bang, and the can still there. Not like when Hartono demonstrated.

But they improved every day. Hartono was pleased on the second day. "I knew that you would get the hang of it. You are sportswomen. You have the eye ..."

Hartono was gentle but uncomprising. One day, they sat on the beach and he went over the tasks again. The tide was up. Bertha kept looking at the sea while he was talking. When he finished he said. "What about a swim?"

"But we have no swimsuits!" Ethel said in exasperation.

"*Sarongs*," Hartono said.

"*Sarongs?*" Ethel reacted with her mouth staying open.

"Yes. You are going to be *orang* Melayu. So this is practice."

"Haven't you seen how the Malay women can slip a dry *sarong* over the wet one after a bath? You must practice," Siswono added.

Ethel uttered a "Haaa... If you want Malay girls to do the job why don't you get Malay girls?"

"Because I don't trust them," Hartono replied in a low calm tone.

Bertha looked into his eyes. Was this the man whom Siswono said was ever grateful to the Malays? He knew his statement needed a follow up. "It's not that the Malays are unreliable as far as loyalty is concerned. It's that there is a gap between us Jawanese and them. It's better to use people who have no fixed stance against us ... vis-a-vis us. You have no prejudices either way."

Bertha's eyes went to Ethel. She had never forgotten Ethel's sudden statement on the train that she hated the Malays. Ethel's eyes dropped. She was silent.

"I see," Bertha said.

Hartono would not leave it at that. "We from Jawa are different to the Malayans. The Sumatrans have a lot in common with them. It's funny but I think that in some ways the Malays distrust us more than the Chinese," he said slowly.

"Because they don't quite understand you," Bertha said.

"Yes." Hartono waited for a few seconds before he continued. "It's like the Christians in Jawa. They are the same people. Not just Christians but Europeans ... together ... same culture. They know how to talk to us. Many of them have learnt the ways of the Jawanese better than many Jawanese ... But there is distrust between the Lutherans and the *Katoliks*."

"I know what you mean," Bertha said. "It's like my people. They may be united against the *matsalleh*, or the Chinese, but they squabble about the different churches ... in some way."

"Not quite the same, Miss Bertha Rodrigues," Hartono said quickly. "The differences are deeper in psychic terms. Not theoretical religious philosophies ..." Hartono continued, speaking slowly.

It had gone too far for Bertha and Ethel.

"OK LAH!" Ethel said loudly in a tone of mock protest, "Better to swim wit' *sarong* than not to swim lah."

And so they swam and splashed and shouted into the waves rising suddenly in front of them.

They ate well than night, *roti chanai* and mutton curry. *Kachang bendi* and *dhal*. *Achar timun* – cabbage cooked with green chillies, curried and *hati ayam*. They ate well every night. But always at the street stalls or coffeeshops. Not at the rest house. Siswono said he didn't trust any Hainanese cook. They could never cook a truly *halal* meal. Hartono seemed to humour him. "Anyway the *makan* is better outside," he said. There was tension and concentration during the day. The night meal was a release. Both Hartono and Siswono seemed to be more relaxed in the evening. Hartono had a beer sometimes. Siswono would not drink alcohol.

The four days came to an end. They were good days. The Indonesians had treated Bertha and Ethel like "proper ladies" as Bertha's Ma, Mary, would have said. Bertha learnt how Siswono ticked. But Hartono was still a many-part mystery. As Siswono had obliquely predicted, she came to admire the force and the drive in Hartono. If Siswono had not told her about Hartono's war experiences, it might have been different. Bertha was not the sort of person who looked for the golden lining everywhere. When she was looking, she could find the gold in anyone. She could see and sort out the grain from the chaff. When she was looking. When she wanted to. When she was interested enough to want to.

The nights were dreams, finding new parts of her soul she never knew were part of her. She knew the gap between her background and Ethel's. But Ethel had a simple warmth. Ethel was flesh and blood. Human, woman. Rough, but lovable.

Labis was their destination. The area they were going to live in and plot the paths and streams and gulleys in detail. Hartono had a survey department map of the area. He also had a much simpler and easier to see at a glance rough sketch map. In the four days, they got to know the area.

Then Hartono and Siswono took them there. To the shack they were to live in. It was not too much of a shock to them. They had been prepared. It was simple and rough. They took over the maps and sketches. The gun. The tinned food. The quinine. Bicycles.

"Hoi! They have no locks!" Ethel said when she saw them.

Hartono and Siswono laughed. "Hey, Miss Ethel Richards, this is not Singapore!"

"What are all these books about birds?" Bertha asked, puzzled, when she saw Hartono unpacking the bag he had brought.

"Oh. I forgot to tell you. This is the cover story. If anyone asks, you have to say you are doing some research on birds in the area for the University. On birds," Hartono said slowly.

Bertha knew that he had not forgotten. He wanted to tell them the "cover" that way. They would not forget if he said it that way.

As the two Indonesians walked away down the path they had come by, to the car about a quarter of a mile away, Bertha and Ethel stood at the door of their shack and waved.

To Bertha it was like a new life unfolding with Ethel by her side as Hartono's white shirt bobbed about between the trees and the leaves, receding from the broad back to intermittent glimpses of white.

~ *Chapter Twenty-four* ~

Plotting Together.

It was a wonderful three months for Bertha and Ethel. As she got out of her mosquito net every morning, Bertha thought of the new day ahead. The toilet out at the back stank. It was just a hole in the ground. A deep hole. They put a bit of sand into it every day but it still stank and attracted flies. The cold bath at the well, with her bathing *sarong* on, was biting cold. But it woke her up. Coffee and a good breakfast. It was either *bubor* or rice. Sometimes, but not very often, she fried eggs. They could not get a regular supply of bread. When Siswono or another person made their visit they sometimes brought bread.

They packed a lunch of tapioca or rice in two sections of a *tengkat* and with their clipboards, pencils, erasers, compass, camera, binoculars, sketches of birds which Hartono had given them and the *Introduction to Bird Watching in Malaya*, they set out. They soon realised that the programme given to them was easy. They did not have to rush to achieve the day's quota.

Dinner was a big meal. They took turns to cook. The shack was in a cool place with large trees sheltering it from the sun. A curry could keep for two days without getting bad. Rice would get *barsee* if it was kept. Fish was the greatest problem. Salted fish became one of their main meats. But, however simple the food was, they enjoyed their dinners after a tiring day walking through the rubber estate lanes and the paths in the jungle.

Siswono was delighted with the amount of detail they had recorded when he looked at their worksheets on his first visit. "Oh, Hartono will be so pleased."

One afternoon, in their first week, a round chubby puppy came bounding out of the belukar towards Bertha wagging its tail. She swooped it into her arms, and cuddled it. "Berta! Doan!" Ethel called out. "Why Ettel?" Bertha asked surprised at Ethel's reaction. "We can't touch dogs. Hartono said we have to follow the *makhur* also." Bertha put the puppy down. But it followed them all through the afternoon. "Now we have a problem," Ethel said as they sat on a patch of grass to rest. But the puppy later disappeared as mysteriously as it had appeared.

Bertha studied the bird book every night in the light of the pressure kerosene lamp. She started developing a strong interest in the birds around them. When she had first arrived there, she could only identify the white-breasted kingfisher. Soon, she was able to identify a great many birds; the *burong chiak padi* (streaked fantail warbler) in the *lallang* rising up suddenly with its sharp, scolding, clicking calls, the *burong mambah kera* (racquet tailed drongo) whistling out to each other and mimicking the calls of other birds, the crested tree-swifts with their metallic blue-green crested heads and black plumage and their wings curved like a crescent moon in flight, the *but-but* (crow pheasants) like a crow with its chestnut-brown back and wings and its black head and underparts, and many, many others.

Ethel too began to have an interest in the birds. It probably started the day they saw their first weaver-finch's nest swinging on a tree. Next to it were two unfinished nests. Bertha told Ethel they were "cock-swings." Ethel laughed loudly. Bertha explained that they were built by the cock-birds to induce prospective mates to join them.

"Like having a house before you get married hah?" Ethel commented.

Christmas 1959 was upon them in their second week. They had forgotten dates. There were no Sundays to mark the weeks. They only knew it was Christmas when Hartono appeared with Siswono in the evening. They brought the food and cigarettes for Ethel.

And Hartono had a small block of ice in his bag. And a bottle of brandy. "Wow! Brandy!" Ethel exclaimed. "What's the occasion?"

"Don't you know? It's Christmas today," Hartono replied.

"Good heavens!" Bertha exclaimed.

"We have forgotten the dates," Ethel said.

"You shouldn't, you know," Hartono said gravely and smiled suddenly. "But it IS your Christmas and we are here to celebrate it with you."

"Oh, how wonderful of you!" Bertha said and kissed him on the cheek. "Whether you celebrate it or not, here's a Merry Christmas."

She tried to give Siswono a Christmas kiss but he ducked his head giggling and blushing. Hartono kissed Ethel and then he opened the bottle. They had only three cups. "That's enough," Hartono said. "Siswono doesn't drink."

They drank a toast to Hartono. He turned to Bertha, "I'm sure you must miss your family today."

"Yah. But I'm a big girl now," she replied.

"What do you all do at Christmas?" he asked.

"Oh. You really want to know?" she asked, ready to tell him.

"Yah," nodding his head.

"Well it begins weeks before. My mother would start making pickles and cakes. And little tarts with pineapple jam."

"And agar-agar," Ethel added.

"Then, on Christmas eve, my sister and I would take the tree down from the top of the cupboard with the trinkets. Eric would check the lights. We'd put up the tree and talk about the presents we would get," Bertha continued.

"That was when you were small, I suppose," Hartono said.

"Yes. But even when we grew up Beryl used to come over to put up the tree. It was much more fun when we were little of course. Because Pa would be there too, organising everything. You had to ask him if you wanted to tie anything on. He wanted it to look balanced, he used to say. Then we dressed up and went to midnight mass. You know about that?"

"Yes. I have many friends who are *Katoliks*," Hartono replied, smiling to see Bertha getting excited with her talking about Christmas.

"And after midnight mass we would go to our grandparents' place. Ma and Pa would have a few drinks. They would sometimes sing carols. Grandpa always had a turkey. And a ham. And lots of other things too."

"And *feng*," Ethel interrupted. "Got to have *feng*."

"What's that?" Hartono asked. Bertha explained.

"And all during the day friends and relatives would come over and drink and eat tarts and pickles ... The next day we would go visiting."

"A real family feast, eh?' Hartono commented.

"Was it the same for you Ethel?" he asked.

"Yah ... But not so posh. My Pa usually got drunk. And Ma would shout at him. One Christmas he actually vomited at the communion rail, Ma says. She was so mad."

"And you got presents?" Hartono asked Ethel.

"Yes. The real present was my dress. Or shoes. Then there were some *kanas* and maybe a kite. I never got dolls. I used to prefer those Dinky toy cars," Ethel said.

"Always a tomboy ha?" Hartono said laughing.

"And doan ferget the gambling," Ethel said.

"Yes ... very often the old folks used to start a card game. Twenty-one or something like that," Bertha said.

"My Ma's favourite was *chap-ji-ki*," Ethel added.

"And everybody kissed everybody, ah?" Hartono asked.

"Yes. We used to have a mistletoe in our house," Bertha said.

"Not at our *pondok*," Ethel added. She looked blank for a few seconds and said, "At one time I remember my rich aunt used to come to the house every Christmas. Just about breakfast time. She used to bring me a small present. And she brought pickles she had made. Or tarts. She and her husband were so swankily dressed. Even their little boy, a real cissy, used to be dressed up. The little bugger was dead scared of me. My father used to say when they left, that's the annual visit to see their poor relatives. And Ma used to get angry with him. 'At least she come to see me once a year. And gives me some money.' Then Ma would give me a big note and send me to the *kedai* to get a quarter bottle of brandy or rum. Rum was cheaper. And I could buy some *gula-batu*," Ethel said.

"Ah. *Gula-batu*. I know that," Hartono said. "Like our *Hari Raya*," he added.

"Sparklers, Berta. Did you have sparklers when you were small?" Ethel asked Bertha.

"Oh yes. And Chinese crackers," Bertha replied.

"Did you pull the western style crackers?" Hartono asked.

Bertha and Ethel answered simultaneously. "Yes!"

"But der bes part is *feng* ... when my Ma made it," Ethel said slowly.

"Oh Ettel ... *feng* is so delicious! But the Hocquards never had *feng*, you know," Bertha said.

"Don't know them," Ethel said.

"But you don't visit the graveyard ... and wish all your dead relatives. We do at *Hari Raya*," Siswono spoke after listening silently to Bertha's and Ethel's stories.

"Yes. That is a wonderful thing. To remember your relatives who are gone when you are happy," Hartono said.

"You know, if a Chinese went to the graveyard on his new year's day, he believed that he would have bad luck for the rest of the year," Ethel said. "They are so afraid of det."

They talked of the jungle and the birds. Hartono asked if they had met anyone. "No one so far. We see tappers now and then. They don't really look at us," Bertha said.

"We are on the edge of a big rubber estate, aren't we?" Ethel asked. Hartono looked at Siswono.

"Yes," he replied.

"These people had a terrible time during the Emergency." He turned to Siswono, "Tell them about Mr. Bussens."

"Oh. He was an estate manager. One day, when he was driving through that cutting near Labis, the car was suddenly sprayed with bullets. As he turned the bend, he saw a tree trunk across the road.

He had a big Ford V-8. It was armour plated. He had two special constables with him. They started shooting back. It went on for a long time. Then the communists had an idea. They rolled hand grenades under the car. They must have known that there was no armour plating there. Mr. Bussen's legs were riddled with bits of metal. They weren't big wounds. Small little ones. He said that, months later, a piece would work itself out now and then."

"They were very brave, those Englishmen," Hartono said.

"But did they really stay to defy the communists or had they no other job or place to go to?" Bertha questioned.

"Perhaps you are right," Hartono said.

"Did you know him?" Bertha asked Siswono.

"No, I knew the HA at the Estate," he answered.

"What's HA?" Ethel asked.

"Hospital Assistant. They were like doctors on the estates."

"Yah," Bertha added. "My Dad says that some of them thought they WERE doctors. Strutting around with stethoscopes around their necks."

The subject drifted to the jungle, as Ethel lit the mosquito coil muttering about the "mozzies."

Siswono then livened up. He had spent a part of his teenage in the jungles in Java, he said. He talked about the tracks of different animals. The black panther with its eyes gleaming in the dark as your torchlight, he used that word, swept across the trees. The deer. Very hard to see. You must be downwind. Bertha had heard similar talk sitting in the verandah when her father returned from his hunting trips with his friends. Then Ethel told a story about her cousins who went to Bahau.

"Only my uncle an der boys. Jerry was the eldest. Maybe about twenty den. One day dere fadder, my uncle had to go to Seremban for someting or arther. Dat evening, as dey were seeting aroun, dey heard a tiger roar. Der hut dey lived in had no door. Dey had no gun in dose days. Jerry stood up slowly and drew der curtain across der door! Jus dat!"

They laughed weakly. Bertha could see that it was a great family joke-story that had been repeated dozens of times bringing out roars of laughter and slapping of thighs. But tonight it was just an odd story. She laughed louder than the others deliberately.

Bertha also saw that the brandy was going to Ethel's head. Ethel had slipped into the dialect of her past. She too was getting the floating feeling, as she described it to herself. But it was good floating into the past with company. She was grateful to Hartono for coming to them and bringing the brandy. It was a different Christmas. But she knew they would remember it for a long, long time.

Hartono and Siswono left when the brandy was finished. Bertha kissed Hartono again on the cheek. He kissed Ethel. Siswono stood back deliberately, smiling. He put his hands up and said "*Selamat malam*" as Bertha moved towards him.

"*Takut ka? Takut chium?*" Ethel teased him.

"Berta, you didn't kiss me a Merry Christmas?" Ethel said after they had gone. They hugged each other, laughing.

Two days later, Ethel was looking for another eraser in Bertha's bag when she found an envelope. It was marked "To the Commander in Chief, The Malayan Races Liberation Army." Ethel knew that the "Liberation Army" was what the communists called themselves. She stared at it in surprise. What was Bertha up to? Why? As she stood with the letter in her hand Bertha came up behind her. Ethel turned round and faced Bertha. She looked into her eyes expecting to see the embarrassment from the fright of being discovered.

"Put that away, Ettel. That's the letter we have to give the commies if they try to kill us or capture us."

"Hartono gave you this?" Ethel asked.

"Yes. When you went to the toilet at the rest house in Batu Pahat," Bertha replied.

"Has he got anything to do with the commies?"

"No. I doubt it. He hates them," Bertha replied slowly, seeing Ethel's suspicions.

"Then how can this letter help us?" Ethel asked.

"He told me that he has a friend of a friend who is a big shot in the PKI. He said that man wrote the letter when it was explained to him what Hartono wanted done here at Labis. He said he wasn't sure if it would work," Bertha said.

"How do you know he hates the commies?" Ethel asked.

"Siswono told me ... I think ..." Bertha replied hesitatingly.

"He told me that too." Ethel paused and continued, "I wonder if that is true ..."

"What were you looking for anyway, Ettel?" Bertha asked, ending the conversation.

One day, Bertha saw a *pipit batu* (grey wagtail). It was hopping in short impulsive rushes near a little stream they had passed every day for the last week. As it was moved, its body seemed to flash with almost a whole spectrum of colour. The yellowish-green of its rump, its yellow breast, the brown-grey plumage with streaks of white and black and the white curve over its eyes, tumbling and mixing as it made an occasional sudden jump to catch an insect held Bertha and Ethel dazed with its beauty.

"Oh Berta, it's beautiful!" Ethel whispered. "What is it?"

"*Pipit batu*. Grey wagtail in English. It doesn't belong here. It comes here from Europe for the winter."

"Whoa! All der way!" Ethel gasped softly.

"We are lucky to see it. They should be going home soon. The cock changes to a clear grey with a black patch on its throat before it goes off. They gather in flocks before they fly back home."

"Like to travel in groups, ah? ... Like me." Ethel said.

They only used the bicycles in the first week. As Siswono had advised, they started with the squares furthest from their shack. After the first week, they decided that the walk to the area they were going to work in was not too bad. The bicycles had to be pushed so often anyway. So they stopped using them. One evening, Ethel suggested that they ride to the village they had seen in the distance. Kampong Lankap. But Bertha would not agree. "If this is so secretive, we should not show ourselves unnecessarily," she said. Ethel pouted and walked out of the door.

Bertha put down her bird book and followed her out after a few minutes. Ethel was standing facing the jungle path going west, her back to the shack. Through the trees, the bluey white evening sky was visible in patches. A squirrel dashed up a tree trunk as it heard Bertha approach. It was still and the only sound was the distant call of the *wak-waks* in the mountains to the east. There was a faint scent of crushed grass. Bertha put her hand on Ethel's shoulder. "Ettel, getting bored ... are you?" she said softly.

"No lah! ... Maybe jus tired today." She turned and smiled at Bertha. "Then let's go to bed early tonight, Ettel," Bertha said.

"Not jus yet. Lessit here a while."

The mosquitoes were the biggest nuisance. They were not afraid of malaria. They took their quinine pills every day and slept under a net. It was just the irritation, the itchiness and bumps on her arms the next morning that annoyed Bertha. Siswono brought some cream when she asked him to. But they both didn't like the feel and stickiness of the cream on their skin and did not use it.

One day, as they were sitting on the ground after lunch, trying not to move so that they would not frighten any birds away, Ethel turned towards Bertha and put her finger to her lips. Bertha listened. A large animal seemed to be moving near the stream which they knew was about a hundred and fifty feet in front of them. It didn't worry Bertha. She believed that the carnivorous animals only moved about at night. But Ethel was clearly tensed and frightened.

It was the sounds of bush branches being pushed aside and small dry twigs on the ground snapping. Then they heard a soft splashing noise, as though the animal was wading in the stream. Bertha motioned to Ethel with her forefinger, stood up and started moving forward slowly. One of them stood on a dry twig. It cracked loudly. They froze and waited. There was silence from the direction of the stream for a second or two. And then they heard the animal jump through the belukar. And the sound of hooves running. It was hooves, not soft paws nor pads, Bertha thought.

They went to the stream. They knew it had gone. Ethel went to the water's edge and began to look for tracks. She found several at once.

"Deer. Berta, it was a deer," she said loudly, releasing the tension in her.

An idea came to Bertha at once. She slipped the *parang* which Hartono had given each of them out of its leather sheath and went to a clump of thin bamboo near the stream. She cut a piece and then cut off a section of it so that she had a length with two nodes.

"We're going to call it to us tonight, Ettel," she said the Ethel.

"How? You going to make a magic flute, ha?" Ethel said mockingly.

"No. I heard my father's friends talking about it. We're going to make a small hole in it and fill this with salt water. And tonight we will hang it near our shack. It'll bring the deer," she said pleased with herself.

That night they used the mosquito cream and sat quietly in the house watching the tree from which Bertha had hung the bamboo filled with saline water.

"It's so dark, maybe we won't see it if it comes," Ethel said.

"Shh ..."

They waited for nearly two hours. "I'm going to bed. Coming?" Ethel whispered with her ear almost touching Bertha's. Bertha stayed watching for another half-hour. Then she went to bed.

Siswono came early the next morning. He arrived frightened. An army patrol had passed him in the rubber estate. He was frightened because he had fish, eggs and vegetables with him. It was a serious offence to be found carrying more food than one meal.

They told him about the bamboo. He reacted at once. "You're *gila*! Yes, you'll bring the deer. But with the deer will come the tiger! Or other fierce animals. Don't you ever try that again."

The girls looked at each other. Ethel defused Siswono's anger at once with, "And please, Siswono, bring some salt next time. We've finished our salt."

He laughed. "*Gila*!" he muttered.

"Do you believe what they have told us?" Ethel suddenly asked Bertha one night after dinner. Bertha was silent.

"Do you? Berta?" Ethel repeated.

"Yes I do. I thought about it. The commies don't want this information. They know the jungles all over Malaya better than anyone except perhaps the Sakais, Semangs and Temiangs. I also believe that if someone built a hotel nearby and left this area untouched, it will be a tremendous tourist attraction," Bertha said.

"That's what Hartono tole me," Ethel said.

Ethel was quiet as she drew on her cigarette. "Den … we should be looking for tings that will interest a Europin'," she said.

"Guess you're right. And recording all we see about the birds," Bertha added.

"Yah, maybe they tink we're not good enough for dat," Ethel said.

"Probably bring in an ornithologist later," Bertha said.

"Please Berta. Not dose big words. Means birdman I suppose?" Ethel said.

"Hey listen!" Ethel said, her finger in the air.

"Tock-tock bird!" Bertha said, her face lighting up at hearing something familiar. It was only the owls that they heard at night. The slow hoots, the "popkh" of the *burong jampok* (collared scops-owl), the "kant-kwik-kek-kek-kek" of the bay owl and the plaintive, melancholy "koo-lick, koo-lick, koo-lick" of the *burong punggol* (hawk-owl). It was the first time that they had heard the "tock-tock" call of the nightjar.

"It's a lowland bird," Bertha said. We're not really in the lowlands here."

"Wanna play a game?" Ethel asked.

"Guessing the number of 'tocks,' right? … Okay … three," Bertha responded.

The bird clucked two "tocks."

"Tree!" Ethel said. It was her turn.

They counted seven "tocks" and laughed.

One day, after they had been there in their shack at the jungle edge for nearly two months, Bertha was thinking to herself as she finished writing "telephone wire pole" on her clipboard sheet, that they had met such few people so far when she looked up at the sound of rustling leaves and saw a huge Alsatian dog sniffing in the bushes, about fifty feet from them. She froze. To her, the Alsatian was a wolf; only kept by the crazy Europeans.

As she watched it, a tall European with flaming red hair walked into view. Quickly, she flipped the sheets over so that the half finished sketch of a bird in pencil that Hartono had given her was on top. She muttered, "…tel" and Ethel looked up.

He walked up to them smiling. The dog followed him. Ethel moved up to Bertha at once and pressed her body against Bertha's in fear.

"*Jangan takut*," the European said. He was wearing a white shirt, white shorts and white hose. "BRUCE! Here!" he called out loudly and sharply to the dog. It went to him at once. He grabbed its collar. He smiled at them.

"*Sudah makan*?" he asked in a polite tone.

Bertha nearly burst out laughing. He thinks we are Malay, she said to herself. She smiled with a little laugh.

"*Belum* …" she replied.

He came nearer. His eyes opened wide as he saw the sketch on Bertha's clipboard.

"Good heavens. Bird watchers," he exclaimed.

"No lah …" Bertha said. It was the first phrase that came to her mind.

"Artists then? You speak English," he asked.

"Yah. A leetle," Bertha replied, deliberately mispronouncing the word.

"Are you studying birds?" he asked. His voice strong and forceful.

"Yah. Not stardying, but recording," Bertha replied, shyly.

"Studying? Students?" he asked, again with his loud voice.

"No lah. Working for the university," Bertha answered. She was herself now, remembering the cover story Hartono had outlined.

"Working? Good heavens! What kind of work is that?" he thrust at her with his insistent tone.

"We have to write down all the birds we see lah. Even if it's the same kine. An der time … An where …" Bertha said.

The dog stirred. Ethel clung to Bertha.

"Please sir, your dog," Ethel said.

"He's all right," he answered. He put his hand in the pocket of his baggy shorts and took out a short leash. He buckled it to the dog's collar and said, "What an interesting job."

"Can do lah," Bertha replied to his comment.

"And what pretty girls!" he added with a gleam in his eye.

They hung their heads down. Ethel still clinging to Bertha as a child to her mother.

"You do this every day?" he asked. Bertha saw his eyes smile as he spoke. They were a beautiful light green.

"Yah … for a month," Bertha answered.

"You must tell me about it. Most fascinating," he said. Like a school teacher Bertha thought.

She did not reply.

He smiled and spoke again. "I'm Tosh. Gerald Macintosh. Tosh to my friends. I'm at the Harrison's estate up there. I'd love to have a chat with you about birds … sometime when you're free. Why don't you drop in … any time. I'm always free … Just ask for me, Tosh. They'll know."

He didn't hold out his hand. He's been out in Malaya for enough time to know that Malay girls don't shake hands, Bertha noted. He smiled. He looked into Bertha's eyes. Ethel began to feel foolish clinging to Bertha. She stood up straight.

"I'll tell the conductor to show you to my house any time you show up. Who shall I say?" he thrust again.

Europeans are like that, Bertha thought to herself. I'm behaving like a bloody American, Gerald Macintosh thought to himself. He's after us, Ethel decided. Or rather after Bertha.

"You must come … sometime. Please, it will be nice to talk to someone in English," he said. Bertha saw his eyes waiting for a reaction.

"Thank you, sir. It's very kine of you," she said, inserting the "sir" deliberately.

He stood looking at Bertha silently. The dog stirred again.

Ethel saw that he didn't look at her. Bertha is so tall, she said to herself. The uneasy silence continued for a another few seconds. He smiled again. A wide, forced, friendly grin. But Bertha saw that he was not comfortable. She realised then that he was as embarrassed as they were. Perhaps he was lonely up there in the large estate manager's house.

She smiled at him.

"Well, I've got to go. Can't keep old cookie waiting, you know. Tootle hoo! ... Please don't forget. Do come when you can."

He turned round and walked away with the dog on its short leash.

"My, so handsome!" Ethel said with enthusiasm as soon as she thought he was out of earshot. To her alarm, he turned around and waved as soon as she she spoke. She clasped her hand over her mouth.

Bertha looked at her. "Ettel!" she said. Ethel saw that she was smiling.

Bertha knew that she looked taller and slimmer in the *sarong* and *baju kurong*. There was no mirror in the house large enough for her to see herself, but Ethel had said to her the first time she put on the *sarong* that she was "beauuuutiful, beauuuutiful, beauuuutiful ..." She was standing in *sarong* with her breasts bare then. She knew that to a European she would look different, sexy, beautiful in her *sarong*.

They walked back with their own thoughts. Bertha cooked that evening. Ethel sat alone on the rough wooden seat at the front door while she cooked. She did not fuss around or start meddling with the pressure lamp as she usually did. To Bertha, she seemed to angry and morose. But Ethel smiled into her eyes during the meal and said it was delicious. "You're wonderful, Berta," she said.

Siswono didn't come as he was scheduled to the next morning. It was unusual. After breakfast, they set out to the square on the grid that the programme had set. They went through a different path. The trees were taller and larger, Bertha thought. About half an hour after noting the features of the zone, Bertha began to feel her body itching. She looked at her arms. They were red with a rash. It wasn't mosquito or flea bites.

"Ettel, look. What's this?" she called out to Ethel.

"Hiyah! Rash lah. What did we eat last night?" Ethel asked.

"Cannot be last night. Must be breakfast or something," Bertha replied.

"We only had *bubor* ... with the tinned *tung-chye* an' *tau-hoo-jee*... an aig," Ethel said. "Cannot be dat."

"It's so itchy," Bertha said.

"*Gatal* huh?" Ethel said and burst out in one of her raucous laughs.

"Don't joke, lah. It's no joke," Bertha said, rubbing her chest under her breasts.

"Doan scratch, Berta," Ethel said.

She watched the discomfort in Bertha as Bertha tried to ease the itch by wriggling her body.

"It's all over me, Ettel," Bertha said.

"Come, we'll go back an I'll rub cole watter over you. Der well watter's cole," Ethel said.

They made their way back. The itch seemed to ease off as Bertha walked back. But as they arrived at the shack it came on fiercely again. "Oooo ... Ettel it's come back," Bertha said to Ethel.

Bertha stripped her clothes and panties off and lay on the matting on the wooden plank bed. It felt better when there was nothing touching her skin. Ethel got a kerosene tin of water from the well and bathed Bertha's naked body with a rag soaked in the cool water. It soothed her pain and somehow excited her. "Oh thank you, Ettel ... that's so good," she murmured.

The itch slowly died away. Bertha lay relaxed and dozed off. She woke up with a start. A mosquito was buzzing in her ear. The bright daylight was fading. Then she saw a man standing at the door. It seemed to her that he had just walked in and stopped rigid in his tracks. It was Hartono.

Bertha gasped. She sat up at once and grabbed her *sarong* at the foot of the bed.

She heard him breathe out loudly. "Bertha, you're beautiful," he said, and abruptly turned on his heel and walked away.

She put on her panties and her *sarong* and her *baju kurong* and went to the door. Hartono had his back to her. In a soft voice she called to him, "Hartono … We didn't expect you."

He turned around. He seemed relieved to see her clothed. "Siswono could not come this morning." His voice and face were dead serious. "I'm sorry." He hung his head down.

"What for, Hartono?" Bertha asked.

"For seeing you … for what I said," he stuttered.

"We weren't expecting you. It's not your fault. But thank you, Hartono … I heard you," Bertha said softly and gently.

He avoided her eyes. She saw his body was tensed.

"I brought the provisions … and some *roti prata,*" he said as though he was grasping for a straw to stop himself drowning.

"I'm sorry," he repeated his apology.

Ethel appeared at the door. "Hey, Hartono!"

Her voice was like an explosion crashing into the silence that seemed to weave a web around Bertha and Hartono. Her voice wrenched them apart, wrenched Bertha from her thoughts and tore Hartono out of his cringing apologetic mood. Hartono explained again that Siswono could not come in the morning. Ethel told him about Bertha's itch. He mumbled an "Ah" as though it explained her lying there nude on the bed. Ethel went through the possibilities of what they had eaten and expounded her theories. Then he asked Bertha to show him her arms. She went close to him and held up her arms so that he could see the underside of her upper arms, her body almost touching his. He seemed embarrassed again. He looked at the rash without touching her arms.

"I think I know what it is," he said.

They waited for him to continue.

"Did you go by a new way today?" he asked.

"Yes. Why?" Ethel asked.

"It's the *rengas* rash. Some people get this rash when they pass under a *rengas* tree," he said.

"A big tree?" Ethel asked.

"Yes. Very big," he replied.

"But how?" Ethel asked.

"It has a very strong juice. But only some people get the rash if they pass close to the tree ..." he said.

Bertha was silent. Her head was swimming. She felt her body hot in some sort of way. But it was not the rash any more.

"Stay for *makan*. I'm cooking," Ethel said. He agreed, shyly. His eyes avoided Bertha's.

Bertha wondered if they had enough for three. She knew what a big eater he was. She went to the kitchen corner of the shack to help Ethel but Ethel said sharply to her, "Hey you know it's my day. Go away! Talk to Hartono."

Hartono had gone outside. He stood with his back to the door almost in the same place that Ethel had stood that night when Bertha had refused to go to Kampong Lankap. She realised how broad his back was. And what a powerful man he was, standing there with his hands in his pockets.

"The *wak-waks* are early tonight," she said softly.

He turned to her and smiled, "You sound just like my adopted father. He was a man of the jungle He used to say every evening if the owl was early or late. Or if there was more scent in the air that evening."

Bertha leaned against a tree next to him. "Your adopted father?" she questioned.

"Well ... How do you say that in English. The man who adopted me," he answered.

"I donno ... You were adopted, Hartono?" she asked softly.

"Three times," he replied.

"Three times! Good heavens," she responded loudly.

He gave a little laugh. "It's not unusual in Jawa. People are very poor. But they also treat children well. And relatives have this responsibility," he said.

"Were you adopted by relatives?" she asked.

"Yes. But twice by distant relatives," he said.

"How extraordinary," Bertha sighed.

"Not for Jawa," he repeated himself.

"Which part of Jawa were you brought up in?" Bertha asked.

"In a place very few people know about. Or perhaps I should say very few people want to go to." Hartono paused for a few seconds. "My father was a Baduis."

"What's that?"

"A tribe in West Jawa. The Baduis are thought to be the original Sundanese. Their language, they say, is the original Sundanese. They isolated themselves hundreds of years ago when the Islam conversion began. In fact, they had to run to the hills."

He lit a cigarette. Bertha watched him silently. Watched the way his hands moved. Slowly and deliberately.

"My real father, who I cannot remember, and my first adopted father were Baduis. The Baduis had their own culture. They believed in pure nature. They will not use tools. No *changkols*. They will not teach their children. Education is bad, they say. They allow singing but not dancing. The only colours they wear are black, white or blue. Dark blue, that is," he said.

"Gosh. Are there any Baduis left today?" she asked.

"Yes. That's the wonderful part about Indonesia. Tolerance. The government have left them alone. They have a special zone of their own. The centre of it is called Badui Dalam. Those who stay there never leave it. Around it are several Badui villages."

"Huh. Tolerance. You fight each other so much," Bertha said aggressively.

"But, Bertha, we also compromise so much. We do have tolerance, Bertha." He seemed to be mentioning her name in a different way today, Bertha thought. A softer, more intimate way.

He continued. "This country, Malaya, has not got the tolerance we have. We have to live with many Christians in Jawa. In fact, the address of our largest mosque is Cathedral Street. A general once took me to the roof to see the view from up there. He pointed to a delicate old Christian cathedral across the road and said, 'Look, this is Indonesia. The Christian church across the street.

Side by side with our largest mosque.' "

"Huh," Bertha huffed, "Didn't they build the mosque there purposely," she asked pointedly.

"I guess they did. To show how we live side by side," he replied aware of her reaction.

"Huh," Bertha mumbled.

"The eyes see what the mind tells them to see, Bertha," he said softly. Then he added, "In most things."

She looked into his eyes. He met her look with a tenderness she didn't expect. "Tell me more about the Baduis," she said.

"They believe in complete purity and simplicity. No writing. No rearing of cows, pigs, horses, goats, ducks, even fish in ponds. Maybe, when I'm an old man, I shall go back to the land and lifestyle of my ancestors."

"Will they accept you, Hartono?" Bertha asked softly.

"I don't know, now that I've *masok* Islam."

"Will they allow you into the inner area … the Badui Dalam?' she asked.

"No. Never," he answered.

Bertha changed the subject. "Is that why you're not so strong a Muslim?" she asked.

"Who said I'm not so strong. That isn't true," he answered calmly.

"You drink …" she ventured.

"Ah yes. And I don't stick to many of the fringe rules. But I am truly Muslim, Bertha."

"The test is probably when you fall in love with a Christian," Bertha said. It was dark now. She could not see his face clearly.

"Are you a strong *Katolik?*" he asked.

"I dunno. I don't think so. My generation is different from my parents."

"But they probably have little tolerance for the Muslims, right?" he asked in the Singapore way of making the statement and then adding the questioning word.

"You've been around, haven't you, Hartono?" Bertha asked.

"Yes. I had a hard time during the war."

Bertha did not comment. What Siswono had told her was probably in confidence. Or was it? Was it true?

"In Indonesia?" she decided to prod.

"No. In Singapore, but it's no use talking of the ..."

"DEEEENER!" Ethel roared from the doorway.

"Come, Hartono," Bertha said gently, "Eat with us. Just something simple."

Ethel was in a good mood that night. She was in high spirits. Hartono praised her curry. "Only because you brought fresh mutton," she said. They talked of Malaya. The jungle. Birds. Bertha brought up the subject. He smiled. Bertha could see his pleasure in their new interest. He only knew the sea birds in this area, he said.

"I think the most beautiful thing in the world is the *lang laut*, the white-bellied sea eagle. It is so big. When you see them soaring high up there with their white wings and the black edges, it's complete relaxation. And when you see them swoop down, it's power, force, lightning. And they are so clever. They drop crabs onto the rocks to break their shells. But the most beautiful thing about them is that when they mate, they mate for life," he said with rising excitement.

"A simple life, hah?" Bertha commented.

"You seem to have seen a lot of them?" Ethel asked.

"Yes. A long time ago. Sitting on the beach in Betting Kusa."

"Where's that? Jawa?" Ethel asked.

"No. Singapore."

"Never heard of it," Ethel said.

Bertha watched the moth flying round the the kerosene lamp, keeping her thoughts to herself.

She curled up in her corner of the mat that night away from the real world, isolated in the mosquito net from the darkness, from the night, the hooting owls, and Ethel's snoring. The rash had gone.

"Three days more!" Ethel said bright and sparkling as Bertha opened her eyes one morning. She made a gruff noise of response and turned over to squeeze a minute more of sleep, to curl up and forget the world for just a minute more, only one minute ...

That was the day when their months of isolation and privacy was broken into. As they were returning to their shack, Ethel suddenly gripped Bertha's arm. "Berta!" she muttered softly. Bertha saw Ethel's eyes staring at their shack. She looked up and saw the European planter in his white clothes standing at the door. He had his alsatian dog on the short leash by his side.

"I saw him come out of our house," Ethel whispered.

He had not seen them yet. Bertha went down on her knees at once and Ethel followed. That way, the bushes blocked his view. She motioned Ethel to the thicker bush on their left and they crept into it slowly and quietly. Bertha's hand went to her *parang*. Then she remembered that the gun was in the bag slung on her shoulder. She reached down into it and moved it to a corner where she could get to it quickly. They waited, frozen, motionless as statues. Bertha put her forefinger to her lips as a warning to Ethel. They listened. He was apparently standing still. The birds above them twittered nervously. If he had been in the estates and jungles for some time he would have noticed the unrest. Bertha looked up. There was a nest on a branch above them.

Then she heard the dog. It was running around the bushes. He must have unleashed it and it had got their scent. She unsheathed her *parang*. It was in front of them in the next second, barking madly. The European came running up. Bertha lunged at the dog with her *parang*. It stepped back but turned to her left and started to to encircle them. Ethel had her *parang* out now. She stood up and moved so that she was back to back to Bertha. "Kill the bastard," she muttered.

The European shouted out, "BRUCE! Stay!" The dog stopped where it was. He came up to them. Before he could speak Bertha spat at him, "Take the dog and go, you dirty thief. Or we'll kill you and your bitch." Her eyes were blazing.

He saw her anger. "Now come on. No need to get so shit scared ... And I only went in to look for you."

"Get out of here!" Bertha shouted and advanced towards the dog. He took two long strides to the dog, fixed the leash to it and pulled it away. Bertha could see the sweat on his brow. He walked away. "Bastard," Ethel muttered loud enough for him to hear.

The incident upset them badly. They opened a can and ate a hurried dinner. They went to bed early. Bertha checked the gun that night and put it under the bag she used as a pillow. Ethel saw that Bertha was still fuming. She had cooled down. She whispered to Bertha in the dark, "Berta, didn't you see his cock?" and she giggled.

"Ha?" Bertha queried in a surprised tone.

"The dog's cock lah. It wasn't a bitch."

Siswono came the next evening. It was his last visit, he said. He gave them instructions about moving out. But as he was talking to them he saw that they were uneasy.

"What's the matter?" he asked.

Bertha told him about the planter. Their first encounter with him and his intrusion into the shack. Siswono was tense with attention. He asked Bertha to repeat the man's name. Then asked her if she was sure. Siswono left with the moving out instructions unfinished. He appeared to be more worried about the incident than they were. They were silent after he had gone. Both were now deeply worried. They didn't know why. It was Siswono's agitation that had got into them. Suddenly there was a footstep at the door. A figure appeared out of the dark. It was Siswono again. He had come back.

"Listen. I'm going to the village now. But I'll come back. I don't want the two of you to be alone. We'll leave tomorrow," he said.

"But we haven't finished," Ethel said.

"Only one more square left. Doesn't matter," he said.

He turned to go. Then he stopped. "Look, get your bicycles. You come with me to the village. I just want to telephone. It will take us an hour there and back. Come. Let's not delay."

Bertha started to look for her shoes. She hadn't put them on for three months. "What are you looking for?" Siswono asked.

"My shoes," Bertha replied.

"No need for shoes," Siswono said.

They followed him through the jungle in the dark. Only then did they realise the same jungle they now knew so well by day was so frightening at night. There were sounds they could not identify. They got to the village sooner than they expected. He pointed to a shack. "That's a coffee shop. Go get yourselves some coffee and wait there for me."

"Money! Oh, we didn't bring any money," Ethel said.

"Have you got the gun with you?" he whispered. "Yes," Bertha whispered in reply. "Here's some money."

They ordered coffee. There were only two people in the shop. They stared at the girls. One was an old Malay. The other a young Chinese. Bertha was uneasy about him. A commie, probably, she thought to herself. Bertha gave the order in Malay. Then she whispered to Ethel not to talk in English. Ethel frowned. But when the coffee arrived, her eyes lit up. She took a sip and glowed with pleasure. "It's delicious!" she said in English loudly. Bertha glared at her. She took a quick glance at the young Chinese. She didn't see any reaction in his eyes.

The coffee was delicious. The richness of the milk. The bitterish taste of the well-roasted coffee powder. The sweetness. It was nectar to her. And a bit of condensed milk sticking to the spoon to be licked off.

Siswono returned to them and they set off for the shack. He had a bundle with him. It looked like a rolled mat. It was, they discovered later. He had brought a mat and the same kind of red blanket that they had. It was cold in the jungle foothills. He stayed with them, sleeping on the floor that night.

The night passed without incident. They packed up the next morning and left. They could not take everything with them. When they had first arrived, there was Hartono to help them. Another pair of hands. Siswono said not to worry. He would come back one day with someone.

When they got to the village, they found European soldiers

carrying sten guns standing around. Bertha began to get worried about the gun. Maybe they will search them, she thought.

She had noticed that, as they came out of the bush, the leader of the small group of soldiers had stared at them cycling towards him. When he saw them with *sarongs* he had turned away. Looking for Chinese, she thought to herself. But the gun in the bag still worried her.

There was a battered Ford Anglia waiting for them. They loaded the car while the soldiers look on from a distance. A youngish Malay man had brought the car. Siswono didn't bother to introduce them. He appeared to be nervous at the sight of the soldiers. They loaded up quickly and went off.

"What's the matter here?" Bertha asked Siswono in Malay as soon as they started. "I don't know," he replied. The young man who was driving turned to them and spoke, "The *orang-puteh* manager of Harrison's estate on the hill was killed by the communists last night."

~ *Chapter Twenty-five* ~

Batu Pahat

Siswono had arranged for them to be driven to Batu Pahat. It was a long and stifling hot drive in the old car. The young man, whose name they learnt later was Saleh, was a very bad driver. Although the car could not go very fast, he swung round corners at breakneck speeds. He seemed to apply his brakes at the very last moment and it was always with a jerk. With the depressing thought of the Englishman's death hanging in their minds, the end of the nearly three months of living in bliss together had turned into an unhappy finish. They hardly spoke during the long drive.

They did not even stop for a meal. Siswono seemed anxious to get to their destination as quickly as possible. They did stop twice though. Saleh went out and bought bottles of Coca-Cola. The silly fellow, Ethel said to herself, stops so far from the coffee shop. Siswono's nervous, Bertha thought to herself. He doesn't want us to be seen.

They also turned off into a small earth track once. Siswono said they were going to *buang ayer*. The men went off into the bushes, one at a time. Then Siswono told Bertha the area was quite deserted and they could go and "throw away their water" there, speaking in Malay.

But the end of the journey brought a pleasant surprise. Saleh drove into a little house with a large garden full of flowering shrubs. It was a timber house in the Malayan style, on stilts with a small verandah in front. It looked well kept and clean. They could see the outhouses of the servant's quarters and kitchen, flat on the ground behind it.

"You are going to stay here tonight. It is a friend's house. He is away. His wife will look after you," Siswono said as a plump woman in a bright *sarong* and *baju kurong* appeared at the front door.

"Only tonight?" Bertha asked.

"That depends ..." Siswono replied. "Hartono will come up from Singapura tonight or tomorrow and will decide."

Ethel looked at Bertha for a reaction. Bertha shrugged her shoulders.

They went in. Their first impression of the house was right. It was spotlessly clean. Amazing for a Malay house, Bertha thought to herself. Che Fatimah seemed to be a happy-go-lucky type of person. She greeted them with great big smiles and fussed around them from the start. Bertha was relieved in a way but, after being alone for so long, she realised that they would have to fit in with other people again. They were back to civilisation, as Ethel said that night.

After a bath in the bathroom, pouring buckets of water over her naked body after months of bathing in a *sarong*, and changing into fresh clothes, Bertha felt better. She went out to the verandah and, as she expected, Fatima was there.

"It's a small house, but it's clean," she said in Malay.

"It's a beautiful small house. And it's really so clean," Bertha replied.

"Your friend Berta is ready?" she asked.

"I'm Bertha. She's Ethel," Bertha said smiling.

Fatimah burst into peals of laughter, her plump body quaking, and apologised for her mistake. It was a huge joke to her.

"You have no children?" Bertha asked.

"Got. They are at their grandparents place for two days of utter spoiling," she replied with another laugh at her own remark.

Ethel joined them. Fatimah told her how she had mistaken Bertha for "Ettel" and went into a short fit of laughter again.

"I must remember. The besar one: Berta. The other one *etek* Ettel, auntie Ettel," and laughed at her cleverness.

She took them round her garden pointing out the bougainvillea she had got from her husband's sister. From a cutting. One has to spray the hibiscus often. The insects love it so much. And the snails. This place is full of snails. I get up every morning early to kill them. Like my father does, Bertha said. Oh! Your father loves plants too? I always say that if you love plants your life would be a happy one. My relatives call that Fatimah's proverb. The periwinkles, cannas, flocks, marigolds (*bunga tahi ayam*, or chicken's dirt flower in Malay, because of its smell), asters, michaelmas daisies, ixoras, climbing clematis, morning glory. She seemed to have a whole botanic garden here. But no orchids. I always say that orchids are too swanky. Not for ordinary people. Yah it is the flower of our country but it's so stylish, Ethel said. Another of Fatimah's proverbs? Bertha asked and Fatimah went off into another quaking and laughing fit.

But Bertha enjoyed being taken around the garden. She realised that however beautiful they had thought the Malayan belukar and rubber estates were, they had not seen the strong, bright almost gaudy colours of Malayan flowers together in such masses for a long time.

"Lovely blozzoms," Ethel said. Bertha winced. That was what Ben called, "zedding" the "s." She knew Ethel was just trying to be polite. Ethel had not the slightest interest in flowers or gardening. Ethel liked the physical down-to-earth pleasures of life. Even the intangible feelings she enjoyed were clear earthy pleasures; speed, action, food, sex. Bertha sometimes wondered if she could love in the romantic sense.

Hartono arrived with Siswono in a small car that evening. He looked tired. Fatimah greeted him and went to the back, returning with bright-red, sickly sweet drinks. She then left them alone.

"What now?" Ethel surprised Bertha by her impatience.

"I'm sorry that you had to rush off quickly. Siswono did the right thing. But you had really completed the job. And very well done too. We are all pleased," Hartono said.

He paused. He saw their expectant faces and continued quickly. "I have another job for you, that is ..."

Ethel interrupted, "… if we are willing to do it, right?"

"Yah …" His voice trailed off.

Ethel spoke without looking at Bertha. "As for me, I want to go home."

"OK. We'll take it one by one. Are you sure? The money is good. I am giving you five thousand dollars for the Labis work," Hartono said.

Ethel opened her eyes wide, "Whoa!" But her face changed at once. "But I don't want to stay here any more. I want to go home," she said.

Bertha looked at her. Ethel avoided her look.

"Please yourself, Miss Ethel Richards," Hartono said. He turned to Bertha. "Better if I talk to you afterwards." Then he spoke to Ethel, "If you are sure, you can come back with me tomorrow morning. But I have another suggestion for you. We are very pleased with your attitude towards work. We have job for you in Singapore if you want it. It will be twice your salary at the hospital."

Ethel did not hesitate, "No thanks. I don't want to sound ungrateful, but I don't like all this secrecy, lah. I'm happy in the hospital kitchen. Simple. Everything is clear."

"That's a lot of money, Ettel … Why don't you listen to what Hartono has to say about the other job?" Bertha said to Ethel.

"Is it in Singapore?" Ethel asked Hartono.

"Yah," he replied.

"Is it a ting full of secrets?" she asked again.

"Not quite the same as the last job … but, like every job with responsibilities in the business world, there is a certain amount of confidential matters," Hartono said slowly and deliberately.

"No tanks den. Back to my ospital," Ethel said with finality and leant back in her chair.

Hartono put his hand in his pocket and took out an envelope. He handed it to Ethel. "*Gaji*. There's a receipt inside. Please sign it and give it to me. Tomorrow morning will do," he said.

Bertha noted the show of trust. It was deliberate. Ethel looked into the envelope. She counted the fifty dollar notes. Then she kissed the wad of money. Her eyes were shinning. "Wow! *Terima kaseh banyak-banyak*, Hartono. Gotta pen?"

Siswono handed her a ball-point. She signed the paper and passed it to Hartono.

"Thank you," he said softly. "Pity you don't want to work for us. You'll go far."

Ethel put her hand to her breast and said with a frown that her *hati* was not *puas* doing work that was not clear to her.

"No money for me?" Bertha asked turning her head to one side, half in jest.

"*Ada lah*," Hartono replied. He offered Ethel a cigarette and lit it for her. Then he turned to Bertha, "I suggest that we talk at my hotel. I have some things to give you. Then we'll come back here and pick Ethel and go out for a *makan besar*. What you say to that?" he asked Bertha.

"OK, *tuan*," she replied smiling.

They got up. Siswono, Hartono and Bertha.

"You don't drive too fast, ha! Look after my good fren," Ethel shouted a parting shot.

As Hartono walked up to the desk to get his key at the small Chinese-style hotel, Bertha saw that the receptionist, an attractive Malay girl with big breasts and her *baju* tight against them, was giving Hartono the glad eye. Siswono said he would wait downstairs. Hartono winked at him and jerked his chin towards the receptionist. Siswono made a a sound like "chek" and turned his head away in a gesture of annoyance. Hartono grinned.

"She's after you, Hartono," Bertha said as they walked up the stairs. Hartono made a gruff sound in reply.

He opened the door and waited for her to go in first, western style. She saw that he had not unpacked. She stood waiting for him to shut the door. He turned round and put his hand in his pocket and handed her an envelope. "Receipt inside. Please sign it some time. You were the leader so you get fifty percent more," he said.

Bertha opened her mouth and left it open with surprise. "Hartono! Thank you!" she said. She went up to him and kissed him on the cheek before he realised what she was going to do. He seemed embarrassed and upset. She stepped back, unsure of herself now.

"I'm sorry. I forget that I should act like a Malay girl," she said with a serious expression. Then she added, "Or is it because you're married that I embarrassed you?" she asked.

He looked at her sheepishly. "No. I'm still a bachelor. *Tidak biasa*. It's just that I'm not used to that." He smiled.

"But thanks for the thanks," he added.

"It's more money than I've ever had, Hartono," Bertha said.

She sat on the bed. It was the nearest thing to sit on. Her legs seemed weak all of a sudden. Hartono stood in front of her and looked into her eyes for a few seconds. Then he sat down on the floor in front of her.

"Please. I'm not the queen," she said.

"You are as beautiful as a queen, but it's just that I'm comfortable here," he said.

He told her that he had a similar job of plotting details on a map. This time it was along a beach. Much simpler. And not in a remote place. She would live at Fatimah's. Fatimah is a good cook. That's the bonus! And we'll give you a car. A dirty old VW. It works, though. About two months. You won't have Ethel to help you and be your constant friend, but you won't be living in the *ulu*.

Bertha listened. Once again things seemed to have started rushing at her.

"Bertha, over these last few months I've got to know you a little bit. I know your problem about the Jag and all that. The fact is that you can't go back to Singapore without getting arrested. We can help you because we now know for sure that you are an intelligent and reliable person," he looked at her, searching her eyes for her reactions.

"This job now gives you time to think also. Being with Ethel, you were not really alone," he stopped. He seemed to be looking for the right words.

"What about Mr. Vandyke?" she asked.

"He knows what's happening. He wants to know everything you do. He's like a father to you, you know," Hartono said.

"Between us and him we'll see that you come out right," he added.

"Yes, Hartono. I believe you. Somehow I trust you. Not because I have no alternative. I know I have no alternative now. But I have come to trust you ... You know what I mean?" Bertha said, slowly and haltingly.

"I do. I am very conscious now that I am in a position to take advantage of you."

He hung his head down. Bertha leant forward and put a hand on his shoulder.

"You're a strange man, Hartono, but a good man I believe."

He stood up and lit a cigarette. He took the ashtray from the bedside table and put it on the floor. Then he resumed his position on the floor in front of Bertha.

"There are details ..." Hartono went on with the details of the task. They were similiar to the Labis task and simple enough to Bertha. She asked him if it was safe to keep the cash with her at Fatimah's house. Yes, he said. Fatimah's husband was doing a management course in Sumatra. He would be away for another three months. In your organisation? she asked him. Yah. Just a monosyllabic answer.

She would keep the gun for the time being. And continue to dress, act and pretend to be a Malay woman. Minimum contact with the town people, please. Fatimah will do anything Bertha wanted her to do. But Fatimah only knows that on some days you will be doing some work for the university at the beach. Gathering specimens. And sending them off every day. So Fatimah won't see anything. Take the gun with you everywhere you go. You've still got the police permit?

I'll come up now and then. This is Siswono's phone number. But only for emergencies. He stays at Muar.

I'm so glad you and Ethel got on so well. She's a good girl, that girl. Knows what she wants.

"Not like me ..." Bertha added.

"Not yet. But give it time, Bertha," Hartono said.

"I hope you're right."

"The sun rises every morning, every morning." he said with a wry smile.

He looked at his watch. "Gosh. It's taken us longer than I expected. I'm thirsty. Let's go down and have a drink," he said getting up from the floor. "Poor Siswono, sitting there waiting. He's shocked with me all the time. My drinking and eating ..."

"But he told me he's very tolerant, almost like a *haji-bir-ham*, he said," Bertha told Hartono.

"That's not true. He only said that to put you at ease. He was worried about you that first day. I think I over-stressed the fact that you may be highly tensed up. I didn't know you then," Hartono said.

The girl at the reception glared at Hartono when he handed in the key. There was no come-hither look for him.

"Thanks, Bertha. You've solved a problem for me," Hartono said smiling to her.

"And created others?" Bertha replied at once, smiling.

They had a good dinner that night talking about Malaya and the jungle. Ethel and Bertha went to bed exhausted. After her bath in the morning, Ethel bent over Bertha who was lolling on the mat delaying her getting up, and kissed her goodbye.

Her body smelt fresh and clean and her flesh was cool and firm after her cold bath.

Hartono was there to pick Ethel up. He said Siswono would come at ten with the VW. She saw Fatimah's eyes darting from Bertha to Hartono as he spoke to her in English and waved a goodbye.

Bertha watched the car disappear with a heavy heart. A woman who had come through the rocks that had been scattered through her life, clean and pure in so many ways under the harshness and unschooled crudeness of her veneer. Ethel Richards, she said to herself, I'll never ever forget you.

"Nice man," Fatimah ventured as the car drove off.

"Very good man," Bertha said firmly. "My boss. Very good boss."

Bertha went to the beach every day when it was not raining and plotted the pipelines, the seawalls, buildings, estimating their dimensions by eye, checking her estimates now and then when no one was looking by pacing. She filled up little bottles with sea water when someone was watching her, and emptied them when no one was around. She swam and lay on the beach in the early morning. There was no restriction on leaving too early to avoid rubber tappers. In fact, on many a morning she watched the fishermen bring in their catch and sometimes bought fish for Fatimah.

Fatimah did wonders with the fish. The *ikan-parang*, the bony fish, grilled with *belachan* and chillies was truly *sheok*. And Fatimah's *fish asam*. To Bertha's surprise Fatimah could also do a *fish moolie*. It was an Indian dish. Fatimah said the Hylam cook at the rest house had taught her how to do it. Even the simple fried slices of *tenggiri* were suberb when Fatimah did them. Fish was Fatimah's forte.

Bertha could not eat Chinese food openly. She longed for a pork chop done with onions and green peas with a flour-thickened pale brown sauce. And for a real Hainanese *prawn-sambal*. Or *quay-teow* with fish balls. But that was taboo while she was posing as a Malay woman. She often had a good Indian curry or a *beryani* at an Indian stall near the beach. The wonderful thing about her new circumstances was that she was now mobile.

And there was the comfort of Fatimah's house. There was electricity and she could read at nights. And the radio. It was always on the Malay waveband, but there was music. And Fatimah kept it on all the time, humming to the tunes she knew.

Siswono dropped in now and then. His visits were brief. He was not as sociable as he had been at the jungle shack. He seemed to be afraid of her. Perhaps he had seen the easy relationship between her and Hartono, Bertha thought to herself. One day, he suggested that there was no need for him to come and she could phone him if she wanted anything. Hartono was always too careful, he said. His telephone was quite confidential. As long as she didn't leave messages with his wife or anyone else. That was a relief to her.

Fatimah was so very friendly. She had prodded in every direction in the first week, but gave up after that. Bertha learnt so many things about the ways of the Johor Malays from her. Hartono had briefed her to say that Bertha was from the Lake Toba area of Sumatra. She was not a Batak, but her Bahasa Melayu was poor. It explained Bertha. A Muslim, but not good in Malay. It gave her an escape when Fatimah's relatives who seemed to be constantly visiting her, and her friends started asking questions.

One of Fatimah's regular visitors, an old man, Pak Ridzwan was most interesting to Bertha initially. He discovered a listener for his tales of hunting in the jungles. He used to sit and talk on and on while Fatimah was getting the dinner ready of his good old days. How he had helped the Sultan as a beater, driving the tigers to the guns. The men with guns were usually on platforms which were built for them in the trees. He explained to her that it was not just for their safety but the tiger would not smell their scent if they were up above the ground. And it gave them a better view. He told her how they cut the undergrowth for the shooters to have an open strip in front of them. How the beaters tied a piece of wood across their spears so that the tiger could not get at them if their spears got stuck in his body. How the tiger always came around to the rear of an animal or man moving through the jungle.

Once, he was one of a party of two hundred beaters. That was a great hunt. Three members of the Sultan's household and two *orang puteh*. It was one of his longest and most detailed of his reminiscences. Ah, yes, those were the days.

And the *seladang*. It was the only beast in the Malayan jungle that attacked without provocation. It was huge. It never gave up once it had decided to attack. But Bertha remembered her father's friends ridiculing the belief about the *seladang* attacking without reason or provocation.

He had been a *punkah puller* for several years after he got too old for more active work. If only he had understood English, he would have heard all the secrets of the the state pulling the *punkah* while the dinners were going on. And the Sunday tiffins. With the mems half naked with bare shoulders and backs. Oh there were some beautiful white women then. Nowadays they seemed so fat.

But it came to a point when Pak Ridzwan's stories were more of a pleasure to him than to her. The trouble was she never knew when he was coming.

Hartono came about three weeks after she started her beach survey work. He drove to the house before going to his hotel. Bertha saw how hot and sweaty he was and suggested that they go down to the beach and swim at once. It was a great idea, he said. So they went. She swam in her *sarong* as she had learnt to. He had a thin pair of loose cotton shorts. She had learnt to roll her sarong up and leave her legs free to swim a breast stroke as soon as she was in the water. She saw that he was a powerful swimmer. They went out in the pale evening light, far out where they could hardly see their clothes on the beach. When they came back the sun was sinking. They sat on the beach watching the sky turn to flaming red and orange and the glow on the clouds suddenly fade. They could have sat there waiting for the moon, but the mosquitoes drove them off.

Hartono had asked her about her childhood when they arrived at the beach and she had talked and answered his many questions as they swam and lay at the frothing water's edge watching the sun go down.

"Oh, Hartono. I wish I could see my Ma and Pa again. Even if it's only for a little while," she said as they picked up their clothes. He stood still and looked at her.

"Bertha. Your fairy godfather will grant you your wish. I will take you to Singapore for a day. It's a risk, but I know how much it means to you. I understand, Bertha," he said watching her silhouetted against the last streaks of light above the horizon.

"Oh, Hartono!" She put her hands to her face. Tears welled up in her eyes. "Oh!" She whispered. "Oh, thank you, Hartono."

She was standing close to him. He put his hand round her

shoulders and gripped them tightly.

"Don't cry, baby, you're a big girl now," he whispered with a little laugh.

He suggested they go to his hotel. It was the same hotel, but the sexy receptionist was not there. She showered in the bathroom. It was wonderful to feel the spray of the shower on her body again. She came out wih the towel around her, her hair wet. She saw him looking at her body. He stood rooted to the spot for a second or two then he said, "OK, my turn," and went into the bathroom.

They ate at a street stall. They were alone by themselves in the noisy crowd. He continued to ask her about her family and friends in Singapore.

"You are different people," he said.

"Yes, Hartono. But this is still our country. We are not outsiders. Singapore is my country," she said to him.

"I understand," he said softly. It was his favourite phrase, she said to herself. But it's true. He does.

When he dropped her off at Fatimah's, she leaned across the gear lever and kissed him lightly on the cheek, as she said, "Thank you for a lovely evening."

"Cheh," he whispered and looked at the house. She saw that the corner of the curtain of Fatimah's bedroom was raised. "*Alamak!*"

They settled the plan on the next morning. Next week. She would get the battered VW checked up. She would drive down to JB. He would meet her in the evening by the seaside wall at JB. If there were any hitches, Siswono would contact her. The *nasi lemak* was delicious but the thought of going back home even if only for a day was swimming in her head.

"Till we meet in JB!" were his parting words.

~ *Chapter Twenty-six* ~

Singapore 1960

James Rodrigues walked up the steps to the verandah. Mary was at the front door to meet him. She looked worried.

"Wassermatter?" James asked.

"Nothing very serious. I broke the last sherry glass. That's the last. Thirty years, we've had them. Mrs. Schooling's wedding present, if you remember."

"Whoa ... thirty years," James muttered.

He kissed her on the cheek in a distracted perfunctory way and went straight to the sideboard. He poured himself a whisky. Mary looked at him. It was unusual that he went for a drink at once. She went to the fridge to get a soda, without a word. He saw her go to the fridge and went out to his verandah chair to wait for her to bring the soda and ice. When she came he saw that she had got herself a sherry in an unfamiliar glass.

"Testing the new glasses?" he teased.

"No lah," she mumbled. She sat down beside him and waited. There was something to tell, she had guessed from his mood. If he didn't ask what was for dinner now she would be sure.

"We're supposed to go to Auntie Ester's place tomorrow, aren't we?" he asked, appearing distracted.

"Yes. Herbert's birthday," Mary replied.

"Well, we'll have to cancel it. We have to stay home," he paused, looked at Mary, and continued.

"I got an odd phone call today. From Mr. Vandyke, of all people. Asked if he could come round tomorrow night. Said he wanted a quiet talk with us. Then he said that he really had to bring round some money he owed our Bertha," James said slowly to Mary.

"Her pay … she didn't collect her December pay?" Mary said.

It surprised James. It worried him that Mary was still thinking about every detail of Bertha's last few days with them.

"That's right. That's what he said … I asked him to stay for pot-luck. He agreed," James added.

"Does he eat curry?" Mary asked.

"Of course. Didn't you see him wallop the *kurma* at Bertha's wedding? Loves the stuff," James said. He continued after a sip of whisky soda, "Said he'll come round about seven."

"Wonder what else he wants?" Mary said to herself audibly.

She answered her own question, "Maybe he has some information."

James sighed deeply and pointedly. He lit a cigarette and spoke to Mary, "Ma, it's no use worrying about Bertha. I know she can look after herself. She's run away from the problems here. I'm sure she can find her feet in Malaya. She'll be OK, Ma. She doesn't need us any more."

"But I do wish she would write," Mary said.

But James was pursuing his own thoughts. "You know, when she first started working for him I thought the old bugger had his eye on her. Still a bachelor, you know. But I think he is genuinely fond of our Bertha … I don't think he has any information. I guess that he just wants to kick around possibilities with us … Or maybe he thinks he'll get some dope from me … being in the police."

"Just over four months now," Mary said softly. She didn't have to finish the sentence.

A car drove up the drive. "Now, who is this?" James said. Mary thought there was a little annoyance in his voice. It was not like him to be upset with unexpected visitors.

She recognised Sheelah's car. They had been seeing more of Sheelah recently. The car parked in the porch and Sheelah got out. From the other door a tall man got out. He was fair skinned, but not as fair as a European. James recognised him at once. Lionel

Mettah from Penang. "Hey, Lionel! What the hell are you doing here?" he shouted out.

"Come to visit you, lah," Lionel Mettah replied.

"Hello, Sheelah!" Mary and James greeted her.

"Well, well, well, it's been years, old cock," James said as he gripped Lionel Mettah's hand. Mary glared at him. Sheelah took it in her stride.

Whisky and soda, for Lionel. Sheelah? Same? Another one for me, Ma. Mary got the drinks.

"What brings you here, Lionel?" Lionel had come down with the PRC rugger team. Three days. They talked of the chances of the Penang team. The fullback bugger wasn't so good, James thought. But our stand-off and scrum half will knock the hell out of you bloody Singapore buggers, man. The three-quarter fellow, whassis name … Xavier. You have to see him, Lionel …

James changed the subject to hockey for Sheelah's sake.

"I see your goalie is back," he asked. Sheelah murmured a yes, and avoided his eyes.

It didn't work. Lionel was not the least bit interested in hockey. Lionel asked about Singapore. "How's the PAP treating you, James? Not bad.

"Not what I expected when they first came in. They have their own troubles, mind you, Lionel. Squabbling within themselves."

"Yeah, I heard about that Woodhull fellow standing up for the civil service and writing in their magazine … and Lee Kuan Yew replying with his 'open letter,' " Lionel said.

"That was some time ago. And it wasn't really just the civil service. It was the English educated. But I don't know about Woodhull. He's a smart bugger. There's more than meets the eye when he opens his mouth," James said. He looked at Sheelah. She always had her own opinions. But Sheelah did not speak.

"There's something else. They've finally found out that little runt, Ong Eng Guan. They're trying to throw him out at last," James said.

"Ong Eng Guan?" Lionel asked.

"The mayor fellow. The bloke who threw out the mace," James replied.

Mary laughed. "James keeps on and on about the mace," she said.

"He's standing up against the Party. You got to give him the credit. Taking the giants on. You mark my words, within six months he'll engineer a reelection. He'll resign and challenge them to fight him. And what's more, the little runt will win. I'll put my money on it. It worries me," James spoke with feeling.

"You reckon these guys will pull through, James?" Lionel asked. He didn't wait for an answer. He added his comment, "Bunch of reds, aren't they?"

James bristled. "Who do you mean? The PAP ?" he asked. Lionel read his strong reaction. "Yah ..." he answered timidly.

"No, Lionel. This is the first bloody time we've had politicians who aren't interested in themselves. You know, I was bloody upset when they cut our COLA and all that. But now I realise that these buggers are genuine. You probably don't see the rubber trees from the wood ... up there, up-country." James said beginning with intense seriousness and backing off.

"You probably think these guys are just Chinese up there, don't you, Lionel?" Sheelah asked.

"It looks like it. They hammered the English educated, when they got in, didn't they?" Lionel asked.

"Stay for *makan* ..." Mary interrupted. She had slipped away to the kitchen to check on the amount of food they had.

Sheelah looked at Lionel. He raised his eyebrows. "OK by me, Mary," Sheelah said. "You're OK, aren't you, Lionel?"

"Don't want to have a late night," he mumbled. "You're sure it's not upsetting the household?"

Mary closed the subject with the clincher, "I've got *jering* tonight."

"How the hell ...? We can't get it these days in Malaya," Lionel asked.

"Mr. Mettah, we have connections," Mary said with her nose in the air.

The talk moved to the Emergency. "Finished, lah," Lionel said.

"Then we can go shooting again?" James asked.

"Not yct, lah."

"They don't trust our PAP, do they?" Sheelah asked Lionel. James noted her adjective, "our." One never knew with Sheelah. One minute with the *orang puteh*, the next minute defending that crazy chap Sukarno ...

But Lionel didn't want to pursue the subject. "Eh ... How can you expect the Malays to trust the Chinaman who won't speak Malay, I ask you? ... Must tell you, James, my friend Van Geyzel says he saw Bertha in Batu Pahat recently."

James sat up as though he had been struck by a bolt of lightning. "Is he sure? He only met her on that hockey tour," he asked, looking hard at Lionel.

"So he says lah," Lionel again tried to slip out of the subject.

James kept at him. "Where did he see her? When?" he asked.

"Dunno. Jus' said he saw her ... Didn't speak to her. Saw her in a car ... Las' month I think, he said. ... Yah, in a car, in Batu Pahat ... that's not so far from Seremban ..." Lionel replied in broken phrases. Just like Lionel, James said to himself. Never ever exact. Bloody teacher.

Sheelah looked into James eyes. "No news?" she asked softly.

James shook his head. She kept her gaze on him after he answered. He had thought of Mr. Vandyke's phone call and felt uncomfortable. Sheelah saw the doubt in his eyes. She dropped her eyes away from his.

"Dinner!" Mary called out cheerily. They walked into the house from the verandah. As she passed a desk Sheelah saw a book on it and read the title, *Mandarin for Beginners*.

"Good God, James! Mandarin! What is this book doing here?" she asked loudly.

Mary answered, "He's studying it. In his old age ..."

"Gotta move with the times." James added.

Lionel Mettah from Penang heard him and frowned. These

Singapore Seranis are changing, he thought to himself. Even old James.

Their visitors went off early. And James was up early the next morning. He walked round the garden with a *punkis* picking up snails. Now and then he muttered a, "Ha, ha. Gotchyer." He didn't mutter to himself before. He was fifty-one now, and fighting fit he added, if he had to give his age. He was acting DSP. Had been acting for six months. But he was not a man to sit in the office all day. Gotta keep in touch was his excuse to move around and drop in on the units under him unannounced. He was slow with his written work and brought more and more work home. Keeps him out of mischief, Mary used to tell the ladies. She really meant keeps him away from the club bar.

But the reassuring fact to him, as the last eleven months had gone past, was that unlike Moreira and Dengah, he had been able to see the new game play. He had been able to appreciate what the PAP was pushing for. It might have been painful to them in the short term, but he was now sure that it was for their own good in the long run. He wouldn't even think of migrating as Moreira was planning to do. There's nothing left for us Serani here, James, Moreira had told him. James had not taken him on. He's the type who cannot change with the times, James thought to himself, reassuring himself that he was still young enough to adapt. His mind wasn't set. Not like Mary's.

Some of these thoughts went through his mind again as he stirred his tea on the verandah. But he had other worries. That Inspector Hamid. Fighting in the bar. The disciplinary committee was sitting today. Damn good man. Sort of thing the British OCPD would forget in the old days. If you could show him that the bugger performed. And Teoh, hitting the secret society chappie. In the bloody station too. Why the hell didn't he do it before he brought him in. That's the only way to treat the bastards. But things are not the same as they used to be. Sheeesh! The fellow spilled the beans. Poor old Teoh's had it. Damn good man. Going to lose him.

He came home that evening with the decisions on Hamid and

Teoh on his mind. As he had predicted. Then he remembered Mr. Vandyke's visit. Seven, he said. Better have a bath and put on a clean shirt before I have a drink.

He was on the verandah at a quarter to seven with his whisky soda. Mary came up from the kitchen at seven.

"No sign of Mr. Vandyke," she said. James was used to this. Mary saying the obvious. He had stopped making sarcastic counters years ago. Mary continued.

"I saw a fellow hanging around the front from about six, James. Malay bloke. Don't know if I'm imagining but he gave me the feeling that he was watching the house."

James grunted. It didn't worry him in the least. "Probably a bloody CPIB spy. Can't even do a surveillance job without being obvious." James was convinced that the force had given the CPIB their rejects. He had nothing to hide. The bugger should be watching George's place, he thought to himself.

An MG Magnette came up the drive. That's him, James and Mary thought silently. The car stopped and the door on the left swung open. A young woman rushed out of the car and ran up the steps. He heard Mary gasp, "Bertha." And in the next second Bertha was in Mary's arms.

"Ma, oh Ma," she kept repeating as she hugged Mary. Then she turned around and threw herself into James's arms.

"Pa!"

"Oh Berberbertha. You're berberback!" James stammered.

Over Bertha's shoulder he saw the tears of joy running down Mary's cheeks.

The black MG Magnette slipped into gear and drove away quietly. Bertha stepped back out of James' arms and grinned from ear to ear at the both of them. "Gee … It's good to see you again," she said.

"You look good, Bertha. But so brown!" Mary said.

"Been in the sun a lot," Bertha replied.

"Where's your bag?" Mary asked. Bertha did not have a handbag with her.

"Didn't bring one," Bertha replied showing her open hands.

"I mean your suitcase. Your clothes?" Mary asked again.

Bertha put on a serious look. "I've only come to visit. Just for tonight," she said.

"It's seven, Ma," James said. "Mr. Vandyke will be here any moment."

Then he turned to Bertha. "Is this a secret visit? Or are you ..." Bertha cut him short. "Yes Pa. I cannot stay. I only came back for one night to see the two of you. You can report to them tomorrow afternoon, Pa."

He ignored her last sentence.

"Then you better get in before Mr.Vandyke comes," Mary took Bertha's arm and started walking her to the door. But Bertha stopped while they were still on the verandah. "Mr. Vandyke is not coming. I asked him to make the arrangement to make sure that you would be at home."

"Oh Bertha," Mary interrupted. Bertha continued, "And to make sure there'll be dinner for me!"

"Let's get out of the verandah light anyway," Mary said.

"That's OK, Ma," Bertha said.

"Sit with your back to the road, then," James said. He suddenly thought of the man hanging around the house that Mary had told him about.

"Does anyone else know you're here in Singapore?" James asked Bertha.

"No," Bertha said looking into James's eyes, wondering why he asked.

Mary let her arm go. "Drink? Mr. Vandyke?" James asked.

Bertha laughed. "Yes, Mr. Rodrigues, a brandy soda please."

"I'll get it," Mary said at once.

"You sit here, Ma, and get all the news. I'll get it," James insisted.

"Now tell us. But first, how are you?" Mary said to Bertha, smiling now and relaxed.

Bertha told her what Hartono had suggested. That she had

worked with a surveying party in Kedah. A big group. Bertha did most of the administration work. And some field recording. No mention of Ethel Richards. But saying there was a Eurasian girl named Ethel. Just in case something slips out. Then the party did another job at Morib. Ordinary survey work, but in more detail for hotel development. Chalet type developement. "You work the details around that, Bertha," Hartono had said.

James came back with her drink and a sherry for Mary.

"Now tell me," he said.

"No, James. I'll tell you tomorrow. Let's not waste precious time with repeating stories," Mary said.

"Yah," James said. "Did she say what happened to the Jag?" he asked Mary.

"I sold it," Bertha said.

"How could you? You didn't have the registration book?" he said.

"Yes, I did. If you remember Heng was going to sell it. Even the transfer forms were signed," she replied smiling.

"Yaah. That was lucky," he grinned. Then he sat up. He remembered what the police had told him. "But the sale was not registered," he said.

"I knew the fellow was a crook!" Bertha said frowning.

"You went all the way to Ipoh?" he asked cross-examining her as though he was at the station.

"Yes," she replied getting a little uneasy. "How did they find out?" she asked.

"From the petrol stations you stopped at," he replied, "Kajang, Rawang and Slim River wasn't it? But they couldn't fathom out why you needed to stop so many times. They went back and asked the attendants whether you filled her up and they said yes," he added.

"Not quite right, Dad. I stopped once for air. For a rest more than anything else. And I never filled the tank right up. I was short of cash. Didn't want to get more juice than necessary," Bertha said.

James looked into her eyes. He frowned a little and said, "Goes to show. Witnesses are never reliable. Always try to get corroboration, I tell my boys."

Bertha saw James' face change. The muscles tightened and she knew he was about to ask her something serious or unpleasant. But at that moment old Muthu appeared at the door, grinning at Bertha. She hailed him like long lost friend but there was no hugging or touching. It wasn't done. Not with the servants. They asked after each other's health and they were both pleased at the interest each showed in the other. There was an intimacy in their meeting, but it had to be expressed in the subdued manner they both understood and respected. He said dinner was ready.

"*Kurma*," Mary said, "but not so hot. I thought Mr. Vandyke was coming."

"Eric?" Bertha asked, her eyebrows raised.

"He won't be home," Mary replied.

"Did I chase him away by asking Mr. Vandyke to say he was coming?" Bertha asked.

"No. He's in the army now," James said.

"Army?" Bertha asked with surprise in her voice.

"Yes," James said. "He could not pass his exams in the Harbour Board. I mean the British MOT exams. So he joined the army."

"Why not the police?" Bertha asked.

"He said one Rodrigues in the police was enough!" James said laughing.

Bertha grunted a "huh."

"It was the maths, Bertha. He was never good at maths," Mary said softly.

"But he's well off in the army," James added.

"The British Army?" Bertha asked.

"Good God, no. They won't take him. He's joined the Singapore army."

"I didn't know that there was such a thing."

"Of course there is. Whaddayer spect? The Malay regiment to defend us?" James said sarcastically.

Bertha did not reply. This was not a night to start arguments.

"Here, Bertha some *pulang hari,*" Mary broke the conversation thread offering Bertha the pickles.

"Wow! And *kachang bendi*!" Bertha said smiling.

Mary was bursting to tell her the news. "Theresa Pestana's going to have a baby."

"How's Beryl and Ben?" Bertha asked. They had not said anything about Beryl. "Are they OK?" she asked.

"Fine. Robert's coming up with the cutest things these days," Mary said.

"Oh yes!" Mary continued, "Desmond Froist is going to marry Felicia's daughter."

"Really! She seduced him I bet!" Bertha said.

"Just like the old Bertha," Mary chuckled.

"Sheelah was here last night," James said looking into Bertha's eyes.

"Oh, yes," she said.

"And Uncle Dennis died," Mary said. There was so much to tell.

"Knocked down by a taxi," James added.

"More curry, Bertha," Mary said. "James must always give the gory details. I suppose he's going to tell her about his hip bone next."

The dinner conversation went on. The Serani news.

Then James came up with the question that was hanging on lips since Bertha arrived on the doorstep, "What are your plans now, girl?"

Bertha noted the intimate word from her childhood.

"I'm not coming back to Singapore." She saw Mary's face fall with disappointment. "Not at the moment, anyway."

"We can drop the investigation ..." James said weakly.

Bertha interrupted him, clearly and firmly. "No. Dad. Don't compromise yourself for me. As it is I'm asking you to report my appearance late. I'm all right. For the moment."

James looked hard at her. She thought for a moment she saw anger in his eyes. But maybe it was something else.

"If I need your help, I'll ask for it." She said it an a soft open way. Not in a haughty stand off manner. Both James and Mary understood.

"How's things up there?" James asked. She was afraid he would. She had not followed the political events while she was at the Labis shack. At Batu Pahat, she had heard the news on the radio but she had not understood it all of it. They used so many Malay words she did not know.

"I really can't read what the Tengku wants, Dad," she said. "On one hand he has said that he is impressed by the 'Malayan' character of our PAP but yet he referred to the 'China-minded' outlook of some people in Singapore."

"I reckon he's afraid of us," James said.

"The political machine's too good," Bertha said, "The PAP will beat the pants off the Alliance in KL and Ipoh."

"Dunno about Ipoh ... There's those two Indian brothers there. Seenivasagams. Or is it Sreenivasagams ...? It's amazing what support they've got. Two bloody Indians in a completely Chinese town," James said.

"It's their honesty," Mary added.

"Yah," Bertha said. "And their wealth helps ... the people know they are not looking for power to make them rich."

"Are they that rich?" Mary asked.

They talked of Singapore. James gave his views about the struggles Lee Kuan Yew was having within the party.

"Dammit, the bugger's good," he said when he finished.

Bertha looked at him. "So you think he's a great guy now, do you?" she asked, half mockingly. "You didn't before," she added.

"He's sharp and ruthless. He's the guy that'll clean out the bloody reds," James said.

"James!" Mary objected to his "bloody."

"But is he winning now?" Bertha asked.

"Dunno ... I think he is," James frowned and answered.

Dinner was soon finished.

They moved back to the verandah. "Port?" James asked.

Mary went to the phone. She dialled someone a few times and came back to the verandah. "The phone's dead, James," she said.

"I'll call them from the office in the morning," James said.

Then Mary related a long story about Arumugam, the gardener, and how he got drunk at the *toddy* shop and started throwing his weight around saying that he worked for the DSP. And the story of his sister's illness, the poor thing. Muthu's not so well either. Diabetes, I think it is. We're all getting old.

It drifted to the secret societies that James was now struggling with in his job. Then to hockey. And the Selangor rugger team. And back to hockey. Then Mary remembered that she had not told Bertha about the De Wind boy getting into the university and doing brilliantly. It was just as it used to be, Bertha thought to herself. I'm home.

And suddenly the MG Magnette came up the drive. Bertha stood up. "Gosh! It's twelve already! I have to go now."

The car stopped in the porch. "Ask your friend in for a drink," James said. Bertha saw that it was not his normal friendly invitation. The policeman in him was thinking.

She went to the car. Hartono leant over and rolled down the window of the front passenger's seat. They talked.

"He won't stay for a drink, but he'll come in to say hello," Bertha said. She was surprised that Hartono had agreed. Wants to know everything about me, she thought to herself.

She waited for Hartono to come to the top of the steps. She saw him looking closely at Mary. "My mother, Mr. Hartono," she said. He bowed. "My father …"

Hartono turned and looked directly at James for the first time. His eyes widened and his jaw dropped. He stood in shock, staring at James for a second. Then he dropped to his knees and bent down to the floor till his head touched the wooden boards. Bertha dropped down beside him, on one knee, her hand on his back. "Hartono!"

"Sir!" he muttered, his voice unsteady with emotion. "You saved my life many years ago. I owe my life to you."

James stared and frowned. Then his face lit up. "You're not

Tono? The Jawanese boy?"

"Yes, sir ... Many, many years ago," Hartono mumbled.

Bertha looked at her father. He must have been the Malay Inspector Hartono had told her about. She stood up. Her knees were trembling.

James dropped to the floor on one knee. He gripped Hartono under the armpit and pulled him up.

"Oooi. Steady!" he said.

Hartono stood up sheepishly with his head bowed. "I owe my life to you, Mr. Inspector," he said.

James turned to Mary. Not to Bertha. "This must have been the little scruff I told you about. From the Rochore canal death line ..." he said.

Then he said to Hartono, "Please ... It was my duty ... my job."

"I know it wasn't," Hartono said. "I know, sir."

Bertha had never seen Hartono so submissive. So crushed and meek. She stared at him.

The four of them stood in silence for a while. "It's a small world ..." Mary said softly. No one heard what she said. "Please sit down," Mary said.

Hartono straightened himself. He looked at James. "I can at last repay my debt, by the grace of Allah. Mr. Inspector Rodrigues, I will look after your daughter as if she were my own child. I promise you," he said slowly and deliberately.

He turned to Bertha, "We must go now. They are waiting for us," he said.

James went up to him and gripped his hand. He put his other hand on Hartono's shoulder. "You don't know how happy it makes me to see you ... alive. I thought you'd never make it. It was God's will ... and to think that you would meet my daughter. It's, it's, it's ..." he stammered, lost for words.

"We must go," Hartono said.

Bertha went up to Mary and hugged her. She broke away after a second and kissed Mary on the cheek. "Bye, Ma. I'll be back soon. Don't worry."

James hugged her. He gripped Hartono's shoulder as a last parting gesture in silence.

Bertha reached out for Hartono's hand as the car turned into the street. He didn't respond. He was gripping the steering wheel. His eyes stared at the road ahead. She put her hand on his on the wheel.

"Who do we have to meet?" she asked after a few minutes.

"No one," he replied, not looking at her.

When they got to the hotel he turned to Bertha. "Please excuse me if I do not see you to the door," he said. His words were slow in coming and uncertain. "I want to drive around a bit."

"I know, Hartono," she said. She took her hand off his. She had let it stay on his at the wheel going back to cover his large hand every time after he changed gears all the way back to the hotel. "Goodnight."

Bertha sat for a long time at the dressing table in her bra and panties thinking. It was hot.

Then the phone rang. Hartono, she thought at once.

"Bertha! This is Sheelah."

It hit her like a sudden punch in the face. She gripped the phone not knowing how to react. She held it away from her with her mind spinning round and round. She heard the crackling voice, "Bertha! Bertha! ..." And then a click.

She put the reciever back on its cradle. It rang at once, the sound crashing into her ears like an explosion. She stood by the phone in an agony of indecision. It went on and on. She didn't know what to do. No one knew where she was except Hartono. Yet she so wanted to say sorry to Sheelah again. Sheelah had done so much for her. But she was vulnerable now. Exposed. Then it stopped. Her tension dropped back. She sat on the chair by the telephone. A new agony twisted inside her. She should have talked to Sheelah. Now Sheelah would think that ... The phone rang again. Once, twice, three, four, five times ...

~ *Chapter Twenty-seven* ~

Benny Yap

Bertha had very little sleep that night. Hartono picked her up at four-thirty in the morning and took her to Lim Chu Kang Road with another Indonesian-looking man who sat in the back and did not utter a single word. That was the way she had come yesterday. Then they went down some earth tracks and came to the sea.

It was still dark. She held the collar of the black coat she was wearing, drawing it tightly round her neck. It was cold and damp with dew. She thought she recognised Pulau Sarimbun. She had swum there a few times many years ago.

The same little sampan was waiting for them without any lights. Hartono held her hand as she climbed into it after the little Indonesian. She only noticed that he was a small man after she got out of the car. Hartono sat beside her. With the boatman there were four of them.

It was quiet and calm. Only the subdued noise of the oars dipping into the water and the squeaking of the ropes holding the oars to the two wooden uprights. She could see the lights of Johor Baru across the narrow straits.

"You all right?" Hartono asked in a whisper.

"Yes," she answered, and after a second added, "Thank you."

She wanted to reach out and take his hand, but she did not know who the mysterious Indonesian boatman was. She moved so that their bodies were touching. Hartono turned and looked at her.

"You heard what I said to Mr. R?" he asked softly.

"Yes," she answered.

"I mean it. It was a great shock to me, I mean surprise. And now

now I am grateful that I can repay him in some small way."

She looked into his eyes and remained silent.

"You can trust me," he said.

"I told you before, I trust you," she said quietly.

The sound of a motor boat made him sit up and look in its direction. The little Indonesian sitting in front of them turned round and looked at Hartono. There was fear in his eyes. Hartono concentrated on the boat. Only the red port light was visible. It was too dark to see the shape or size of the boat. The boatman stopped rowing.

Hartono told him to continue in Malay. "Too small for a police boat," he added.

The boat passed and Bertha could see the little Indonesian relax and assume his humped position again. They finally arrived on the beach in Johor. Hartono handed some money to the boatman and held Bertha's arm, leading her to a road. The little Indonesian followed. A car was waiting for them. They got in and, after a short drive, the car stopped in a carpark in the town. Bertha saw her VW. Hartono got out and walked with her to the car.

"I have one or two things to tell you. You go back and finish the beach job. It's nearly done, isn't it?"

He didn't wait for an answer. "When it's finished, I'll go to Jakarta with you."

"Jakarta!" Bertha exclaimed.

"Shh ..." Hartono whispered. "Someone will call on you and give you the details. OK?"

"Yes, Hartono," she replied.

"You have to go now. They've checked the car and filled her up. Drive safely, Bertha," he said.

She put out her hand and touched him on the chest. He took her hand as it pressed on his chest and held it for a second. Then he let it go.

"If you have any trouble on the road, ring Siswono. You have his number?"

"Yes. Bye and thank you again," Bertha said.

"'Bye ... and please don't worry," he said and turned round abruptly. Bertha watched him go to the car. She found her keys and opened her VW door.

The sky was grey and the clouds thick and black when Bertha went down the sea the next day. The water was a greenish-grey, tossing and churning, frothing like a restless animal caught in a trap. The wind was strong and the coconut tree leaves thrashed around in the air. Now and then, there was a crackling and a thump as a palm-leaf or a coconut crashed to the ground. The wind drew her *sarong* and her *baju* tight against her thighs and her breasts. It was as if the whole world was angry and restless.

It deepened her depression. But yet there was an electric crispness in the air. On the beach, with the salt spray on her face, she felt as though the raging animal inside her was going to break out. It was not like the hollow empty nothingness of the depression she felt sitting in her room the night before.

She walked the beach for three hours without stopping. For lunch, she bought three dry-fried chicken wings and pickles from a passing little boy and ate them sitting on the beach. It stayed one hunger in her, but something else was turning round and round inside her stomach. She checked if she had brought a spare *sarong*. She had. She went into the heaving, angry sea letting the waves buffet her body with their sudden, strong but gentle blows.

She wanted to take her *sarong* off and feel the sea and the sand it stirred up against her skin. She looked back to the beach. Two elderly men were standing there. Probably wondering why that *gila* woman was out in the sea on a day like this.

She didn't know what was consuming her. She didn't try to think about it. Fate, the Malays said. The forces of nature. Face it. Don't try to understand it. You never will, she told herself. It is just what we are. The way I was born.

Two days after she had got back, she noticed a blue BMW parked outside Fatimah's house as she drove in from the beach at about six o'clock. Fatimah was at the top of the steps to meet her.

"That rude fellow is waiting to see you," she said. "I asked him to come in and wait here but he didn't even say thank you and went and sat in his car."

Bertha had seen a Singapore number plate. She didn't say that to Fatimah.

"When did he come?" she asked.

"About half an hour ago," Fatimah replied. "So rude. Nearly came into the house with his shoes on. Lucky I saw him before he came in. Cannot even speak Malay. All he could say was Berta, Berta, Berta ..." She made a sour face.

"I think I know who he is," Bertha said. "Probably someone from the university. Those university people are all like that."

"What's the use of brains if you have no manners?" Fatimah said.

"Another of Fatimah's proverbs?" Bertha asked smiling. Fatimah smiled. "Aiyah! You always tease me." She was pacified now, Bertha thought.

As they were talking a young Chinese man came walking up to the house. He was slim and fair-skinned. Well dressed and he walked with a confident stride. Probably late twenties, Bertha thought.

"Miss Berta?" he asked.

"Yes," she replied.

"May I talk to you in private?" he asked.

As he came up to the house Fatimah had moved inside. But Bertha knew she would be behind the door trying to listen even though she knew hardly any English.

Bertha went down the steps of the verandah and pointed to the gate. He turned round and walked beside her.

"I've come to give you the details. The password is coconut water," he said.

"Oh yes. In a can," Bertha replied.

"Right!" he responded, rolling the "r."

"Let's go out to dinner and talk," he said.

"OK, but I'm dirty from the beach. Let me change," she said.

"Oh. It doesn't matter," he said. "Let's go now."

Bertha looked at him. He looked so young but she knew he couldn't be as young as he looked.

"I'll go and tell Fatimah then," she said turning away.

"Don't bother, let's go," he said.

Bertha stopped in her tracks. She turned to him and raised her voice, "That's just plain courtesy, which I believe you haven't got! Wait for me!"

He was taken aback. He did not reply. She went in and called out to Fatimah who appeared at once at the door that she would not be eating in tonight.

"Aiyah! Fried *selah* with *belachan* ..." she sighed.

"And *sayur chukop manis*," she added.

He was in the car when she went out to the road. She opened the door and went in. It smelt of new leather.

"What's your name?" she asked.

"It's confidential," he answered.

"Don't be an arsehole!" she said. She saw him reel with the shock of her word. Then she added, "I know how these things work. But you must have a bloody name to use." She was mad now. She went on. "And you better learn a few things right now. The stupidest bloody thing is to be rude to people."

"Was I rude?" he interrupted her.

"Yes. To Fatimah. They notice you then. And parking outside the house was really the end. The whole *kampong* will know, if it doesn't know already that the Batak girl at Fatimah's had a visitor from Singapore. A rich man with a big BMW," she said in a rush of words.

He was silent. She could see that he was upset by her tirade.

He drove on in silence.

They got into the town and Bertha could see that he knew his way. He stopped at a row of shophouses and indicated with a jerk of his head that they were getting out there. She followed him. He walked along the five-foot-way and started to turn into an air-conditioned Chinese restaraunt. Bertha grabbed his arm.

He stopped. She released her hold. "I can't go into a Chinese restaurant." He looked at her surprised. Then he said, "Ah! Of course," and turned to her. "Where to?"

"Roadside stalls. You can have what you want and I can eat Muslim food. Follow me."

Can't they send someone better than this nut, she thought to herself after she had ordered her *roti chanai*, mutton curry and longbeans. She called the man back and added a chicken liver to her order. He got up and walked around the stalls before he decided what to eat.

When he came back he said to her, "I'm Randy Lim."

"You know my name," she countered.

"Yes. Well, as you were told there are some details which I have to brief you on." He went on talking.

The food came. Bertha started eating. He continued talking. He appeared to eat very fast to her. Even though the *loh-mai-kai* seemed to be piping hot. He kept talking all through the meal. Now and then he paused to ask, "You understand?" Bertha muttered a yes, usually with her mouth full. The chicken liver was particularly delicious today, she thought.

He stopped his briefing once. He looked at Bertha and asked, "You eat curry?" It took her with surprise. That he had only just reacted. She was already half way through her meal. "Yah, sure. What makes you ask?" she queried.

"Oh. I thought you were Eurasian, not Malay," he said.

"So. What do you think Eurasians eat?" she asked in an aggressive way.

"Oh." Her question surprised him and the way she said it shook him. "I thought you ate western food," he said, not sounding convincing.

"You mean you've never thought about it, right?" she thrust again.

"Yes. I only knew one Eurasian. At the university. But I never got to know him well. He was always drinking with the Englishmen," he said.

"Englishmen? Were you studying in England?" she asked.

"Yes. At Oxford," he said.

"And you don't drink?" she asked again.

"No," he replied.

"Against your principles?" Bertha asked.

"No. I get so red when I drink."

"Ah. I see."

"Do you drink?" he asked her. She felt he had almost asked her if she committed mortal sins.

"Yah. Love it," she answered, exaggerating to rattle him.

He was silent.

"Tell me about this bloke Pratono," she asked.

He went back to his briefing. She wanted him to. She felt nothing in common with him. For one thing, he was so stylishly dressed. With a fancy gold watch. Probably something terribly expensive, she thought. She wouldn't have a clue what the grand brand names were. These things didn't matter to her. They mattered to Eric, though.

He was precise and clear. But there was no comment or smile from him. It was facts he had to convey. And some slogans that sickened her. For the good of the country. We must all try our level best. He spoke well. But there were the occasional "Singlish" howlers that used to unsettle Ben. "You muzn't" was one.

He had not finished his briefing when she finished her meal. She called out to the Indian drinks man and ordered a *teh aliah*. He broke his train of briefing and asked her, "What is that?"

"Tea with ginger," she said.

"Tea with ginger?" he asked incredulously.

"Yah. It's been around before you were born, old chap," Bertha answered, superciliously.

It hit him. He muttered a "Never heard of it" and continued what he had been directed to tell her.

In spite of her dislike for him, Bertha listened attentively. And finally he completed his briefing. It was late. She had had a second *teh aliah*.

He paid. They got up and left. He went straight to his side of the car. Hartono had the Western graces that Bertha was brought up to expect. This flashy young pup didn't. It seeded another feeling of dislike for him.

He took her back to Fatimah's and left with, not a "Goodnight" but a "Doan forget what I've told you."

The next morning, she chatted with Fatimah about him in a nonchalant way. It seemed natural for her to talk openly to Fatimah about her first unknown visitor. The university fellow, she called him. So young and fumbling. So rude. Fatimah went along with her. The rude Chinese. Especially the Singapore types. Not like the Malacca people or Penangites. It's the city people, Fatimah said. Even some *orang melayu* in Kuala Lumpur were behaving like animals these days. What in God's name is the world coming to!

It's not being a big-shot, Fatimah said. Our Sultans and the *orang puteh* in the old days were not like the new civil servants. Our Sultans and their family, though they were so much above us, never behaved in such a way. Fatimah sailed on, her sails billowing, enjoying herself. She just loved these heart to hearts.

Bertha worked fast and furiously for the next seven days. It distracted her from thoughts she did want to dwell on. She covered more ground than she had ever done. She dropped onto her mat dead tired every night, her stomach happily contented with Fatimah's wonderful food.

One evening, after a good day's surveying and recording work was done, she sat on the beach and decided to watch the sunset. Fatimah would be a little worried and upset with her being late but once in a while, she said to herself, was all right. As she sat waiting for the sky to redden and the clouds to burst into flame, she saw the sea eagle. It was gliding so beautifully and serenely over the sea. Bertha was thrilled with the sight. She felt her whole being rising into the sky with the sea eagle. It was Hartono's favourite bird. It made her feel sad but calm and gliding in a strange way. Against the grey sky, with the first tinges of orange, the *lang laut*.

"*Lang laut*," a voice said behind her. She turned round to see a short young Chinese man standing on the beach a few feet away from her. He had a nondescript white shirt on, the sleeves rolled halfway up his forearms. A baggy khaki or yellow-brown pair of trousers. Black unpolished shoes.

She smiled at him. "Yah. I know," she said in Malay.

"A beautiful bird," he replied in English.

They watched the sea eagle for a second or two.

Then it dropped. Dropped like a stone down to the sea. They could only see its talons and a flash of silver of the fish skin as its feet dipped into the frothing water and it rose again into the sky.

"Whoa! See dat!" he said in excitement.

"Yah" Bertha responded.

His excitement was almost childish.

They smiled at each other, sharing the delight of the unexpected dive of the sea eagle.

They watched it in silence as it flapped its huge wings slowly gaining height.

"That's why I like to come down to the beach in the evening," he said.

"You live around here?" Bertha asked.

"No. Just visiting," he said.

"Where're you from?" she asked.

"Medan originally, now Jakarta," he answered.

"Fancy meeting an Indonesian here ..." Bertha remarked. Then she remembered that she was being herself against what she should be. Don't get familiar with the town people, Hartono had said to her.

"You speak English so well," he said, dropping his voice off as he spoke.

She left it. She ignored the call for a comment or answer.

"You ever been to Indonesia?" he asked.

"Yah. Once," she replied spontaneously.

"Dirty, inefficient, but friendly ... Yah?" he prompted.

"Yah. Wonderful country," she responded.

"One day it will be like Singapore, or KL but not in the country areas ..." he said.

She controlled herself and kept silent.

"The key question is, would you like to go back, even for a short visit?" he asked. She noted the way he framed it. This was no ordinary *kampong* man.

"Yes, I would," she replied.

"You should also see the rest of Indonesia. Such a huge country. So many people. So many different kinds of people. All people with a history. All people with feeling. Warmth. Mountains. Volcanoes. Rivers. Jungles. And beaches like this," he said softly and slowly.

"Oh yes. I've read about it. I do want to see, feel Indonesia one day," Bertha replied without thinking.

"There are many parts of the world that are as beautiful. And as harsh, but that is my home," he said looking into the sky. The sea eagle had gone. They had not seen it go.

"You speak English so well …" Bertha said.

"Not as good as yours," he said.

"Where did you learn it?" Bertha asked.

"At home … and later in Singapore," he replied.

"Singapore?" Bertha asked.

"Yes," he said, "A wonderful place … in some ways."

"Only in some ways?"

"Yah. Not perfect. Not everything I would like Jakarta to be."

"What don't you like about it?"

"You're from Singapore?" he asked.

"What makes you ask?" Bertha replied.

"Don't know. Maybe it's the way you talk. Like an American. Like a man."

"Hah!" Bertha ended the exchange with the exclamation.

He smiled at her in a patronising way.

Then he took two steps and came right up to her.

"I'm Benny Yap. *Chin chin semut*."

Bertha heard the password Hartono had told her. It came as a shock to hear this relaxed man with the baggy pants say it. She returned the second line.

"*Siapa sakit jangan naik.*"

He laughed loudly and sat on the the beach in front of her. He tossed his head back and laughed again as he settled down on the sand. His small round stomach shaking.

"Hartono's passwords and replies are always so clever!" he said, chuckling.

She smiled at him. "The details of the Jakarta trip?" she asked.

"Yah. But no hurry. What about tomorrow?" he asked.

"Fine," she said. "Meet you here at the beach at five," she suggested.

"Later better. Maybe we can see the eagle again," he replied.

"OK," she agreed.

"Oh I like it so much here. It's so peaceful," he said.

"Yah," Bertha agreed. She looked closely at him. His comment about the peaceful beach was spontaneous and genuine, she thought. He was not trying to probe her thoughts or test her. He was just happy sitting there.

A mosquito buzzed in her ear. "The mosquitos have arrived. I must go," Bertha said standing up.

"Excuse me not seeing you to your car. I want to sit here for a while," he said. He stood up. "See you tomorrow then. Six-thirty. This place. It seems quiet enough."

Then he added, "We'll go and get some *makan* while we talk, if that's all right with you."

"Good. Thank you," Bertha said.

"Goodnight then. Sleep well," he said.

"Eat first, then sleep," Bertha said smiling trying to make a joke. She walked away.

The next day Bertha put a dress in the bag she took to the beach every day. And her make-up. She hadn't worn a dress or make-up for months and somehow she felt that an occasion had at last arrived.

Benny Yap turned up about fifteen minutes late without an apology. She rose to greet him but he told her to sit down.

"We'll watch the sun set before we go," he said.

She agreed. She liked sitting on the beach at that time of the evening.

"Well," Benny said after he had settled himself on the beach, "so nicely dressed, Miss Bertha Rodrigues."

"Please call me Bertha, without all the fussy bits," Bertha said.

"Yah. Sure, if that's the way you want it." he replied.

"It's better for security too," Bertha added thinking that she may have sounded a bit brassy for Benny Yap.

"And I am Benny," he said.

"Ah! Our *lang laut*," Bertha said pointing to the sky. The sea eagle was there gliding serenely above them.

Benny watched it in silence for a minute. Then he asked Bertha, "What would you like to eat? Chinese, Malay or Indian or even Western if you want to."

"I haven't eaten Chinese food for ages," Bertha replied.

"And since you're not a Malay girl today, we shall eat Chinese. But we'll drive to Muar, I think. You are not known there," he said.

"Good. That's where Siswono lives," Bertha said.

"I don't know him," Benny said in a serious voice. He looked at her for a second or two then continued, "If he's Hartono's man, you shouldn't have mentioned him. Right?"

"Yah. My slip. I'm sorry," she said.

"Now you have really slipped! Bertha you have to be much more careful, you know," he said.

"I am. It's only that I'm relaxed with you," she said.

"Anyway, shall we eat Chinese then?"

"Yah. If you think it's OK."

"Do you like Chinese food best?" he asked.

"You mean compared to Western, Malay, Indian and all that?"

"Yes."

"I don't know really ... It's difficult to choose," Bertha said frowning. She had never thought about it.

"Between Asian and Western, then."

"Oh, Asian, for sure," Bertha said.

"Now it's easy to choose, Malay, Indian or Chinese?" he said.

"I really don't know. I like them all," Bertha said.

"Supposing you went to hospital, and they asked you what type of food you wanted. What would say?" Benny pressed on with his question in another form.

"Ha! Malay I guess, if I was allowed to eat chilli ..." Bertha replied after thinking for a second.

"Ah," Benny said softly.

"Why is it so important? Nobody's asked me that before," Bertha asked.

"Just want to get to know you," Benny answered.

"You mean European or Asian style?" Bertha asked.

"That's one thing," he replied.

"I suppose food does reflect culture. But on the other hand, the Jews in Singapore eat curry and rice but their way of life is I think still more European than Asian."

"Yes. They are an interesting minority. Like us Chinese in Indonesia," Benny murmured, looking at the sea eagle still gliding above them.

"Yah. You are a minority there. I suppose it is a factor that makes you different from the Singapore and Malayan Chinese," Bertha commented.

"Yah. That's why the Eurasian community interests me," Benny said slowly.

"You know any Eurasians? In Singapore I mean. Or Singapore and Malaya," she asked.

"No," he replied.

He did not say anything more. She left it.

The sun was low over the sea now and the clouds were red and orange in patches. But it was not one of the best sunsets she had seen on that beach. Odd chap, this Benny, she thought to herself. In some ways. But better company than that Randy Lim bloke. Or Siswono. And Hartono? He's different.

When she looked up again, the sea eagle had gone.

"OK. Shall we go now?" Benny asked standing up and dusting the sand off the seat of his trousers. The same baggy pair, Bertha now noticed.

He was driving a large Morris Station Wagon. Fairly new, Bertha thought. He drove slowly and carefully. With a little smile on his face all the time, Bertha noticed.

He turned to her after they had gone a few miles.

"I know a woman in Medan who has Dutch blood. I suppose you'd call her Eurasian. Though she really is a Chinese."

"You mean she lives a Chinese style life?" Bertha asked.

"Yes. She's a strange person. I think she's beautiful. In some sort of way. One day, in a fit of anger she tore up a picture of Sukarno, stamped on the pieces and threw them out of the window," Benny said smiling.

"Good heavens! What on earth for?" Bertha asked.

"Because she couldn't get an exit permit. She wanted to go to Holland."

"Crazy woman. Did she get into trouble?" Bertha asked.

"No. Only a man selling nuts saw her she said. He went away laughing."

Benny continued after a short pause, "She had a terrible shock not many years ago. Her brother was an officer in a regiment that went against the government in North Sumatra. They found him in the family house one day and shot him dead in the garden. Right in front of his parents, her and his sister."

"God! What a shock it must have been. I can understand her hate against Sukarno now," Bertha commented.

"But there is no Eurasian community in Indonesia as there is in Malaya," Benny said.

"And Singapore," Bertha added.

"But didn't all the Eurasians in Singapore come from Malaya originally?" Benny asked.

"The ones of Portuguese origin did."

"Like you?"

"Yes. But there were many families who started from a mixed marriage or liaison in Singapore. The minority perhaps."

"As I said on the beach, you are like us Chinese in Indonesia,"

Benny said, smiling.

"Only in that we are both minorities," Bertha said.

"Because they couldn't or wouldn't be absorbed."

"I think in the case of the Eurasians in the Straits Settlements, couldn't."

"Into the Malay community?" Benny asked.

"Yes. Nor into the the European. Because they would not accept the half-castes."

"Whether Christian or not, huh," Benny said.

"That's the English. I believe the Portuguese did accept the half-castes as equal human beings."

"Yah. You're right. In Timor they accepted them, I think. But it's the Asian community acceptance that us Chinese in Indonesia and you Eurasians did not get," Benny said.

"Because of religion," Bertha said softly.

"Yah. We learnt the language in Indonesia. The Malayan Chinese didn't really get down to it the way we did. In fact, didn't they create that funny bazaar Malay?"

"Maybe. Or was it the colonials?" Bertha asked.

"But knowing the language and not adopting the culture kept us from being absorbed into Indonesian society. You can understand the culture of a country if you learn the language, but you don't absorb it unless you want to," Benny said.

"Yah. Like the Canadians and South Africans. They learn two languages but stay in their own cultural shells," Bertha said softly. Benny saw that she was getting bored with the subject. He drove on in silence.

Benny asked her what she wanted to eat when they sat down in the restaurant. It was a large pleasant place. Not top class, but one wouldn't get a top class place in Muar, Bertha said to herself. They argued about the dishes and finally settled for a steamed pomfret, *fu-yong-hai* and a vegetable. To her delight, Bertha heard him telling the waiter to cook it with abalone.

Benny talked to her about the trip to Jakarta during dinner, in an easy chatty way. He would go with her. From Penang. To

Medan first. But they would not stop there. They would then fly to Jakarta. "In one of those Dakotas from the war days," he said. It didn't mean anything to Bertha. He had finished his job in Malaya. They had something for him to do in Jakarta.

"For how long," Bertha asked.

"I don't know. You don't ask those things," he said.

Money? Or dedication? Bertha asked herself. Benny didn't seem to be an ambitious man. Nor the madly loyal type. It wasn't worth dwelling on.

He went on to talk about the different fruits one could get in Indonesia when he had finished talking about the Jakarta trip. For how long, Bertha was not told. The snake-skin looking fruit, *buah salak*. Avocados. Sapodillas. She had to ask him what he meant. *Chikus*, he explained. Vegetables. The small cucumbers. And they drifted to food.

"Oh, what would I give for *burong darat*!" he sighed.

They had eaten slowly and talked for a long time after the meal was over and the fruits Benny had ordered were finished. Then he offered her a brandy. She jumped at it. They lingered with neat brandy and Chinese tea.

As soon as Benny passed the town speed limit cancellation black diagonal stripe sign, he turned to Bertha, "Did you ever hear the story of the Eurasians of Timor? The Topass they called them."

"No. Topass?" Bertha said.

"I believe the word comes from 'topee'. But there is also a theory that it could have come from 'Tupassi', interpreter. They seem to have come with the Portuguese from Malacca."

"But that must have been much later, if they were adult children of the Portuguese mixtures," Bertha commented.

"Yes. Fifty years after the Portuguese captured Malacca. They seem to have taken a long time to decide to come to Timor."

"What were they looking for?"

"Trade. Sandalwood, gold, beeswax. And Timorese horses."

"Horses?" Bertha asked.

"Yes, horses. There is a special pretty kind of horse in Timor.

But the interesting thing about the Eurasians there, or Topasses as they called themselves, was the family feud that went on for years and years."

"Huh?"

Benny related a long involved story about a feud between the de Hornay and the da Costa families and how the Topass people became a major force fighting both the Dutch and the Portuguese in east Indonesia. It didn't hold her attention. Yah, these people were mixed-bloods like the Serani, but it all seemed so remote in time and distance to her.

He seemed to go on and on, "… then the Portuguese came back. There was a lot of trouble. The locals and the Topass were united against the Portuguese. There was one long siege."

Bertha suddenly saw a dark object in the headlight beam on the road in front of them. As she opened her mouth to warn Benny, he swerved and avoided it. He braked hard. The car stopped and he rushed out of the door. She turned round and saw him pick it up and walk back to the car.

"Ha! Durian!" he said grinning from ear to ear.

"Gosh, you gave me a fright rushing out like that!" Bertha said.

"We have durian! Ha," he repeated still grinning. He put it in the boot and drove off.

"Now where was I … Oh yes, the siege. The Portuguese held out for eighty-five days. They survived eating leaves of trees, powdered horse bones and vermin," Benny laughed.

"So that was the end of the Topass?" Bertha asked. The story was really dragging on. Perhaps he's just showing off his history knowledge, Bertha thought.

"… that was in 1749 …"

"You remember the dates, don't you?" Bertha said.

"Yah, some of them. I think it was in the seventeen sixties that the Topass records die out. But I don't know …"

"Fascinating," Bertha remarked, and realised that she did not sound convincing.

"So you see the Eurasians in Indonesia were once a force that could even take on the Dutch and Portuguese," Benny said.

They were silent for some time after Benny finished his story.

Bertha kept her eyes on the road. They were driving through *kampongs* and past paddy fields. There was a moon. The water in the fields glinted with the reflection of the moon now and then. It was still early but the *kampongs* were dark and quiet. She remembered her nights in the forest shack with Ethel. It was now as far away as a dream. It made her wonder what the future had in store for her. Would she see Hartono again? Yes, she told herself, she would. Perhaps she should fish for information from Benny. No. Benny would see her probing at once. He was not as simple minded as she had first thought. Laid back and unsophisticated, but not the happy-go-lucky, humble man his manner led one to believe.

Benny turned towards the beach when they got into Batu Pahat. Bertha knew the layout of the town well.

"Hey. You should have turned left at the school," she said.

"Going to the beach," he said.

"The beach? At this time of the night?" Bertha asked. What was he up to now? The question suddenly arose in her mind. Oh No!

"We'll eat the durian there," he said , smiling.

Bertha laughed. She'd forgotten about the durian. "But we've been drinking brandy, Benny," she said.

"That was some time ago. Don't worry, it's safe. Old wives tale," he said.

"It's not, you know. There was a fellow in Penang who died in the hotel room after drinking and eating durian. It was in the papers."

"Yes. I know about that. Did you read how much brandy he had drunk? Anything would have killed him after all that."

"He also had sex," Bertha added.

"Yah. Terrible fellow," Benny laughed.

Bertha did not know what to make of his remark. "Have you got a knife to open the durian?" she asked.

"It's split open. But I have a screwdriver. And a rag."

"Yah, must always have a rag." Bertha said with a little laugh.

"Maybe it's not a good one," Bertha said after a few seconds.

"Smells first class," Benny said in reply.

It was first class. "Absolutely wonderful, A-1 topside!" Bertha said, "Mmmmm ..."

"Yah, super," Benny agreed.

This is living, she thought to herself as she licked her last seed. The hushed sound of the waves gently lapping the beach, the cicadas' muffled screeches somewhere in the distance. The cool night air. The soft breeze. The moonlight on the sea. A ship's light just visible on the horizon. And above all the durian.

As she lay on her mat that night she relived the pleasure of that moment, burping the smell of the durian.

~ *Chapter Twenty-eight* ~

Jakarta 1960

Colonel Darso picked up a book from his desk, opened it at a page marked with a matchstick, and read to Bertha, " 'It was here and now, on the edges of central Java, moving closer each day into the heart and drama of Indonesia's being, that I began to understand how finely balanced is the spiritual and emotional machinery of this enigmatic, paradoxical republic; and how cleverly and delicately has this strangely great man Sukarno maintained the equilibrium of a national nervous system that is subject to the most diverse and violent influences ...'

"That is a good summary of us. And of President Sukarno."

He looked over his reading glasses and under his bushy grey eyebrows into Bertha's eyes. He saw that he was holding her complete attention and continued, "That was written by an Australian, Maslyn Williams. We had invited him to our country to see everything and report to the world. I think he has felt the core of the country in this paragraph. It is not the statistics that constitute a country. And for Indonesia especially, the emotional, the illogical myths and beliefs must be understood if you want to feel the pulse of Indonesia. If there's one thing I can teach you in our all too brief sessions, it is this. You must grasp both the myths and the realities."

He smiled benignly at Bertha.

"And that is what President Sukarno grasped? And used to get where he is? Isn't it?" Bertha asked.

"Yes. And this is the wisdom that enables him to understand the *ra'ayat*, the people, and communicate with them."

Colonel Darso paused to let his words sink in.

"Just take one aspect," he continued, "religion. I mean religion itself. Not confused with the animistic and other primitive beliefs of some Indonesians. The President understands this fully. The soul of the Indonesian must hold a belief in a God. Not just Allah of the Muslims. We have a freedom to choose. But there must be a God in one's heart. Article 29 of our constitution states that the state is founded upon the belief that there is one God. It is fundamental to our way of life."

He stopped to light a *kretek* cigarette. Bertha waited. She saw that he was overflowing with thoughts he wanted to express.

"One fellow in the department of religious affairs puts it in a rather silly way; 'by law, it is not possible to be an Indonesian and not believe in God,' he says. But the point I want to make is that our President Sukarno saw the importance of this keystone of our Indonesian psyche."

"And he used it?" Bertha interrupted.

Colonel Darso ignored her comment. He stretched out across his desk and picked up another book. There was a matchstick marking the page. He opened it and, looking over his spectacles before he read from the book, he said, "This is from one of his speeches. It shows his deep personal convictions. 'I came out of my palace and looked at the sky and saw the sparkling of the stars. I was affected. I was moved. I said, "O God, my Lord, these stars are Thine own creation and each gives worship to Thee. Thou art the God of these stars. Thou, O God, art the Lord of all human beings, of the animals, the trees, of this grass which I step on. Thou art God of the sand and of the atoms which can only be seen through a microscope. Thou art the Lord of the whole world, O God, my Lord, creator of the universe, of the sun, the moon and the uncountable stars. And what am I? I am a small thing." ' "

Bertha waited for the colonel to drop from the excitement he had felt in his reading of Sukarno's speech extract.

"I appreciate the fact that, er ... President Sukarno (She had nearly said 'Sukarno' without the president prefix), saw the depth and force of religious belief in the Indonesian. Whether he is a Muslim or Catholic or Hindu er … I mean Buddhist. And what you have just read is beautiful rhetoric."

Colonel Darso's face showed his reaction to "rhetoric," but he let her continue.

"But what I cannot understand, Pak Darso, is how he can reconcile religion with communism."

"It is very complex in Indonesia. The connections between religion and politics," Colonel Darso said.

"Yah. It confuses me," Bertha added.

Colonel Darso smiled enigmatically.

He continued, "I should really have said the overlap. The lines are not clear in Indonesia. First, the attitudes to religion are different. Though religious feeling and conviction are so deep and powerful as I said, there are a great many people who do not draw clear lines between different religions. You may see a Muslim, for example at Borobudur touching the Buddha's hand. And you could probably see him again at Prambanan, the Hindu temple. And our communism is not the original Marx-Lenin brand."

Bertha interrupted him. "But doesn't Aidit want it to be that?"

His eyebrows raised a little in surprise that Bertha knew the name of the communist leader in Indonesia.

"That is true. But I myself believe most of the communists here hold a set of principles which are not truly Russian communism. But we needn't go into that. What is more important is our stance vis-a-vis them. We can live with philosophical conflict. Like the Japanese in some ways. To us there is day and night, but day is day and night is night. There is life and there is death. They go together as good and evil co-exist. We have to learn to live with both. This is what many westerners cannot understand. We accept paradoxes. We do not agonise about drawing sharp lines between black and white. We also know that evil, and the communists, cannot be destroyed completely. You can see this in our shadow plays."

Bertha frowned. "I know that is the president's present attitude but it confuses me. I mean your explaining the acceptance of the communists in those terms. In Singapore many think that Lee Kuan Yew is running with the communists ... He's not. It is straight political expediency. President Sukarno, in my opinion, is playing the same game. He's just giving them enough rope to hang themselves."

Colonel Darso smiled his smile of disagreement showing the little hooks of his dentures round his canines. "There are many who would agree with you. But behind your confusion at my explanations is your very Christian tunnel thinking of good and evil. There is no compromise to you. You see, you Christians have to separate the two because you have to save your own souls. Our concept of fate makes us think in less selfish terms. I mean less individualistic terms."

"I take that point, Pak Darso," Bertha said. It was one of James' favourite concessionary phrases. She continued, "Going back to what you said earlier about the myth and the reality, one can discover these characteristics of the Indonesian psyche by being here, talking to the people ... but doesn't one have to go back to the past, to history, to understand how this has grown?' Bertha asked.

"History explains. But being in the midst of the people makes you feel and believe within yourself that illogical and mystic forces are still around."

"Yah, *bapak*. That's it," Bertha replied. She herself wasn't sure of what she had said. What her "it" was. She felt that she had to complete her statement of reaction, and continued, "Pak, you are the philosopher I said you were ... wisdom."

"Wisdom, not just the logic of Kant and Hegel," Colonel Darso completed her sentence to his own satisfaction and smiled.

"We have talked for too long, Miss Bertha Rodrigues. I'd better call Wideh. He'll take you back ... it's been a real pleasure."

He picked up the telephone.

Bertha sat back in her chair and sighed inwardly. Ah, for a bath, a good meal and bed.

Back in the little hotel, or guest house as they called it, she thought of her last two hectic weeks in Indonesia. Here she was in Bandung at the military college meeting the list of five people who were to brief her. It had been a series of discussions intermingled with lengthy monologues on Sukarno's thoughts. Or rather what he had said in his speeches. She had learnt to make that distinction. His mind moved along a track that was parallel to his utterances. Roughly parallel. Diverging at times and suddently converging unexpectedly.

It was wearing. But she was learning a lot and her mind was opening to concepts and opinions she had never encountered before. It was not just the new and enchanting world of Indonesia. It was the politics and the way the men who were briefing her talked about politics in Indonesia. They seemed to be flying high, far above the down-to-earth topics that were tossed around over the dining table at home. But in many ways, Bertha thought, they were talking of the forces and power behind the surface of practical politics. New doors were opening to her.

It seemed like the long journey that started after saying goodbye to Fatimah had not yet ended.

Benny Yap had chatted about almost every subject under the sun in his slow drawling way from Batu Pahat to Penang in the train. With his hearty chuckles in between. Indonesia, the different kinds of people, the different terrains, mountains, plateaus, alluvial plains, islands. Food. Customs. Religion. Economics. Politics. Not just Indonesian politics. The Philippines, Thailand, Malaya and Singapore.

"I take it, Bertha, that you're Roman Catholic in your core," Benny started the discussion that they continued all through the flight from Penang to Medan.

"Yah … though I'm not a practising one now," Bertha had replied, knowing that she had given up in her mind so many tenets of the church, but also knowing that the deep-seated forces of her culture would never ever allow her to shed the Catholic in her.

"Once a Catholic, always a Catholic," Benny said expressing her own thoughts.

"This man's no fool," Bertha said silently to herself.

She did not respond. As she expected, Benny had commented to give himself a stepping stone to move on to something else.

"So you can never accept communism."

"I can't but a Catholic could ... as a total reaction against his past."

"But you. You can't. Can you?"

"Yah, I can't."

Benny did not say anything more.

"I also do believe that communism is not the answer to our political problems. Not just Singapore's. All Southeast Asia's."

"That is important," Benny said softly. He paused and went on, "These days we all have to sort out some basic things. The colonials have gone. That is as far as Indonesia is concerned. So the power is in our hands. We have to know who believes in communism, who believes in a God, who is interested enough to do something for his people. His country. Who is only looking for money. Or power."

Bertha turned and looked at him sitting beside her in the plane. This was not the Benny she had known.

There was a strange smile on his face as he continued, "I think you are one person who believes and feels ..."

She did not respond. She waited.

"You are the kind of person who would go out of your way to help people in need. Right? You would sacrifice personal time and profit to do so. A rare person. We need you . . . But most of all your young country half way to independence needs you."

"What do you mean?"

"Let me put it this way, if you were in a position to influence a drift of Singapore to disaster, you would take time off to do so, wouldn't you?"

"Yah. I reckon. If I was ever in such a position."

Bertha could not quite follow the drift. What was Benny driving at, she asked herself, but got no answer.

"You could be in such a position, Bertha."

"How come?"

"There is a possibility that Tengku Abdul Rahman may try to get Singapore into his clutches. Make it a part of Malaya."

"Cripes, no," Bertha reacted at once.

"It's racial and economics. The Malays cannot have a nation with a Chinese majority on their doorstep behaving in a very Chinese way. Neither can they lose the harbour and trading centre which has been part of the Straits Settlements. They will pull Singapore into their net. And keep her under control."

"You know, Benny, I've talked about this with my father and my brother-in-law many, many times. I myself am convinced that it would be a disaster if Malaya absorbed us. By sheer population numbers we would be swamped."

Benny smiled. He did not seem to want to say anything. Bertha waited for a few seconds, then continued.

"Neither do we want to be absorbed by Indonesia, Benny. We have to stand alone."

"Squashed in between the giants?"

"The giants will never work together. It's like the Liberals in English politics. They are hemmed in between the Tories and Labour. But they could hold the key card."

"That's different, Bertha. That's gentlemanly democratic British politics. We're talking about might. Force. Power."

"All right. We won't have the joker to play. But we won't be reduced to a municipality toeing the line KL dictates."

"Are you being realistic?" Benny asked.

"Yes. That's just what I am being. The Singaporean as a person will disappear off the face of this earth. We will just be the harbour workers and the traders for the first ten years. Then we will be an insignificant satellite."

"But what is the Singaporean? Isn't he just a variety of the Malayan species?"

"No. He or she is a city type. Diametrically different from the rural Malay or Chinese smallholder."

"Aren't you taking this stance because you're a Eurasian; a minority community."

Bertha flared up. "For Gawds sake Benny, we're talking about whole countries. If you think I'm incapable of seeing beyond my Eurasian community, my family, my personal coconut shell, my sex ... then it's not worth talking to me!"

"Sorry. I didn't mean it that way. I mean a small group naturally looks for survival ... er ... er "

"If it has resources to allow it to survive."

"And what resources has Singapore got? Not even water."

"People. And a leader," Bertha said glaring at Benny.

"Yes. Different people. Different from the Malayans."

"At present."

Bertha was not settled inside her. She moved against Benny's remark again. "Benny. Get this straight. You may explain why I think in such and such a way because I'm Eurasian, or Catholic, or woman, or uneducated but we're not analysing me. We are talking about what I and you think. Whether you're a Chink or Melayu or Mama."

"Yes, Bertha, you're right."

Benny left it at that. But not for long.

"It is a very critical thing for the region. Whether Singapore remains an independent country. If Singapore becomes part of Malaya, then the physical, political and economic border, and potential source of friction is between Indonesia and Malaya. And God knows how the Malays have fought each other in the past. The Achinese attacking Malacca. That Java fellow also having a go at Malacca. Let's not forget they all took a crack at Malacca because it was the trading pivot of the region. The Singapore of the sixteenth and seventeenth century."

"So you want a soft little pillow between you and Malaya?"

"It's very entangled, Bertha . . . We ourselves have doubts about the Sumatra people. They have a lot of affinities with the Malays of Malaya."

"Yah ... entangled and unpredictable," Bertha said.

"In one of the old Buddhist books someone says, 'Tangle within, tangle without, mankind is entangled in a tangle. I ask this question, Gotama, who disentangles this tangle?' "

Bertha sat up in her seat. Was this the Benny with the baggy pants she met on the beach?

"And what was the Buddha's answer?" she asked.

"I can't remember. Something about solving it all with virtue and concentration and wisdom."

It went on in that vein till they touched down at Medan. She got the feeling that Benny kept hanging onto the subject like a dog with a bone, gnawing, biting, licking, sucking at it long after the last traces of pleasure and taste had gone. She wasn't sure if he was trying to thrust his views on her, or poking and probing to see what makes her tick. But she was tired. It wasn't worth thinking about.

Then Jakarta. Learning to her surprise that she was not going to stay in a hotel but in Kebayoran Baru in the home of an elderly government servant. "You'll be more comfortable there," they told her. "And safer." They were right. Mononutu was a kind and friendly grey-haired man. A perfect host. She had the run of the house. Two servants. And a gardener. And Mononutu was so often away on some government business.

Meeting Hadi again. Seeing his genuine pleasure in greeting her as an old friend. But later, seeing his coldness in many ways, it didn't ring true. Hadi seemed to have decided to keep her at arms length. He was part of the organistaion. But he did not appear to have a key role to play with regard to her task in Jakarta. He briefed her. Probably because his English was better than the rest of them. Benny was to remain her main contact. Like a boss. But not quite. He was the information conveyor. It was only later that she found out who her real boss was.

Hadi did not do the full briefing. Major Abdulgani gave her the outline of her involvement with the Indonesians which she could not help feeling she had been sucked into. Like getting caught in a whirlpool. A quicksand.

Major Abdulgani was the epitome of sedateness. He could have been a senator, a judge, a Buddha, a God doling out the sweets and punishments without the slightest trace of emotion. Old enough to have been educated in the Dutch disciplines, she said to herself. Like a German. A European with machine-mind efficiency and precision. Definitely not an Indonesian. But later she found that her first impressions were wrong.

"Benny has told us about your political views," he said.

"Gees … I don't really have a political faith in anything, *bapak*."

"Perhaps I should say your political feelings. It's feelings that have the force. Convictions."

"Yah."

"So, we have found the niche that you fit into without your knowing it, and will be to our advantage. There is a lot of common ground. We are lucky."

"Both of us?"

"Yes. But let me get down to it. Two viewpoints. First you. You are a person (Thank God he didn't say girl or woman, Bertha said to herself.) who has not yet found your niche. You have brains. You have not used them. You have passions for ideas, causes, righteousness. You have not used them … yet … and you have an upbringing that is very special."

Bertha's mind raced along several directions and pulled back to start again. The major was inscrutable.

"You are a Singaporean. A Singaporean from a minority. You do not belong to either of the two main racial-cultural groups. You can stand outside their closed cells and look inside. But you grew up among them. We have been looking for a person like you for some time. We looked among the Indians and the small but very interesting group of Europeans who have lived in Asia for years and years and understand the people they have lived with. But they are not Asians. I mean their minds. Feelings. They have a capability to look at things in a different light but sometimes do not feel the situations as an Asian would."

'What do they want out of me," Bertha asked herself with

growing impatience.

"So, we think you can give us slants in looking at Singapore that we with our blinkers cannot see … and perhaps, also Malaya."

Major Abdulgani leant on his elbows and hunching over his desk looked intensely into Bertha's eyes (Here it comes, Bertha thought, the punch-line at last), "We would like you to stay with us for two or three years and help us to understand Singapore and Malaya. We want you to read everything that comes out of Singapore. Out of their politicians, and give us YOUR thoughts."

"But Pak Abdulgani, that is beyond me …"

"No." His tone was sharp and definite. "You lack two things at the moment. You have not the experience to sort out and put down your thoughts. But you DO have your opinions. Your slants on the different situations. Hartono has told us. Hadi too. A friend of ours who played with you for the GSC team confirms it. Siswono also says you have what it takes to do the job. Did you know Siswono has a Masters degree in Political Science?"

"No."

"Well, he has. We are sure you have what we want. The second weakness is your very superfical knowledge of the Indonesian. The Jawanese, I would say. Not because I am Jawanese but because the Jawanese mind will direct Indonesia for a long, long time. This is a minor problem. We will straighten it out."

Bertha sat rigid. What the hell are they doing to me?

"And above all, Miss Bertha Rodrigues, we are sure you have the honesty, and the true love for the place and people of your childhood and upbringing that makes our interests coincide with yours."

Through the mists and blurred outlines of Major Abdulgani's words, Bertha saw her own interests and the opportunities. It excited her. But she held herself back.

"Yes, *Bapak* Abdulgani, I see. I understand what you are saying in your roundabout Indonesian way … My first reaction is yah! yah! we are together in this. But please … let me sleep on it."

"Of course, Miss Bertha Rodrigues. Take your time."

Major Abdulgani smiled. There was complete satisfaction and calm on his face. "You should know by now that we won't rush you here. And when you say 'the roundabout Indonesian way,' I know you understand one part of us, us Indonesians, us Jawanese."

"Or us Sundanese?"

So the stimulating, but relaxed in some ways, talk with Major Abdungani set the course. She dropped him a note the next day, as he had suggested to signify her agreement. She didn't think of the alternatives. Thanks to the Labis and Batu Pahat payments she had no empty-belly fears bearing down on her. She had a certain freedom of choice that in her wildest dreams she had not forseen.

They left her waiting for some time before Benny came to the reception area and picked her up. The way he looked at her made her sure that Major Abdulgani had been discussing her with him. "Some bits and pieces," Benny said as he drove her to Mononutu's house. "We are arranging for you to study Bahasa Indonesia. You'll pick it up easily with your Malay knowledge. It's almost the same."

He handed her a piece of paper and smiled.

Bertha looked at it quickly. The times and days of the Bahasa Indonesia lessons. All at Mononutu's place. Oh good! she said to herself. Then a programme. The visit to Bandung for briefing by five men who were named. Below that, she saw some figures. She would be paid a thousand Singapore dollars a month. Whew! Board and lodging would be covered by the organisation. They would provide transport. There was also a "settling-in" sum of three thousand dollars. Clothes! she mumbled to herself.

"Yah," Benny responded to her muttering of "clothes." "I'll arrange for someone to take you shopping and show you where the shops are. No more in the jungle now, eh?" he said, smiling.

There was more. The job described. Working hours. Public holidays. It was like an employment contract but loosely worded. And she was not expected to sign anything, she assumed from the way it was written.

Benny saw that she had finished reading the paper and spoke to her, "Tomorrow, shopping and meeting your teacher at three at the house. And tomorrow night I'd like you to have dinner with me and meet an old friend of mine."

"Old, as in long-in-the-tooth?" Bertha interrupted. She was relaxed with Benny.

"No. Old meaning I was in school with him. He's at the university lecturing in history. Interesting man."

"Oh dear, one of those intellectuals?" Bertha said.

"No, no. He's not like that. A human academic."

"Oh good. Thanks Benny."

Benny drove on in silence. After about five minutes, Bertha felt that she should get as much information from Benny as she could.

"You drive on the same side of the road as we do," she said to open up the conversation again.

"Yes. Thanks to Sir Stamford Raffles."

"Stamford Raffles?"

"Yah. He changed the traffic system. Before that, the Dutch had us driving our carriages on the European right side."

"Oh yes … I remember reading he was here … with his wife … sometime or other." She had little knowledge of Indonesian history.

"Yah. Only a few years. 1811 to 1816, I think."

"Well, we have something in common."

Benny laughed.

Shopping was a great disappointment for Bertha. Mrs. Sujitpoh was as pleasant as one could be. She was down to earth and practical. She kept telling Bertha the basics. How much to pay the *betja*, or the taxis. Where one could get the best buys. And a host of other things which were of little interest to Bertha. The only places she remembered after the tiring morning were Glodok and Pasar Senin, the Monday market place. The heat seemed to be intense in the city and the traffic quite impossible. She wondered if she could ever be able to drive in Jakarta.

As they went from shop to shop, Bertha noticed that the men were looking at her. She had a simple silk flowered dress on that showed her figure. It was not very short. She knew she had made up with care that morning. Being in a city again was a change after months in the forest and in sleepy Batu Pahat.

She saw the admiring glances and the lusty looks cast at her. She was sure that she did not appear different from the Indonesian women. Perhaps a little taller. And better built. But she was healthy, her body firm and glowing with a sun-tan. It was not just one or two men. She saw so many men running their eyes over her and following her with their eyes. And then she saw a man who looked like Hartono. She stopped in her tracks. Mrs. Sujitpoh stopped and looked at her.

"Someone you know?" she asked.

It was NOT Hartono. "I thought so ... but it's not," she replied with disappointment in her tone.

"Hah, someone you know well, ah?" Mrs. Sujitpoh probed.

The men's glances excited her. Maybe she had blossomd in these last few months, she said to herself. Or is it the dress? No. She'd seen a good few women dressed as nicely as she was in this area.

Her elation did not last long. She began to notice that the men looked at all the pretty women in the same way. It was not generally a look of lust or desire. It was usually just admiration. But there were the stares and the eyes of men searching for a smile, for a hint of recognition, of friendliness. This was Jakarta, she told herself. Not Singapore where everyone was single-mindedly moving from point A to B.

She saw hardly anything that she liked. Mrs. Sujitpoh began to get impatient. But to Bertha almost everything she saw was ten years behind Singapore. She did, however, buy a pair of shoes.

As she sat waiting for the salesman to bring another pair to try on, she decided that she would have to get her clothes tailor-made and looked at Mrs. Sujitpoh's dress to see if she could rely on her recommendation of a tailor. No, she would have to ask someone else.

That was that. She thanked Mrs. Sujitpoh. Smiling charmingly Mrs. Sujitpoh left, disappointed at Bertha's fussiness. These Singapore women! Aiyah! so difficult. Nothing pleases them!

The Bahasa Indonesia teacher made up for the crowds, the heat, the *betjas* and shabby goods of the morning's shopping expedition.

He was tall and thin. Grey, sedate and handsome, he carried himself upright and straight backed. Almost like a military man, Bertha thought. His English was poor, but that was good she said to herself. He didn't start off well. He told her she needed a dictionary, and some readers and exercise books and that he had taken the trouble to get them for her. They cost ... Is this going to go on and on, Bertha asked herself. She paid him. He spoke to her in Indonesian and she replied in Malay. He was pleased with her accent and knowledge. He said that she would learn fast.

He would teach her at her pace. He was used to adults, he said. And he would teach her the real Indonesian. Not the rough and the crude language of the streets. Not the language of the foreigners. And, God forbid, she must make every attempt to avoid picking up Betawi, the hotch-potch dialect of Jakarta. And of course, forget her Bahasa Malaya. And the occasional words of Singapore bazaar Malay she used. It's full of Chinese corruptions, he said.

She liked him. His name was difficult. Mochtar Dardjowidjojo. But she would get used to it sooner or later. She also saw that he looked at her as a woman as he bowed his goodbye.

~ *Chapter Twenty-nine* ~

Batavia

Dr. Joseph Kusuma lunged at her as soon as they met. He was in the restaurant waiting for them. It was somewhere along Jalan Hayam Wuruk. She was getting her sense of direction of Jakarta.

"Miss Bertha Rodrigues, Dr. Joseph Kusuma."

"Rodrigues? A Portuguese name?" he asked.

Bertha was sure that Benny had forewarned Joseph Kusuma who he was going to meet. Especially since there would only be three of them. It seemed like a prepared reaction to her.

"Yes," she replied monosyllably and looked at Benny grinning his wide Benny-Yap smile.

"Pleased to meet you. You must be one of the descendants of the Malacca mesticos."

"Mestico? No I'm Rodrigues."

"Ha! ha! very good," Joseph Kusuma chuckled. He seemed to be a man alive to the world around him. He was dressed in a flashy batik shirt and was smoking a pipe. From the way he looked at her, she knew that he was not the academic man living in the clouds.

"I don't know who or what you mean by 'mestico,' " she said.

"Oh! I'm sorry. It's the Portuguese word for mixed bloods. Perhaps it has connotations in Singapore … I'm sorry."

"No it hasn't," Bertha said. "In fact I think very few Eurasians would know the word today."

"Are there words which you Eurasians dislike?" he asked. He had jumped into the subject leaving Benny grinning quietly.

"Well, I don't know. Perhaps some object to *geragok*. I reckon Serani is acceptable. Maybe the Hokkien *chap-cheng* has derogatory implications to the Chinese. But I guess no one cares these days."

"But you are really a descendant of the Malacca originals?" he asked.

"Yah. Very much so, I suppose. My mother's Gomez."

"You know, in Jakarta, in the old times there were many people who claimed to be of mixed bloods and who lived in the Portuguese style, who didn't have any European blood in them at all."

"That's the same in Malaya and Singapore. I mean in the old days before the place got so westernised. There were also many Indians and Ceylonese with Portuguese names."

"Yes, the people from Goa and Ceylon. The Portuguese priests made them change their names when they became Christians."

"So I hear," Bertha said.

"It's interesting why they did it. I read somewhere that it was not just that they felt that the names of saints were necessary."

Bertha interrupted him, "But the Catholics did require a saint's name at one time. I remember my mother telling me that the Padre objected to first names like Rex and Dolores which are not saint's names."

"You're right. But doesn't that give the saints a monopoly on names? One could never get a new saint's name."

"Yah. I never thought of that."

"As I was saying, there were other motives. Dilution of national identity was one. In Ceylon they wanted to destroy the caste divisions. Portuguese names would add to the complexities of castes."

"But wouldn't that help them to get out of the caste bloodlines?" Bertha interjected.

"That's exactly it. People branded with the names of the lower castes, I believe, rushed to be baptised and take on new foreign names. It must have done wonders to the convert figures."

"And the Portuguese thought that they could sort out friendly people to trade with by their Portuguese names."

"And probably because Ceylonese names were very difficult for the Portuguese to pronounce," Bertha added.

Only Benny laughed.

The sharksfin came. Joseph Kusuma continued talking as he ate. Benny sat smiling enjoying his food.

"It was part of a grand plan to destroy the customs and cultures of the natives, I think."

"But why didn't the Portuguese do that when they came to Malacca and Indonesia?" Bertha asked.

"Maybe they had learnt that it didn't work."

There was a short silence. Bertha pursued the subject. "You seem to know quite a lot about the Portuguese, Dr. Kusuma. Is it your special area of history?"

"Good heavens no. Military history is my speciality. It's just that the mixed bloods interest me. There are so many fascinating scraps of the Eurasians in Indonesian history. In Jakarta alone, there were many curious Eurasians written up in the history books."

"Were there? Tell me," Bertha was getting interested.

"The most romantic and pitiful of them all is the story of Sarah Specx." He went on with the Sarah Specx story. The horror tale of the daughter of a member of the supreme governing body of Indonesia and a Japanese Eurasian. When she was twelve, she stayed with the governor while her father was away and allowed her lover to visit her there, submitting "to his fervent embraces," as Joseph Kusuma put it. Joseph Kusuma went into all the details of the terrible punishment meted out to Sarah Specx and her lover.

"When was this?" Bertha interrupted. "Did the Japanese come out this way so early?"

"I don't know. It was when Jakarta was Batavia. Probably in the late seventeenth or early eighteenth century."

"What a terrible story," Bertha, commented. "What happened to the girl in the end?"

"She married a Protestant minister and died in Taiwan. As a respectable woman," Joseph Kusumu answered.

"AH! The *burong darat*!"

Benny's loud voice brought them back to Jalan Hayam Wuruk in Jakarta, away from seventeenth-century Batavia.

It was absolutely delicious. Dark brown. Dripping with oil. Soft, rich, juicy. It was everything that Bertha remembered *burong darat* should be. It was the high point of her evening.

The talked about food for a while. Then Benny turned to Joseph Kusumu and said, "Tell her about Tugu."

"Ah yes ... You must get Benny to take you there sometime. It's an important historical spot just outside the city. They found a stone there with writing on it that shows man has been here for fifteen centuries. Fifteen hundred years!" Joseph Kusumu said.

"Ah the Java man!" Bertha interrupted.

"No. He's even older, but the more interesting thing to you would be the black Portuguese of Tugu."

"Eurasians?" Bertha asked, interrupting Joesph Kusuma again.

"They were originally; but later they were Indonesians. Catholics who took on the Portuguese way of life. When the Portuguese first came here they brought several 'mesticos' with them. Some from Malacca."

"Fifteenth century?"

"Yah. The first ship came in fifteen-thirteen. Two years after they took Malacca ..."

Joseph Kusuma was off again on a monologue about the early history of Jakarta. How the Portuguese insidiously moved into the port of Sunda Kalapa as traders; how the Portuguese language lingered on for years after the Dutch took over; the forced conversions of the Catholics to Protestantism and the term they used for the converts, *mardjikers*, the free ones.

"That's the origin of the word *merdeka*, freedom," Joseph Kusuma said.

Bertha interjected with an interested "Ah ..."

Joseph Kusuma continued, "But a great many of these Catholics changed their religion in name only. They attended Catholic mass whenever a priest sneaked into Jakarta. Or Batavia as it was then. They also hung onto the Portuguese way of life. Speaking Portuguese, wearing black, singing *keronchong* ..."

"*Keronchong*?" Bertha asked.

"Yes. You surely know the Malay *keronchong*."

"I do. And I know that the Portuguese brought it to Malacca."

"It came a long way, you know. The Moors brought that kind of music to Spain and Portugal. They developed it from African music. And Tugu today is well known for the guitar type instruments made there, but I was telling you about the black Portuguese. They held onto their lifestyle for years and years."

"But as you said these people were not really Eurasians."

"Right."

Benny had been smiling throughout Joseph's monologue. He sat up and spoke as Joseph Kusuma ended his sentence, "You said they wore black?"

""Yes. It was the Portuguese fashion then."

"Is that why they were called the black Portuguese?"

"I don't think so. Probably to distinguish them from the white ones."

"Funny how the southern Europeans wore black." Bertha commented. "I believe the Italians, Spanish and as you say the Portuguese wore black. Such a hot colour for sunny countries."

"I guess it had something to do with religion," Joseph Kusumu said. "I am not sure."

Benny turned to Bertha, "There are two old Catholic churches still standing. One in Kota and one in Tugu. I'll take you out to see them one day."

I've got to get out of that one, Bertha said to herself.

"But apart from the non-Eurasian black Portuguese, there are many people of mixed Asian and European blood who figure in our history. The Topass people, for example ..." Joseph Kusuma said.

"Benny told me all about them," Bertha said before he launched into the Timor Topass stories.

But Joseph Kusumu pressed on.

"The most infamous of mixed bloods was a man called Pieter Erbervelt ..."

Joseph relit his pipe again and continued, "Pieter Erbervelt was the son of a German father and a Siamese mother. He was a captain of the cavalry in Batavia ..." Bertha looked around the restaurant to see what the women were wearing. She was surprised to see that most of them were Chinese. Then she remembered that this was a sort of Chinatown of Jakarta. The diamonds on one elderly woman's fingers caught her eye. But a plump big-bellied man leant back in his chair and blocked her line of sight.

"… put to death in the most cruel way," Joseph Kusuma droned on, "They were all quartered and the place where this occurred came to be known as Kampong Pechah Kulit, or *kampong* of the broken skins."

She caught the last lines of his long story.

"The most infamous Eurasian in Indonesian history?" she asked. Joseph Kusuma looked at her. She sensed that he thought her tone and reaction very frivilous.

"Yah. But there are many loose ends to the story. Who betrayed them?" He had to round it off.

"Those were bad days, weren't they?" Bertha said, feeling guilty about her inattention. I hope he's done with Eurasian stories, she thought to herself.

But Joseph Kusuma still had more to say about the Pieter Erbervelt stone, "There is a copy of the stone in the grounds of the Jakarta museum. The Japanese destroyed the original during the last war."

As they finished the meal with fruits Joseph Kusuma went back to the past, "You know Jakarta has a long and interesting history. Compared to Jakarta, Singapore is a young place. Eighteen-nineteen was it?"

"Yah. Sir Stamford Raffles …"

Joseph interrupted Bertha. "Yes, he was here between 1811 and 1826."

And Benny said he's not the typical academic!

"Ah, I was trying to think of the dates yesterday," Benny broke his silence.

"His wife is buried in Bogor, isn't she?" Bertha asked, adding, "That's about the one fact I know about Indonesia!"

"No. No. That's only a memorial he erected for her. She is

buried here in Jakarta. At the Tanah Abang cemetery. So many people think that the elaborate memorial at Bogor is her grave."

"I don't know how I picked it up," Bertha mumbled.

"The greatest thing Stamford Raffles did for Indonesian, in my opinion, was rediscovering Borobudur. It had been built in the seventh and eight centuries and had been forgotten. Raffles brought it to life again," Joseph Kusuma said.

"That's a historian's rating. Raffles did a lot more," Benny said. "Apart from the traffic system he reorganised many things. He also wrote a history of Java."

She saw Benny was moving in to ease Joseph Kusuma aside.

"All I know about him, apart from his wife being buried in Java is that he founded two colonies that have survived over the years, Singapore and the London zoo," Bertha said.

Benny laughed.

~ *Chapter Thirty* ~

1961—1962

Bertha looked carefully at her face in the mirror over her dressing table. She liked it. Yah, she said to herself, Hasnah did a good job. I knew it was the right decision. Yes, Bertha Rodrigues, you look good. In fact, Mary Devries, you look stunning. And she laughed quietly but audibly to herself.

She had decided to cut her hair very short. She thought it suited her mood and her role as a woman of action now. It was also cooler for the heat of Jakarta. She saw how it brought out her high cheekbones and her strong chin. It made her look different from the mass of women in Jakarta, she thought. She was pleased.

That was phase one of her new image. She had got herself all the new footwear she wanted. Then her hair. Next, it would be her wardrobe. She didn't want to rush into it. She wanted to look around in the streets, the restaurants, and the office to see how she should fit in and yet stand out. It wasn't just the ordinary woman's desire to be noticed. She wanted to be singled out as the girl from somewhere, who looked, moved, laughed, behaved, thought differently. Strong, fast and beautiful, she had said to herself as she showered one day. Fast, snappy Mary Devries.

Only her hockey. She must get back to the game. She must ask around and join a club. Perhaps there was one at the Ministry.

Yes, Mary Devries, she repeated in her mind, you do look stunning.

She had become Mary Devries. They didn't want her to use her real name, but they wanted her to still be a Singapore Eurasian woman. Hadi had suggested Devries because people knew the name in Indonesia. A Dutch name. And there were one or two mixtures with that name around. She had chosen Mary. Partly because it was her mother's name and partly because it was simple.

She had started on the job. There was so much reading. Not only the newspapers from Singapore, government reports, articles on Singapore from journals, magazines, the British press but also the translations of the Singapore and Malayan Chinese newspapers that Rose Gunawan had done into her poor, barely readable English. She was also given translations of the *Utusan Melayu*. She didn't know who did them but the English was so much better that Rose Gunawan's.

It was sorting out the grain from the chaff that gave her a lot of trouble. Then the even more difficult task of putting her thoughts down on paper. But she stuck to it tenaciously. She was determined to live up to their expectations. They had set the standard and the pace and she had accepted them and taken their targets into her herself as hers.

She had some terrible mental blocks in the beginning. Almost as soon as she had started, there was that meeting between Mr. Duncan Sandys, representing the British government, Lee Kuan Yew and the Tengku, Malaya's prime minister, in December. She had to give an opinion on it from the meagre scraps of real facts and the guesses of the *Economist* and *Observer* correspondents. It was the first stirrings of conception towads a Malaysia; the union of Singapore and Malaya.

And all the internal conflicts of the PAP were coming out at that time. It was the worst of times to start such a commentator's job. But she told herself it was the best of times for her to learn the job. So much was going on. So many changes were taking place. She lay in bed one night and tried to sort out what changes were going inside her. The job had opened up her mind. She was now forced to think along paths she had never been down before. Learning Bahasa Indonesia and living in Jakarta brought new experiences every day. And now she was reflecting on the differences between Indonesia, Singapore and Malaya and making her own judgements.

She said to herself that the new turn in the direction of her life could never have happened if she was living in Singapore. Here she knew nobody. No one would say, "O Bertha, you've changed your lipstick, you've cut your hair, fancy you saying that! That's not like you at all, Bertha!" It was more than that. There were no well worn grooves to snuggle comfortably in. No images cast in her past to live up to. Or to overcome. It was almost like being reborn.

If she wanted to be reborn, she told herself. Yes. Definitely, yes. It was an extraordinary chance to remould herself into a new ideal. Mary Devries was going to be a far better person than Bertha Rodrigues.

Christmas 1960 came upon her before she had thought about it. She was alone. She decided to go to the cathedral and attend midnight mass. It was not a sudden religious surge. It was a sentimental thing and a curiosity to see what they did in Jakarta. To her horror, she found out that she really had nothing to wear. She settled for the dress with the skirt that flared out in the old stlye of the fifties. She went early and sat for what felt like hours while the cathedral filled up.

It was a beatiful church, she thought. Like pictures of French cathedrals she had seen where those ribs from the walls rose up to meet in the roof.

She thought of her last Christmas with Ethel and Hartono, drinking the bottle of brandy he had brought to their rough hut in the forest, laughing and talking of old times while poor Siswono shuffled restlessly in his seat and seemed to make so many trips to pee outside although he was not drinking. And she thought again of the good old days with Eric and Pa and Ma, and uncle Harry, old man Machado, Beryl and Ben ... *feng* and turkey, *achar*, pineapple-jam tarts, mincepies, mistletoe ... But she stopped herself. That was the past. Aren't you Mary Devries now?

Mr. Mononutu appeared to be so pleased that she had gone to the midnight mass. It was her first indication to him that she had any religion in her. He asked about the rituals and the music. He seemed particularly interested in the complicated music the Christians needed for their rituals.

"We don't need it, Pak," Bertha insisted.

"Yah. You say that. But it's like the Chinese, they must have their gongs to have a proper festival. Or the Indians, the Japanese. Or like us," he said.

Bertha distracted him with an account of how she spent Christmas when she was a child in Singapore. The last thing she wanted to discuss over her *nasi lemak* at breakfast, light-headed with her tiredness from the late night, was religion.

She hadn't figured the old fellow out yet. But she knew one thing. His interest in her comings and goings, her half-westernised way of life, and in her Singapore, varied sharply from an apparent dutiful need to enquire and genuine interest. She concluded that he had to report on her at regular intervals. That's OK, she said to herself. It didn't worry her. She was getting used to the double life and secrecy of her new job.

May 1961. The Tengku's talk to the Foreign Correspondents' Association with his surprise, surprise – dropping the first hint that Malayasia was kicking in the womb.

April 1961 brought the PAP defeat in the Hong Lim by-election. Ong Eng Guan beat PAP's Jek Yuen Thong. It was as Pa had predicted. It stirred up much interest in the office. She was sure in her own mind that it did not signal a serious drift. But when the PAP candidate was beaten again in July by David Marshall, her thinking was challenged. She explained it by the personality of Mr. Marshall. She had to defend her views at several meetings.

Most of the arguments that came up were not expressed in writing in response to her written reports. They were oral. They sat for hours on end questioning her. They spoke to her in English. But they often went into a huddle themselves in Indonesian. As her Bahasa Indonesia improved she was able to cut in and correct wrong interpretations of her reports or interject comments. She also used their language at the end of her verbal presentations in the final punch-lines.

The job exasperated her at times. But there were also the days when she left the office elated that her views had got through. Or when she felt she had done full justice to a topic. Like when they asked for a run-down on David Marshall. How could that *Jaudi* command such a following? She was absolutely pleased with her summary of the man. Lying in bed that night with David Marshall on her mind, she realised that she had thrown herself into the subject with emotion and bias. It made her dwell on how she should tackle the job no one had taught her to do. Fumbling in the dark, she said to herself. But later, as she tossed in bed smacking her cheek when she heard the piercing whine of a mosquito near her ear, she realised that it wasn't their simple-mindedness that made them ask her to do what she was doing. They wanted the unschooled, first thoughts of a Singaporean. Of an unusual Singaporean. She wondered if there was a soporific element in the mosquito coil smoke, and whether that beige linen material would suit her and finally fell asleep.

Hadi came to her desk at least once a week. She sat in an open office among people who seemed to be doing similar jobs to hers. But she never found out precisely what they did.

He always said that he was visiting someone or other and came to see how she was doing. He was always polite and charming. And Bertha saw the glint of admiration in his eyes every time he sat in front of her.

"Oh Bertha! I mean, Mary Devries, ha, ha. You look wonderful!" he had said spontaneously when she cut her hair. "It really suits you."

But he never asked her out to lunch or a drink or to dinner. It wasn't the Hadi she had got to know during her first brief visit to Jakarta. There was something forced and different in him.

She joined the office sports club. She said she was mad on hockey in the application form to make them sit up. They fielded her in a little inter-department game a week later. It brought an explosion of joy in her. She rushed to Glodok after work and bought herself a skirt, shoes and socks and even a pair of good tough, decent panties. So that she could fall with her legs in the air and not show too much. Ma would approve, she giggled inwardly to herself, as she paid for them.

She made up her mind to stun them at her first game. As the girls knocked the ball around before they started, she saw that she would be playing with a bunch of near-beginners. She held herself back as they passed the ball to each other with their fumbling weak strokes. But she couldn't resist the temptation, once, to dribble through one of the girls as though she wasn't there.

They let her play left wing. Because no one else wanted the position. As usual, she said to herself.

With complete self-confidence she took her position as the the whistle blew. And almost immediately the ball was at her stick. Her pulse raced. This was it. The old feeling of the holding the trump card, the ace, for that second while the girls from the opposing team converged on her, the thrill of seeing the possible moves, grasping the lay of land and her team-mates positions, the vibrations of the ball against the stick coming through to her hands, to her whole body, raced through her. She realised that she would have no back-up. That dark skinny thing who hadn't the strength to hit a fly, was in the best possible position to take a pass, but she'd fumble. There was no one else. Behind her the solid girl with a mole on her lip would take it, but what would she do after that?

She kept the ball to herself and moved up. Along the side line. Past fatty. Past the buck-toothed girl. Then she saw she could make it on her own.

The adrenalin surged through her. She cut in towards the dee. Two girls were approaching her. No yellow shirts were visible to take a pass. She raised the stick and gave it all she had with a long shot. It went high. For a split second she thought it would go over the bar. So did the goalkeeper. It dipped at the right moment and went into the goal. GOAL!

Her blood was up. Soon after the bully-off there was a confused scuffle. The centre started hacking away with two red-shirts. She got it from them. Bertha shouted. "Dahlia!" Dahlia sent it to her. She moved in-field to the opposing team's surprise. Then across to the right. The yellow-shirt right wing was there almost rubbing shoulders with Bertha. Bertha gave it to her and turned towards the dee. The girl returned it to her. The goalkeeper was out, waiting for her. She seemed to Bertha at that moment to be nothing but two small breasts and two large brown pads. A short flick to the right and she stopped the ball with her stick, with no time to lift it. A ground-scraping flick. Past the goalie. Clunk against the board. GOAL!

She demolished them. She had killed their morale in the first five minutes. She went on and scored five. They beat the red-shirts hollow. Five-nil. Five to Bertha.

She glowed with pleasure, conceit, excitement. They hailed her as a heroine. She was it! She knew it was no great success with those girls but it thrilled her. "Oh Mary! You're fantastic!"

This was her beat. Her game. Ahhh, at last ... the good times are back.

The hockey games became one of the things she looked forward to. A little spice of her new life that was becoming dominated by the challenges of her tasks at the office.

Then she met him at Glodok.

She was shopping. It was hot. Very hot. She was tired. She suddenly felt a hand gripping her arm. "Bertha!" By now she was Mary. "Bertha" was a shock. It wrenched her out of the dirty pavement, the smells and jostling of the Glodok crowds. The tone. The strength of the grip.

"Rudi Schindkunz!"

It was just over four years since she had met him while having lunch with Hadi in Jakarta. She remembered his muscular body and his open friendly look. She had been surprised to hear the surname which sounded like Dutch or German to her and, while Hadi and he talked, she studied his features and thought she could detect Caucasian traces. And she remembered his shy, wide, friendly grin.

~ Chapter Thirty-one ~

Rudi Schindkunz

"Bertha! What are you doing here?"

"Rudi! You! What a surprise!"

"You look wonderful Bertha. It's a wonder I recognised you with your hair so short."

He noticed, Bertha thought to herself. She smiled and looked at Rudi. He was in a simple short-sleeved batik shirt. He looked the picture of health.

"And you too, Rudi. You look great."

He rubbed the big triceps of his left arm in embarrassment. She could see that he relished the comment. More than she appreciated his.

"I've got a job here," she said.

"Well, whaddyaknow. Then we'll be able to see more of you."

"Yah. We must get together some time."

"Sure. Where you staying?"

"In Keboyaran Baru. You'll never find the place. But I'll give you my office phone number." She opened her bag and fumbled inside. He reached for his wallet and took out a card, holding it while she continued to rummage in her bag. She found a little notebook, one of the little "555" books that she had brought from Malaya.

"Here, I've got a pen."

She saw it was a Parker 51, a rare and expensive thing in Jakarta. She tore out a page and wrote her number on it. He held his card awkwardly waiting for her to finish.

"There. That's my office number."

"My card."

She took it from him and read it. Economics Department, Bank of Indonesia, she translated in her mind.

"Ooo ... Bank of Indonesia!"

"Yah." He didn't venture any further information. Bertha saw that he was uneasy. The fellow's shy, she thought to herself. He just stood there grinning at her.

"Oh, by the way, I'm Miss Devries at the office."

"Married?" he asked lifting his eyebrows.

"Yes. And divorced."

"Whew! Why it's only ..."

"Yes, Rudi. It's a long story. I tell you when we meet."

"We've met! Why don't we go and have a cup of coffee somewhere."

"I'm in a hurry," Bertha said. She was not. She wasn't sure how she should react to Rudi. She wanted to think about it. Not that it embarrassed her.

"I'll ring you at the office tomorrow then. I'll ring at ten."

"Wow. That's precise."

"I'm impatient."

"I must run."

"*Selamat jalan*."

He smiled at her. But Bertha saw that it was more than a smile. He was grinning from ear to ear. Like a little boy in front of the Christmas tree.

She walked away briskly. After about fifteen seconds she turned around. He was standing on the sidewalk still grinning, as she expected. Grinning to himself. He saw her turn around. He waved.

Jees ... she said to herself, he's a beautiful hunk of a man. As big as Hartono. But more muscle. More powerful looking. Younger. Tall, dark and handsome her mother would have said.

She almost sat with her hand on the big black phone from five minutes to ten. It rang at ten.

It was his deep voice, speaking in Bahasa Indonesia, asking for Miss Bertha Devries. Hell, she said to herself, I forgot about the

Mary bit.

"Yes, Rudi," she replied.

There was a brief silence. She read the silence at once. Her answering the phone had stumped him.

"Bertha. What about tomorrow night. Dinner?"

"Yah, Rudi, *terima kaseh.*"

"Where shall we meet. I thought we'd go to the Oasis and have a Dutch meal."

The Oasis, she repeated in her mind. The fellow's rich! Or stupid. Or crazy about me.

"Wow!" she said.

"Oh, it's nothing, I dine there three times a week. But only with beautiful women," he said in a haughty, joking tone.

"Yes, me Lord."

He laughed. "But where can I meet you?"

"What time, Rudi?"

"Seven?"

"Good. I'm playing hockey at five. I can be cleaned up and perfumed by then. What about the lobby of the Hotel Indonesia?"

"Yah ..." his voice trailed off.

"But it's crazy to drink there. We musn't."

"Yah, fine. How will I recognise you?"

She laughed. "I'll be baring my teeth, with ..."

"Baring your teats?" he interrupted.

"Rudi!"

He giggled. Yes, she decided later. He actually giggled like a schoolgirl.

"You've been there before? The Oasis?" he asked.

"Yah."

"So you know what it's like? It that OK by you?"

"Yah. It's really posh, isn't it?"

"Yes. A beautiful place to dine with a beautiful lady."

Oh God. The corn! she thought.

"That's it then. Seven. The lobby."

"Listen, I'll take a taxi there and rush in, grab you and rush out.

How's that?"

"Good. See you tomorrow then."

He looked even taller and squarer in a suit. He had such wide strong shoulders. Bertha was wearing the dark blue dress she had decided to make on an impulse. It had one bare shouder. It hugged her hips. She had picked the design out of the book the tailor had brought with him. She changed the neckline. After she had tried it on, she went to the dining room to get Mononutu's opinion. He had raised his eyebrows. Aduh! It's stunning, he said. The old fellow's not so old, she had said to herself, smiling happily.

Rudi told her she looked stunning too. But he was so full of that sort of jazz, she said to herself. It was a long time since she had dressed up and been out to a posh place. She looked around. It was the poshest place she had ever been to.

"What's this with the hockey?" he asked.

She told him about the department team. She was down to play for the ministry next week. Whoa!

She saw he knew his European food. But then, she remembered, he had gone to university in Germany. He ordered a bottle of wine. Bertha's knowledge of wine was limited to port and Wincarnis. And the few thing she remembered from Heng's courting days. And sherry, of course. She knew the different sherrys.

He was polished. He was confident with his orders and his choice of the wine. But he was so boyish in his manner towards her, she thought.

"Now tell me. How the Dickens did you come to change your name, Bertha?"

"I'll tell you one thing more. My name's not Bertha anymore."

"Beautiful, unpredictable woman. You keep surprising me."

"Briefly. I got married. He was the slickest man in town. He danced like a dream. He had everything. But … but … it didn't work out."

"The dream collapsed?"

"He started playing around."

"Idiot! Didn't know he'd struck a goldmine?'

"Hah! Not all that glitters, Rudi."

"You are the real McCoy, Bertha."

"Mary!"

"Mary. Actually, I prefer Bertha."

"So, as I was saying, I left him. It was a bit more than that. I stole his car. I mean, I drove off with it. To Malaya. The beast reported to the police. I'm a car-thief now. I'm a wanted woman."

"God! Honeybun. That you are!"

Bertha laughed. He had all the oozy stuff, but that was good!

"So that is why I'm using a different name here."

She saw Rudi knit his brows. She knew from their first meeting he had a quick and sharp mind that his puerile flirtatious nonsense concealed. She had to be careful.

"I'm sorry to hear that," he said in a serious tone.

"It's all water under the bridge now, Rudi."

"Yah-lah."

She looked at the candle flame. She saw him looking at her in a different way.

She asked him about his job to change the subject. Economics. World trends. Money values. The rupiah against the US dollar. She was learning. It wasn't just politics. There were the realities of finance.

The flambé distracted them. "Oh, Rudi, it's wonderful!"

He asked her about Singapore. She could see his surprise when she laid out the political situation as she perceived it clearly to him. She could see his admiration of her and not only her body. It was something new to her too.

"So it's Lee Kuan Yew fighting the tiger that carried him through to his battle against the old order. And the question is whether he'll beat them or get eaten up," she said.

"Swallowed. As Sukarno may be swallowed up by Aidit."

"No. Here it would be chewed up, Rudi."

"Yes. You're right. There's none of the British gloved fist fighting here. You see, the Dutch hacked at us with heavy cutlasses. They set the pitch of violence and treachery. We had to fight them head-on. The British wheedled their way with the Sultans. They drew up unequal treaties and whispered different things to different rajas. The threat of the rapier thrust was more dramatic than the the showdown. You had teenage Chinese students in the front line. A few riots. Ten, twenty killed. That was enough. We had the bloody wars. And I mean wars. The Achinese wars way back. Then after the war, the full scale army battles. There was so much blood lost, Bertha."

"Mary."

"Mary ... And to my mind, the last of the bastards was that bloody Eurasian bastard, Van Mook."

"This is strong wine, isn't it Rudi?"

"Sorry. But he was a pig."

"A Eurasian?"

"Yah."

"Like you and me?"

"More like you."

"Why do you say that?"

"Because, I'm not an Indo, not really."

"You are, aren't you, by blood?"

"But not in my bones."

"What do you mean?"

"Bertha. I know a little bit about you people in Malaya. You lived as a community."

"Not now."

"Yah, but before and the past still lingers. I am an Indonesian. I should really say I'm an Andalas man."

"Andalas?"

"The old word for Sumatra."

"You are saying that you were brought up as an Indonesian, not as an 'Indo?' "

"Yes. Indo is an old word, honeybun."

"So you are Indonesian? And you say I'm not Singaporean?"

"I didn't say that. Coming back to the point ... what was the point anyway? Ah yes, I was saying that the last of the Dutchman who fought us with his brand of treachery was a man of mixed blood ... But he was a man to be admired in some ways. He wanted to create the United States of Indonesia. He was genuine. But Van Mook was the product of his time. A little more open-mindedness and compromising would have brought Sukarno and Van Mook together to build the United States of Indonesia earlier without all the bloodshed."

"And kept the communists out?"

Rudi Schindkunz frowned. He looked into Bertha's eyes and stopped talking.

Bertha had the communists on her mind. She was committed to do all she could to prevent the formation of Malaysia. In fact, this was the task that Benny had hinted at during the journey to Jakarta. Now the communists had decided that they should attack the proposed merger of Singapore and Malaysia. The PKI had made their stand by condemning the idea of Malaysia as NEKOLIM, neo-colonialism, at the end of 1961. She was sure that it was only a matter of time before the Indonesian government followed the communists' stand on the Malaysian issue. It was a sort of repetition of running with the reds for expediency. It unsettled her.

She suddenly realised that her mind had drifted far away from the candle-lit room. Rudi was saying, "No one can ride the tiger and not get eaten. Confucius says ..."

She laughed.

"Tell me about you," she said to Rudi.

"You took the words right out of my mouth, Bertha. Or Mary. Heck! You are Bertha to me."

"No, Rudi. Help me to change my life, my image."

"I see." He paused with a dead serious look on his face. "Well, tell me about your precursor ... from day one."

"There's nothing much to tell. I've told you about the big things. Marriage and divorce."

It was easy for Bertha to make him talk about himself. His childhood. His time in Germany. As he talked, she saw what a self-centred person he was. And that he was completely Indonesian in his approach to life. The new Indonesian, finding new visions in western technology and western attitudes in many areas. But she liked him in spite of his conceit. He had drive. He was alive to the changes going on in Indonesia.

He got a taxi and said he would drop her off at her place first. When they arrived at Mononutu's house he tried to kiss her. She turned her face away. She could see that he wanted to turn her chin around and kiss her on the mouth but he was too shy to do it in front of the taxi driver.

Three days later, he rang her. "Mary, did you know that Jakarta is playing Palembang this evening? It would be a good match."

"Yes. I saw it in the papers."

"Shall we go?"

"Oh Rudi, that would be wonderful!"

"Good. Where do I meet you?"

One thing about Rudi, she said to herself, he doesn't chit-chat on the phone. She told him that when she got to know him better. "Heck!" he said. "In Jakarta you're lucky to get through. You've got to cover the essentials before you're cut off. Besides, there're probably hundreds of people waiting to use the line."

It was not the answer she expected.

In the taxi to the stadium, he put his hand on her knee. "Aduh!" he whispered into her ear, "Your skin is so smooth."

She moved his hand away firmly, with, "Like all women."

They enjoyed the game. She was thrilled with the standard of play. She had not watched a good hockey game for years. They had dinner at a small eating shop. Rice and curried food. He ate with his fingers. When she saw that he intended to, she decided to eat with her hand too. It pleased him. He said something to the effect that she was a daughter of the soil.

They began to meet regularly.

Rudi was a relief. In spite of his ego. He loved his body. He told her he jogged every morning and did weightlifting two or three times a week. He also seemed to read a lot of journals on economics, in English and German. But so much of what he told her went over her head. They had settled down to a relationship that Bertha was happy with. They met once or twice a week early in the morning and ran round the field of a club he belonged to. Then they had breakfast together. He was at his best then. Natural and open. Flushed and handsome.

They met and had dinner together about once a month. Bertha though he was at his worst after his third Bintang Baru or his second whisky. He started his drooling over her. She chuckled to herself one night as she lay in bed after having a delicious rice and curry dinner with him. It's a pattern. One night trying to screw me. Then two nights being nice and brotherly. Wonder if he has noticed that. Slow-slow-quick. Come to thimk of it, he has never asked me to go dancing.

She thought about him for a long time that night. He had the looks and the body. He had brains. He could lay on the charm when he wanted to. But he could also be painfully shy. He could be absolutely clear in seeing the problem at times and could be utterly naive now and then. He hasn't got his act fully together yet, she decided. But she loved the way everyone looked at them when they were together. Women look at him. Then the men notice me. Or is it the other way around? She nearly giggled.

But there were too many things on her mind to dwell on Rudi now. The unexpected change in the West Irian conflict was one of them.

She remembered how the shape of the island of New Guinea, somewhere between Australia and Java, had provoked her in her schooldays to add reptilian feet to it in her school atlas and it looked like a cross between an iguana and a turtle. Half of it was coloured yellow. The same yellow as the Dutch East Indies, now Indonesia.

Indonesian troops had been fighting the Dutch on the island. Indonesia claimed that West Irian, as they called the western half of the island, belonged to Indonesia. Bertha was not quite sure if the people there were the same kind of people as the Indonesians.

Sukarno had made much capital out of the conflict. It was a

fight that drew the nation together. Volunteers from Malaya and Singapore had also come over to fight with the Indonesians. But she knew they were a motley collection of communists, opportunists and rejects of society.

Then on the fourteenth of August 1962 it had all ended. America had acted as the peacemaker and the fighting stopped. The Indonesian part of the island became West Irian.

The settlement of the dispute brought an emptiness into the political anti-colonial air. It was like a calm before a storm.

The wind had suddenly dropped out of Sukarno's sails.

The meetings at the office on the possible merger between Singapore and Malaya into the new state of Malaysia became a new focus.

Major Abdulgani pointed out the increasing strength of the communists in Singapore. He quoted A.W. Scott, the retiring Chairman of the Singapore Chamber of Commerce, "the orgy of strikes, go-slows, sit-downs, etc."

"Therein lies our hope. Or rather, mine. The communists could stop the merger," he said

Mr. Lee Siew Choh of the Barisan Socialis, a regular commie in Bertha's opinion, had recently stood up in the Legislative Assembly and made a marathon speech against the Malaysia proposal. He had spoken for seven and a half hours over two days. It indicated the weight the reds were putting on their campaign against Malaysia. It was a natural. It would be easy to stir up the Chinese fears against Malay domination. They were going to go all out on this.

It appeared to her that the opposition parties in Singapore had not thrown in their votes with the Barisan against the formation of Malaysia only because the reds had taken the initiative to lead the attack. Party politics were clouding the key issue. Only Mr. Marshall had voted with the Barisan Socialis.

She had faith in the PAP leadership and organisation but the way they were fighting the reds worried her. There was a lot of off-the-centre slamming at the Barisans.

She told the unit that she thought the PAP would go further

along these lines and could foul up their image with their determination to achieve the merger.

Nyoto, one of the committee, praised Bertha for seeing how the PAP would move. They had called for a referendum to make it clear that it would be a decision of the people. It bore out her predictions. The voting form was couched in terms too difficult for the common man to comprehend. There were A and B and C options to select. Not a straight yes or no to merger with Malaya. And to cap it all, they were doing the dirty trick of saying that blank votes meant alternative A. That was nasty, Nyoto said.

"Even the symbols on the forms are designed to sway the vote. They are loaded. This isn't democracy. It is conning the people," he said.

"Let's ignore the little details," Abdulgani said, "What we really want to know is where the power lies within Singapore today. Which way will Singapore go? Will it be an appendage of Malaya or a buffer for us?"

At the end of one session, Hadi with a chuckle said that we are all wasting our time; we can take Singapore any day.

Hadi played a fairly important role in the unit. She wasn't sure what it was, but she knew he had a certain amount of "pull."

He gave her some assignments now and then.

One morning he came up to her desk with an armful of files.

"*Selamat siang*!" he greeted her smiling. They exchanged pleasantries. Then he selected a file from the bunch he was carrying and handed it to her.

"I have an interesting file here for you. It is a job you can do for us."

She looked at the title, SIN/OPS/JAM/62, and opened it at once in front of him.

The first lines came as a surprise:—

"James Andrew Mckay; born in Penang in 1933
Father: Scotsman, Master Mariner, A.J. Mckay"

~ *Chapter Thirty-two* ~

Captain James Mckay

James Mckay stood on the bridge leaning against the rail, looking out to port. Kedah Peak was just visible, rising above the Malayan coastline, grey-green in the early morning light. The sun was still behind the mountains and the air still damp.

He had stood many, many times on the deck, and later on the bridge, looking at Kedah Peak as they steamed into Penang. Ten years in these waters. Aden, Bombay, Calcutta, Penang, Singapore, Sandakan, Hong Kong, Medan, Batavia ... they were all familiar to him. The sea lanes, the charts, the islands, landmarks, lighthouses; he had seen them change. Singapore and Hong Kong in particular.

But Penang was still the same: Georgetown was as sleepy a hole as ever. Even the pilot and the harbourmaster seemed to have been there since he had first sailed in.

Soon it would be different for him. In a sense, he would be dropping his anchor here. Tying himself down to Doris and sinking new roots into the ground at Pulau Tikus.

"Good morning, sir." It was the steward bringing him his regular morning tea. He would have a late breakfast today. He had got "sparks" to ask the agent to have breakfast with him when they got in. They could clear all the odds and ends over breakfast. He wanted to get it over and done with so that he could get to Sungei Nyor as soon as possible. Jones could get her alongside the wharf. There were no complications in Penang.

He walked over to the bridge telegraph and with the clang of bells told the engine room to drop the speed. They were almost there. In the distance, he could see the Butterworth ferry near the mainland.

"Morning, sir. Gonna be a nice day." Jones had come up to the bridge.

"Aye. Looks like it ..."

"How long are we going to be at the yard?" Jones asked.

"Don't know. That's why I want to go out there this morning with Savage. Make sure they don't mess around and get us out as quickly as possible," the captain replied.

"Savage reckons three days but, as always, says he's got to see the guts of it after they've open her up to be sure," Jones said.

"Aye," the captain grunted.

James had all the confidence in the world in his "chief." If there was ever a man who could feel an engine, it was Ronnie Savage. It was almost uncanny at times. Ronnie was sure that he had some sort of sixth sense with engines. But they are always like that. One bloody superstition or another. Never get it out of their systems. He reckoned Ronnie Savage used their irrational fears at times to get them into line, the crafty bugger.

Aye, the lad was a wonder with the men too. He'd got them working as a team in the engine room as soon as he had come aboard. No more back-chat from Noor. Whole-hearted co-operation. Bloody Robbie couldn't handle Noor or any of the cocky greasers. Tried to impress them with his muscles only. Damn good thing they took him off the ship.

Aye, Ronnie Savage is a good man. A "white man" at heart. God knows when the company is going to see that some of their best men are the local boys. Perhaps Savage has opened things up now that he's proved himself as chief. They've seen the figures. McTavish had come aboard at Singapore and had seen how he had got the burners going as they had never worked before. Fixed them as soon as he took over.

If he were a "white man," I wouldn't have to go over to the yard today. He'd be able to fix it all up with Scott. Bloody Scott. Bottle a day, they say. Yet, he runs a good show out there at Sungei Nyor. Forgets the dredging now and then though. Hope he hasn't allowed the silt to clog up the channel this time. Aye, Savage is one of the best. Never forget the time he went ashore at Bangkok with Graham on his first trip with us. Didn't want to do anything. Drove Graham mad. Only wanted to post that letter to his best girl. Then the Thai girl at the post office. Putting her hand on his as she slid the change towards him. "Sleep me?" Ha, ha, ha. The captain chuckled to himself. If Graham hadn't been close enough to hear it, we wouldn't have known. And Graham cussing the poor lad because he wouldn't "sleep me" with her.

Or that time when the bearing went. Reckon that's when he got the engine room completely on his side. They saw that he could do any bloody job they could. And a thousand times better. And faster. Make someone a wonderful husband, he would.

He could see the buildings now. The clock tower of the railway station; the railway station without a rail-line. Opposite the Prai railway ferry. Hah! Horses on the railway ferry. The races must be coming up in a day or two.

James scanned the shore front. There were still old junks there. And the clumsy, big-bellied, Indian one-masted boats. One was pulling out. Going up some river with crates all over her deck. Lighters by the dozens, small motor boats with their canvas roofs chugging around, towing the lighters loaded with bales of rubber.

The *Kampar* is in, James noticed. Wonder how Linggard is getting on. Bet he had his elbows on the E.& O. bar last night. A big Greek ship was anchored next to the *Kampar*. Twin screws, James noted to himself. Probably vibrates like hell. Waste half their bloody energy fighting themselves, churning up the bloody water. It's a wonder they don't shake their rivets loose. What's that? Beauty! President line. Oh, the *Jackson*. One of them new-fangled diesel driven things. Not in my bloody life. Wouldn't take one of them anywhere if they paid me a million pounds. Ah, the *Perak's* in too. Or is it the *Kinta*?

He looked at the ships anchored closer to the shore. The *Kajang*, the *Kamuning*, and the little *Rasa*, looking like a tanker with her superstructure way back aft. Must be nice to run those little coasters.

Up and down the coast, like driving a bus.

The *Ganges* is raising steam. Hasn't got her Blue Peter out yet. Pretty heavily loaded.

He looked at the large mass of the Penang hills. His eye ran down to where Pulau Tikus would be. Dear Doris. Yes, it's time I got m'self a good woman. Mum would be happy at last. She wouldn't care if the woman was black, brown or yellow. It's only the bloody shits out here. Or worse still in Batavia.

He cleared all the business with Sandy Harris over breakfast. Sandy had his early morning *gin-merah*. It was far too early for James. Sandy brought him up to date with the news. The U.K. news and the company gossip.

O'Leary's finally got the sack. Gone absolutely blotto at the Christmas party. Actually, he was very funny. Kept shouting "Happy new year dirty-dree," when Peter Dreeman was giving his speech. But he really crowned himself when Mrs. Gray was giving out the prizes to the staff. He burst out singing, "Whatever happened to the old grey mare." Nineteen thirty-two Christmas will never be forgotten at head office!

The company launch came up to the ship at nine. James recognised it. The *Ian*. Bloody Scotsmen, he always repeated to himself when he read the name on her bows. Giving her a name like that. The *serang* and the *klassis* said it one way and the bosses and officers said it a different way. And a masculine name at that!

The *Ian* took Sandy Harris back to Penang and turned off towards the Prai river mouth with James and Ronnie Savage. He had done the trip several times before. They would chug away slowly across the channel, with the porpoises leading them at times, often following the Penang-Butterworth ferry initially and then bearing more to the north towards Prai. He recognised Mitchell Pier, the Bagan Dalam slipway and the pretty row of Straits Trading quarters. At the wide river mouth they would pass Prai docks, with the huge cranes that sat idle most of the time on the wharves because the big boats they were designed to load and unload could not come alongside the empty wharves. They were sterilised by the silting up of the Prai river mouth.

Then down the river. From now on it would be mangrove all the way. No villages on stilts, no large, brown, wooden warehouses, no flimsy jetties. Just mangrove swamp for the next fifteen minutes. They would sometimes pass one of those heavy-bellied Indian boats, like junks, only less delicate in their lines, moving downstream slowly with their hulls filled with bales of rubber.

Sometimes there were monkeys in the swamps. They said there were crocodiles there and he was sure they were right, but one never saw any when the sun was up on the banks of the wide river. Scott had told him that they went up the little creeks and tributaries. Scott had also told him of the otters around the dockyard. And the monitor lizards.

As they turned round a bend he saw the "shearlegs," the tall three-legged crane of Sungei Nyor Dockyard. It was a landmark rising above the flat mangrove landscape. The yard crept into view. The rusty looking crane on the wharf. The ancient dredger tied up at the entrance to No.1 slipway. The corrugated iron stores and offices. A wisp of smoke from the foundry at the back of the machine shop. The stacks of coal, little black hillocks with the latticed timber ventilation shafts sticking out of them. A rusty half-built boat on the chocks. Stacks of brown steel plates. Rusting girders. Old life boats, lying on their sides, abandoned. Condemned anchor chains. Twisted ventilators thrown on the mud. An old funnel. Ash heaps from the foundry. A capstan. The garbage of shipyards.

And in the distance the chain-ferry, like a house on the water, loaded with trucks and cars going to Penang.

James felt strangely happy and contented on seeing the familiar castaways of a shipyard. They were things he had lived with. From his earliest days at the fishing village in Scotland, and later at the shipyard in Glasgow where he had started his working life on a moulder's loft. When he was heavy with whisky and talking of old times he always insisted that he knew ships better than any seafaring man because he had started at the beginning of it all, on the moulder's loft, where the lines, the character, the way she behaved in the sea; the way she cut through the waves, the way she listed when her holds were not trimmed, the way she pitched and rolled and responded to the rudder and the thrust of the screw were determined.

The dockyard scrap, the smells of tar and paint and smoke from coal and coke fires, the clanging of hammers against steel, the rumbling of the little railway that went around the yard all reminded him of his days in the shipyard in Scotland. But James was not a sentimental man. He left the past behind when he sailed across the Red Sea, every time he stepped onto a new boat, every time he left a bar, a girl, a port.

Neither was he a man who brooded over things or lay awake trying to analyse and sort out problems. But there was some kind of rough philosophical roundness in the way he lived and thought. Men like us, he often said when they were passing the Akavite or Scotch bottle around the table, who have battled with the elements alongside our fellow men should have no truck with petty differences of opinion. It's a funny thing about being at sea. You get to know how a man ticks. You live with your shipmates for days and weeks. Then you go ashore and deal with people for an hour, fifteen minutes, ten minutes ... and you forget all you have learnt about human nature. "Get caught by some biddy, eh?" someone usually added at that moment.

But he was pensive today. He had been caught, as they would say. And by some half-caste at that. The wedding was next month. He was sure that Doris was the woman for him. He had met her at the PRC. The night they came into Penang three years ago, Savage had said there a dance was on and asked James if he'd like to go. He agreed and had a great time at the bar and on the dance floor. She was standing in front of him at one of those Paul Jones dance games. In her red dress. Like the Indians, he thought, wearing those screaming bright colours contrasting sharply with their dark skins. She was so shy. He had to draw her out. Ah yes ... sweet, dear Doris.

It didn't worry him that she was not one of his kind. In fact, it was a stroke of luck that he was a Roman Catholic and the greatest possible objection her parents could have had did not present itself. They didn't mind his being a seaman, in spite of the old man's jokes about a wife in every port. Doris's brother was at sea. Fifth on a Blue Funnel. And so was her cousin. On deck. On the *Tapah*. Nice boat that.

It would be good to have a home after all these years. And Doris waiting for him. And a ripe age to get married, he said to himself. Thirty-nine. With a master's ticket. He was proud of what he had achieved, but he kept his pride quiet in his heart.

It was a fairy tale, a dream, a blessing from Our Lady to Doris Coehlo. A Scotsman. A captain. A Catholic. A he-man, with those clear blue eyes and golden hair. A house of her own. She swelled with pride as she told them about her "Jamie" and saw Jean and Norma's envious faces. Yes. It's all fixed. Wednesday the third of February, 1933. But he's fourteen years older than you, Doris. What is age when he loves you, she had replied. She giggled at her haughtiness when she thought of it later. But pride was bursting out of her. She had found a dream-man.

But when they came down from Maxwell Hill after the honeymoon was over and Jamie was packing his bag, the dream faded and the terrible pain of separation tore into her like a *kris* thrust into her belly. She hung onto him, kissing him, pleading with him to remember her love, half-crazed with fear and jealousy. Then he was gone. Back to the sea. The sea that was part of him. A part that she knew she would never ever fully understand. She cried into her pillow and hugged her bolster, wishing it was her Jamie every night for that first ten days of their separation. Never in her sheltered life had she been wracked with such pain.

It continued for the next ten, twelve trips. The same terrible pain. The same tearing fears of losing him. Her Jamie. Her wonderful, wonderful Jamie.

He's a wonderful man, Mrs. Coehlo said to Aunty Peggy. He adores her. Practically worships the ground she walks on. And he's so gentle. So understanding and attentive. No fuss and nonsense. Eats anything. *Belachan* and all. No man could have made her happier. Oh, Peggy, I'm so lucky.

The pain of parting eased as time went by. There were strange new changes in her body. She had missed it once, twice, but Doris had always been irregular. It used to worry Mrs. Coehlo until Dr. Reutens told her it was nothing to worry about. Some women were like that. Then the nausea in the morning. Her craving for sour *kanas*. Dr. Reutens confirmed it. She was "carrying."

"Fast worker," Hector Coehlo had said, to the great annoyance of his wife. Pregnant within the year.

Doris Mckay, nee Coehlo, was as strong and tough as they came. There was no trouble. James Andrew Mckay was born on the fourth of November 1933, wet, slimy, red-faced and screaming but utterly beautiful to Doris.

The family had argued about the child's name after Doris told them what Jamie and she had decided. It's none of your business, she had said, but they ignored her and debated the name while she sat there, as though it was no concern of hers. Ma and Pa, Uncle Ambrose, Auntie Peggy, Auntie Vera, Auntie Pearlie, and even that busybody Auntie Constance, Mrs. Constance Spykerman. Her Pa won the argument defending their choice. He was the real traditionalist. Stephen had been saddled with Stephen Sequeira Coehlo because he had insisted on the old Portuguese tradition of his mother's surname being carried by the eldest son. Poor fellow, they kept asking him "Hey! Are you Sequeira or Coehlo?" every time he filled in a form. So Pa had understood Jamie's Scottish style of putting the common name the boy would be known as in second place. Anyway the two names were both good saint's names.

She didn't tell Jamie about all the fuss they had made about Andy's name.

~ Chapter Thirty-three ~

Doris Josephine Mckay nee Coehlo

James Andrew Mckay was a beautiful baby. Round and full with a thick head of hair. It was brown, fine and downy. Both Valma and Norma went into ecstasies over his hair. They kept running their fingers through it and were thrilled with its softness and texture. They said how pink and white he was. Auntie Peggy thought he had a touch of his father's eyes. They were grey-green. Not blue. Mrs. Constance Spykerman said he had his father's wonderful strong jaw. Uncle Ambrose said he looked like a regular *orang-puteh* but he had his mother's smile. Nobody said that he had a good round, flat Malay nose.

Jamie was almost delirious with joy when he saw his son three days after his birth, when his ship came in. He was embarrassed with his pleasure of seeing the baby. Andy brought so much happiness to Doris and Jamie. He was perfect. They almost fell over each other to get fresh nappies, to wipe him clean, to burp him. And while Jamie was in port, the bathing of James Andrew Mckay was a whole new delightful experience.

Doris soared with happiness. She felt a pride in her bringing into the world, delivering to her Jamie, a bouncing baby boy. And a pride in her delivering seemingly endless volumes of milk to James Andrew Mckay from her tight, swollen breasts, which Jamie told her were beautiful.

The baby grew by leaps and bounds with every return of the S.S.*Irrawady* to Penang. The baptism was timed to coincide with the S.S.*Irrawady*'s schedule. It was a major social event in Pulau Tikus. Almost as big as the wedding, Jamie thought. The months flew by. Every day, James Andrew Mckay did something new. There was so much to tell Jamie when he walked up the wooden steps of their house verandah with his bag, grinning and with his arms wide open to embrace Doris.

The bringing up of James Andrew Mckay involved so much. There was so much to organise and plan. And to guard against. Doris and Jamie talked about him for hours on end. But through the euphoria of their first born, some shadows began to fall.

Wind in his little belly was one of their first differences that came up. Doris was absolutely firm in her faith in *minyak urat* as the solution when the little fellow screamed blue murder with wind pains. Jamie wasn't quite sure if that was the right thing. It's an internal thing, he said, the cure must surely be putting something into the nipper's tummy.

There was more. For gawd's sake, Doris darling, crying is natural. It's nature's way of developing the lungs.

And in between all the fuss and bother with James Andrew Mckay, Doris and Jamie started little bickerings. "Why do you tell him to *chium* you and to kiss me, sweetheart? Isn't he going to speak English?" … "Daddy! luv, I'd rather be his Daddy than his Pa." … "It's not cold, Doris my luv. There's no need to wrap him up like that."

So they taught him to call Jamie, Dadums. It was a happy compromise.

With all the getting up at his faintest squeak, Doris caught a chill. Jamie walked in one night from the ship to find her red-eyed and snivelling. "Better call Dr. Reutens."

"No, darling, it's arright. I'm taking *liang char*."

"What the hell is that?"

"Herbal tea, sweetheart."

"For Crissake!"

Fussing over James Andrew Mckay clouded other differences. "Jamie, darling, why did you join the Penang clup?"

'It's a good place, luv. We can go there and have a drink and dine when I'm in port. And it's club, luv. Cluber, ber, ber, ber, ber."

"Please, Jamie. No need for me to tok like a Europin."

Jamie had joined the Penang Club soon after he got married. It would be a nice retreat, he said to himself. Cheaper than the E.& O. And some good blokes there. Ashley's joined the club.

They had met Ashley who was the manager of a rubber estate somewhere near Sungei Patani one day at the PRC. Jamie had taken to Ashley's easy Manchester manner, and Ashley had married a Chinese girl. She was brown for a Chinese. She knew the Kedah (she pronounced it in a way Jamie could not recognise) Eurasians and had played hockey with them. They were at the PRC because the Kedah team had come down for some game or other. Ashley had convinced Jamie that he should join the Penang Club.

One had to rely on the chappies who knew the country better than an in-and-out seaman, Jamie said to himself.

But it was at the club bar that Jamie had felt the first jolt of his unconventional decision.

Sandy, the agent guy, had suggested that they meet at the club as soon as he docked to clear up a thing or two. He knew that Jamie was now a member. Jamie agreed. He would drop in on his way to Pulau Tikus. He had walked into the bar and saw that Sandy hadn't arrived. Probably held up at the office. There were two "white men" at one end. He went to the other side and ordered a *stengah*. Scotsmen, he said to himself. One's from Edinburgh.

He could see that they had been at it for some time. Slurring and running out of conversation.

Then he heard the voice, thick-tongued with alcohol, unaware of the loudness of his speech, saying to the other, "Captain Mckay ... the *Irrawady* ... married some native woman ..."

It hit him like a thunderbolt. He had to force himself to stop shouting across the bar. His head throbbed with blind anger. The bar swayed. He gripped the edge. He could have smashed the bastard's face in. And kicked him in the balls when he was down!

It was only after the next trip, about a month later that he was able to take it into his mind again and talk about it. He told Ashley. They were by themselves at the club bar and Jamie had had about three before he brought it up.

Ashley smiled calmly. "He was wrong. Your woman's only half-native. Mine's full native. One hundred percent *Chink*."

Jamie looked at him, not knowing whether to laugh or argue with him about humanity and all that gefuffle. But Ashley added after a few seconds, "And a wonderful *Chink* at that. A rose by any color or name."

Jamie chuckled. Her name was Rosemary. Ashley had told him how he had managed to change her way of saying it after many months. But the family still called her "Rows-mare-ree." Except Johnny, her young brother.

"Yes, Jamie, there're a lot of things I'd like to change in that girl."

"Such as?" Jamie asked. The subject was his, not Ashley's, he thought.

"Nutty superstitions. When we were first going out, I stepped on the ashes of some blooming joss paper fire. You know that paper money they burn by the roadside. She almost went berserk. Crazy."

"They've all got their Asian superstitions," Jamie said.

"Damned if I'm going to live with them. Just learning what's what and when you shouldn't do this or that is one helluva business. I told her, I'm willing to accept your old Chinese ways, but those absolutely idiotic superstitions, no. There's a limit."

"But shouldn't you go native the whole hog?" Jamie asked. Ashley had been married almost exactly a year before Jamie.

"Heck, no. It's a halfway thing. Mind you, I'm quite happy going utterly native on some things. Curry and rice. Dirty street stalls. Bare chested at home. And burping loudly, of course."

Jamie laughed. "You didn't say *sarongs*."

"Oh Jees no. You've gotta have an oriental inner calm to sleep in a *sarong*. Believe you me, capt'n, I've tried it. End up with the bloody thing working itself upwards round my waist and leaving me lying there with me do-dah all exposed."

Jamie laughed. "I'm determined to sleep in a *sarong* one day. That's the acid test of going native. Isn't it?"

Paul Cooper came up to them. “Hullo Ash, Where you bin? Haven’t seen you around the club for ages.” Ashley introduced them. Paul was an accountant with Henry Waugh. Been out East for years and years.

“Good to meet a man from the sea here. Not many of you lot get as far inland as the club,” Paul said.

“Jamie’s gone further that that, Paul. He’s sinking his roots in Pulau Tikus. Married a Penang girl.”

“Oh, congratulations!”

Jamie was not sure if Ashley should have come out from the start like that. But he knew Ashley was always diplomatic and alive to the differences in people. Jamie could see that Paul had reacted with no colonial hang-ups.

“Reckon he got tired of knocking them off in every port, eh?” Ashley said with a chuckle.

“Not quite. I just fell in love.”

“Well said, man!” Paul responded at once. “You deserve a drink for that. What are you chaps drinking?”

They had a good time for the next hour. Jamie liked Paul.

He thought of the exchange with Ashely in jest as he stood with his arms over the rail one moonlight night as the *Irrawady* steamed down the Malacca Straits. He realised that Ashley was saying more than his words literally carried. After all he WAS English. “Meet them halfway,” or something to that effect. Doris and he were not meeting halfway. They were moving along their same tracks, in happy parallel courses. But they weren’t constantly as parallel as the parallels of latitude. The lines crossed at times. And collided. Aye, that they did.

Small things at first but, recently, bigger things. Like the way she brought up wee Andrew. Her way was fine for those days, but …

Then suddenly he saw what the difference between Ashley and Rosemary, himself and Doris were. They weren’t living together. They would come together when he was in port and meet. Clash and compromise. Meet halfway as Ashley had said. But when he went back to the ship he became Captain James Mckay again, the Scotsman. And Doris went back to the bosom of her family and the friendship of Valma and Norma. Back to her Eurasian life. Aye, there's the difference.

He had changed her ways a little. He remembered when he first took her to the Runnymede for dinner. He saw how she was overawed by the waiters. It wasn't that she was not familiar with the cutlery or the menu. It was just the atmosphere. With all the Europeans around. He had leant forward over the table and whispered to her, "See that haughty head waiter over there, he wears baggy striped Hylam underpants."

She had roared with laughter attracting the attention of the whole sedate dining room and nearly blew out the candles. But it broke her nervousness. She actually didn't care about her burst of laughter. He smiled. Aye, that was a night. She was wearing that strapless black gown. With the pearls I had given her. Dear, sweet Doris.

But these were small things. There were still the deep-rooted, semi-religious, illogical images that loomed up unexpectedly in her. Funny how these half-breeds clung to old Malay beliefs after all these generations. Or were some of them Portuguese?

The big one he had won was ... He smiled when he thought of her reaction to his surprise present. He had come off the ship, pleased as punch with himself and announced that he had this surprise for her. A Java pony.

"A HORSE! ... Jamie you're not serious!"

"Not a horse, sweetheart, a pony. A lovely pony with big liquid eyes."

"But what the dickens would I do wit a horse or pony or whatever it is? Gallop down Farquhar Street? Wit a gun slung on my hip?" she laughed.

"No, luv. He'll take you down in style pulling a gig or gharry."

"But I don't know the least thing about horses or ponies."

"Ah. I've got you a man to look after the pony."

"A man!" Doris said with surprise.

"Well, a young man, a lad really. He's from Java. I brought him to look after the pony. He knows the job and he's cheap."

"Is he going to stay here?"

"Aye. In the syce's quarters."

"Ah Far wouldn't like that."

"Well it's just too bad. But I tell you what, she'll be tickled to death to be driven to market in style."

Doris giggled. She threw her arms around Jamie and hugged him. Then she suddenly pushed him away, still holding him, so that she could look into his eyes, "That's not my birthday present, is it?"

"No, my love. That's a piece of equipment for the house."

"Where's the horse, Jamie. I mean pony."

"Reckon she'll be coming down Kelawi Road by now ... clippety clop, clippety clop."

"Oh, Jamie. Andy will be thrilled."

"Aye. That he would," Jamie replied smiling.

"I hope that pony-fellow is OK."

"He'll have to be. You're the boss, I told him. They call him the syce, not pony-fellow, please. His name's Yon."

"That's a funny name."

"It's Javanese. Actually it's short for Suryono."

"And what's the pony's name?"

"Itam. He's a lovely black colour."

"Aiyah! What an awful name. Can't we call him something else?"

"Better not. He knows his name."

"A he, is it?"

"Aye."

Doris' acceptance of the pony was not as smooth as the way their first discussion on the subject ended. First, there was the location of the stable. Then she discovered to her horror that the pony left droppings around. Yon was given the strictest of orders to pick up everything Itam dropped immediately. And I mean immediately, Doris repeated, her eyes opening wide to show that she meant it.

But Itam looked at her with his big brown eyes and she saw that he was a truly beautiful animal.

Suryono settled down quickly and so did Itam. Jamie loved the pony and squatted for hours watching Suryono brush him down or just watching him eat.

Suryono lived in the back room next to the black-and-white servant's room. He was not fussy about eating food cooked with lard. And he didn't complain about anything. Ah Far treated him with utmost contempt, as though he was an animal. She gave him the very minimum *lauk* to eat with his rice but to her annoyance he seemed to relish his meals tremendously. He told her one day, after he'd been there for a month, that her cooking was "*banyak, banyak baik*." She received the compliment with an absolutely inscrutable face but she began to put more *lauk* on his rice.

Doris saw all this happening and did not interfere. She saw how Ah Far treated Yon and scowled inside. Bloody hard-hearted Cantonese bitch. Her sympathy for Yon was stirred by his servile acceptance of anything handed out to him. He bowed when he received an order and carried it out quickly and efficiently. Not like the Malays, Doris remarked to Jamie. Jamie merely grunted a reply.

What she didn't like was the smell of his cigarettes. It was not that she objected to smoking. She herself smoked a cigarette now and then. It was not a habit. It was a pleasure to be enjoyed occasionally, like a brandy or a glass of stout. Her mother and her grandmother smoked in the same controlled way. Grandma had switched to cigarettes when chewing *serai* began to be frowned upon.

Yon smoked a tobacco with a strange and strong smell. He rolled his own cigarettes with some kind of leaf. That seemed to be his one pleasure in life, until she thought she discovered another. A vice.

"Jamie. I'm sure Yon goes to the brothel every month after I give him his pay."

Jamie laughed.

"It's not a laughing matter, Jamie," she said, annoyed at his reaction.

"Well. You can't be sure, so we can't do anything about it."

"Can't you talk to him ... as a father?"

Jamie laughed loudly. "But, Doris, how do you know? In fact, how do you know he hasn't found a girlfriend?"

"He goes into Georgetown every night on his payday. The next morning the whole of the servant's quarters is smelling of Dettol."

Jamie chuckled. "Well at least he knows it's a dirty thing. You must be buying a lot of Dettol, Doris."

"It's not a laughing matter. He buys his own."

Jamie related the whole matter of the pony's introduction and gradual acceptance to Ashley over a few beers one day. "We're getting used to each other's ways," he said as he ended.

"Hey, don't get confused, fellah!" Ashley commented. "That's got nothing to do with different cultures."

"Aye. You're right, Ash."

He thought about that too at the ship's rail. And he thought about the row he had with Doris concerning Sunday lunches.

Doris had started a routine of having her family over to a curry tiffin after church every Sunday. She had taught Ah Far to cook excellent curries and the family looked forward to the weekly tiffin with the gossip. Mr. and Mrs. Coehlo enjoyed playing with their first and, then, only grandchild. Valma and Norma were included, although they were not family, and they cuddled Andy and treated him like a doll. There were cold beers for the men. Uncle Ambrose often dropped in. Sometimes Mrs. Constance Spykerman also came. They were always impressed with her house and the interesting things Jamie brought back from Indonesia, Hong Kong or Borneo. They ate well and had a good time.

When Jamie was in port the routine was maintained. He enjoyed being there at first, listening to the family chatter and the week's yarns about soccer and cricket. Only Uncle Ambrose irritated him. He insisted on calling him "Jock," because Uncle Ambrose firmly believed that every Scotsman should be called "Jock," and every

Irishman "Paddy," and every Welshman "Taffy." It was one of the immutable rules of the British social system as far as he was concerned.

Jim Jansen also began to annoy him because he always exaggerated any bit of news he had. And that young Balfour Sheperdson would pick an argument with anything.

One Sunday when Jamie's boat was in, he told Doris that he would go to the Penang Club and have a few drinks with the boys. Ashley had said he would be in town.

"But it's Sunday, Jamie. Church and lunch."

"Aye. I'll go to church with you. Then Yon can drop me off at the club."

"You won't be late for lunch, will you?" Doris said looking at him from the corner of her eyes.

"I won't have lunch at home. Must try their Sunday roast."

"But all the family will be here."

"That's OK. They won't miss me."

"Of course they will. They'll think we had a row."

"Tell them something or other."

"What? What can I tell them?"

"Oh for goodness sake, Doris, you're jolly good at making up excuses when you want to."

"That's not a nice thing to say to your wife. Besides, why do you not want to stay with me today?'

"I'll be back after lunch, Doris," Jamie smiled as he saw storm clouds gathering.

The storm clouds burst. Their tempers flared. There were tears and Jamie punching his right fist into the left hand. He said he'd had enough of some of those pain-in-the-arse fellows.

She called him a conceited European pig. He stormed out of the house. He didn't even go to church that day.

Attending mass on the Sundays he was in port was more than a pleasant outing to Jamie. It was going back to the days of his childhood and youth. Doris did up her hair and wore her finest dresses. Wee Andy was all spruced up and gurgling. He sat on

Jamie's knee sucking his latest rubber toy. They nodded to everyone they knew as they walked in and, after mass was over, knots of people formed and chatted. It was just like in his little Scottish town.

One day, while the Padre was mumbling a particularly boring sermon with his Portuguese accent, he felt Doris's hand on his knee. It was not a gentle touch of friendly intimacy. She was caressing him. It shocked him. This was the house of God. Hasn't the woman got any sense! The Perera's are behind us.

They had a row over it. "I was only thinking of you last night and feeling loving, Jamie," was Doris' simple explanation. Later, he thought, how sitting there in the church had brought back the codes of his past that his stern father and mother had drilled into him. He was sorry he had got annoyed with Doris.

Sometimes, Jamie thought that he was getting too impatient with Doris. Not always. He was sure that he was right that Saturday Doris had dragged him to the funfair. She announced it as soon as he walked in and hugged her. "We're going to the Convent Funfair tomorrow afternoon."

"Oh no!" he said in subdued exasperation.

"Andy will love it."

"But what about me?" he pleaded.

"You!" she snapped back. She glared at him for a second. Then she said, "It's fixed. I've bought the tickets. Norma will be meeting us there."

"With her timorous, cowering, sleek beastie?" Jamie added referring to Norma's present "intellectual," teacher "beau," as she called him.

"Aiyah, Jamie, why you so intolerant lah."

"I'm not. I'm bloody well not intolerant."

"You are."

"I'm not."

"You are."

"I'm not."

"Well, sometimes."

"So are you at times, Doris."

They went to the funfair. All horribly amateurish, Jamie thought but kept his thoughts to himself. Wee Andy was delighted with everything. And there was a bar. As he counted out his coupons for his whisky, he heard the painful voice of Uncle Ambrose, "Hey! Jock! You're in port, eh? Splicing the mainbrace, huh?"

Jamie winced. He turned round and greeted Uncle Ambrose civilly. He looked over Uncle Ambrose's shoulder to see if he was with anyone else who might have diluted Uncle Ambrose, and saw that Uncle Ambrose was alone. But over Uncle Ambrose's shoulder he saw Doris and wee Andy in the distance. They were standing behind the guess-the-cake-weight-stall. Then, to his disgust, he saw Doris pull down wee Andy's pants to let him *pee* on the grass in front of everybody.

Jamie blew up when they got home. He restrained himself while they were being driven by Yon but Doris could see that something had "got his goat," as she usually said. She put her hand on his but he did not respond.

It ended with her shouting at him, "Now who's being intolerant!"

He wasn't thinking of that when he wondered if he was getting too impatient. He was thinking of the night they had dinner with Ashley and Rosemary at the Penang Club. Doris had been so tense. "Aiyah, do I really have to go to that European place?"

"The food's excellent, luv."

"Yah ... but those women."

"Rosemary will be there."

Doris was uncomfortable all night. It surprised him at first. They had often dined at the E.&O. and the Runnymede, which she had described as European places. She had got used to the atmosphere there. But the club seemed different to her.

She enjoyed the shrimp cocktail, and said so enthusiastically. But to Jamie's embarrassment, she took out a cigarette as soon as she had finished it and lit up. He looked around surreptitiously to see the reaction of the *mems*. To him it was the height of bad manners. Smoking between courses.

Ashley read his reaction. He smiled and turned to Doris, "Well, Doris, you're really in. That's the style of the "in" set in London these days."

"Yah," Rosemary added, "it's become fashionable for the women to smoke, with long cigarette holders ... You've got to get one of those, Doris ... and at anytime, even before the king is drunk, if you are one of those out to change the world." Jamie looked round. There were no stares of righteous shock. There were some sickly smiles. He kept silent, confused. Were Ashley and Rosemary having me on?

Ashley and Rosemary were a tremendous help to Jamie, in that they helped Doris to adjust to the world of colonial society in Penang. Paul's wife was a wonderful person. She took Doris under her wing and chatted with her at the house for hours over endless cups of tea, all the time slipping in a subtle education. She did it with a zeal born out of her conviction that East and West must meet socially, and it was through the women of this world that new bonds could be forged. She was one of those, Jamie said to himself. But she's a gem. She was undeterred with her failure to interest Doris in bridge. Jamie thought Doris would be able to play bridge quite well, seeing she played a crafty game of gin-rummy or whist. But Doris just closed her mind to bridge. Jamie knew that she knew that it was the social game of the *mems*.

Just when he thought Doris had opened up, the chairman's dinner thing happened. The chairman of the company was doing a "Far East tour." They had organised a dinner and ball for his visit to Penang, and the *Irrawady* would be in port on that day. The Mckays were invited. Gilt edged invitation card. Black tie. Doris got a dress made.

Jamie was in one of his humming moods. He sloshed gallons of water over himself after he had shaved, and slowly dressed, brushing his hair carefully, trying to hide the first few grey hairs that had appeared. He was ready, shiny shoes and all, well before Doris was and poured himself a whisky soda. He stood on the verandah, his hands on the rail, the way he stood by the rail on his ship, humming very softly.

Five minutes later, Doris came out. She looked beautiful. But there was something in her eyes. Fear.

"Jamie, darling. I can't go!" she said suddenly in a tone of pain and collapsed into his arms.

"Why, Doris? What's wrong."

"Narting. It's jus dat I doanna face all those people."

She was crying, pleading. His heart went out to her. He was annoyed and frustrated, but he saw the terrible conflict raging in her.

"I'll go if you really wan me to, Jamie, but, please, please … can I stay at home?"

He knew he loved her at that moment.

He went alone with a heavy heart. With a mixture of love and disappointment. A feeling of failure and a throbbing sympathy.

"Poor Doris is down with influenza. It came so suddenly."

He rushed back as soon as it was decent to leave and held her close in his arms that night. This was the woman he married. She was his. And his responsibility.

But he knew that Doris had a strength in her that was as strong as the steel of the hulls of ships he had taken through seas which raged with the fury unleashed by the gods and the winds. He had seen her steel, and it was part of his total admiration that made him love her and want her as his woman for life. He had watched her take over the arrangements of Valma's wedding with an iron hand. She had planned and dictated the moves and sequence of everything. She had ruthlessly cut down relatives trying to change her scheme of things. She had cajoled, badgered, barked out the orders and screamed at anyone who dared say it couldn't be done.

And he had seen the clash of minds between Ah Far and her. He knew the Cantonese woman. He had intervened so many times in domestic eruptions between the Cantonese fitters and their women; wives or mistresses. He had helped to sort out the complications when the sonofabitches in his crew had got themselves into strife with Cantonese dance hostesses and bargirls.

Ah Far had the diamond hardness of the Cantonese woman in her. He knew she came from Shunde in China where they spun the finest silks. He had heard of the ritualistic cutting up of hair in front of the whole village to signify their acceptance of lifetime celibacy. And a lifetime of work with a devotion to their task as fanatic as that of a Catholic nun. These were strong women, now driven out of China with the collapse of the silk boom to seek employment in Southeast Asia.

Ah Far had subtly pitted herself against her young mistress. He had seen Doris slowly but surely grip her and bend her to her own will. But that was in her own environment. She danced and darted, twisted and feinted, then lunged like a fish in the waters she was familiar with, but out of her water, out of her depth, she wasn't the Doris he had met on the dance floor seven, eight years ago. She was still a child bewildered with ogres and rainbows of an unknown world. When he took her to his home in Scotland, the harsh truth of this, of the differences in their upbringing hit him.

The trip was a disaster from start to finish. He had looked forward to it like a schoolboy going to his first scout camp. Seeing his mother again after so many years. Bringing home the bride he was so proud of. His "neater, sweeter maiden from a cleaner-greener land." He knew Uncle Gordon would love her. He knew Jeannie would take Doris into her heart like a sister. But it didn't go that way.

Poor Doris was seasick all throughout the four weeks at sea. On top of that, the blithering idiot of the ship's master broke almost every rule in the book. And the first officer wasn't any better. Gawd! The bloody man didn't understand the sea.

Then the confusion in Tilbury. The bloody boat train problems. The Godamned customs. And even the Flying Scotsman was late.

She hated the cold. It was as much her fault as it was the Gods who brought the winter forward that year. Doris sat huddled in front of the fire almost right through those three weeks that he had looked forward to so eagerly. He kept telling her that if she wrapped up warm and tight, and walked briskly with him, her blood would flow and she would feel so much better.

She did come out with him one afternoon when the sky was blue, as blue and as cloudless as one never sees in the tropics. They had walked the field footpaths and he had pointed out the different kinds of sheep to her. He had seen walls that he had known as a boy. Rough stone walls he had climbed over, sat on, stood on, kicked, leaned against, that were still there. The old croft where McGaw lived was still there. They had let the mill go and crumble to ruins. The field at the bend of the road near Mrs. Harris' cottage, where he had kissed Mary Mcbride, the pond Donald had nearly been frozen to death in had all gone. But the heather, the coarse grass, the streams rushing and gurgling, the old tree on the top of William's Hill were still there.

Doris had enjoyed that wonderful afternoon. It was one of the parts of that huge dream of a visit he had painted in his mind that had materialised. And it was as beautiful as he had dreamt it.

But, after that afternoon, she returned to her hunched position in front of the fireplace and stayed there till they left.

"She's lovely, Jamie, but the poor lass is nae happy here." his mother had said. She was right.

They crept back across the Bay of Biscay, spewing wrath and tossing the P.&O. boat like a cork, through the Mediterranean, unusually cold that year, through the blistering heat of the Red Sea where not a breath of wind could be felt. They stopped at Aden. He wanted to show her the places he knew but she was sick of it all. He was gentle and understanding. They stood together on deck watching the brown dry land recede. One more step nearer home. Her home, he said to himself.

The she was as sick as dog again in the Indian Ocean. Bombay was terrible. He lost his temper with a beggar when they went ashore. It didn't help. But at least the "old man" on that boat knew what he was up to. Jamie could see this was a man who knew the Indian Ocean.

Doris stood beside him as they approached Penang. The very thought of home had revived her. And the warmer weather. He put his arm around her shoulder and pointed out Kedah Peak. Kedah Peak, standing high above the grey-green Kedah coastline he knew so well. She turned to him and smiled. The wind was blowing her hair into her eyes. "I love you, Doris," he suddenly said.

Somehow the day he had stood on the bridge looking at Kedah Peak came to his mind. That trip when Savage was still on the *Irrawady*. Ronnie Savage. Aye, that was a good man. The time when they went down the Prai river to Sungei Nyor together on the *Ian* to talk to Scott. Scott, he's gone now. Poor bastard. Shot himself one night in his house on Pantai Road.

~ Chapter Thirty-four ~

Wee Andy

James Andrew Mckay was throughly spoilt by his grandparents for three months while Doris and Jamie were away. Jamie had warned Doris what to expect; the deterioration of James Andrew and his possible coolness to them when they got back. In spite of telling her his predictions, she was upset that the boy received them with a certain standoffishness.

But Jamie bundled him into the carraige and Yon whisked them home. He still had a few day's leave before the *Irrawady* came back, and it only needed one sound smacking on his wee bottom for the sharp little fellow to realise that he was back to his real home where he could not rule the roost.

But his naughtiness seemed worse. Naughtiness, Doris called it. Bloody cussedness, Jamie thought and kept it to himself. Jamie was really mad the day he saw wee Andy make the Sureens' four-year-old girl cry her little heart out. He had been dozing off in the verandah on the rattan armchair with a glass of ice water in the hole of the chair arm, idly looking at the hedge. He saw wee Cynthia Sureen through the hedge with great concentration planting a cutting in a little flower pot. Her tiny hands pressed the soil down a million times. She watered it with her small, red toy watering can. Then she sat back on the earth, soggy with the overflow of her watering, and looked at her handiwork. She had a lovely little smile on her face. He dozed off smiling.

He was aroused by a sharp pleading cry, "Pleees, Andy doan … doan." He saw wee Andy on the Sureen's side of the hedge. He was holding Cynthia's little pot and, as Jamie watched, he turned it upside-down with a diabolical grin on his face. Cynthia had stamped the soil down too well. Nothing happened. So wee Andy gave it a mighty thump with his podgy hand and the cutting and the earth fell out into a slushy lump on the ground. Cynthia burst into tears.

Jamie was on his feet in a flash. "ANDY!" he roared. The boy was too frightened to disobey. He crept back through the hole in the hedge. Jamie grabbed him, shook him in anger and spanked him soundly. Doris came out to the verandah on hearing the uproar and snapped at Jamie. He roared at her to "shut up."

Then there was the time wee Andy made Doris mad and embarrassed Jamie. The D'ranjos came over for a drink with their little boy who was about wee Andy's age. D'ranjo was Chief on some Blue Funnel boat. Jamie had met him at the Seamen's Club in Singapore, which was really an officer's club. D'ranjo was taking up the invitation Jamie had made. Doris was delighted to see Kathlene D'ranjo. She was a Campbell. The Taiping Campbells. D'ranjo was a "Penangite." Doris knew them both from way back but hadn't seen them for years.

Jamie listened to D'ranjo's pet theories on operation of the superheaters and condensers and, later, to his agitated relation of the governor problems he had when he was on the *Achilles*. D'ranjo loved his whisky soda too. Everyone was enjoying themselves when the D'ranjo kid came running in howling with a scratch on his cheek. It was bleeding. The women fussed and rushed for iodine. Young Vernon howled. Through his screams he said that Andy had done it. Jamie got to his feet with a deliberate slowness. He caught Doris' eye. It said, "Jamie, don't." He called out softly but firmly, "Andy!"

Vernon insisted that wee Andy had scratched his face with a penknife. Wee Andy with equal insistence affirmed that Vernon had rushed at him while he was holding the penknife. "What the hell is the little bugger doing with a penknife?" D'ranjo had said. Jamie remained calm. Kathlene got more and more agitated and holding wee Andy by the shoulder asked him to tell the truth. Her manner upset Doris. But to Jamie's relief, Doris remained calm. It seemed to go on and on. Then D'ranjo downed an almost three-quarter full glass of whisky soda in one gulp and said they'd better take him to a doctor at once. There may be tetanus germs on the knife.

"Oh, come on, Chief. You damn well know how many cuts and scratches happen in the engine room ..."

"Yah. But there's oil there. It kills the germs."

"For Ffff ... for Pete's sake!" Jamie muttered.

D'ranjo kept an exterior cool. He saw Kathlene was working herself up. They left. Doris grabbed wee Andy. "Now, tell the truth."

"Leave it, luv," Jamie intervened.

She looked at him. He repeated the message with his look. She read it and let wee Andy's shoulder go. Andy slunk away.

"Aiyah!" Doris sighed flopping into the cane chair.

But Jamie was sure. The little nipper had scratched Vernon.

There were times when Jamie wondered if he had brought a little ogre into the world. And at other times, he knew he had fathered a genius. It's not just my brains. Doris has plenty of brains. Only she didn't go beyond primary two. And she was seldom pushed to use her head.

Grandpa Coehlo was beside himself with wee Andy's retort to him when he tried to give the little fellow a moral lesson because he saw wee Andy biting into a blown-up balloon. "You must try to make things, Andy, not break things," he said in a slow, clear voice.

"But I am making something, Grandpa. I'm making a hole."

The story was repeated on Sunday for Mrs. Constance Spykerman and Uncle Ambrose. It sent Norma and Valma into stitches of laughter. And Doris laughed again wholeheartedly with them. It became one of the items in the family repertoire.

Soon after wee Andy had started school, Jamie took him out into the garden one dark night and crouched on the grass with his arm round wee Andy. He pointed out a few stars.

"You mean they have names, Dadums?"

"Aye, that they have, Andy. And they each have their own ways of moving. Some run fast. Some run very slowly."

"You mean they move?"

"Aye. But very slowly. Come here. Look, we'll stand under the frangipani. Just here. We'll make a mark where we are standing. And see, that star is just touching the branch up there."

They went back to Jamie's marks later and he showed wee Andy how the star had moved.

It started something that James never imagined would grip the wee lad's interest and drive him on and on to discover more and more about the stars.

It fascinated Doris too. Wee Andy told her what he learnt and, together, Doris and wee Andy started on an adventure of exploration, discovering the night sky, something which was to go on for years until Andy left Doris far behind in his discoveries.

Jamie saw the interest he had aroused that night. He exploited it. He had done the same for so many young cadet officers over the years. He used to roar at the agents when they sent him men with hardly any experience at sea. "You–son–of–f … g–sea–cook, do you think I'm running a kindergarten on the bloody bridge!"

He had succeeded in sending some back. But when he lost the fight, he had taken them under his wing without resentment if their attitude was what he thought was right and taught them the finer points and the tricks of his trade. And always, he searched for their interest and exploited it. Terrence Roberts, fascinated with shapes of the coastlines and the hills. He taught him more about the shapes of the seabed than any first officer knew. Ignatious Marsh, shapes of different hulls and how they responded to the rudder. Cosmos Nicholas, currents and tides. Jock Donaldson, the law of the sea. Anthony Lange, charterparty problems. Guy Pembroke, the tall laddie, the perils of alluvial river mouths. Aye, he was someone special. He would go far, that young Pembroke.

English boys, Scottish lads, Eurasians. But no Indians, Malays or Chinese. They couldn't get into the game in those days. If only they had let some of the Malay lads in. He would have given them masters to man their whole bloody fleet and who would bring them home through the north-east monsoons and the typhoons of the South China Sea.

So now he became a teacher to his son. He drew the orbits of the planets. Later, he slipped in the mathematics of their courses.

He bought him a telescope. Many a night, the wee lad went to bed exhilarated with what he had seen. But there were more nights when he stamped his foot on the grass in front of the telescope because the clouded sky had made observations impossible.

From his interest in astronomy, Andy came to develop a fervent interest in mathematics. But only because Jamie kept relating the boring formulas and rules to the stars every time he was home. Andy kept topping the class in mathematics.

But he got miserable marks in English. Bloody Eurasian grammar, Jamie used to say. It's not Serani grammar, Doris insisted. It's the Chinese boy's talk. Huh! The arguments went on.

One day, Norma said to Doris, "Hey dat son of your's is not Serani, eh? So good in mats, and lousy in English! And also he cannot sing! Aiyah, all Serani can sing, Doris!"

It made Doris very angry when she thought about it the next day as she walked round the garden. Yes. Somehow wee Andy had a bad ear for music. She added another to Norma's list. The lad isn't the least interested in sports.

Doris raised the question of Jamie calling him wee Andy when he was about seven. He was a big boy for his age. He had the large bone frame of the Mckays. Doris had seen his mother and his sister. They were strapping women. Jamie agreed at once. But it was difficult for them to drop the adjective. It had become an intimate thing. Like Mrs. Constance Spykerman calling her children, our Molly or our Patrick or our Doreen.

But, while they swung from delight in Andy's progress at maths in school to frustration at his dreadful marks in English, his total absorption in changing crazes, like in beetles, or kite flying; his attempts to cheat Doris with pocket money payments, taking advantage of her poor memory, or adding onto the money he paid for exercise books and other school requisites; his hitting Romauld Paulo with a spanner; they squabbled heatedly over the upbringing of James Andrew Mckay.

Then Doris got a fresh thought into her head. The lad's like this because he's the only child. He was seven then. A sister to soften his wild ways would be the answer.

Jamie was sick of their bickering about the child they both loved so much. He could not face the same thing all over again. Her maddening superstitions about pregnancy, or confinement as she called it, and the stupid rituals she believed in. Un-Catholic, un-Christian, uncivilised and heathen!

They fought over it many a night. The Catholic morality of birth control which Doris had happily and conveniently closed her eyes to all these years became an issue. To Jamie, it was terrible to even discuss those intimate things. He was adamant. No sister for wee Andy. And anyway, how in tarnation do we know it will be a girl.

One sunny afternoon, as he leaned on the bridge rail and looked at Cape Richardo before they passed Malacca, he muttered to himself, "Shit! To think that I dread coming back to Doris these days just because the same old ballwash about the baby will come again! We were so happy before she got the bloody thing into her stupid head."

He'd forgotten about the other differences. He'd forgotten that he was transformed into Captain Mckay, lord and master of the S.S.*Irrawady*; God's representative when he read the funeral service, prosecutor and judge when he doled out justice as he went up the gangway. He'd forgotten that he kept returning to his floating kingdom of another world leaving the harsh, dry land where people were drifting away from and forgetting the wonders and the cruelness of nature.

Then the world went to war. Neville Chamberlain's promise of peace was shattered. His prime minister had brought back the treaty to England and was greeted by the cheering crowds. He saw it on the Pathe news in Penang. It thrilled him when he saw another clean British diplomatic victory. Neville Chamberlain had done it!

But it hit him like a typhoon twisting in his guts when the war suddenly crashed down on them. His mother. Frail and waiting. Up there in Scotland. Gawd!

It decided the question. We cannot bring a child into this world erupting into global war.

Doris accepted it.

Nineteen hundred and thirty nine. Maginot and Siegfried Lines. They gathered around "sparks," twiddling the knobs in the radio room for the BBC news. Holding their glasses, beer and scotch. Tense. Just holding their glasses, not taking gulps as they used to when they ribbed each other and told dirty jokes. Jamie scanned the faces of his men. He saw how the strain of the unknown hung on them. They had families out there. Then Dunkirk.

But even as he lived with his officer's tension and concern for the happenings in Europe, when the *Irrawady* dropped its anchor in Penang, he climbed into the Morris, greeting Yon with a grunt (Yon was now the driver, still called syce), winding his feelings down slowly as the car raced to Pulau Tikus. He returned to his home and his Doris and his son, away from the war in Europe. To Pulau Tikus, Penang, west coast of the Malay Peninsular, Asia.

After Dunkirk, the European war receded from his mind and his men's minds to some extent. But a letter from his mother brought him back to the realities of the war. One of his school friends, Cameron McNeice, had been shot down during his very first wartime mission over the North Sea. A bullet had ripped through his lower jaw. He was still alive but they weren't sure if they could patch up his face. Or whether he had the strength to take the long drawn series of operations that had to be done.

Another friend from his schooldays, Harvey MacFadden had shot himself. He had applied to join the army but had been refused. When he got the news of his brother's death in France, just before Dunkirk, he had plunged into a deep depression and shot himself. These two tragedies shook Jamie. Doris could see how badly upset he was when he told her. It was not that he had kept in touch with them after he left Scotland. He only met Cameron once after he had left home. And the last time he saw Harvey was about ten years ago. Doris could not understand why Jamie reacted so badly.

Their life deteriorated to endless little bickerings and periodic major rows. It was almost always about Andy. But it was also Jamie's irritating attempts to correct Doris in her way of speaking, her habits, which he considered crude; like the way she liked to curl her legs up, squatting on the dining chair when she was really enjoying her food; her superstitious fears, and her new style of shrieking when she heard an especially good joke. There were many other little things. "You used to say that was cute when you were chasing me," she often retorted to him. He had no answer to that.

Between their fights, Andy struggled to grow up. He developed into a loner. Jamie saw this and brooded to himself that he, Jamie, was a loner at heart too. There would be many who remembered Jamie as the life and soul of the bar, or the man who could build a strong personal relationship with his crew; but he knew that his thoughts when he was alone in his cabin, on the bridge at nights, or at the rail on the deck looking at the distant land masses and islands they passed, were completely isolated from his friends and his shipmates. That's why I could break with convention and marry Doris, he said to himself. Andy was following him. His brilliance and insatiable passion for mathematics and his dislike for sports or music distanced him from his peers. What worried Jamie the most was that he thought he had detected attitudes in Andy that were very different from the boys he went to school with and the Eurasian sons of his mother's relatives and friends.

Jamie also brooded about the possible war in Asia. He was getting old. He followed the Japanese invasion of China with much concern. He had talked to royal navy men and army officers, at the Raffles, the Union Jack Club and sometimes at the Cricket Club in Singapore. Their confidence worried him. He'd seen that same kind of cocky overconfidence ruin many a skipper.

One day, as his ship steamed into Penang, he saw the Butterworth ferries loaded with new trucks and armoured cars that had just arrived from Britain. All the ferries seemed to be running. The *Bagan*, the *Tanjong*, the *Kulim*, and others whose names he couldn't remember. The trucks they were carrying were all painted a pale desert-sand beige. Would they have time to repaint them? There were hundreds of them being moved to the mainland.

Then it came. The Japanese invasion of Kelantan. The bombing of Singapore. And the attack on Pearl Harbour. It confirmed his fears about British overconfidence.

Contingency plans had been made for the merchant fleet to assist if there was a war. He had said that his Chief Officer, Alfonso Frois, could take over the *Irrawady* any day although he did not have a master's ticket. They had accepted his statement and he was taken off the ship and drafted into the Royal Navy. He left the ship at Penang. He had three days' leave and was to go to Singapore on the *Kedah*, that vibrating twin-screw pride of the Straits Steamship fleet, to get his orders.

The Japs swept down Kelantan faster than anyone had expected. Then the sinking of the *Prince of Wales* and the *Repulse* on the tenth of December. Jamie and Doris had sat together listening to the wireless when they heard the terrible news. Jamie had shouted out in anger. It frightened Doris. She had seen him in his fits of blind anger a few times, but this rage seemed to be different. And she was helpless to defuse or console him. Andy heard the shout. He ran into the drawing room. Doris told him. He stood silently, watching the rage in his father. But there was no fear in him.

The Japanese bombed the airfield at Butterworth. They put the RAF out of action. Jamie heard that crates of Spitfires had arrived and were being unloaded at Sungei Nyor Dockyard because they would have been seen by the Nips if they were unloaded at the Penang wharf. It gave him a shred of hope.

Then one night, Jamie came home after spending the afternoon in Georgetown. Doris saw that he was driving the old Morris Ten in a way he never drove before.

"Pack some things, Doris," he said rapidly as he came up the steps. "We're leaving. We can get seats on the train."

"Only what we can carry," Jamie added. "I'll take Andy's things in my bag. And don't put too much in yours, Doris. We may have to carry our bags a long way."

Ah Far came up the steps from the kitchen weeping. She said that she was going to the hills before the Japanese bombed the whole town flat. She told them to put on as many layers of clothes as they could. That's what her friends had told her about the way people fled from the towns in China.

They got to Church Street Pier. It was pitch dark. A British soldier was directing them. They got out of the car and joined a crush of Europeans in front of the wharf. Jamie saw that it was an unruly queue. His heart sank. The soldier shouted out to him to leave the keys in the car. He knew why. They were going to drive them off the wharf into the sea. "Scorched earth," they called it. Dog in the manger. Being smart after you've lost the bloody fight.

They queued for two hours before they set foot on the crowded ferry. Jamie kept his arms round Doris and Andy so that they would not be separated. When they got on the ferry he pushed and manoeuvred them to a place beside the rail. He didn't tell them that he had worked his way to a spot beneath the lifejacket racks.

About ten minutes after the ferry had left the wharf, Doris saw Jamie frown. She saw the annoyance in him. Before she could find out why, he snapped out gruffly, "Stay here with Andy. Don't move from this place, Doris. I'm going to the bridge. I'll be back as soon as I can."

She clung to his arm, "Why Jamie ... Doan leave us, please."

He saw that there was more than just fear in her eyes. He saw that she wanted him there in the darkness beside her.

"Hell, they don't know where they're going to. It cannot be the regular *serang*."

He was off pushing his way through the crowd, shouting, "I'm a captain, please make way!" He heard a shout. "Mckay!" It was Sandy with his wife and his three girls. He saw that they were wearing their mother's garden party hats. He pressed on.

He was completely surprised to see a "white man" on the bridge. He introduced himself and gave the man at the wheel directions without asking the skipper's permission. He saw in the dark that he too was also a European. A navy uniform.

"Gawd am I glad to see you. You obviously know these waters. I haven't a clue. There are no charts. All I know is that we've got to get to Proi."

"Prai, man!" Jamie corrected him. "And it's that bloody way!" He thrust his finger out, pointing to the north in anger.

"OK, OK … we're taking your instructions, captain."

Jamie softened. He pointed out some landmarks which were barely visible, but he knew the skipper would now be able to set his course.

"How the hell did they put you bloody ignorant lot on the ferry, without any local …"

The skipper cut in. "Listen, captain. You're the bleeding angel of our deliverance. We don't know where the hell we are. All we know is that they picked us out of the sea, and here we are. We're grateful for that. Then they raced us overland and put us here."

"Out of the sea?"

"Aye. Some of us were swimming … we're from the *Repulse*."

"Godstrewth!"

Jamie gave him directions. He got him to repeat them. It was too dark to write. Then he said he had to get back to his wife. The skipper put his hand on Jamie's shoulder and stopped him. He called out to two ratings and told them to push through the crowd and get Jamie to his family then bring them to the bridge.

They got to Prai. Then on to the train. It wasn't as packed as Jamie had dreaded. The bottleneck was obviously at the Penang ferry pier. They flopped down onto the third class seats, dead tired. Doris sat beside wee Andy, opposite Jamie. She smiled weakly at him. He grinned. But he prayed that, when day broke, the Jap planes would not be looking for the railway lines.

The journey to Singapore was a mental hell for them. Sitting in the train at Ipoh and listening to the drone of the Jap planes were the worst moments for Jamie. The heat and the hunger, the filth of the toilets, the Europeans staring at her, dragged Doris to depths of depression and sadness she had never known. Andy was tired. But he had never been on a train before. He forced himself to keep awake, looking out of the window, fascinated with the padifields and rubber estates rushing past.

Pulling into Kuala Lumpur station and seeing the tables of food laid out, the camp beds and the British wives there to greet them, their fellow countrymen on the last train out of Penang, brought a sudden surge of joy and relief to Jamie. It also brought hope in some illogical way.

Finally, Singapore. Jamie telephoned Doris' sister, Nora, who had married Tertullian Hendricks, a surveyor with the PWD.

They moved into their place at Wilkie Road. But it was only moving from frying pan into fire. Jamie reported to the navy office. He packed his bag and kissed Doris goodbye. She was dry-eyed and dazed. Andy hugged him with an equally dazed absence of emotion as he said "ta-ta Dadums."

Jamie was bewildered with the sudden disorientations, the unknown duties ahead of him, the relief of having "Ter" to take Doris and Andy in. He did not see the tearing feelings going through his one and only child. To Andy, his father was deserting him. Leaving him and Ma in this strange four-storied building without a garden, where Uncle Ter and Auntie Nora told them what to do and that swine of a Bernie hounded him throughout every waking hour.

The world started to collapse around Andy. Sirens, wailing like *pontianaks*. Bombs. Later, the whine of shells. The smell in the air raid shelter down the road. Everything was dark. There was nothing to read. He curled up at night on the floor mattress with Ma and sighed with relief because another day had gone. But tomorrow Bernie would be taunting him again.

Then the smoke that covered the whole sky, no water from the taps. The grown-ups' talk. Surrender. The plump Japanese soldier, with a sword hanging from his belt. Ma pleading with the man. Auntie Nora packing a bag. Thrusting it into his hand. Ma crying. Squeezing him till it hurt. Uncle Ter pulling Ma away roughly. The soldier smiling at him with his gold teeth. The truck. The European woman asking him, "Where's your mother?" The crowds. Jostling and pushing. That large woman holding his hand. Her small daughter holding his other hand. The Indian man telling him to go into the other truck. The large woman hugging him, crying. Gripping his bag. The bumpy road.

They took him in as a civilian internee. Doris was somehow not taken in. He was big for his age. They didn't believe the paper he was told to hold on to. They sent him with the men. "Where's your mother?" everyone seemed to be asking. They didn't ask about Dadums.

He remembered years later, how he stood there beside the truck holding his bag. The men were moving away. Then a thin, tall man looked over his shoulder and saw him. He looked at Andy, stopped, turned back, and walked up to him. "Where's your father?" he thought the man said. Andy gripped his bag till his hand was numb. The thin man took it from his hand. He put his hand on Andy's shoulder and pushed him. Andy turned round to look for the truck that had brought him there. It was gone. The thin man's hand was hurting his shoulder. He had taken his bag. The other men had gone ahead and were quite far away now. He looked at the thin man. He suddenly saw that he was European. He had green eyes like Uncle Ash. He yielded to the force on his shoulder. He followed the thin man.

Saul Hawkins. Bloody good-for-nothing, they called him. Been out here for bloody years and not a thing to show for it. Must have pure alcohol in his veins by now. Living with some native lass. Aye, but there's no one who knows the spun-pipe business like he does. The what? Spun pipe business. Don't you know that they make concrete pipes by spinning them. Good God! Do they?

Saul Hawkins,"Umpteen and a half generations from the convicts and still with the manacle marks on me ankles," as he described himself, was Auzzie to the core. He had come out when the company started in 1927, a foreman, to teach the locals the job. And he was still a foreman in 1942, as far as he was concerned, although they called him factory manager.

"A decent bloody wage, good beer and a skinny Chinese sheila" were all he wanted from life. But he didn't say that his life was inextricably tied up with his work. His evenings after dinner were bent over plans and figures or filing down some part of the machine in the kitchen. No company could have had a better man in the factory. But even after fifteen years in Singapore and Malaya, he called his bosses "bloody pommies."

His children in Australia had grown up and married. The Far East assignment was the escape he had dreamt about. He never went back. He sent his nagging woman a small sum each month and lived happily with a clear conscience. Except that he missed his children.

But Saul had a mind as sharp and quick and clear as any of "them four-eyed-pillars-of-goat-shit" who sat in the design offices and the executive management offices peering through their spectacles. He could do all their mathematics. He had sweated it out through night school in his apprentice days. He talked a lot to people. He didn't read much. Sexton Blake and Zane Grey. But he sat with his beer and thought about things. "All kinda things from elephant's foreskins to why me bloody Dad called me Saul, and when the flippin hell the Auzzie worker is going to have his bloody say," as he used to reply in his crude way to the "penny-for-your-thoughts" question.

And when he knew he had to go into the internment camp, the terrible restriction to his freedom, the idleness of prison, the absence of Swee Leng and her wonderful Cantonese cooking, all worried him.

Without his realising it, Andy was the answer to his unvoiced prayer. He devoted his attention to the lad all through the years in the camp. And to his delight, he found that the lad liked mathematics. He taught him all he knew about engineering calculations.

He was a godsend to Andy. Andy hitched himself to Saul Hawkins, listened to everything he said, his orders and the zillions of fascinating things he told him about how one could actually calculate when steel would snap, how water flowed, how the same rules of centrifugal force that kept planets in balance were used to spin concrete and cast iron pipes. But although Saul slowly grew to love the "little fellah," he could not feel any deep emotional response from Andy.

He was hurt the day Andy called him a dirty old man when he discovered Saul's cigarette tin of water. The tin that he used to dip his finger into and wipe his eyes every morning when he got up, a ritual which constituted his entire morning toilet. It was boiled water, Saul pointed out.

It was a strange relationship. The men in the camp talked about Saul's devotion to Andy and held him in high regard because of it. But they whispered that the "selfish young blighter does not appreciate what the crude old son-of-a-gun was doing for him."

Then, suddenly, it ended. They were in Sime Road then. It was too confusing for wee Andy to sort out. What struck him most was the doctor and the soldiers who were dropped by parachute into the camp. The Nip guards were still outside. The barbed wire was still there. But these British soldiers had fallen out of the sky into the camp. And they said Mr. Pender had pulled through because they had given him a shot of some new drug.

One day, the gates were opened and hundreds of Singaporeans poured into the camp. He saw Malays, Indians and Chinese, strange faces to him after the three and a half years, who were now allowed to come into their camp, hugging and kissing the men and the European women. He sat with Saul watching them laughing and talking loudly and handing over food and clothes. Saul and he seemed so isolated from the eruption of tears and laughter all around them.

Then Saul stood up. Andy saw him staring at a thin Chinese woman walking slowly down the path between their timber dormitories. He saw Saul's knees trembling. The woman was looking to her left and right, her face blank. She turned her head towards them and blinked. Then she shouted, "Sol! Sol!" She rushed at him and Saul held her in his arms. He was startled to see Saul crying. Saul, the toughest man in the camp, who never let any bad news get him down. The man was weeping, crushing the skinny woman against his bare, bony chest.

After what seemed ages to Andy, Saul turned to him and said to the woman, "Swee … this is my son. My son of three and a half years."

She did not know what to say. Andy stood up awkwardly. He forced a smile. He saw Saul brushing the tears away from his face with the back of his rough hand. He saw the tears still flowing down Saul's cheeks. It upset him.

"Has he been a father to you, boy?" the woman asked him.

"Yes," he answered.

His monosyllabic answer and his blank face stopped her. She looked at him in silence.

Saul smiled at her, "He's been my concrete pipe machine."

She gave a little laugh, "Your love, Sol …" and she put her arms round him gently and hugged him with her face on his chest, turned towards Andy.

Then Saul kissed her. Full on the mouth. Right in front of him. As though he was not there. As though he was a tree, a rock, a part of the ground, the soil, the dirt.

Something shot through him. Something snapped. He dropped his eyes and stared at a blade of grass. Then he slowly bent his knees and sat down on the ground again.

The next morning, Mr. Davies, the tall man with the yellow-blonde hair, who did the sewing for them because he had a needle, came panting up to him. "Andy, your mother's looking for you! Quick, she's at the guard house. Hurry lad!"

Ma was there. She was almost unrecognisable. Thin and haggard. Like Grandma. Her hair long and dishevelled. Brown and sunburnt. "Ma," he said softly. She rushed at him and hugged him. She kissed him on the mouth, on his cheeks, on his neck. He felt that every man in the camp was looking at him. He was happy to see Ma, but the embarrassment of her kissing overwhelmed him.

"Oh, my Andy. Oh Andy," she kept repeating.

"How are you, Ma?" he asked. The words sounded strange to him.

"My, you've grown so beeg!" she said. Her way of saying it was unfamiliar to him.

"I'm twelve now," he said. He didn't know what else to say.

She cried. She held him tight and cried. He didn't know how to put his arms round her. He wanted to. Like the way Saul hugged the thin woman. He was a man now, he said to himself. But he wasn't sure.

"How's Dad?" he asked.

She released him. She stood back and looked into his eyes. He met her look. He saw his mother was frightened.

"I don't know," she said.

He felt numb. He stood motionless and silent.

"Do you remember after he left the flat the navy fellow rang? He asked where Pa was?"

He remembered. Ma had said that Dad had gone to the navy HQ. The man had said that he had not arrived. She said he was going to see a Captain Tibbets. Oh, the man said. That's not who he should have reported to. I'll check. Some bloody cock-up.

"Well. ... that's the last we have heard of Pa, Andy."

The war ended. To Doris' horror Andy decided to take up the offer of a passage on a troopship to England, to be repatriated to his family, to Scotland, to his grandparents. She cried. She pleaded with him. Uncle Ter shouted at him for being so ungrateful to his parents. He didn't know what Uncle Ter meant. There was no news about his father. Saul had gone, he didn't know where to. He had given him an address, but Andy had lost it in the confusion of leaving the camp. Mr. Pender was on the ship. He was a familiar face in the camp until he got the "runs." But he was a face Andy had known for three and a half years. Mr. Flannagan was there too.

~ *Chapter Thirty-five* ~

File SIN/OPS/JAM/62

One morning, Hadi came up to her desk with an armful of files.

"*Selamat siang*!" he greeted her smiling. They exchanged pleasantries. Then he selected a file from the bunch he was carrying and handed it to her.

"I have an interesting file here for you. It is a job you can do for us."

She looked at the title, SIN/OPS/JAM/62, and opened it at once in front of him.

The first lines came as a surprise:

"James Andrew Mckay; born in Penang in 1933

Father: Scotsman, Master Mariner, A.J. Mckay"

He let her read the first two lines, then he spoke, "We have found a man who has the brains and the commitment to play a leading role in the field for us. A Singaporean. He is charged with fire to stop the formation of Malaysia."

"A communist?" she interrupted.

"Yes. But he will work with us. It doesn't matter what his present gods are, we want him as a field man; a fighter."

Hadi paused to let his words sink in.

"This is a file on him. Top secret. I want you to study it. We have made plans for you to get alongside him. Win his confidence. His friendship. Try your very best. Put in everything you've got."

"Why me?" she asked.

"Aaah, because it fits so neatly. He's a Singaporean, a Eurasian."

"A Eurasian?"

"Yes. Who could do a better job of winning his friendship than you? You've got to woo him, win him."

Hadi smiled. He continued along the same line, repeating the message, "It's important. We must make him one of us. We know you can do it. Woo him. Win him."

"Huh!" Bertha mumbled, surprised at the turn of job direction. After a moment, she added sarcastically, "Seduce him, you mean ... with my body too?"

Hadi sat up as though a knife had been thrust into him. His face darkened. Bertha saw his expression change from surprise to anger in the next instant. She saw him boiling inside struggling with himself. She knew he was waiting to calm down before he spoke. She regretted her words.

"I'm sorry ..." she started but Hadi cut in, in a low voice thick with feeling.

"If he touches a hair on your head, Hartono will kill him!"

His eyes were bloodshot with emotion. He saw her startled reaction. He got to his feet and snapped, "I'll come back in the afternoon."

Bertha put her head into her hands with her elbows on the desk and closed her eyes. Hartono, Hartono, Hartono. What are they doing to me? Oh God, I must learn to keep my mouth shut. I'm getting overconfident.

But why was Hadi so upset. Had he meant to say "I will kill him?"

She went to the toilet and sat there for a long time to restore her calm. A thousand other thoughts kept thrusting themselves into her head. What the hell is this job coming to? What can I do now to get out of this trap? I've lost my freedom. What the hell am I getting so worked up about the merger issue? It's not my business. Oh Hartono, can't I work beside you? Where are you, Hartono? There are many others who can carry the torch. Why must I be pigeon-holed by my birthmarks like this? Who is this bloody Eurasian anyway?

She went back to her desk, unlocked her drawer and took out

the file. Going through it may shut out the thoughts raging around inside her. She opened the file and started reading.

"James Andrew Mckay; born in Penang in 1933
Father; Scotsman. Master Mariner. A.J. Mckay
Disappeared during the war.
Mother; Doris Josephine Laker-Smith, nee Coehlo, Eurasian, born in Penang. Married George Humphrey Laker-Smith in 1952, after Captain Mckay's death was legally accepted.

Laker-Smith was with Wearne Brothers in Singapore. The Laker-Smiths returned to the U.K. with their baby daughter in 1956.

History; Spent his childhood in Penang up to the war. Was interned alone. Went to Scotland after the war. Lived with his grandmother for four years until she died. Then with his small legacy lived with a friend's family in Glasgow. The father of the family was a shop steward.

Obtained a B.Sc with first class honours from the University of Manchester in 1954. Chairman of MU Socialist Club, 1952–1954. Returned to Singapore 1954. Joined the Education Service, 1955.

Classification; A4/1/1/8

Report by T397

I noticed subject speaking with much conviction and emotion, but not very articulate at two successive meetings of the Socialist Club and at the next meeting introduced myself as an Indonesian who had studied abroad and suggested we have a drink together.

Drank with subject, who has a capability to drink much liquor, for several hours, and talked of politics in the region. Established that subject is deeply anti-British, had read a great deal about the overthrow of colonialism in many parts of the world, that subject has much potential and recommend that he be recruited.

Bertha looked at the photograph. At first glance he looked European even in the black and white picture. But as she scrutinised his face, she saw his Asian nose. A hard mouth, she thought. And intense eyes. She went back to the written reports.

Report by G301

A very, very interesting chap. Not the typical Eurasian. Not an intellectual in the sense of one seeking knowledge and personal conviction of theories for satisfying his own needs. Strange in many ways, but one must consider his background, his past, to really understand the fellow.

Perhaps your files have all this in them, but at the risk of providing redundant information, I shall put down my impressions. To understand all this you should note that I met him socially, and not at some high-brow or over-heated political meeting. From your data I got onto Peter, whose surname I won't mention for security's sake, and he engineered my invitation to a social "do" at the house of a teacher bloke who knew Andy. Quite a pleasant fellow, Ben Machado.

There was a lot to drink, as there always is at these Eurasian gatherings, and I started talking to and observing Andy. My impressions were developed from that long night. Not only listening to him and observing his reactions to the thoughts of others, but also talking to him, alone, for about an hour in the Machado's dining room. (You see, the main body of the party was in the verandah.)

I reckon his psyche was cast in his earliest days from his strong father who was not always there at home. His father's influence came in sort of waves, off and on, when the old man was in port. And, reading between the lines, I think there was conflict between the old man and his spouse in waves too. (I refer to him as the old man to emphasise the age difference between the captain and his spouse.)

Some events hit the bloke hard in his youth. His being alone in the concentration camp. An old Australian codger looked after him while he was in the internment camp. Andy told me laughingly that the old fellow was always bitching about the Australian worker not getting his due. The other thing that hit him was how different his mother and his aunt and uncle appeared to him when he came out of the camp. (You will note, of course, that he spent about three formative years of his life in the camp with the kwei loh *colonialists.)*

I reckon he decided to be a Scotsman after the war. Perhaps he did start becoming one in the village he lived in with his old (very old, I should say) grandmother. But when he went to Glasgow, he saw the worst effects of the industrial revolution. He tells me he hates Glasgow. He hates the city, the people, the way they talk, the overcrowding, the ghastly slums which the British, with all their wealth, are doing nothing about.

The hardest blow he faced was returning home. He found that he was not a Scotsman. He tried to get expatriate terms but they wouldn't consider it. Actually, I said to him at that point, that he was crazy to even ask, knowing his mother was not a European. I think that upset him. I don't know why. We were getting along fine up till then. But all said and done, I reckon he got himself screwed up inside and anti-colonialism is now his religion.

In conclusion, I must say that he certainly has the deep-seated drive against the colonial-capitalistic order. It is a force we can use. I have seen it strong in him.

I recommend he be recruited.

There was a hand written note under this: "Who the hell is G301?"

Report by D22

JAM is a man with exceptional brains and intense drive. He put these two qualities into his academic work and proved that they can work together in him. He is a man who needs a goal. Now that he has been disillusioned as a teacher, because he pitched his goals too high, I believe he is in desperate need for a goal, a cause. I think he may have found it. I am not sure.

He has been dabbling with communism as an interesting set of ideas, a pattern that brings new thoughts to the problems of capitalism, that fits within itself. Like a new mathematical series. But theories are not enough to fire him. He got his first at Manchester not only because he was engrossed in the beauty of mathematics, but because he wanted to get a first. He is a man who needs a practical goal. Igniting students in school to burn with a passion for maths was to him better than developing new relationships between mathematical functions at the university.

This is an important aspect of the man.

On the other hand, he is a narrow person. He would select a particular objective, a practical one, and concentrate on it without looking again at the broader environment changing around him.

He has this drive but he lacks loyalty in person–to–person relationships. He cannot hold a girlfriend for long.

We can use him. He is a rare find. He will be an excellent operator. But the direction must be clear and practical. He can plan, but he cannot inspire men. If we understand these limitations, he can be a valuable man to us.

Recommended that we recruit him; but for special, particular tasks.

Report by J887

I friended subject using info H gave me. It was not easy. He took me out to deener and I worked on him. Unfortunately he was more interesting in telling me what bastards the PAP and the British, Tengku and Tan Siew Sin of Malaya were while drinking heavy. But subject was always in full controls of hisself.

I was wearing a low-cutted red blouse and a tight skirt with golden earrings, but subject, I tink, did not notice. After dinner I tried the usual and even a bit more so, but no good.

Subject is not interesting in girls. I don tink he's the "pondan" type either.

She thought about the file as she had a *bakmi* lunch alone at a street stall. Somehow, she felt sorry for him. He had had a rough time and had not been able to rise above the events that dragged his spirit down. Now he had found a direction. But what a direction, she said to herself. In spite of that she felt sorry for the man.

She wondered how much his parents had contributed to his present state. Or was it just the environment he grew up in?

Hadi came to her desk after lunch. His face was serious. He opened up with, "I hope you understand now, Bertha."

"Yes, Hadi. I'm very, very sorry I opened my mouth without thinking. I really didn't mean it. I'm sorry. I'm sorry I upset you so much, Hadi. I'm sorry."

He accepted her apology without a word. He got on to the subject he had hinted at.

"We are going to give you a break from this desk job. It is connected with the need to get close to that man. We have code-named him *kerbau*."

She supressed a smile. It was an apt codename she thought; the buffalo.

"We are going to put you into a group who are being trained for guerilla warfare. It is mostly physical. Shooting, some unarmed combat, explosives and a little bit of tactics. Very little. Let me finish." He saw he open her mouth to say something.

"I know you are thinking about the roughnecks we have been training in Sumatra. But this training is for picked people. It will be done here in Jakarta. There're only about twenty in the team. Three, including you, are women. There will be no difference between the women and the men in the course. I'm sure you can take it. You are fit and strong. And in the long run it will benefit you a great deal. You will see how terrorists operate. I know what you are thinking. You don't want to be a terrorist. But one day you may be involved in suppressing terrorism … perhaps."

Bertha was silent. It would be a relief in a way to get out of the stuffy office. She was sure it would be most interesting to her. But where it led to worried her.

"Take the problems one at a time, Bertha." She noticed that he had slipped back into Bertha. "I learnt that from Hartono. By the way he knows exactly what is going on. He has seen every report you have put up."

"Is he still in Singapore?" she asked.

"He's moving between Singapore and Malaya," Hadi replied. Then he added as an afterthought, "But not in Kalimantan."

Bertha read it as an important appendage, but she didn't know why.

"I wish I could see him," she said.

Hadi looked into her eyes. His expression was serious. He kept silent.

Then he took an envelope out of his pocket and handed it to her. "One detail we had left dangling. That Glock you still have. Here's a permit for it in the name of Mary Devries. Hold on to it as a personal item. Don't tell anyone in the unit about it."

"I suppose *kerbau* will be one of the men in the course."

"Yah. You take it from there," he replied.

A military jeep picked her up from Mononutu's place the next Monday morning. The young driver saluted her. She smiled at him in return, and commented that it looked like it was going to rain. Her talking to him in Indonesian seemed to surprise him. They talked a little. He was from Semarang, he said. But she saw that he was not comfortable chatting while driving. Or he thought that she was way above his level in the order of things.

The rest of the course participants were in the room when she arrived. She saw him at once. Conspicuous with his fair skin. She saw that he was much better looking than the photograph. The two girls studied her closely when she walked in. They were both Chinese and very young, she thought. They were short and stocky. There were two or three Chinese men. The others were Malay. She noticed that there were only a few well-built men. She would be one of the tallest in the group. A captain, as she read from his shoulder pips, greeted her. He introduced himself as Slamet Yamin. He got down to his task as soon as she arrived. They moved to a room with chairs arranged like a classroom with a blackboard.

He spoke in English with some Bahasa Indonesia words thrown in here and there. They were to be known as team A. That was for the course. It didn't mean that they would be operating together later. Their rank was "recruit." He was the course *direktor*. The *nonya-nonya* would be treated the same as the men, except that they had separate sleeping rooms and washrooms.

Then the pep-stuff. Bertha saw that Slamet Yamin was experienced in that sort of briefing. They were asked to introduce themselves after he spoke. She noticed that he said his name and "Singapore" softly with an accent more English than Singaporean and a touch of the Scottish "r," like one of Mr. Vandyke's visitors. She resisted the temptation of looking at him when she gave her name, saying that she was from Singapore and Padang, as Hadi had told her to say.

Then there were medicals. Even her teeth. She was surprised. But it was a nice new experience for her to sit in a dentist's chair without any anticipation of pain. Uniform issues. Boots, belts, a knife in a leather sheath, sweaters (for cold nights in the jungle, she knew) and a knapsack.

At ten o'clock they were asked to change into shorts and tee-shirts and put through fitness tests and other physical tests. The Malay boys (she thought of them as boys now that she had seen them at close quarters) cheered when she did her hundred metre run. She joked with them in Malay, taking care to show an Indonesian accent and choice of words. But by lunchtime she had not said a word to him. She saw him looking at her. That woman's report is wrong, she said to herself. He's no exception to the bloody rule.

A concession was made to the Chinese at lunch. They were asked if they wanted Chinese food during the course. But, sorry, there would be no pork. The cook's Muslim and, if we make the cook unhappy by asking him to cook pork, you'll never get tasty food, the sergeant said laughing.

She ate with her hands like the Malay boys. He was behind her during lunch. She was dying to see how he ate. Or if he had chosen Chinese food.

At lunch, she made friends with Yasin and Mafus. Both Malayan. Yasin had a ready quip for almost anything.

He came up to her after dinner. While they had a "smoker" break before the last lecture of the evening.

"Hello, you're from Singapore? I'm Andy." A wide smile.

"I'm Mary. I was from Singapore. My people are in Padang now."

"Eurasian, aren't you?" he asked.

"Sort of ..."

"Well, all Eurasians are sort of's or all sorts of ... liquorice of sorts eh?" he said trying a joke.

She grinned. "Your first time in Indonesia?"

"Aye." The word surprised her.

"Hey, how come you use that word?"

"I went to school in Scotland."

"Good heavens, did you?"

"My father was a Scotsman."

"Yah. I see it now. That's where you got those big bones from."

"My mother was a Coehlo. From Penang."

He is a Eurasian, she thought. Going through the introductory rituals. She decided to play to the rules.

"Then aren't you related to Mrs. Nora Hendricks?"

"Yes. She's my aunt. Why, do you know her?"

Bertha was just about to say that Nora Hendricks was one of the GSC coaches when she stopped herself.

"No. Just knew that she was once a Coehlo. You know how it is when the old folks start talking about who married who."

"Aye. That they do."

"Surprised to see a person like you here," he said.

"I'm here because I'll do everything I can to prevent Malaysia being formed," she replied.

"Hey ... that's what I like to hear. Must talk to you later. They're calling us."

She watched him closely for the next few days, whenever she could without his knowing it. She thought she saw something that had been reported incorrectly. When they broke up into teams for their first hand gun practice, she saw that by the end of the two hours he had taken over as leader of the group of five. Her observation was confirmed when they did a competitive cross-country run. He was urging the short Chinese girl on. She was the slowest. He was pushing his team. He had taken over again.

He was not articulate in class, except when they had a lesson in tactics. He spoke out then. He made points that the instructor did not anticipate. Not against what the instructor had said, but reinforcing his statements. She saw that Chalid, the instructor, was pleased. She knew it would go down in Chalid's report on him.

He made a beeline for her table one day at lunch. She saw then that he did not know how to eat with his hand. He was trying, poor fellow, to be one of them although he obviously had had little experience eating with Malays. She didn't like the way he concentrated his talk and attention towards her during lunch so she kept bringing Mafus into the conversation. He forgets the surroundings when he's after something, she said to herself.

She was in the top three for hand gun target shooting. But only seventh with the Sten guns. The Chinese girls gasped and came up to her to praise her. It was difficult talking to them. Their English was very bad. She wondered how much of the training they were absorbing. But it didn't matter. They seemed to be charged with the zeal of religious fanatics.

After the first week, a note was slipped to her during a lecture. Phone call. Urgent, the office.

It was Hadi. He wanted a report. She was at one of the telephones in the open office. She saw that all the clerks were looking at her and trying to listen to what she was saying in English.

"I can't talk here," she said.

"Just the key points. Be vague. I'll understand."

"Good. I can do what you want me to but honestly, I think there should be another front."

"Hah, I understand. Not getting to him?"

"I am, but ... can't you get one of the same people to work on it at the same time?"

"I don't understand."

"One of the same type."

"You don't mean Singaporean, do you ... Ah! I see, a PKI type."

"Yes, yes. That's it. Like one of the family."

"Ah! I see. Common water is thicker than blood, eh?"

"Yah, that's it."

"OK, I'll see to that. But you continue."

"Sure. I will. I'm doing my best, but there are barriers."

"Barriers?"

"Yah. Think about the differences, Hadi."

"Differences? But you're the same people."

"But, Hadi, there's always fifty percent of one and fifty percent of the other ..."

"Ah! male and female. You mean he's some sort of odd asexual person?"

"No, no, try again."

"Ah! The Asian attitude. You're a woman, not serious, not important. Or is he shy of women? Ber ..."

"Yes. It's more like what you said."

"Asian ...?"

"Yah."

A clerk at a desk near the telephone was listening with a frown on his face. Hadi had got the message anyway.

"I understand. Second front eh? We'll fix it. But you keep at it."

"Sure. Never say die."

~ Chapter Thirty-six ~

Eruptions

Gunung Agung, Bali peak, the king mountain, erupted in early sixty-three. It hurled rocks and fire into the sky, and molten lava poured down the mountain slopes dividing into two streams, killing thousands of people, demolishing houses, burning and scarring the land. It was a major disaster. The Red Cross rushed to the aid of the victims but their resources were severely strained. The papers were filled with stories and photographs of death and damage for days.

Gunung Agung had not erupted for centuries. Gunung Batur on Bali had blown up several times in the last century but Gunung Agung, the greatest of the Bali volcanos, had been dormant as far as any living person could remember. In February 1963, there were rumblings deep down inside the mountain but they said that the Gods were only whispering to each other. Then in March, Gunung Agung exploded with three eruptions darkening the sky as far as Surabaya three hundred and fifty kilometres to the west and the people could not see to work at noon. The subsequent earthquakes continued for three months.

Apart from the physical damage, the horror was that Gunung Agung had erupted because the gods were angry. They discussed it at length in the office and by the street stalls. A ceremony to honour the gods of Gunung Agung had in fact just been completed. It was a ceremony of major importance, the Karya Agung Eka Dasa Rudra, the great rite of the eleven directions of the eight major points of the compass and up, down and centre.

Bertha was not sure of the real facts. Whether the ceremony was performed every ten years and whether these were calendar years or years reckoned by the Balinese year of one hundred and eighty days. But the harsh fact was that their supreme deity, the home of Siwa, the navel of the world, the Northpoint of their island had erupted in anger.

A few days later, Mononutu returned from where he had been to on some mission or other. He talked to her about the Gunung Agung disaster for hours while sipping Chinese tea. The volcanic eruption had shaken him. He gave her the figures he had accepted although she had read the papers and knew that no one really had the exact numbers. Two thousand killed. Seventy-five thousand displaced and homeless. A quarter million people with their land temporarily sterilised by volcanic ash.

Mononutu sighed, lit another *kretek* and said softly, "The sad fact is that in spite of all the efforts of the Balinese Hindus, mankind has not yet succeeded in restoring the balance of nature in purification and renewal which brings harmony and happiness to the world."

His face was pained and serious. Bertha kept silent. This was her friend and landlord who she thought was a man with a clear and logical mind. This was the Indonesia Pak Darso had spoken about.

He went on and on. She remembered his telling her that the relief work was organised by a woman. "Yes, Miss Mary Devries, here in Indonesia we do not have the prejudices of the world against the other sex." (She noted the "other" adjective.) He told her the story of Miss Paramita Abdoerachman who had done so much for the republic in her younger days as a social worker, as a medical assistant, living in the mines recording evidence of Japanese atrocities, collecting information of mass executions, organising medical supplies for the revolutionary army and eventually rising to Secretary-General of the Red Cross. President Sukarno had called her in to organise the Gunung Agung relief. An extraordinary woman who sacrificed her dreams of being a sculptor and a pianist for her country.

It was a simple story about an outstanding person, but somehow it struck deep inside her.

Benny and Joe Kusuma sat around a restaurant one evening with her, soon after the disaster, talking about Bali. Benny had his theory that when the Buddhists and Hindus came to Indonesia, only central Java and Bali were civilised enough to absorb their teachings. Later, most of the rest of Indonesia was ready to be converted to Islam when it arrived. But there were pockets that the Islamic wave did not get to because they were not ready, not advanced enough, to accept the new philosophies. The Baduis, the Bataks, and others. The Christians then came and converted people like the Bataks who were by then able to take on Christianity. But there were still people who were living with their primitive religions in the remote parts of Indonesia, he said.

"Like the Javanese?" Bertha chipped in. They laughed. They knew what she meant.

"Like the Japanese," Joseph Kusuma added.

Joseph Kusuma told Benny that he was wrong. As early as about 200 A.D., he said, Hindu culture had swept all over Java and Sumatra. Their writing and their mythology were still alive in some way in Indonesia. By the sixth century A.D., Buddhist influence was all over Java and Sumatra. It was far more complex than that, he said to Benny.

The talk went back to Bali. Joseph Kusuma told her of the strange battle that had occured when the Dutch massacred a Raja and his warriors, proceeding to battle with all his retinue in pomp and refinery.

"In the early days of Batavia, the Balinese population was a large part of the city. That's why there are many Balinese words in Bahasa Betawi," Benny said.

They told her of the arts of Bali; the paintings, the carvings, the temples, the dances. "And don't forget to tell her about the fighting cocks," Benny added. As usual he was quite content to listen to Joseph Kusuma talk, sitting with his coffee, smiling.

"They're crazy about cock fighting," he said. He told her how the cock fights were carried out, how the men fussed over their prize birds and treated them even better than they treated their wives.

"You can see them sitting under the shade of a tree in the afternoons dreaming of the next fight, holding and stroking their cocks," he said.

Bertha burst out laughing. Benny roared out with her. He thumped the seat of the chair next to him several times enjoying her reaction immensely.

It was not only Bali that erupted in 1963. There were major upheavals in Singapore, Malaya and the island of Borneo.

The first was at the end of 1962, on December the eighth, the uprising in the tiny Sultanate of Brunei. The British reacted quickly and troops were flown into Brunei from Singapore by the evening of December eighth. The rebellion was squashed in a few days.

But the British also reacted by arresting many Chinese in the neighbouring state of Sarawak who were believed to be members of a clandestine communist organisation. It caused about a thousand five hundred young Chinese to flee across the border to Indonesian Kalimantan.

Then in February 1963, the Singapore government made an island wide sweep and arrested a hundred and thirteen pro-communists; members of the opposition party, the Barisan Socialis, trade union leaders and undergraduates.

"Huh!" Hadi said. "They say 'detained.' They call it *Operasi Cold Store*, implying that they'll let them go again. Huh!"

Bertha was delighted with the swoop. Now the PAP can get down to it. And now they have television to help them. But the Indonesian reaction to the swoop worried her.

The eruptions of 1963 came rapidly one after another. On the twelfth of April, Indonesian troops crossed the border of Sarawak and seized the police station at Tebedu, close to the capital, Kuching. The undeclared war, Confrontasi had started.

It was to become a strange undeclared war. Indonesian troops infiltrated the jungles of Sarawak and fought a guerilla war with the British and local armies.

But it wasn't Sarawak that interested her. It was Singapore. Her country. The next targets surely would be Singapore and Malaya. She knew there were about two thousand Chinese from Sabah and Sarawak, 300 from Singapore and about 200 from Malaya being trained in Indonesia for subversive activities. So many new elements were being thrown into the pot as it began to boil.

She read with much pleasure that the first frictions of Malaysia were beginning to show before Malaysia was born. The dream that Lee Kuan Yew had nurtured for years wasn't going to be all wine and roses. Tan Siew Sin, leader of the Malayan Chinese took a swipe at him in July, saying that he was making himself out to be the only man who could champion the cause of the Chinese in Malaya. Oh, she sighed to herself, if only the man would see that the old commonality of Malaya and Singapore has gone. Maybe it's the frightening thought of Singapore standing alone that he cannot subconsciously face.

The United Nations had insisted that a referendum be held in the two States in Borneo island, Sabah and Sarawak, to ensure that the people there wanted to be merged into Malaysia. It had thrown a rock into the Malaysia planners' path.

Then Lee Kuan Yew's impatience. Declaring the independence of Singapore from the British, a new free state, a part of Malaysia on the thirty-first of August before the United Nations report confirming Sarawak and Sabah's agreement was officially out. Or was it a subtle master-stroke; like Napoleon grabbing the crown from the bishop, or archbishop, whoever he was, to place it on his head himself? Or like the Indonesian declaration of independence while the Japanese were still in control of the country after they had surrendered but before the Dutch returned?

The fact was that he had caused much irritation by his premature announcement. It was significant, she thought. Another omen.

The sixteenth of September, 1963. Malaysia day. Lee Kuan Yew's birthday. The demonstrations in Jakarta outside the British and Malayan embassy, protesting against the new state of Malaysia. The counter protests in Kuala Lumpur where a crowd of over a thousand stoned the Indonesian embassy and burned a picture of

Sukarno outside the embassy gates. To her surprise, Devan Nair, one of the key figures in Singapore politics, stirred up racial emotions by describing the maltreatment of the Chinese in Indonesia. The eruptions continued.

The twenty-first of September general election in Singapore coincided with the problems Singapore and Malaya were having with the establishment of Malaysia. Lee Kuan Yew's PAP won the election. Thirty-seven out of the fifty-one seats. Forty-seven percent of the votes. They had beaten UMNO. She was elated with the results. The Malays had voted for the PAP, a Chinese dominated party. They had voted across racial barriers.

This was the Singapore she believed in. Christ! Can't they see the scene had changed?

But on the other side of the coin, the pro-communist Lee Siew Choh had lost to the little PAP giant, Toh Chin Chye, by only eighty-nine votes. The pro-red support was still there. It was a worrying thought, with 45,000 looking for jobs each year and Aidit with his communist PKI so strong here in Indonesia.

Upheavals, eruptions and the mountain throwing out red-hot molten lava in Bali. Disruptions going on everywhere around her. Then the bombshell came, direct at her, from across Muljadi's desk.

He had asked to see her. The boss of the unit. She had met Muljadi at meetings but had never talked to him one to one. She really wasn't senior enough for him to talk to her. She knew he spoke to Hadi, Benny and Major Abdulgani. He was on top because he was an able man. Not like some of the bosses of other departments who had wormed their way to the top by flattery and never saying no. Sycophants and bullies. She respected his opinions. She had seen him toss out a thought now and then right off the track they were arguing on, but relevant and parallel to it. And, unlike the other Indonesians, he was blunt and direct. But perhaps that was only to his underlings.

"I asked to see you because we're going to send you on a very important attack mission. You have been trained. The reports on your performance at the training school are excellent. You are the person we need for this mission."

She sat waiting. He paused and looked deep into her eyes.

"We are going to bomb the British top-dog's house in Singapore. We are not sending any of those riff-raff volunteers on this mission. We have selected three of our best people for this. Hartono, you and Andy Mckay. Every detail has been planned. You leave for Singapore tomorrow. It's a bit early, but a car will pick you up at five-thirty from Mononutu's place tomorrow morning."

He paused again. Bertha'd head was swimming. She kept silent.

His lips curled in a little smile, "I see you take the news with an exterior calm. That's good, Miss Mary Devries. In this envelope are the details. You will read them tonight and digest them fully. You haven't got a date tonight, have you?"

"No, *bapak*."

"We know Rudi Schindkunz is busy tonight ... But as I was saying, the details are here. There is also another envelope inside this. You will seal these notes in it and hand it to the driver when he picks you up in the morning. This is absolutely top-secret. I don't have to tell you that no one else must know. The unit will be told that you were sent to Palembang to interview a man from Singapore for a few days."

He stopped talking and looked at her. She felt she should say something.

"I understand."

"You will take orders from Hartono when you get to Singapore. Needless to say, you cannot contact anyone when you are in Singapore. The temptation to speak to your parents will no doubt be strong. But I know we can trust you. Hartono has the highest opinion of you, Miss Mary Devries. And Hartono is one of our best."

"I have the highest respect for Hartono, *bapak*."

"Good. That's all."

He reached for his pipe. She stood up. He smiled at her. A genuine broad smile. He was pleased with himself and with her.

But Bertha was excited and taut inside. She smiled and spoke, "It's only on the outside, *bapak*."

He grinned. "If this assignment didn't excite you, didn't provoke a storm of feelings and thoughts, you would be a cold fish, an unfeeling cold fish. And you would be of no use to us. The adrenalin must flow."

His words stuck in her. She dipped her head in a symbolic bow and left. Her eyes were shining. Her pulse was racing.

~ *Chapter Thirty-seven* ~

Confrontasi

A private car picked her up. The young driver asked for the envelope and handed her another in return. She opened it in the car. It contained a Malayan identity card with the name of Mary Devries. He took her out, down the road through Cengkareng. She remembered hearing of a military runway at Halim. She didn't talk to the driver.

In the pale dawn light, she was taken immediately to a six-seater aeroplane. It was full. Two middle-aged men in uniform. Three civilians, one dressed in a full suit. And her. No one seemed to want to talk. It was odd. Perhaps everyone of us is on some terribly secret mission, she said to herself. Anyway, she was in no mood for idle conversation.

About an hour later, the plane landed. It was a small deserted runway. As it taxied to the timber shed which was obviously the terminal building, she saw coconut trees by the side of the runway. It had been too cloudy for her to see anything as they descended.

A sergeant was waiting for her. "Miss Mary Devries?"

"Yah."

"Good!" One syllable.

He led her to a car and they drove off. The car stopped in front of a house by the sea. She saw a jetty in the background. A round smiling man met her, "Ahh, so pleased to meet you," in perfect English. "Breakfast time, my dear."

She grinned. It was such a warm welcome after all those silent drivers and passengers. "Goody-good!" she said. "I'm hungry."

"Just call me Harry," he said. "It's not my real name of course, but one needs a name to be human, doesn't one? I meet so many code names or numbers, like A4/907, or "*tikus*" which are so unhuman. So, my dear, make up a nice name and we'll use it for the hour or two we'll be together."

Bertha laughed. "What a lovely idea. I can finally be what I want to be! I know what! Lamour!"

He chuckled. "Very good, very romantic and politically so apt!"

"Politically?"

"Yah, *Terang Bulan* ..." he started to hum the first bars of the Malaysian national anthem, which was the same tune as a song sung in an old Hollywood film starring Bob Hope and Dorothy Lamour, in one of the "Road to ..." series. It was a tune that had been on the air recently, reminding the Malaysians of the old love song. It was one of the "*Ganjang Malaysia*," crush Malaysia, stream of attacks on Radio Indonesia.

Bertha burst out laughing. "Oh, Harry."

"But you must not be too familiar with me, you know."

"I won't, Mr. Harry ... Oh! I see Harry!"

She laughed again. It had suddenly registered that it was Harry Lee Kuan Yew whose name he had taken.

"Come, there is the best *nasi lemak* and the best *otak-otak* in the whole of Indonesia Jaya served in this house."

She saw that his house was spotlessly clean. The furniture was pre-war but it had been maintained well and everything seemed to be in its proper place. She complimented him on the house.

"My house and garden is one joy. The other is meeting people on their way in and on their way out. They are always so tense. So I enjoy myself fooling around with them. But, you know, some cannot relax and laugh as you do, Miss Lamour," he said chuckling.

She thought that the *nasi lemak* was superb. The fish and the *sambal* were truly delicious.

"Home made?" she asked.

"But of course. And caught by my man."

"*Tersangat sedap, tuan.*"

"Thank you. And I must say, I haven't entertained anyone as

beautiful as you for a long time."

"*Terima kaseh, tuan.*"

"Hey, please … I'm Harry."

She laughed again. "How wondeful to meet you here … wherever we are."

"We are nowhere. It is a lovely restful place. Not like Jakarta or Singapore. Now, let me tell you. There is no hurry. After you have eaten, and, my dear, you should eat well in Harry's house, a motor-boat will pick you up. It will take you to a larger fishing boat, which will be smelling to high heaven of fish. They will be a Chinese crew. They will take you into Singapura. After that, I don't know."

He made an exaggerated act of washing his hands.

She was sucking the spine-bone of the fried fish. She smacked her lips and smiled with her eyes. When she had finished with it she asked him, "How long have you been here in paradise, *Tuan* Harry?"

"Forever!" he replied at once.

"Cannot be, lah! Your English is so good."

"Because I lived in England for a few years."

"In England!" she repeated his words with surprise in her voice.

"Yah. And in America."

"In America!"

"Yah. I was with the foreign service, Miss Lamour."

She turned to him smiling with a handful of rice, ready to bring to her mouth. She was enjoying the *nasi lemak*. "Please, Harry, call me Dorothy."

He laughed loudly.

"Yes, I was in the FOREIGN SERVICE." He said it with capitals.

"And you left it?"

"Hey! You ask a lot of questions, ah?"

"I'm just amazed at how good your English is, Harry."

"Yes, I was going up the ladder, then I made a mistake."

"You?"

"No need to flatter me lah, Miss Dorothy. I am human, we all are … It is important that we never forget that."

She looked at him. This was another side of "Harry."

"I once dreamt that I would follow in the footsteps of Adam Malik. Hero, lah!"

She thought she should not press him further. Just a little bit more, then that will be enough … God, it's good! Absolutely delicious!

"Yes I made a mistake. If I didn't have friends in high places I would be riding *betchak* in Jakarta today. But I had friends. So they gave me a small job here. It is the most wonderful thing that could have happened to me. I don't want to be Adam Malik anymore."

"Happiness, *bapak*, that's what counts."

"Don't you *bapak* me! I'm young enough to be your husband, Dorothy!"

"Please take it as a sign of respect. Not of relative age, Harry." She stressed the "Harry," smiling.

"It's such a pleasure to be able to talk English to someone again."

"Harry," the man feeding her in transit, in the "nowhere" island was what she needed after her night of tossing in bed and the silence of her fellow-travellers in the plane. When she had finished eating he walked her round his garden. It reminded her of Fatimah in Batu Pahat. Only Ethel wasn't there getting bored with it all. It also reminded her of Pa who walked the relatives who were interested in plants round the garden at their Sepoy Lines home. Then they walked down to the beach.

It was beautiful. The sun was still low in the sky and the sweltering equatorial heat had not come down to them. Harry told her of the storms that whipped up the waves and sent them crashing to the verandah steps of his house in the wet season. The winds that tore the coconut palms off the trees and sent them flying across the beach to dash against some house or some fruit tree in the compounds of the houses along the beach.

And he told her of the sunsets. Harry was exercising, airing his English. He waxed poetical, overdoing it for humorous effect. He saw her enjoyment of his company and went on to quote *pantuns* and scraps of his fading memory of hackneyed English and American poems.

"You must be a Sumatra man, Harry?" she suddenly asked.

"Yes. I know the Malay of your accent."

"And the *pantuns* of Malaya."

"Yah. I was always interested in language."

"You speak Dutch?"

"Jangan lah! I'm not that old, lah!"

They smiled at each other. Then with a serious face he said, "Maybe it's because I never learnt Dutch that I can appreciate English?"

She let it ride. It was not her beat.

The sky was still clear. The boiling clouds of the afternoon had not yet built up over the sea. It was that time between the calm of dawn and the fierceness of the afternoon, Bertha thought to herself, remembering Batu Pahat and the many days she had walked the beach, lazily, without a hurried purpose. She would never forget those days.

"In the evenings it is so nice here. On that island over there is a *lang-laut*. Sometimes he comes over in the evening and looks at us. And we look at him. Do you know the *lang-laut*?"

"Yah. I do."

She did not add, "and it has special memories for me." The thought of Hartono, skinny, half-starved on the beach at Betting Kusa watching the *lang-laut* rushed at her. Hartono, who had grown out of the pit he was cast into. Hartono. Hartono.

And Benny. Watching the sea eagle gliding, sitting beside her on the beach.

"It's a beautiful bird," she said.

"Yes."

As they looked out to sea, they saw the little motor-boat come chugging in.

"Well, my beautiful Lamour, your transport has arrived."

"Harry, or whatever rose-name you go by, this has been a morning I will not forget. Thank you." He wasn't listening or he wanted to show he wasn't listening. He had turned to signal to the house boy to bring her bag out to them on the beach.

"Bye, Lamour."

"Bye, Harry, and thank you … not just for the *nasi lemak*."

His eyes showed that he understood and felt her gratitude. He had enjoyed her company and his communicaton with someone with a kindred soul in some way. They were pleased and sad.

Fifteen minutes, bouncing up and down on the waves, climbing up the rope ladder against the pitching trawler's side, the smell of fish, as Harry had said, then sitting on deck. Hearing Hokkien again, shouted and cursed. Seeing the outline of Singapore slowly come into view. Sweating. Tanah Merah. Changi beach. Changi Point. Rough, slimy fisherman's hands helping her up. The timber jetty. Back on solid land. Her legs still swaying with the pitch and roll of the boat. The sun blazing down. Back home. In Singapore. Back home, in a way.

Hartono was at the end of the timber jetty. He looked huge and powerful to her. He smiled at her and asked her how she was. Then she noticed another Indonesian or Malay man beside him. He did not introduce him. Later she heard Hartono call him "Mat." She looked into Hartono's eyes, searching. She saw that he read her look.

It was a dirty little car that took them into the city. He sat at the back with her. She put her hand on the back of his and asked him how he was. He let it lie there. He answered he was fine in a formal way and asked her how the journey was. It was like talking on stage with Mat as a whole audience, listening intently.

To her surprise, they drove up to the Hotel Singapura on Orchard Road. She raised her eyebrows at Hartono. He smiled and nodded in silent reply. When she left Singapore, it was one of the best hotels. She registered at the desk. He followed her to her room and tipped the Malay boy who brought her small bag up.

Her bladder was bursting. She rushed to the toilet. It was beautiful. Sparkling. Gleaming. So clean. So shiny.

When she came out, Hartono was standing at the end of the

small room looking out of the window. She went up to him and let her body touch his. She put her hands round him and felt his firm arm muscles tighten against her arms as she held him. Her chin was on his shoulder.

"Hartono ..."

"I've missed you, Bertha."

He was tense. Every part of his body that she was touching seemed taut, stiff. He didn't move.

"Hartono ..." she whispered.

The afternoon sky was dazzling bright and the clouds were spread out white, hot, blinding, in full rounded clumps, smooth, soft, like pillows. Like waves of a restless sea, like steam, bursting out, white eruptions out of the earth, far above the horizon.

The phone rang. The noise crashed into her. Hartono turned around and said, "That's Andrew Mckay."

Bertha moved away from him. She dropped into a chair. Her soaring spirits collapsed with her into the chair.

It was Andrew Mckay. He came up. He grinned at her, pleased to see an old friend, but she could see that he was distracted. He was more edgy than she expected him to be. It was heightened against Hartono's calm. Hartono's exterior calm. She saw the fire still raging in Hartono's eyes as he talked quietly about the plans of their mission. She saw that in his indirect way he was reassuring Andy Mckay.

She listened to the discussion, struggling with her own thoughts. Then she heard, with much disappointment, Hartono reluctantly offer to go with him to the scene again. She had learnt from their talk that they had been there a few times before. He stood up awkwardly and spoke to Bertha.

"I'll come for you at eleven o'clock tomorrow night. You have the details. I'll have the equipment. Mckay and I have to sort out one or two things now."

He looked at her and then dropped his eyes.

"Siswono's in town. He said he'll take you out to dinner tonight. Early dinner. He'll call for you at six. Informal. You know Siswono

..."

They left together. He said "Bye'" to her through the closing slit of the door.

"DAMN!DAMN!DAMN!" her thoughts, her body, screamed at her as the door closed. She sat slumped in the chair angry, dazed.

Siswono was dead on time and surprisingly friendly and open. They had dinner at a street stall in Tanjong Pagar, near the docks. You won't meet any of your friends here, he said. Part of his friendliness was explained, she thought to herself, when he commented that she was regarded so highly at the HQ. But the way he opened up on the mistakes the unit was making seemed out of character to her.

"That fellow Partono ... he's really messing up things."

"Partono?"

"Lieutenant Bambang Partono, assistant naval attache at the Indonesian Embassy here. The fool is recruiting the most useless and unreliable of characters. Why in God's name can't they see it."

"Is he?"

"Yah. Look at that clown, Nordin bin Lemon. Ex-boxer, bum.

"Never got past standard two. Dishwasher, laundryman. Now he's a key contact man with his coffee stall. I know how much they gave him to set up the stall. Eight hundred dollars! They're crazy. Where's most of that money gone to? Huh! Clothes for his wife. I reported it. They won't believe me. Aiyah! I wish you were staying here longer. I'll show you."

"But *mas*, we all make mistakes," she said using the Indonesian familiar, *mas*.

"That's just one. There are so many others ... Kassim bin Ahmad. Idiot. Says he's madly anti-Chinese, so Bambang recruits him. They give him money for the operations and he fritters it away. What's more, he had the cheek to ask for money for the mosque. Then they make him Lieutenant-Colonel of the Tentera Nasional Republic Malaya. We're getting the wrong men."

Bertha knew what that was all about. The so-called "National Army of Malaysia," a guerilla group that Indonesia was developing.

"Hmm, that's no good. I wonder if the chief knows."

"You mean Muljadi? I think he suspects, but the naval fellows have the ear of the people on top. It's terrible."

He sighed. But he started again almost at once.

"And they want to get men who are well known for their political activities. Like Bong Kahar. Sure we can use men like that for political work. But not for undercover operations. They are known people! Partai Ra'ayat Singapore, Peninsular Malay Union, Malayan Peoples Social Front. The Singapore Police Special Branch is watching all those guys, lah!"

Bertha frowned. He appeared to be a frustrated man. But that didn't worry her. It was the team they were going to work with tomorrow night that worried her.

"Are we going to have to work with second-raters then, tomorrow night?" she asked Siswono.

"No, no. This is *kerbau's* team. That fellow knows what to do. As soon as he came back from Jakarta, he backed out of all political parties. He wasn't seen anywhere. If they had ever suspected him before, it looked as if he had lost all interest in politics. And he has recruited the best men. He works quietly. Professional, man! He is going to be the top man in the campaign. Mark my words. And I must say the training in Jakarta seems to be very good."

He looked at her. She didn't indicate that she had gone throught the same course.

"I know you've met him," he said in a whisper.

"Are you one of tomorrow night's team?"

"No. I'm not in the squad. I've fixed the logistics."

"Yah. You must be good at that. You certainly looked after us up there. And brought those curries now and then."

He laughed. "I liked it there. And I think you did too, didn't you?"

"Yah … Just long enough."

"And that was the first time in my life I sat with people celebrating Christmas."

"That wasn't a real celebration."

"But I heard how you celebrate it that night."

"I enjoyed myself that evening."

"Half-drunk eh?" he laughed loudly. The thought of her slightly tipsy seemed to amuse him immensely. His laughter baffled her.

They had an early night.

Hartono rang early in the morning using the code words of "my aunt has moved" to say that HQ had changed the target. Could they meet in her room at nine? Hartono, Andy and a short man who was introduced as Kaslan came at exactly nine. Amazing punctuality for Indonesians, she thought as she opened the door. But perhaps it was Andy who organised them.

Hartono was in jeans and a tee-shirt. He smiled at her. A beautiful smile, she thought. Then he put on his serious face and said HQ had now directed that they go for a key telephone exchange in the city. They had sent a new set of detailed instructions. It included a sketch plan of the area.

Why? Why? Bertha thought quietly to herself. Why change the target at the eleventh hour? Dammit! I know they are better organised than that. Then it struck her. She had wondered why they had included among the various contingency code expressions in the note Muljadi had given her, "my aunt has moved." She had thought that was unnecessary.

They knew it from the start! The British High Commissioner's house was a red herring for security.

Hartono spread out the sketch plan of the new target area. Bertha recognised the telephone exchange at once when she saw Hill Street on the sketch plan.

The three men hunched over it, discussing the operational details.

Andy will drive his car taking Kaslan and Bertha. They will pass the telephone exchange on the other side of the road and stop a little way down to let Bertha out. She will cross the road and walk back up the road to the exchange.

She will go up to the sentry with a camera slung round her shoulder and a map in her hand and ask directions to the Padang.

Hartono handed over the camera and map. Yes, yes, he knew it would be late at night, but there were always crazy tourists trying to cram in as much as they could every night. A man known as "*nombor satu*" would then approach the sentry from behind and strangle him with a rope. If he got into trouble, Bertha would knock out the sentry.

"The neck chop, remember?" Andy said.

As soon as *nombor satu* attacks, Andy will turn the car around, pull up in front of the exchange, and he and Kaslan will leave the car with its engine still running and go to the main door of the building. There was a very small carpark between the gate at the street, where the sentry would be and the main building. One or two guards sat near the main building door as reserves. They would either be smoking and chatting or sleeping on the bench. They had rifles.

Andy and Kaslan had silencers on their guns. They will kill the two guards as quickly as they can.

Hartono will be waiting in another car across the road with two men, "*nombor dua*" and Charlie at the wheel. They will see the gun flashes. Charlie will then make a U-turn and stop the car in front of the exchange behind the first car. Hartono and *nombor dua* will carry the bomb out of the car. It needed two men to move it quickly. It was a big bomb. Siswono had provided a basket for carrying it.

The guards outside had the door keys. If the keys weren't on them or if they took too much time to locate, Kaslan would put the charges and detonators he was carrying and blast the door open. They would have to stand well back, especially Hartono and *nombor dua* with the bomb. The sketch map showed where they would stand.

Meanwhile, Bertha will get into the first car driving seat, her gun ready to help the others if they had to fight their way out. There will also be a sten-gun on the floor, in front of the seat next to the driver, if she needed it.

After all, Andy said with a smile, she was the best shot among the whole lot of them. Hartono turned to her with his eyebrows raised.

They continued. Andy, Kaslan, *nombor satu* and *nombor dua* will go in and place the bomb. Andy will set it. Hartono will be on guard outside.

Their places in the getaway car were decided. Hartono in front beside Bertha. Andy and Kaslan behind in fixed places. *Nombor satu* and *nombor dua* would run down a backlane as indicated on the sketch plan. They knew the area.

Bertha queried whether this idea of HQ's was sound. Would it not cause more confusion and delay? HQ should not try to fix every move as though it was a stage musical.

Kaslan and Andy looked at Hartono. They obviously agreed with her.

"In fact if a real problem arose, Andy and Kaslan could get into the other car," Bertha added.

No, Hartono ruled. HQ's plans must be followed. And it's ridiculous to suggest anyone getting into the other car. Charlie would be in it, reeking of brandy, to ram any vehicle that might chase them. Charlie, Hartono explained, was clean, in the sense that he had no political connections. He was also know to be a playboy around town.

"That's why he needs the cash," Andy interrupted with a smirk.

"He's reliable," Hartono said looking hard at Andy.

"Hope the bugger doesn't drink it," Andy continued. "It's supposed to be perfume, not to be drunk."

"Don't worry," Hartono added with some impatience. "I know he's reliable. That's my responsibility."

Contingencies, Hartono said. They discussed HQ's contingency alternatives. I don't like it, Hartono mumbled.

"I'll be carrying the bomb with *nombor dua*. No way will he and I be able to get our guns out if there are more than say three guards at the door."

"They say their men have observed the place night after night," Andy said. "There are only two."

"Who were those guys?" Hartono asked, speaking to no one in particular, "They use such *dungus* sometimes."

"That's not good enough for such a key exchange," Bertha said.

"They're just complacent."

Bertha chipped in again, "But I'll be at the sentry box to help."

"No!" Hartono said sharply. "You have to be in the driver's seat as soon as possible. That you must not forget."

"But isn't Charlie's car the reserve getaway car?"

"No, no. We've purposely got that huge old Volvo station wagon so that he has a heavy car to hit any vehicle chasing us. And he'll have all those old telephone directories at the back for more weight. He's even promised to deliver them tomorrow for evidence if it's necessary."

"Poor Siswono had one hell of a time getting them." Andy chuckled.

"Now," Hartono cut in abruptly, "Kaslan, you're to go through the bomb setting with Andy again today. If anything happens to him, you have to set it."

"Yah."

"Siswono will be checking the car tuning this afternoon. He's got the super fuel."

Hartono handed out cigarette packs. There was a small radio alarm in them. You all know these things. Press the red button, the pyramid-shaped one, if there's real danger. And I mean danger that makes it necessary to abort the mission. Everyone will get the signal. The green button, the rounded one, to stop the buzzing as soon as you've heard it. Now get this straight. This thing's too simple. Because only I can decide to abort. So you only press the red if you're absolutely sure. It means you are giving the abort order over my head. Understand?"

They nodded.

"Bertha, do you understand?"

"Yes, Hartono."

"Kaslan?"

"Yah!"

"Andy?"

"Aye."

"And Andy, let me repeat. These explosive things are not my game. I put the brass bit inside and screw it tight in, right?"

"Aye. As soon as Bertha gets out of the car when we arrive."

"Should we bother about the keys?" Bertha asked. "Shouldn't Kaslan fix his door-opener at once?"

"Yah," Andy responded. "Tell you what, Kaslan, as soon as we've knocked out the door guards, you start fixing the thing. If I or *nombor satu* find the keys ..."

"No, boss. Once I put it in, you can't take it out."

Hartono was considering Andy's suggestion seriously. "No," he said, "Kaslan's device is a contingency."

"I hope those silencers are really silencers," Bertha said.

"At that point it doesn't really matter," Andy replied to her, frowning. Then he snapped his fingers. "What I need is a kind of alarm that I can start as soon as we enter the building. If we haven't found point X here on the plan, within three minutes, we'll have to leave the bomb wherever we are."

"Good idea," Hartono said, "Siswono can probably find one by tonight."

"Too many gadgets, lah," Kaslan said.

They discussed more contingencies. Then Hartono put up both his hands. "Okay, we stop here. We've covered the main possible problems. We can go on forever. It is important that we don't build up our tensions. We break up now. See you tonight."

They went out of the room. Bertha held the door open, looking at Hartono. He looked at her and said, see you tonight.

"I'll come a few mintues earlier."

She saw Andy's eyes narrow and a shadow seemed to pass over his face.

She flopped into the chair beside the little table at the window when they had gone. She could feel the tension rising in her. She sat there for about twenty minutes, doing nothing, staring mindlessly at the hot bright sky outside the window and the fluffy clouds, white, blinding white. Then she stood up suddenly. She put on her roughest clothes. Plain cotton shirt, jeans and flip-flops. She picked up the camera Hartono had handed to her and the map. And she walked out of the hotel, turning right down Orchard Road. Not more that a thousand dollars she said to herself. WOW! Her eyes shone. Wow! I can actually blow a whole thousand today! Oh Ma, if only you could see me now. Wow … Maybe a bit of jade? Something for Benny. And Rudi, dear Rudi. And Mononutu. Fatma? And of course, if I see him on the way back, Harry, my wonderful surprise!

And for lunch, *siew yok*! Or *babi tauyu*? *Mui chin*? Or *Swee Kee*? Would Hartono ever learn to enjoy pork if I broke him in gently?

Ten o'clock. Ten fifteen. Ten thirty. Ten forty. Ten forty-one, two, three … She sat watching it, with the bed-side radio loud. That cigarette pack alarm. The red button is so sharp. It would probably cut my finger if I had to press it. Hell, it's only ten forty four.

Hartono knocked. He smiled nervously.

He walked in shyly and sat down.

"I've heard the most flattering things about you, Bertha."

"You don't need to hear them, do you Hartono?'

"You're right, I don't."

He sat nervously in the chair opposite her.

"Are you all right?" he asked.

"Yah, thanks"

"Nervous?"

"Yah … but mostly about Andy. He's so young in some ways."

"So are you, Bertha."

"But Hartono, I know I can think and move fast. I learnt that on the hockey field."

"Yah. That's true.'

"Oh, Hartono, please be careful …"

"You too. You're a very precious person."

"To you?"

"Yes. I have a promise to your father, besides that ..."

Bertha saw his struggling.

Then the phone rang. She picked it up, listened, snapped a 'No lah!' and put it down

"Huh?" Hartono asked with a grunt.

"Stupid wrong number."

"In this hotel?"

"Woman. Soliciting."

"I thought the hotel filtered those calls."

"Not if you're soliciting from the lobby phone."

The phone rang again. She picked it up.

"OK. Andy, we'll be down. Hartono's just arrived."

She put the phone down.

"Andy ... in the lobby?"

"Why the 'just arrived?' "

"I not sure how much I can trust Andy."

His eyes narrowed.

Bertha didn't ignore his reaction. She looked directly into his eyes and thrust, "Do you?"

He looked at her in silence. The room suddenly seemed cold.

As she got out of the car, she noticed that there was an almost full moon. I never thought of it, she said to herself. They must have. She saw *nombor satu* in the five-foot-way. She guessed the figure leaning against the brick pillar smoking was him.

Away from the car. Cross the road. Back down the road. The sentry. A kid. Smooth faced. Baby faced.

In her best mock-Australian accents. Getting him to look at her map. The she saw the cord. The muscles of *nombor satu's* hand. But in a flash she noticed it. The cord didn't sink in. He had something hard under his collar. But he seemed to choke with just the pressure on his neck. His knees buckled and he slid down to the ground without a sound.

Andy and Kaslan were in the car park. The guards were slumped on the bench. Two of them. Their guns flashed. Thump. Thump. In the corner of her eye she saw Charlie's car make a U-turn.

Andy and Kaslan bent over the bodies looking for the keys. Andy's voice, "Ah!" Charlie's car now at the gate. Hartono and another struggling with the heavy basket with a big lump of black in it. Andy and Kaslan taking the basket. *Nombor satu* and *nombor dua* going into the building with them.

Then Hartono shouting at her. "Bertha! To the car!"

Damn! What's wrong with me?

She rushed into the car. Why the bloody hell didn't they let me take it out for a fast run today! God, they say they thought of everything! Shit!

Then the alarm hoot went off. Flustered, she pressed the green button to silence it. Muffled sounds of shooting from the building. Hartono rushed into the car. She saw the Volvo in the rear view mirror. Andy came running out of the building. His eyes were blazing. He didn't get into the car through the back door which Hartono had opened. He stood there and shouted at the top of his voice.

"They were waiting for us!"

Hartono stared at him.

"Get in you fool! Where are the others?"

"They were waiting for us!"

Hartono saw Bertha push open her door, get half out of the car and stand with one leg on the road. She had her gun in her hand.

He heard her shout to Andy as they faced each other across the roof of the car, "And you got away … you bastard!"

He heard Andy start to say "Swine …" but a burst of gun shots cut his word off. He collapsed onto the road. Hartono had his gun ready for the men he expected to rush out of the building. The car lurched forward. The opened door crashed shut. He turned round and saw Bertha gripping the wheel, her lower lip curled down.

"Bastard! Bastard! All of them bastards!"

It wasn't the Bertha he knew. His head spun.

The car screeched round a corner. He heard a dull quick crunch of gears as she slammed it into third after they rounded the bend.

"Two faced-bastard! Traitor!"

He tried to put his hand on her arm but the car screeched round another corner and he was thrown heavily against the door.

He forced his body up. It looked like Beach Road. He looked at Bertha. Her eyes were blazing with fires he did not understand. He felt the car surge as they went into a straight road.

"BERTHA!" he yelled.

"Bastard! Traitor!"

He drew in a deep breath. The car was steady, but it was tearing along the road at a breakneck speed. He turned around to see if they were being chased. There was a car behind them. But no sirens. He blinked and looked again. A Volvo. Charlie.

"Bertha! Slow down. You'll kill us. It's only Charlie behind."

"Bastard. Pig!"

His head was clearer now.

"Bertha! We're not being followed. Slow down! You'll attract attention speeding."

"Bastard!"

He put his hand on her arm and gripped it. Her foot relaxed on the accelerator pedal.

"Slow, slow. There's no more danger now. Drop your speed."

The car slowed down a little. He saw that they were passing the large gas tank at Kallang. The road was deserted.

"Pull over. I'll drive."

She slowed down a little more.

"PULL OVER! It's an order!" he yelled at the top of his voice. She turned and looked at him. She saw the frenzy in his eyes.

She pulled up on the side of the road near Sin Koh Street. He saw the Volvo pass them and stop about two hundred feet in front of them.

Bertha bent over the wheel. She was trembling. He put his hand on her shoulder.

"Bertha."

"Bertha."

"Bertha."

"Bertha. Move over. I'll drive."

He had to give her a hard shove before she lifted her leg over the gear lever and start moving her body across. He got out quickly and walked round the back of the car.

Charlie had run up to them.

"Anyone hurt?"

"No, Charlie. Follow me."

He drove off. Bertha had slumped down in the passenger seat. She was still muttering.

He drove towards Katong. The Volvo in his mirror. To Siglap.

Past Still Road. Past Parbury Avenue. Charlie following. Bertha still cursing.

He stopped at Bedok. He got out of the car and walked round to Bertha's side. He opened the door and gripped her arm. "Come on, out!"

In a daze she followed him. He walked to the beach. Across the concrete paved area near the eating stalls. Over the rough grass. He pushed her down onto the sand. She sat down. He sat beside her and put his arm round her shoulders. His grip relaxed her a little.

Charlie walked up to them.

Hartono started so say something but Bertha suddenly sat up straight and spoke rapidly.

"If they were waiting for us, they would have had a car to chase us. Or they would let us go and follow us. Hartono!"

He looked at her for a second and spoke, "No, Bertha. They were too cocksure."

Then he turned to Charlie, "You didn't see anything following us, did you?"

"No. I was looking."

"But Charlie, you'd better go. The two of us on the beach at this hour are not suspicious. Three of us are."

"Right. Goodnight."

The mysterious Charlie walked away.

Hartono sat with his arm round her shoulder for some time in silence. Then he said slowly, "If it was a trap, why did they let us kill their men?"

"That's it!" Bertha said suddenly, "Somehow I thought that the sentry did not drop naturally. There was something ... the way the cord didn't dig into his neck."

"But the door guards?" Hartono muttered. He answered himself after a few seconds, "Bullet proof vests ... But ... surely it was a risk."

"Maybe expendables," Bertha said.

"Are you all right now, Bertha?"

She turned to him and burried her face in his chest.

"Oh God! Did you see the blood spurt out from his head? God it was horrible! It just burst open ... Oh God! I can still see it."

"Bertha," Hartono said slowly and softly. "Do you know you put three shots into him in the same place. That's almost impossible to do."

"Oh Hartono, hold me."

He pressed his hand on her head as she closed her eyes with her face against his chest. She wanted to cry, but there was something stuck inside her, choking her.

She leant against his chest until her back started aching. Then she sat up.

"Why?" Hartono said to himself audibly, looking out to sea.

"Money?" he mumbled. He saw she was listening.

"No. That's not him," she said.

"They played on his Singapore loyalty?"

"No. I think they must have played on his worry about Indonesia. He was such a meticulous person. He couldn't distinguish between the bad and the good in Jakarta, I think."

She paused. Hartono waited for her to continue. "Because he saw the mass of problems in the streets, he couldn't see that there were men and systems as sharp and efficient as the best in the West hidden behind the stinking mess of garbage and disorganisation."

Hartono turned and looked into her eyes. "Yes. I think you're right."

"Oh God! Hartono. His head exploding like a volcano ... bits shooting out. Oh God!"

~ *Chapter Thirty-eight* ~

Malaysia 1964

Jakarta seemed hotter and dirtier when she returned. She had her bath and flopped into bed as soon as she got back. Mononutu's place seemed so tumble-down and primitive after the hotel in Singapore. Not just compared to the hotel, she said to herself, it's crummier than most houses in Singapore. But the physical and mental strain of the last few days had sapped all her energy. She fell asleep at once.

There was a note on her desk when she went to the office the next day. Muljadi wanted to see her at nine.

"How's Palembang?" Fatma who sat at the desk next to her asked.

"Donno … Actually I never spent any time there. As soon as I arrived, they took me out to an army camp outside the town and I stayed there all the time."

"Successful trip?" she asked again.

"Yah, got a lot of information … useful stuff."

Muljadi wanted a verbal report from her. He'd heard, but only the bare key facts. He was not smiling today. His face was grim.

She related the events, briefly, clearly.

"It's a disaster for the unit, Miss Mary Devries. It's our fault. We did not take enough note of your warning about Mckay. I should have read between the lines of the other reports. In hindsight, we can see that the man was unstable. Or should I say undecided yet. Finally his past caught up with him, in the sense that he returned to the loyalties of his past."

Like me, Bertha thought. Muljadi appeared to read her thought.

"You are different. You never rejected your past. You work with us because your objectives coincide with ours at the moment. Am I not right?"

"Yah, *bapak*."

"And you killed him because you cannot tolerate a two-faced thing. Also because he was a communist, right?"

"I'll never know why, *bapak*. It was a snap decision."

"A predictable decision, to my mind."

"But the mission failed," she added.

"Yes. It's a terrible failure for the unit. But we have learnt a lot."

"I'm sorry. I should have pressed my point about not feeling at ease with him."

"You yourself weren't sure, were you?"

"My feminine intuition was sure. My logical mind was not."

"Hah!" It was a loud outburst. "There's no such thing! There is intuition but not feminine intuition, Miss Mary Devries!"

She got worried that she had upset him. Must watch my damn mouth, she said to herself.

He was speaking to her when her mind returned to the room.

"I myself believe that when he came here for the basic training he was not their agent. I reckon they worked on him after he returned."

"Come to think of it, *bapak*, I suddenly remember a piece of conversation I had with him while we were together in the training camp. He asked me why I was here in Indonesia. If I believed that Malaysia was detrimental to Singapore I should be at home fighting it there. I said that we could not fight alone. We needed assistance. Support. Support from a strong hand. He said, Huh! Indonesia! I told him that he was behaving like a typical narrow-minded Singaporean. He did not know the force and power of the country. In fact, I suspected that he knew very, very little about Indonesia. No matter how poor and disorganised they were at present. Over a hundred million people, I said."

Muljadi was leaning over his desk with concentration on her words. He interrupted her.

"Did you not ask him why he was here?"

"Yah. To be trained, he said. But isn't the party here an inspiration to you? I asked. No, he said. Aidit is not a nationalist. He's a Moscow man. But *bapak*, Mckay was not well informed on the PKI." She ended quoting a Malay proverb about the frog under the coconut shell.

"That's very interesting," Muljadi said. Bertha was silent.

"Well, there's a limit to how much we can learn from our mistakes. The pressure of the present and the future is with us. Thank you for your report, Miss Mary Devries. That's all."

She rang Rudi as soon as she came out of his office. She needed a distraction. She could not face the night alone in her room at Mononutu's. Muljadi had shown her that he had fully approved of her killing Mckay. Perhaps, admired her quick decision. But his words kept going through her head, "Your objectives coincide with ours at the moment ... at the moment."

They put her back on the job of reading the newspapers and reports on Singapore and Malaya, or Malaysia as it was now, and giving her analysis.

She saw more signs of dissension between Singapore and Malaya. Rajaratnam in Singapore taking Tan Siew Sin of Malaya to task openly in the *Straits Times* for saying the PAP was "supposed to be socialist."

Then Dr. Toh Chin Chye's shock statement on the first of March, 1964. A shock to the Malayan Alliance. He said that the PAP were going to contest the April elections up-country. One more point to buttress her belief. But she was badly disappointed that the PAP was so impatient. Or was it Lee Kuan Yew? Couldn't they wait?

On reflection she was not sure about whether they should wait and let Malaysia settle down before they moved into Malayan domestic politics. They were showing their hand now. The communists would have waited. But the fact was that they had upset the Tengku. And he was really the key man in Malaya. He had cancelled Lee Kuan Yew's visit to the USA, to lead a team to place the facts of Malaysia before the Americans.

And Tan Siew Sin had leapt into the fray saying that his Malayan Chinese Association was accepting the challenge from the PAP for the representation of the Chinese in Malaya. Lee Kuan Yew rubbed salt into the wound unintentionally when he rose to speak in a pre-election rally at Suleiman Court in Kuala Lumpur. He was given a three-minute standing ovation before he started speaking. It thrilled her to read it. But she knew how Tan Siew Sin would react to the same news. The more the PAP clashed with that prickly fellow, the sooner Malaysia breaks up, she said in her report.

She was disappointed to see that the PAP only got one seat of the nine they stood for. "And an Indian ..." Nyoto had said at the meeting. "That's irrelevant," she countered.

"You mean voting is not communal?"

"No. It's still very much communal."

"Then what did you mean by irrelevant?"

"I'm sorry. I withdraw that. I was thinking of something else."

"What?" he asked. Nyoto would never miss an advantage.

"That perhaps the personality of the man swung it, rather than the party."

"Huh. Like you once said of David Marshall. Who was this Indian anyway?"

"Devan Nair."

"Ahh, that fellow. Miss Mary Devries, sometimes your feelings, or should I say hunches, overrule your mind. Don't they?"

"Yes, *bapak*."

Muljadi chipped in, to her defence, in some way, "When we are judging people, we should understand signals that the unconscious sends out. But this is not assessing how the man ticks. It's dissecting an event that has happened."

She didn't know how to take it. She left it.

It seemed to Bertha as if the turbulence of 1963 was continuing. The *Sukarno ganjang Malaysia*, crush Malaysia, propaganda depressed her. It was getting to the people. Sukarno was getting to the hearts of his people again. The radio poison beamed at Singapore was even worse. At home, Syed Jaffar Alba of UMNO, the United Malay National Organisation, hitting out at what he called the "fate" which had befallen the Malays in Singapore, telling them that if they were united, "not even a thousand Lee Kuan Yews would break them," was bad enough. The Indonesian radio went further. "We call on the Malays to free your country from the bondage of Lee Kuan Yew and his friends who have robbed Singapore which belongs to the Malays." "Malays, wake up! Take over Singapore which has been seized by Lee Kuan Yew and his friends." Why do "his friends" keep coming in? she asked herself.

She would throw herself into stopping Malaysia before it went too far. But not this way.

Then her faith in the man she respected so much dropped. He called over a hundred Malay organisations together and explained to them their position as Singapore Malays in Malaysia. These were bitter truths for them to swallow. She had been in Indonesia for a long time now and was sensitive to the bluntness of "no's" and direct confrontations. She had learnt to understand the gentle Indonesian way of softening the head-on clashes. Lee Kuan Yew's giving it to them straight from the shoulder was so utterly wrong to her mind. And for five hours!

It erupted the next day during the procession for the Prophet's birthday. She could not trace how it was triggered off. But that didn't matter, she was sure how it had been fuelled. It was ghastly to her. Her people fighting each other, the police, her father in the streets again. Hadn't they learnt? Will people never learn?

She poured out her feelings to Rudi that night. Oh Rudi. If it wasn't for Rudi ...

Then one day in late August, Muljadi sent for her again. It was another mission. There were no details this time. She would be going to Malaya. Tomorrow. They didn't give one any notice, did they? she thought to herself. I guess it's secrecy. But that's not right. I could tell someone tonight. Just lowers the risks I suppose. They could be watching me tonight. They should if you think about it.

Hartono would meet her. Her heart missed a beat. Oh, to see him again. He would brief her. It was an easy mission. They only needed her this time because of her special knowledge.

Muljadi smiled a small mysterious smile. She knew she shouldn't ask, but she did.

"My special knowledge?"

"Yes. We'll leave it at that. But as I said, this is an easy mission."

"Excuse my saying so, *bapak*, but that's when things go wrong. When one thinks it is easy."

"Yes, Miss Mary Devries, you're absolutely right. You've taught me something. I meant to tell you not to worry. But I shouldn't have stressed the ease of the task. One cannot relax in this game, as you no doubt know. And of course, the adrenalin must flow for the whole mind and body to work at its best. Thank you, Miss Mary Devries. That's all."

As she was leaving he added a parting thought, "It's going to be a significant mission. One day you'll look back and remember how you were there when history was made." He smiled.

~ Chapter Thirty-nine ~

Out of the Blue

A half moon hung in the sky. Bertha lay on her stomach on a small rise looking down at the valley below them. There was very little moonlight as the clouds kept blowing across the moon. All one could see were the tops of the rubber trees below them. To their right was the fringe of the jungle. The line of the river was not visible from where they were, but Bertha knew where it lay. She had studied every inch of the ground four years ago. She could locate Kampong Batang Merbau and Lenga and Pagoh from her knowledge of the terrain. She wasn't quite sure where Kampong Baru Melayu was.

As the clouds passed, the half moon and the changing light made the scene appear even more beautiful. It was dry. The air smelt dry to her. The tree leaves rustled. There was a breeze up there but not where they were on the ground. It was still and hot. And silent.

The forests seemed more silent than the days she had lived in them. Tonight, there was only an occasional owl or a soft rustle in the grass as some tiny creature moved about them. It was so quiet and serene, she thought.

She looked at Hartono lying on his stomach on the dead leaves beside her. They spoke in whispers. She pointed out the villages and the lines of the paths she remembered, killing time in idle talk. Hartono was anxious. He didn't want to talk much. Bertha read his mood and only spoke now and then to break the tense silence.

After some time, he said softly, "There was trouble in Singapore today, Bertha. I heard it on the radio before I left my place."

Bertha looked at him, waiting. He did not appear to be worried about his news. "Riots," he said.

"Riots?" she asked incredulously.

"Yes. Racial. Chinese and Malays," he replied.

"Oh Lord," she muttered.

"It seems that they started with some Malays dragging an old trishaw rider off his trishaw and killing him," Hartono said slowly and softly.

"Oh Lord. Not the July riots erupting again," she said.

They remained silent for some time. Hartono reached out to the black radio next to him and checked a knob for the tenth time that night.

"Don't fuss, Hartono. It's working. We've checked it enough number of times," Bertha said to him.

Bertha put her head down on her arm facing Hartono and asked him, "Are you sure that the marines were not all wiped out?"

"We'll never know. But as I told you, it was their plan to go into hiding as soon as they landed," he replied.

"The papers say that the Malaysian and British troops have rounded them all up," she said.

"We've been through that, Bertha," Hartono said. "Maybe they're deliberately misinforming to let the Indonesian marines think that they've stopped searching."

"Shit," Bertha muttered under her breath. "How could they make mistakes like that ..."

Hartono had told her how the Indonesians had changed the landing point of their coastal invasion at the last minute. They had decided not to land on the Batu Pahat beach that she had surveyed four years ago. They thought there had been a leak. So they had landed at Pontian with only the survey department maps to guide them. And they had left the islands off Sumatra too late. It was already light by the time they reached the beach. They lost the cover of darkness and part of the element of surprise.

"Yet, I guess that the Malayans also got information after the decision to change the landing point. It seems strange how quickly they moved their forces into the area," he had mused aloud to himself.

"Still, one never knows ..." Bertha had said. "The whole thing might have been a red herring for tonight."

Hartono did not talk for a long time. Bertha left him to his thoughts. They had sat together side by side like this years ago for many nights, leaving each other to think quietly, yet feeling an intimacy in just being together.

Then suddenly Hartono put up his finger. "Listen," he said.

She heard a distant drone of planes. "Hercules," he said. "For sure."

They were here. The night they had been waiting for for so long had finally arrived. They had placed the two radio beacons in the forest and the rubber estate and were waiting beside the main central radio beacon for the contact. Bertha searched the sky. She could not see anything. There was a lot of cloud.

"There!" Hartono said excitedly, pointing north-east.

She saw them. Tumbling out of the planes which had come out of the clouds. Like little ants falling from the sky until the parachutes opened. It was a beautiful sight. The white of the parachutes seemed to gleam in the moonlight. The sky was flecked with them.

A plane roared low over them. A little further on another bunch of men started falling out of the plane. As if it was dropping stones one by one. The parachutes opened but she could see that they were not going to land near them. Near Pagoh, she thought. She looked at Hartono. He was calm now. But not smiling. His job was not yet fully done.

She pulled her handbag slowly close to her and opened it. Her hand found the Glock at once. She drew her legs up and with a quick movement sprang up standing about two feet away from Hartono.

Her voice was sharp and loud. "Put your hands up! You're surrounded!" she shouted pointing the gun at him. He spun round still lying on the ground. His jaw dropped open. He stared at her. "No tricks ... I'll shoot."

He was too shocked to act. He muttered, "Bertha ..."

A shot rang out, the sound crashing through the stillness. Bertha had fired a bullet hitting the ground twelve inches from his chest.

"That's to show I mean business. No tricks, Hartono."

Her eyes were hard. He saw them alive and watching him with intense concentration. He shook his head in disbelief.

Bertha spoke loudly, "OK Sheelah ... Come and get him."

"Sheelah? Shshsh ... eelah?" Hartono stuttered.

The bushes near them crackled with sound as three men and a woman rushed out of them. Hartono turned his neck to look at them. All the men had guns in their hands. He was still lying on the ground, too bewildered to move. One of the men rushed up to him and started searching him at once. He found his gun and took it.

Bertha continued to stand there with her gun levelled at him.

"Bertha ..." he murmured.

The woman spoke. "She's our agent, Inche Hartono. Come quietly." He recognised her. Sheelah Cornelius. He had trailed her when they were checking Bertha out.

He stood up. The dead leaves were clinging to his clothes. He shook his head again. There were sounds of automatic gun fire close by. And explosions like hand grenades going off.

He looked at Bertha. He looked into her eyes.

She was trembling now. She dropped the hand holding the gun and let it hang limp by her side. With her lips quivering she stammered, "I love you, Hartono."

He stood reeling with the new shock.

"Bertha. You trapped me. And you say you love me ..."

A cold shiver went through Bertha. She saw Sheelah in the corner of her eye standing tense a few feet away from her. Sheelah was now holding a gun.

Hartono muttered "An agent for your country. And you love me ..." His eyes were red.

He swayed and said softly to her, "I love you, Bertha."

Bertha dropped the gun and rushed into his arms. He held her and whispered again and again, "I love you, Bertha, I love you … Oh Bertha, I love you."

"Oh! Hartono …"

Then Sheelah's voice rang out like a whip-crack through the air. "Search him again, Tong. Cheok, search her. Everywhere. The crotch too. Raju, pick up her gun."

They stood apart with their hands in the air submissive while they were searched. Their eyes held each other's.

Sheelah snapped out loudly again, "Now get to that bush and keep them covered. Leave them alone to themselves till I get back. If he tries anything, kill him. Cheok, come with me."

Hartono took her gently into his arms while the men in the bush twenty feet away stood watching them in the pale moonlight embarrassed and uneasy.

Tong Say Lee looked at Raju. He saw a tear run down his cheek. "Careful with the gun, *badak*," he whispered.

§

Epilogue

Sheelah sipped her BGA and looked at James. Sitting there on the verandah of his house in the fading evening light, he looked old. Fifty-five, he said he was. Maybe it was the slanting sunset rays. Or the mental strain that he gone through these last four years, Sheelah thought to herself. But now he was relaxed and contented. Bertha was safe. Back home in a way.

"I'm really glad you're being seconded to the SID, James," Sheelah said. "I can talk to you openly. It's such a relief to be able to talk to someone."

"I guess so, but I'm not so sure I'm pleased about the posting. Security Intelligence Department is not really my style," he said.

"It is. You'll soon find out. They need you there. There are too many young pups there who think they're the cat's whiskers," Sheelah consoled him.

"So, Sheelah. Tell me how the hell did you get mixed up in this? And you pulled Bertha in, didn't you?" James asked, one question following the other rapidly.

"It's a long story ..." she sipped her drink, "It really began with my job at the Borneo company. The Singapore Intelligence people found out that my boss was a CIA agent on the side. He tried to recruit an informer and messed it up."

"You mean an Englishman, a CIA man?" James asked incredulously. "Yah. They approached me ... to watch him, tell them of his overt appointments. I went further, you know me, and got a whole load of dope on him," she grinned proudly. "So they asked me if I would join them permanently. I was in the right frame of mind. But what pushed me into it was your bloody daughter."

"Oh yeah," James said weakly.

""Yes. That day she shouted at me like a regular whore in the office. Made me look like a whore too. That did it. I left."

James was silent for a few minutes.

"You won the lottery then, isn't it?" James asked.

"No. That was a cover," Sheelah answered. "I wish I had."

"And the publisher's agent job was a cover too?" James asked.

"No. I did that job. It wasn't much. Just acted on their instructions. It was a good cover. And extra money."

"Enough for a Sunbeam Alpine eh?" James interrupted smiling.

"Yah," Sheelah said.

"Let me get this straight. You mean the publisher's agent job had nothing to do with the Intelligence people?"

"Yah."

James grunted and went back to his questioning.

"What unit did they put you in?"

"They knew that the commies were getting more sophisticated. Our people were also learning new techniques from the Americans and British."

"And Israelis?" James interrupted again.

"I suppose so. I don't know. I was to start a new independent unit. Background research and field work in the same unit. It would be isolated from the rest of the organisation. I started recruiting ... And here is another funny coincidence."

James waited for Sheelah to sip her drink again.

"I don't know if you remember many years ago there was an attempted suicide jump by a young Eurasian lad. Chap called Kenneth Jerome Rozario. Well, this fellow was brought up by an unusual woman. She had a only little money, but she was a big-hearted soul. She looked after him and let him and his wife stay with her when he got married ... She was a wonderful woman in my opinion. She drank like a sailor and swore like a trooper, but inside she was a gem."

"Yes, yes, yes ... I remember, a Miss Morera," James said.

Sheelah related a long story about her recruitment of Kenneth Jerome Rozario and his wife Annie as agents.

"Husband and wife team?" James asked, when she had finished.

"No. They never worked on the same case," Sheelah replied.

"So the bugger turned out all right.," James muttered, more to himself than to Sheelah.

"About this time, they started watching Mr. Vandyke. They couldn't figure out what he was doing. The Inland Revenue people thought he was hiding some profits, but it didn't worry them too much. It was small stuff, if any. It was the Indonesian contacts of his that made the organisation suspicious. The PKI was strong then, if you remember."

"Never knew much of what was happening there," James said.

Sheelah continued, "That fellow Hartono seemed to be very active meeting people and going in and out of Malaya and Indonesia. Then out of the blue, Ethel Richards rings me one night and says she's going to Malaya ... and refers to hockey fixtures that didn't exist. It wasn't like her. It puzzled me. I reported it to them. That same night, I heard of Bertha taking off with Heng's Jag."

"It wasn't his," James interrupted.

"I know. So they followed Ethel. And lo and behold not only does she go to Seremban with Hartono but she meets Bertha there. It began to fit. Vandyke was grooming Bertha. The bust-up with Heng precipitated their plans ... and ours."

"They took a bit of a risk, didn't they?" James asked.

"What do you mean?"

"Getting her and Ethel to do the survey job for the landing," he replied.

"They had checked both of them out for a long time. In Jakarta, Hadi had spent a lot of time with Bertha, if you remember," Sheelah said.

"But the only hold they had on Bertha was that she had stolen a car?" James said.

"They didn't use that as a hold or a threat. It was a carrot they offered. An opportunity to get away for a while. They did, however, get an ace later. I don't know if you know that they killed a planter, a Mr. Mackintosh, because he was getting too nosey. They used the gun Hartono had given Bertha," Sheelah said.

James made a face of disbelief. "Her name was not on the gun records, Sheelah," he said.

"But her fingerprints were on the gun. They left them there," Sheelah said.

"They switched guns, then?" he asked.

"Yes. Somehow. I seem to think it was done early in the piece. On Christmas day, I think. When they were drinking and Siswono, one of their team, appeared to be just hanging around bored ... But the need to use the ace didn't arise. Bertha started co-operating wholesale," Sheelah explained.

"Because you contacted her?" James asked.

"Yes."

James frowned. "But there was no need for her to throw herself so enthusiastically into the job."

Sheelah cut him short. "It is a principle in this kind of game, James. Your plant is told to do brilliantly in his or her job in the organisation. If he gets to the top, well and good. Because that prevents someone else from getting there. He must throw himself in fully. Whether or not his brains are used against us. Provided, of course, the information continues to flow. That fellow, Law Teck, during the war, I suspect was a British agent on the same principle."

"Hah! A Japanese agent you mean!" James said provokingly.

"We'll never know. Some think he worked for both the Japanese and the British. Anyway, my point is that he went to the top," Sheelah said.

"I was told to get as many Serani as possible. They had the advantage of not being aligned to either the Malays or the Chinese," Sheelah continued along the line of her own thoughts.

"You said, 'had,' Sheelah."

"Yah. It's changing now ... As I was saying I tried. Got some good men and women. But had some failures. Well, not in the sense of their falling down on the job. In the sense of wasting time and effort working on them. Ethel Richards was one. A woman of strong loyalties, but we couldn't find the weakness or fire to operate on. She had no ambition whatsoever. Though she needs money. Pity. She could be a real stalwart. Muriel de Souza was another."

"Her!" James interrupted with surprise in his voice. Sheelah thought there was also anger and hate in his tone. Everyone knew about Heng and Muriel, and James, the pig, had probably taken the man's side without thinking.

"Yes, her. Didn't have enough brains or morals," Sheelah said, with a little sigh.

"Why didn't you use Heng?" James asked.

"Good heavens, no. He was too open a person."

"Open? That bugger?"

Yes, James … in his way." Sheelah moved on, "We already had one of those types. A good man but without that personality for undercover work in the field. You'll meet him. Fellow called Randy Lim. He was either too open or he clammed up. Useless with people. But a good head. We had to give him a backroom job. And he did brilliantly, thinking quietly, sitting out in the cold, as the chief used to say."

They were silent for a minute. Then Mary came out of the living room into the verandah with a glass of Wincarnis and sat down.

"Was Mr. Vandyke involved with the Indonesians?" James asked.

"No. They used him. But he was no fool. He got a defence contract now and then, and he slipped them information now and then. It wasn't a clear trading business. He knew, I think. But that's where the Indonesians are so good. The unspoken agreements, with both sides knowing. *Tahu sudah tahu* (Once you know, we both know)." Sheelah said.

"So Bertha can come back and live in Singapore?" Mary asked Sheelah.

"Yes. But …"

Mary didn't hear the "but," or didn't want to. She continued with another question.

"I didn't see anything in the papers about what James told me," Mary said to Sheelah.

"What do you mean?" Sheelah asked.

"About Bertha catching the Indonesian spy."

"Oh no. That's confidential. She didn't exactly catch him, Mary. And he wasn't really a spy."

"Well, whatever ..." Mary mumbled.

"In fact, Hartono is a very fine man ... And a very good man in planning detail. That night Bertha came to visit you, he had the house watched as soon as Vandyke put in the call. He had your phone cut while Bertha was with you. Only he couldn't arrange for the hotel phone to be cut or tapped. That was the night I contacted her," Sheelah said slowly. They looked at her, expecting her to continue.

She was silent. She did not want to tell them how Hartono, acting on a hunch from Vandyke, had fixed Bertha's surprise visit to the Balmoral Road flat.

She did not tell them how she had rung Bertha in her hotel room at the Singapura just before the Indonesian attack on the telephone exchange to check if there were any last minute changes in their plans, and Bertha had replied with her "No lah!" as arranged.

She would never ever tell them, or anyone else, about the killing of Andy Mckay. It wasn't planned. Bertha had acted when she saw his eyes blazing, accusing her of treachery. It was either him or her.

"Another?" James asked.

"Isn't it *makan* time?' Sheelah asked in reply.

"Never mind. As you wish, Sheelah," Mary said.

"OK, thanks," Sheelah decided.

"What will happen to Hartono now?" Mary asked when James had gone into the house. "Will they shoot him?"

Sheelah laughed. "Good heavens no. It's not like that any more. We've got to see how the Indonesians react. They may choose to ignore him. Poor man," Sheelah said.

"Why do you say that?" Mary asked.

"He was a very frustrated man towards the end. You see … I'll wait for James to hear this."

James returned with a drink for Sheelah and one for himself.

Sheelah continued, "Thanks. You see, Hartono began to see that they were not handling the Confrontasi properly from the military aspect. They were using bums to plant their bombs. So many of them just put the bombs anywhere. Just to get rid of them. And there were a good few who collected their money, stashed it away, planted the bomb in some useless place and gave themselves up. They were quite contented to serve out their prison sentences and pick up their hidden money afterwards."

James added when Sheelah stopped. "And they used the secret societies. Or rather the secret societies used them, didn't they?"

"Yes," Sheelah replied. She put her glass down on the *pahit* table and continued. "Back home in Jakarta, there were internal squabbles about the attacks on Malaya. Ahmad Dhani was never convinced that they could take on the British and the Malayan forces. He tried to discourage Yani, but he didn't succeed. Then he surreptitiously threw rocks in. He organised it so that the campaign was hampered by logistical support. They were short of transport, for example."

"But he put his crack paratroopers into Labis, didn't he?" James asked.

"Yes. But I'm sure he sacrificed them in his own mind," Sheelah said.

"Who screwed up the invasion at Pontian?" James asked.

"Don't know. That was another thing that really upset Hartono. The stupidity of landing after sunrise. But that was not all. I reckon what upset Hartono the most was the use of Malayan communists. He could not accept running with the tiger even when it is to one's advantage," Sheelah said.

"Like Lee Kuan Yew," James commented.

"I don't know if he deliberately went for that, James. He was in a different position. In this case, they went out of their way to use the Chinese communists," Sheelah said.

"When they had consistently mistreated the Chinese in their own country," James said.

"Not mistreated, suspected."

"No, mistreated," James insisted.

Sheelah left it at that. After a few seconds she said, "So I think that to Hartono, the failure of the airborne attack and his capture was a blessing in disguise."

James and Mary looked at her, waiting for more.

She was silent, thinking of Hartono's declaration of love to Bertha that had taken her by surprise that night in the jungle fringe on the hill at Labis. And Bertha. Fulfilling her duty. In spite of her feelings. She would never forget that night.

Bertha, woman, Serani, Singaporean caught in the currents of the conflicts and her past, clinging to her family, her people, her home.

§

Glossary

The words explained here are normally used in bazaar Malay. The standard spelling has not been used because it is easier for a reader to get the correct pronunciation with the English style spelling used in the colonial days. Unless indicated, the words used are of Malay origin.

abang — Elder brother; also used to mean husband.
adat — Customs, manners.
adek — Younger brother or sister.
almeira — (Portuguese) Cupboard.
amah — (Chinese) Female Chinese servant.

Baba — Decendants of Chinese who settled in Malaya or Singapore and had adopted Malay customs. The word peranakan can be used interchangeably to refer to these people.
badak — Rhinoceros.
bai — A word used for Sikhs, which means "brother."
bak mandi — Tub for bath water.
basi — Spoiled, musty, stale.
belachan — A cake or paste of ground and dried tiny shrimps.
bling-bling — A sour fruit.
borak — Bluff.
bosoku — (Portuguese) Scrotum.

chaching kring — A dried worm.
champorisation — Champor is to mix. Champorisation is an anglicised word meaning mixed up.
chang kuda — A Malay game in which boys are carried by each other like riders on horseback.
chap-cheng — (Chinese) Literally ten bloods; a term for Eurasians.

dali — (Portuguese) To hit.

Echigoya	A Japanese textile store before the war in Middle Road.
geragok	A little shrimp, the term used for Eurasians.
jamban	Toilet.
Jaudi	Jew.
Jawa	Java.
Jingli Nonah	A Malay song, originally Portuguese.
katek	Short; also used as a nickname, "shortie."
keronchong	A style of traditional Malay music.
klassi	Sailor.
kondek	A bun or knot of hair.
lauk	Any side dish eaten with rice.
lawyer burok	One who thinks he knows all about the law.
long soup	A soup which has noodles and some meat in it.
makan besar	A feast.
makan kechil	Tid-bits served with drinks.
makhur	In the Indonesian Islamic social code, makhur are deeds which are frowned on.
malu	Shy, embarrassed.
mampost	Death! An exclamation.
mestico	(Portuguese) Mixed ancestry.
minyak urat	Literally, rubbing oil. A well-known Malay medecine.
missi	A term used in bazaar Malay meaning "miss."
momoh	One of the ghosts or devils which were used to frighten children into submission or obedience.
obrigado	(Portuguese) Thank you, when said by a male.
P.K.I.	Partai Kommunis Indonesia, the Indonesian Communist Party.
pantat	The rump, bottom.
ponteng	To absent oneself.
pontianak	A vampire of Malay superstitions that preys on women.
portico	(Portuguese) Porch.
puki	Vagina.
rakya'at	The people, in the political sense.
samfoo	Jacket and trousers worn by Chinese women.
sarpooed	From the Malay sapu, to sweep, used in "Singlish" to mean wipe out, sweep.
seladang	A wild bull

serai	A mixture of betel-nut and other ingredients to be chewed like tobacco.
serang	The first mate, or leader of a crew on a ship.
Serani	A word used for Eurasians, originally meaning Christian, derived from Nazarene.
sheok	Delicious or a wonderful feeling.
shillings	And old Malayan word for coins, from the colonial era of pounds, shillings and pence.
short soup	Short soup is just plain thin soup.
stengah	Literally half. A standard term for half a peg of whisky in the colonial days.
sugi cake	A cake made from semolina.
syce	A horse attendant, a word later used for a chauffeur.
tamby	(Tamil) Little brother. Used as "office boy" in the colonial days.
teh-aliah	Tea with ginger.
temberang	Rigging of a ship; also used to mean exaggeration.
tumbok	Pestle and mortar.
Ten-cent store	A well-known Japanese store in Singapore before the war.
tengkat	A food carrier with containers stacked on top of eachother.
terang bulan	An old romantic Malay song, popularised by the movie, Road to Singapore. When Malaya got her independence the tune of Terang Bulan was selected for the national anthem which was ridiculed by the Indonesians.
tetek	Breasts.
ting-ting man	A hawker who sold a wide variety of goods and announced himself with the sound of the bell.
tock-tock man	A hawker who sold cooked noodles and announced himself by knocking on a piece of bamboo making a "tock-tock" sound.
toh-tee-man	(Chinese) Nightsoil carrier.
tuan	Now used as "mister," or "boss," when speaking or referring to men.
ulu	Literally, upstream of the river, but often used in the sense of a remote rustic place.
wade	An Indian fried tid-bit of mixed beans and lentils; dry and crunchy, eaten with a fresh green chilli.

§

About The Author

Rex Shelley was born in 1930. He belongs to a fading generation of Singaporeans that has seen the last vestiges of the Colonial raj, lived through the Pacific war and the Japanese Occupation, and experienced the trials and uncertainty during the turbulent struggle for independence and the radical changes following it.

Rex is currently serving on the Board of the Public Service Commission and has his own trading business. Besides writing, he occupies his time playing the piano, painting T-shirts and swimming.